Volume 4

Secrets

Satisfy your desire for more.

On **Jeanie Cesarini**'s story: "She has a talent…that makes you want to read her story over and over again (between cold showers) to re-live the wonderful sensations that her words evoke."

— **Lani Roberts**, *Affaire de Coeur* Magazine

On **Desirée Lindsey**'s story: "A well-written tale of forbidden lust and love that will keep you turning the pages. Desirée Lindsey is as hot as it gets!"

— **Kat Martin**, nationally bestselling author of ***Breath of Magic***

On **Betsy Morgan** and **Susan Paul**'s story: "Grab a fan or a ready man. You'll need one or the other while reading this hot, hot, hot story from these masters of the erotic. Wow!"

— **Martha Hix**, multi-published romance author

On **Emma Holly**'s story: "Wicked, erotic, sexy and fun. I can't wait for the next Emma Holly story…."

— **Thea Devine**

Jeanie Cesarini

Emma Holly

Desirée Lindsey

Betsy Morgan

& Susan Paul

Volume 4

Secrets

Satisfy your desire for more.

SECRETS Volume 4

This is an original publication of Red Sage Publishing and each individual story herein has never before appeared in print. These stories are a collection of fiction and any similarity to actual persons or events is purely coincidental.

Red Sage Publishing, Inc.
P.O. Box 4844
Seminole, FL 33775
727-391-3847
www.redsagepub.com

SECRETS Volume 4
A Red Sage Publising book
All Rights Reserved/December 1998
Second Printing, 2000; Third Printing, 2002; Fourth Printing, 2002; Fifth Printing, 2003; Sixth Printing, 2004; Seventh Printing, 2007
Copyright © 1998–2007 by Red Sage Publishing, Inc.

ISBN 0-9648942-4-6

Published by arrangement with the authors and copyright holders of the individual works as follows:
AN ACT OF LOVE
Copyright © 1998 by Jeanie Cesarini
ENSLAVED
Copyright © 1998 by Desirée Lindsey
THE BODYGUARD
Copyright © 1998 by Betsy Morgan & Susan Paul
THE LOVE SLAVE
Copyright © 1998 by Emma Holly

Photographs:
Cover © 2007 by Tara Kearney; www.tarakearney.com
Cover Model: Shayna Kearney
Setback cover © 2000 by Greg P. Willis; GgnYbr@aol.com

Printed in the U.S.A.

Book typesetting by:

Quill & Mouse Studios, Inc.
www.quillandmouse.com

Contents

An Act of Love

※⁀♡‿※

by Jeanie Cesarini

To My Reader:

It wasn't until I read Secrets Volume 3 in print that I thought of continuing the story that began in "A Spy Who Loved Me." Paige and Christopher had triumphed over evil and found their happily ever after. Lewis Goddard would meet justice. I turned the last page with a satisfied sigh — until Shelby piped up, "You're going to leave me a fifteen year old on the lam forever? No way! I want a happily ever after, too!"

Shelby was right. After all she'd been through, it wasn't fair to leave her a fictional loose end. She deserved a chance to overcome her past and find the man of her dreams. Guided by her hopes and fears, I honored her request, and now, dearest reader, just turn the page to find out how...

Take 23

Fractured light slashed across his face. His eyes were shadowed, dangerous. Feral. Shelby Moran issued a moan of half-hearted protest when he pushed the blouse over her shoulders, stripping away her last defense.

Cool air glazed her naked skin, but only for an instant before his strong arms enveloped her, every hard muscle of his body crushing her against the splintered warehouse wall.

"There isn't time," she pleaded, knowing as surely as he must how easily they could be discovered, *killed*. "We'll be caught...."

Shelby tried to talk some sense into him, into herself. He needed to be strong, to push her away, because God knew she couldn't tell him no.

He ignored her. His mouth came down on hers, biting, full of darkness and urgency, his kiss stripping away her last vestiges of resistance.

To hell with common sense. To hell with tomorrow. All that mattered now was the air sizzling between them, the way she ached to feel his hands on her bare skin.

"I'm taking you, baby. Here. Now." His voice was gravelly, rough with unrestrained desire.

Stroking the column of her throat with a calloused hand, he drew the kiss from her mouth as surely as he drew the strength from her legs. "You're worth dying for."

She believed that he meant it. Need skittered across her nerve endings, and she fitted her thigh between his, seared by the proof of his desire, branded by his heat. He would take her violently right on the bare stone floor. No tenderness, no romance, just urgent sexuality.

She would not resist. She wanted him.

And he knew how much. Oh, yes, he knew. He would use desire as a weapon just as he used touch to banish her will.

His hands slid down her neck, over her shoulders. He cupped her breasts greedily, rolling her nipples with rough fingers. She moaned aloud. Her heart throbbed in her chest, almost too hard.

Running unsteady hands over him, she buried her fingers in the crisp curls on his chest. He didn't seem to notice how she trembled. His hard thigh slid between her legs, his hand explored her breast, his tongue made love to her mouth. Just as he would make love to her.

She *should* be tingling by now, riding a wave of desire that blocked out everything but their passion. She *would* feel it if only she could focus, if her heart would stop pounding and let her concentrate.

His mouth seared a path along her jaw, his teeth tugging on her earlobe. A cold sweat broke out on her forehead. A fine sheen of ice that warned of trouble.

Shelby breathed in deeply, a sound much like a sigh. She didn't resist when he dug his fingers into her skin and dragged her to the floor.

Concentrate.

Every inch of his hot skin scorched her as they stretched out on the hard floor, legs twined together, arms grasping.

The pounding in her chest eased slightly, and she closed her eyes to everything except the moment.

Feel. Respond.

He rolled her beneath him. Her legs parted, and he wedged himself between her thighs. A shiver slithered through her, icy sweat flowing freely when she felt his masculine length nestling against her. Goosebumps raised along her arms.

Concentrate.

Stroking the firm roundness of his buttocks, she focused on the play of his muscles as he moved on her, trapped her beneath his grinding hips. His mouth crushed hers. Her chest tightened. She struggled to dislodge the breath that clogged in her throat.

Dragging her hands down his back, she raked her nails until he growled. In a few minutes they would be finished....

Her long hair caught beneath his elbow as they turned together. Her neck snapped backward, not painfully, but so unexpectedly that her pulse erupted in her veins, all her efforts at concentration smothered beneath a blast of emotion.

Fear.

Her lungs burned. She struggled for air. Her heart hammered so hard against her ribs she thought it might burst. Unable to stop herself, Shelby shoved wildly to dismantle one hundred and eighty-five pounds of muscular male from her body.

"Cut!" the director yelled.

The command barely sliced through her panic. She'd blown it.

Bright lights flooded the set, exposing her shame beneath the harsh glare of reality. She could feel their gazes on her—production workers, cameramen, stage hands. When her co-star sat up and stared at her, Shelby covered her bare breasts with shaking hands.

She felt ridiculous, *ashamed*, but those emotions came only in the wake of a frighteningly real struggle to draw one more breath, to stave off a choking black void that swirled at the edges of her vision.

"Cut! Cut! Cut!" The director's voice sliced through her spinning thoughts. He threw a towel at her co-star. "Everyone get back. Give her air. She's fainting."

Shelby wanted to tell him she would be okay, but her throat was so tight, she could only draw in a trickle of air.

Suddenly Wes D'Angelo was pulling her to her feet, wrapping a robe around her shoulders. "You haven't eaten today, have you?" His voice was abnormally loud, but sounded so far away through the clouds in her head. "Hypoglycemia, don't you know. Everyone, take a break." He half-dragged, half-carried her from the set.

The shadowed coolness backstage did nothing to calm her racing pulse, nothing to ease the choking sensation that robbed her of breath.

"God damn it, Shelby. You promised," Wes yelled. "You promised you'd go see your therapist."

She wanted to tell him that she *had*. She'd been seeing Doctor Pich for weeks now, but her throat constricted precluding any attempt at speech. Dark spots whirled before her eyes. Her legs felt like lead.

Wes kicked open the door to her dressing room. "Here, sit down." He pushed her into a chair and shoved her head between her legs.

Mortified that this had happened again, that he should see her this way, Shelby felt tears press against her eyelids. She wanted to shrivel up and evaporate.

"Come on, babe. Breathe deep." He stroked her hair. "Come on. Breathe with me. In, out."

Shelby tried. Her ears rang. Her hands shook. She fought unconsciousness with huge gulps that let in only fragile ribbons of air.

She felt stupid, stupid, stupid.

But finally, after an eternity of false starts and unproductive gasps, the sound of Wes's voice calmed her, and she drew her first real breath.

"There you go, babe. You've got it."

Tears streamed down her cheeks. She could hear the ragged edge to his voice, his impatience. "I-I'm sorry."

"Half the women on the planet would give up their Xanax to get naked with Mr. Hollywood out there, and you have an anxiety attack."

She wanted to curl up and die.

He took pity on her. "They're getting worse, aren't they?"

Nodding, she wiped the tears from her cheeks. This was a nightmare. "I—I'm seeing a therapist."

Wes ran manicured fingers through his stylish long, gray hair and emitted a harsh laugh. "I hate to point this out, but it doesn't seem to be working."

"I'm trying, Wes." She sat up straight. "Really."

He started to pace. "What the hell are we going to do? We still have sex scenes to shoot. *If* we can get the first one on film."

Readying for battle, Shelby thrust her arms through the sleeves of the robe and belted it around her. She recognized his tone of voice. Sarcasm usually preceded intimidation.

"Can you shoot the stunts? Give me a week or so to work with Doctor Pich. I'll be ready by then. Promise."

"Been there, done that, got the T-shirt, babe." He frowned. "It's not only your box office sales riding on this film, but my future."

A flash of anger warmed her. It wasn't her fault that his career was at the breaking point. "Don't you think you're over-reacting? I'm one person. I can't..."

"This movie has to be a success, which means you have to film the sex scenes." He knelt before her and stared into her face, his own clear gaze icy.

"Get a double."

He blinked. "Forget it."

"Why not?"

"Fans are paying to see *you* on screen."

"Fans pay to see Charlie Brent," she pointed out. "But he got a double so he didn't have to show his ass in *Robin Hood*."

"When you earn out what Brent does, you'll have *carte blanche*, too." He swept his hair back with an impatient swipe. "I'm calling an acting coach."

"You want me to *act* my way through an anxiety attack?"

"You're an actor, aren't you?"

The man was an idiot. A brilliant director, but an idiot just the same. "I won't."

"You will."

Gripping the arms of the chair, Shelby leaned toward him until their noses almost touched. She wasn't backing down. "I'll report you to the union."

"I'll sue you for breach and smear your little problem all over the papers."

"Damn it, Wes!" Anger evaporated, and in its place came the sinking feeling of despair. She wanted to tell him to take a hike and storm out of the room.

But her legs still felt weak. Shelby didn't trust herself to stand.

She *was* backing down. "Who?"

Wes stood and smiled at her. "Someone who could coach a monologue from a brick."

A Cameo Appearance

Jason Gage spun away from the computer monitor and snatched the telephone from the cradle. "Gage, here."

"Do I address you as doctor or professor?" The male voice came from another lifetime, no, another *world*, and Jason stared at the receiver, shocked into silence. Wes D'Angelo?

"Are you there, old man?" Wes asked. "I'm ignorant on the nuances of academic address."

Jason's fingers itched to slam down the receiver. Caller ID would definitely be included on his next budget proposal. "How about I solve your problem and hang up?"

"Leaving Hollywood hasn't improved your temper, I see." Wes's deep chuckle only piqued Jason's already strained temper.

"What is it?" Wes asked. "Doctor or professor?"

"Doctor."

"Of what?"

"Psychology," he growled, not in the mood to play twenty questions with someone from a past he had put behind him long ago. "What do you want?"

"I have a problem, Doctor Gage. I need your help."

A dull ache began at the base of Jason's neck, and he rolled his shoulders to ease the tension, wishing he had attended the dean's faculty meeting instead of begging off to work on his lecture. Wes D'Angelo and his problems had always given him a headache. It looked as if five years away from Tinsel Town hadn't changed that.

"Forget it, Wes. I'm on the lecture circuit right now. I'm only in town for a week, and I don't have time for anything except preparing my next presentation."

"You're breaking my heart." A disbelieving snort echoed through the receiver. "You haven't even heard my proposition."

"No."

"No?"

"Whatever it is, the answer is no." Couldn't get much clearer than that. Whatever Wes was, he wasn't deaf.

"We used to be friends."

Jason leaned back in his chair, gaze focused on the computer screen, every blink of the cursor reminding him how much time he was wasting on this telephone call. "We were never friends. You were one of my father's cronies who just happened to insinuate yourself into my career."

"All right. I'll settle for a friend of the family." Wes laughed. "It's been a long time, though. We haven't spoken since you coached Charlie Brent for me and launched him into super stardom. He's getting 17.5 *million* a picture now. We were a helluva team."

Jason couldn't deny that. Whether he acted or coached, his collaborations with Wes always yielded spectacular results. "Does this trip down memory lane have a point?"

"Just trying to jog your memory, so you'll be feeling magnanimous when I ask you my favor."

"I've already said no."

"This is a new favor," Wes explained. "I just want you to listen. Give me five minutes for old time's sake."

Had he really forgotten how persistent Wes could be? He hadn't forgotten. He had simply blocked it out. Wes had gotten him into more scrapes than he cared to recall, had opposed his retirement with more underhanded tricks than Jason could count on both hands. Wes had only been interested in using his fame to stay on top. That had hurt.

But on the other hand, Wes had stuck by him after the accident which had claimed both his parents' lives. Wes had been there when everybody else had turned away. That counted for something.

"Start talking."

"Good. I'd hoped you'd come to your senses." Wes laughed, but Jason didn't miss the relief in his voice. "You've heard of Shelby Moran?"

Who hadn't? The raven-haired beauty had burst upon Hollywood like a storm. Even he was impressed. More than once he had found himself calling in favors at the local video store to get her latest releases. "You've been doing a great deal of work with her lately."

"I'm flattered you've been paying attention." Wes's voice dropped a notch. "Have you seen her in anything? She's good. *Really* good. She could be great."

Jason agreed. Back when he had been coaching, he would have given his right arm for a student with Shelby Moran's potential. But now, at forty-one, he'd been out of that business for five years and had no intention of backtracking.

This conversation was going nowhere. "I'm not interested in coaching *anyone*. No matter how good she is."

"I just need you to teach her some techniques to help her through this problem she's having."

An image of the willowy, green-eyed actress flashed through his mind, but Jason's image didn't involve problems. Shelby Moran looked perfect as far as he could tell.

He shouldn't ask, should just hang up the phone right now and change his number, but the lure of those bedroom eyes was just too much. It had been too damn long since he'd had a date. "What kind of problem?"

"She freaks out during sex scenes."

Surprised, Jason sat up in his chair. "Any history of sexual abuse?"

"Hell, I never thought to ask." Wes emitted an unsteady laugh. "I'm not a psychologist. All I know is that if I don't get her through filming, I won't have an eligible release for the awards."

"Couldn't have that, could we?" Jason glanced out the window, squelching a rush of familiar emotion and letting the serenity of the landscaped university center him.

He knew what it felt like to be used as a vehicle to further someone else's ambitions. Looked like Shelby Moran was filling the bill now.

"Will you help me, Jason?"

He didn't hesitate. No matter how fast his pulse raced when he thought of being face-to-face with Shelby Moran, she'd have to learn for herself what the price of stardom was. "Sorry, Wes. Not my line anymore."

"She just needs a little coaching so she can deliver a decent performance without hyperventilating."

The accomplished young woman he had seen on screen contrasted sharply with the image Wes depicted. "If Shelby Moran has emotional issues, coaching won't help. Get her into therapy."

"She can deal with her problems on her own time," Wes erupted. "Right now I've got a film to direct."

"Compassionate as ever, aren't you?" Jason couldn't keep the bitterness from his voice as he took a deep breath to dispel his distaste.

This situation was not something he wanted to get involved in. Even if the thought of coaching Shelby Moran through sex scenes made his heart beat faster. "Let her go, Wes. Let her get the help she needs."

"You don't understand…"

"I understand completely. Shelby Moran is the most promising actress to come around in a while, and you're riding on her coattails because your last three films bombed."

"Ouch." Wes laughed, but the edge to his voice didn't fade. "You know how this business is."

"That's why I'm out." Jason rocked back in his chair. He stared out at the campus grounds, lush with the green of summer. The serenity of the scene reflected his peace of mind. No matter what the pros and cons of his new life, he was much better off out of Hollywood. "I won't change my mind. Good luck."

A heavy silence greeted him before Wes said, "I'm sorry, old man, but I must ask you to reconsider."

His flat tone made Jason's hackles rise. He braced himself against the ax he sensed about to fall.

"I haven't read anything about you in the rag sheets in what… three, maybe four weeks?"

Jason didn't answer. He propped his feet up on the window ledge and waited for Wes to play his hand.

"You must be enjoying all that privacy. I mean, I know how much you resented the paparazzi dogging you all the time. Even now they don't really leave you alone, do they?"

"So?"

"You're a mystery. Hollywood gifted you with stardom and you tossed it back in their faces. They're fascinated. Helluva career move."

"Your point?"

Wes laughed. "Remember that seedy little blue flick you made back in '74? The one that earned the X-rating and cost your father a fortune to keep from being released?"

Jason remembered very well. It had been one of his first attempts to break free of a career that had consumed his entire life. "What about it?"

"I have a copy sitting in my film vault."

Jason clutched the receiver and struggled to keep the revulsion from his voice. "I don't care if you release that. I was a kid for Christ's sake."

"*You* might not care, but the *paparazzi* will," Wes drawled. "Ready to step back into the spotlight?"

He wasn't, and the bastard damn well knew it. Jason exhaled a harsh breath. "Don't pull this crap on me."

"I asked nicely. You said no."

Was he bluffing? Jason didn't trust Wes as far as he could throw him. It had taken five long years to achieve the degree of privacy he enjoyed now. Five years to be able to walk out his front door without facing the flash of cameras, to drive to the university, or the airport, or the damned grocery store without outrunning the paparazzi.

He had been Chase and Elena's son, Hollywood's golden child whose entire life had been public domain. After his parents had died, the world had grieved with him, then watched him grow into adulthood, delighted, angered and, above all, entertained, by his antics.

Until Jason turned his back on them.

Now he was an enigma. His only defense was the utterly *ordinary*, utterly *uninteresting* life he led.

Was he willing to step back into the spotlight now when, for the first time in his life, he could finally open his eyes without being blinded by the glare?

Jason gripped the receiver so tightly that his hand trembled. "Give me her address."

Star-Struck

Shelby crossed the foyer and cast a quick glance at the grandfather clock. Eight on the dot. The acting coach Wes had hired was right on time. Lucky her.

Stopping just short of the door, she stood with her hand poised over the knob and calmed the flutters in her stomach. The moment of truth had arrived in the form of a stranger, and she was totally unprepared. No matter how hard she tried to gear herself up, the idea of tackling this problem still made her queasy. Maybe she should just give up acting?

But she couldn't give up life. With a little luck, if she could learn how to film a sex scene, she might be able to perform one in real life, too.

Taking a deep breath, Shelby cleared her thoughts and placed herself in the mindset of cordial hostess. *Open the door. Greet the guest.* She could do this.

The doorbell chimed again.

Rolling her shoulders to dispel the last of her tension, she settled a smile on her face and turned the knob.

"Hello." Shelby peered out at the powerhouse of a man who stood on her doorstep, faded jeans slung low on trim hips and expensive athletic shoes bracing long legs firmly apart. Her heart dropped to her feet.

Jason Gage?

No way. The lengthening twilight cast him in silver and shadow, and she quickly took in his casual, but masculine stance, his well-toned body. He radiated intensity, the robust energy of a man in his prime, a self-possession nobody half his age ever quite managed to pull off.

Experience. That's what it was. This was a man who had lived. She could see it in the chiseled planes of his face—a handsome face, an interestingly rough and experienced face. A face she had studied in stark clarity on film. A face she had seen grainy and shadowed on tabloids in the supermarket.

Jason Gage. In the flesh.

"Miss Moran?"

She had heard his voice a thousand times. Deep and strong, like a velvet murmur, his voice conjured up images of dark bedrooms and slick bodies.

Leaning back against the balustrade, he looked terribly roguish, just as he had when he had played Frankie Worth in *The Last Rebel*. He folded his arms across his chest and scowled before Shelby realized she had missed her cue. Jason Gage apparently was not amused by the way she kept gawking at him.

"Are you going to invite me in?"

Heat singed her cheeks with the force of Pepe's Beyond The Border Salsa. "Of course. Please." Feeling really stupid, she stumbled back against the door and allowed him to enter.

Striding past her in a burst of masculine grace that trampled what was left of her composure, Shelby suddenly found herself staring at his impossibly wide shoulders. The torchiere lamps illuminated his hair, thick wavy hair that was neither brown nor auburn, but some wonderful russet color in between.

Swinging back around, he sized her up with brilliant black eyes. "Are you coming?"

Shelby nodded. There was no recovering from this one. She'd flopped. Big time. "I'm so sorry. It's just—well, I wasn't expecting *you*."

"Obviously." His full mouth tightened in a frown.

Get a grip, Shelby. Forcing herself into motion, she pulled the door closed and sailed past him, taking the opportunity to steady her nerves.

Leading him into the living room—a room large enough to allow her some breathing space—she moved as far away as politely possible. "May I take your—" She glanced around for whatever he had brought with him. Coat? Briefcase? Garment bag? "Keys. May I take your keys?"

"No." He hooked them onto his belt loop. Assessing the room in one even glance, he did not look pleased by what he saw.

She had decorated the room herself, just as she had the rest of the house. Stripped and refinished the woodwork by hand, fitted the cornices above the windows, selected everything from the draperies and floral arrangements to the mirror above the fireplace and the cloisonné vase that sat on the oriental-inspired "biblot" table beside the door. The result was a Victorian drawing room washed in shades of pink and burgundy that sent a tingle through her every time she glanced around.

Granted, Jason looked like a stallion in a field of dandelions against the backdrop of curio shelves and ornately-worked étagères. So was it her taste in furnishings that offended him, or did she herself displease him?

"Are you ready to work, Miss Moran?"

"I *was*. Until I saw you." She brushed an errant strand of hair from her face, then forced her arms to her sides. She didn't know what to do with her hands. "I *really* wasn't expecting you."

"Can you handle it?" he asked on the edge of an impatient breath.

"I don't know."

He seemed almost relieved, and she would have bet her bottom dollar that he would rather be anywhere in the world but here.

"How on earth did Wes talk you into this?" she asked bluntly.

"Blackmail." The reply was just as succinct.

That certainly wasn't what she had expected.

"The weasel!" Plopping back into a chair, she eyed him curiously. "Must really have the goods on you."

Those sable eyes bored into her. "No comment."

Yep, she'd bet that Jason Gage would rather be roasting in hell right now.

She tried to act composed, *recovered*, but the breath caught in her throat when he sat across from her, so close she couldn't help but notice the way his long body folded in a neat display of muscle, how he looked oh-so-masculine on her delicate Queen Anne settee.

"Wes told me a little about what's going on, Miss Moran. You sure you're up to this?"

"Absolutely."

Not!

"Then we need to cover a few ground rules." He compressed his mouth into a thin line. "If you want me to work with you, you'll have to agree to protect my privacy. I am not out of retirement and don't want to deal with the backlash of anyone thinking I am. This was one of my conditions to Wes."

"That's quite acceptable, Mr. Gage. I'm not exactly eager for media coverage either."

He blinked, and what she thought might be the start of a smile tugged at his lips. He managed to control it. "I don't imagine you are."

Slipping off her sandals, Shelby tucked her feet underneath her. She needed every relaxation technique she could think of right now, starting with casual posture. "I have a few questions of my own. The first of which is what you think you can actually do for me."

"You sound skeptical." He raised an eyebrow in that wonderfully quizzical expression she remembered so well from *The Longest Day Of The Century*.

He had played a quirky scientist in that one. A comedy that still made her laugh even though she must have seen it thirty times.

"Oh, I'm definitely skeptical. This was Wes's idea."

"But you agreed."

"No, Mr. Gage. *I* threatened to report him to the union." Shelby flashed her brightest smile. "*He* threatened to leak my problem to the press."

Jason let out a snort that might have been a laugh. "He is a weasel, isn't he?"

"Absolutely. But I've decided to make the best of a bad situation. Have you?"

He studied her for a long moment, and when he finally nodded, Shelby sucked in a breath that reminded her she'd almost forgotten to breathe.

"We'll call a truce." He leaned back on the settee and rested an elbow on the cushioned arm. "You had a few questions. What would you like to know?"

In the blink of an eye, all aggression left his expression, and she suddenly faced a man who reminded her of... her therapist.

Shelby laughed. "I was so surprised to see you, I'd forgotten."

"What?"

"You're a psychologist now. I read it in the papers."

He nodded.

"Are you here to coach me or psychoanalyze me?" She wasn't sure she was comfortable with either.

"I'm just here to help." He steepled his fingers before him and offered his first real smile.

Ohmigosh! Her heart skipped a beat, and she struggled to draw a decent breath through a chest that suddenly felt way too tight.

No wonder Jason Gage had been a star. He oozed presence like nobody she'd ever seen before. One smile, and she not only knew she was in the same room with him, but on the same planet.

She was *never* going to be able to work with him.

"I plan to take you back to your acting basics, Miss Moran. Relaxation. Concentration. Then we can move into sense and affective memory."

She didn't know whether to laugh or cry. "I've used every trick in my repertoire. Know any magic?"

"We don't need magic." His deep velvet voice made her chest squeeze even tighter. "You're obviously hung up somewhere. We just need to figure out where and find you some other stimuli to draw from when you perform."

Shelby let out a sigh. "You're talking coaching, not psychology. Right?"

"You'd be surprised at how closely the two are related. But I have no intention of prying. You fill in the blanks whenever you feel it's necessary. Fair enough?"

She nodded, not trusting herself to answer while experiencing such a strange mixture of relief, apprehension and foolishness. Relief that she wouldn't have to take a trip down memory lane. Apprehension because she didn't think she could avoid it. Foolishness because she needed Jason's help but couldn't seem to think straight when she looked at him.

"You're still worried."

He *knew*. As if he could see straight through to her soul, Jason Gage knew she had a horrible secret. But she had already spent years in and out of therapy working through all the emotional baggage from a dark past. She refused to believe that anything constructive could come from rehashing old memories.

Jason must have sensed her turmoil because he reached out and took her hand. "You can trust me, Miss Moran."

Tension melted. His grip was strong, warm, *giving*. Shelby knew in that instant no matter what the paparazzi wrote about the infamous Jason Gage—no matter how surly, ungrateful or selfish they portrayed him—they didn't have a clue about the man himself. This was a man who had been coerced to come here, yet he was willing to help. If he said she could trust him, she could.

And the protective way he held her hand said everything.

Shelby decided right then and there that she was going for the pot of gold at the end of the rainbow.

Her fingers tightened around his. "Can you teach me how to perform a sex scene?"

"Yes."

She lifted her gaze to find him watching her. With concern. And determination.

She believed that he would never hurt her.

Shelby swallowed hard. "Do you think you could teach me how to perform *sex*, too?"

Wouldn't Miss this Show . . .

"Your trouble isn't just with performing a sex *scene*, but with having sex?" Jason kept his voice level and his gaze steady, but it was a damn good thing he was sitting. Otherwise he might have hit the floor.

Shelby tried to pull her hand away. He held on.

"Yes." She breathed the word in a sigh, and something fluttered in his chest at the vulnerability he saw in her eyes.

God, she had beautiful eyes. Greener than the lawns at the university during summer session, her eyes attracted him just like that inviting place did.

"For how long?" He forced the words out, struggling for professional distance when all he wanted to do was stroke away the frown that creased her brow.

"I didn't have any problem filming sex scenes until about a year ago." She shrugged, a gesture that admitted defeat more eloquently than words. "Sex has always been a disaster."

"Always?"

She cast him a crooked grin. "Always."

Blood thudded through his veins. Shelby Moran wasn't at all what he had expected. Not by a long shot.

"Why has sex been a problem?"

Jason felt her agitation even before she jerked her hand away. Shooting to her feet in a fluid motion that drew his gaze along the slender lines of her body, she ran a hand through hair the color of soot and paced before the fireplace. "I don't know why."

"I said I wouldn't pry, but it would help me immensely to know if you have a history of sexual abuse."

"I don't," she answered defensively before turning to face him. "Something happened once. A long time ago. But it's all over now. I worked through it."

"This *something* doesn't have anything to do with your inability to perform a sex scene or have sex, does it?"

"No," she answered decidedly, then shrugged in obvious exasperation. "Oh, I don't know."

At first he thought she was trying to convince him, but he quickly realized she must be trying to convince herself.

Time for a new approach. "You asked me earlier if I thought coaching would help, and I'm going to ask you the same thing now. Do you think coaching will help?"

"Yes."

Apparently she was willing to settle for a sex life based on acting. That said a lot about what she was willing to sacrifice.

This was a problem Jason hadn't anticipated, and they already had a significant one. His professional detachment had vanished the minute she had opened the door. One look at her, and his blood had started pumping double-time.

Shelby Moran was definitely not what he had prepared himself for. She was tall, a bit too thin, a bit too lanky. He knew her runway model body filmed well, yet he couldn't help but wonder if those slender shoulders could bear the emotional burden she carried.

What had happened to her? So many tragedies could befall a beautiful young girl that inwardly he cringed at the possibilities. She must have been really young, because he knew she was only twenty-six now.

She seemed determined, though. He could see purpose in the stubborn tilt of her chin and the firm set to her lush pink mouth.

But Shelby was an actress, and a good one. While Jason didn't think her vulnerability was an act, in his experience, a vulnerable starlet was a contradiction in terms.

"This is more involved than I was led to believe. What do I get out of the deal?" he asked, needing to verify the impression he had formed about Shelby Moran.

Her back stiffened, and her straight black hair glimmered like glass as it swung with the movement. "The satisfaction of knowing you helped someone in need?" He wished she would turn around so he could see her face.

Jason came to his feet. Crossing the room, he stood behind her. Although she was tall, the top of her head only reached his chin. She jumped when he placed his hand on her shoulder.

"I'm no altruist."

"You'll get to have sex with me." Her words stabbed at his conscience.

"That's not much of an enticement. You've already said you're a disaster in bed."

She spun around, and his next challenge lodged in his throat when he gazed down at her exquisite face. Jason knew what it felt like to want. Shelby wanted to work through her problem more than she wanted anything else. He *felt* her longing like an electrical surge through his body. The strength of the connection he shared with her stunned him.

"I guess you'll just get to keep your secrets, then." Her green eyes sparkled, and he suspected she was fighting back tears. He felt chagrined.

"Wes won't let you off the hook, Mr. Gage. He's got a vested interest in me."

Jason didn't point out that he'd get to keep his secrets simply by coaching her through sex scenes. He would help Shelby, and maybe while he was helping her, he could alleviate some of the restlessness he had been experiencing since the start of his current lecture circuit.

Unable to resist, he ran his thumb along the full curve of her bottom lip. Her skin was soft to his touch. Warm satin.

"If I'm going to be your sex coach, perhaps you should call me Jason."

Her liquid gaze met his, and her lip trembled. "You'll do it?"

"I'd be honored." He meant it.

"All right, *Jason*." Her mouth curved upward into a smile. "What about the logistics?"

"We'll work here. I've got my bags in the car."

That seemed to fluster her. "Wow. Great." She ran a jittery hand through her hair and backed away. "I'll go make up the guest bedroom while you get your stuff. Okay?"

He let his hand drop to his side, amused that his skin still tingled from where he touched her. It looked as though Shelby wasn't the only one star-struck.

"I'll go get my things."

Her relief was almost palpable. Spinning on her heel, she disappeared. Jason recognized retreat when he saw it, and for the first time in a very long time, he felt like smiling.

The Divine Comedy

Ohmigosh! Shelby swung into the guest bedroom, the only bedroom besides her own in the oceanside cottage. She pulled the door closed, sorry that she hadn't plunked down more money for a larger place.

But why had she needed more space? Up until twenty minutes ago, the only people who ever visited her had been Paige and Christopher Sharp, her "family-by-love" as she thought of them. After everything they had been through together during the years, she and the Sharps were so close they could have easily sacrificed the second bedroom and held a slumber party in hers.

For the first time ever, her comfortable little home seemed entirely too small. She couldn't get far enough away from the man in her living room to make even a stutter in her racing pulse.

"Calm down, Shelby," she told herself. "*Getting away* isn't the idea here. You wanted someone good. Jason Gage is the best." She stared into the mirror, aghast when she took in her rumpled hair and pale cheeks.

She should have at least put on some makeup. Biting her lips for color, she smoothed the front of her white cotton romper, then dragged her fingers through her hair. Yanking open the door to the cherry armoire she had refinished herself, she selected a set of sheets.

"Shelby?"

She could hear him calling her through the closed door. This house definitely wasn't big enough. "In here," she yelled.

The door opened, and he suddenly filled the room with his sheer masculine presence. As he hoisted the garment bag over the door and placed his briefcase on the desk, she watched the taut muscles play in his shoulders.

This was like living a scene from *Heaven's Traveler*, her very favorite Jason Gage film of all time. He had played the role of Max Brandauer, a grudging angel of sorts, who had appeared to help the cast resolve their troubles—sometimes to very unexpected results.

Her pulse rushed like a tide as she stared at him across the bed. He was tall and beautifully proportioned. The most gorgeous angel she had ever seen with his melting black eyes and rich russet hair.

He was her very own Max Brandauer. An angel who would help her through this mess.

The idea delighted Shelby, but she couldn't help wondering what the twist would be—Max the angel *always* managed to turn the expected into the unexpected.

She shook the fanciful thought from her head along with the flat sheet. "I'm in the middle of a film. Haven't been home much," she said by way of explanation for the unmade bed.

He grabbed an edge of the sheet as it floated down. "No maid?"

"Place really isn't big enough to warrant one. It's only me here."

He cornered and tucked the sheet into place with the practiced moves of a veteran. Shelby was considerably less adept, though not from lack of practice.

She couldn't keep her eyes off him. The tanned cords of his neck contrasted sharply with his white collar. The rugged angle of his jaw stood out beneath a five-o'clock shadow that burnished auburn on his chin. Everything about him fascinated her and filled her with silent expectation.

The sensation was completely unexpected. *Unfamiliar.* Shelby had summoned emotions, coaxed them, stifled them, built upon them—whatever the role she was playing at the time called for. But she had never actually *felt* this way before.

She fluffed a pillow. Jason caught her hand and stopped her short. His fingers twined through hers. His touch seared straight through her body.

"I'm making you really nervous, aren't I?"

Suddenly she was aware of the bed as if it were another living presence in the room. "Yes."

"Do you think you'll be able to work though it?" He cast her a wry grin that stole her breath. "You're beginning to make me nervous, too."

It took a second for his admission to register, but when it did, Shelby groaned.

How on earth am I going to work with him?

But she reminded herself that he was here to help. No need for pretense or artifice. She had already admitted her deepest, darkest secret.

Well, almost.

Laughter bubbled inside. "I really am sorry. I've met my share of fans who lose it when they ask for my autograph. Suddenly I can relate." She tightened her fingers around his. "Maybe the next time I meet one, I'll take his hand, look into his eyes and smile. Let him know it's okay."

Their gazes locked. His sable eyes glowed with laser intensity.

"It is okay, Jason, isn't it?"

"I don't bite."

"I'll be glad about that, I'm sure."

His expression warped into charming, and he turned into Max the angel before her very eyes. "I wouldn't count on it. I see the potential for brilliant results here."

"Really?"

He lifted her hand and brushed his lips gently across her palm. "We have chemistry, Miss Moran, or haven't you noticed?"

"Oh, I've noticed."

A tingle sailed up her arm. Whether it was his touch or his words that made her feel so... *alive*, Shelby didn't know, but that she was able to feel anything at all thrilled her. "Max Brandauer."

"What?"

"*Heaven's Traveler*. My favorite movie of all time," she admitted, not caring if she made a total jerk of herself by acting like a groupie. "I can't help but think of you as Max, coming to help me."

He laughed, his warm breath gusting across her palm and making her shiver. "Are you always so creative in your choice of stimuli?"

"Whatever helps me deliver the most believable performance."

"If Max does it for you, then Max I shall be." He let her hand slide away, and she felt the loss of his touch more intensely than she could explain. "Are you ready to start?"

"Yes."

Grabbing the antique chair from the desk, he placed it in the center of the room.

"I have a studio."

He slanted an amused glance at the bed. "This bedroom seems to be as good a place as any."

He had a point. But when he motioned her to the chair, Shelby had to force herself to sit, all at once apprehensive and excited.

"It's late. Why don't we start with some relaxation techniques? I want to see what kind of control you've got." He knelt beside her, so close that his voice pulsed against her ear. "You're very tense. We'll work through it and tackle more in the morning."

"Okay."

"Go limp."

Shelby closed her eyes and sank into the chair, arms resting on the armrests, head draped over the crest.

While she would have liked to relax at will and impress him with her usually exceptional control, she swallowed her pride and worked each muscle group, knowing that unless she became totally responsive this exercise would never work.

Silence seeped through her body, chased away the nervous tension. She retreated into herself, focusing on the breakers that combed the shoreline with rhythmic harmony just yards beyond her balcony. The steady tick-tock of the grandfather clock in the foyer.

And Jason. She could hear his deep even breathing, feel heat radiating from his body.

Suddenly his strong, warm fingers touched the sensitive skin beneath her bare knee. He lifted her leg and flexed it, and though other coaches had touched her exactly the same way a hundred times before, Shelby experienced a crazy little shimmer that kindled her skin like a sunbeam.

She willed herself to relax, but her mind feasted on this new sensation. She could smell him, unadorned by cologne, yet alluring and male, with his own unique scent. Hear the hushed quickening of his breath as he circled the chair and knelt before her, feel the raspy tread of his palms skimming her hips, nudging her diaphragm.

Only the strictest of control kept her from shivering while he worked his hands up from her waist and along her bare arms.

"Got some work to do here." His fingers glided along the bridge of her nose and over her eyelids. As if it were his pleasure and not his job, he explored her every curve, charted the lines of her muscles, committed his new knowledge to memory. "Open your eyes."

He stood oh-so-close, his face only inches from hers. Their gazes locked. She saw the flare of desire in his eyes, noticed a vein throbbing in his brow, even though his expression otherwise revealed no more than a professional interest.

He traced the curve of her brow with his thumbs, then outlined the hollow beneath her eyes.

"Let the tension drain away." His breath fanned her face like a gentle burst. Intimate.

Shelby let her eyes drift closed and focused on the stillness she had created within.

"Now relax here." His thumb circled her mouth.

She yawned wide, knowing she looked ridiculous, not caring. The last of her tension fled, and she sagged against the chair utterly limp, savoring the emptiness of controlled relaxation.

"Great. You've got it." He stroked her neck, a feather-light touch that tested her control. "Let's work on sense memory. Pick an object. Something simple."

Drawing her mind into the exercise, Shelby summoned an image of the only object she could concentrate on at the moment.

"What are you focusing on?"

"You."

"Why me?" She heard surprise in his voice.

"Trying to focus on a chair or a lamp would be impossible with you in the room."

He chuckled, a husky desirable sound that made her tingle. "All right. Add me to your memory bank."

Sweeping his hand across her eyes, just enough to stir the air and remind her to keep her eyes closed, he said, "What do you see?"

She conjured his image easily. "I see you the way you looked when I first opened my door. Everything about you waiting, impatient. You looked just like Frankie Worth in *The Last Rebel*." She could feel the smile in his laughter and narrowed her focus from the whole man to more specific details. "You're jingling keys in your right hand. Your keychain has the emblem of a Jaguar and the letters XJR-S. Your shoulders are straight. Your legs braced. You wear expensive athletic shoes, and the sole of the left one is worn down from the way you carry your weight."

Jason whistled. "What highly developed observation skills you have, my dear."

"I'm just getting started." Shelby laughed, liking that she had impressed him.

She guided her mind's eye upward along his legs. "Your jeans are just starting to show wear. The cuffs beginning to get thready. Judging by the way you move in them, I'd say they're comfortable."

"They fit well."

Amen. They hugged his thighs just enough to hint at the muscles beneath. And he had a great butt. Not flat. Not rounded. Curved just enough to make her want to touch.

Oh my!

Surprised at where her mind had wandered, Shelby forced herself to focus.

"Your tan magnifies the color of your eyes. Black. Like sable. Burning eyes. You have a strong face, an interesting face with just a hint of arrogance, as if you've seen a lot in your life and are determined to stay above it." Pausing, Shelby sharpened the image in her mind. "Straight nose. Blade-like nostrils that flare just a bit when you inhale. Full, erotic mouth. A mouth that makes me think of… kissing."

"Go with it, Shelby." Was that a catch she heard in his voice?

"You lick your lower lip when you're thinking. Your tongue darts out. It looks soft, textured, sort of like rough velvet."

"What does my tongue make you think of?" His voice simmered with some barely-checked emotion, and the sound slid right through her.

"*Taste*," she answered honestly. "Makes me wonder what you taste like."

The Anticipated Tragedy

Jason sucked in his breath, a reaction that could have been shock at her boldness, or something more, but a reaction that made Shelby realize how much she wanted to know.

Instead of summoning the emotion from the inner well she kept carefully filled at all times, this desire glowed from within. He was having the most amazing effect on her.

"Let's move on to your other senses," he said in a gravelly whisper. "What do you hear?"

"Your voice. Throaty and deep, yet controlled. I like the richness of it. You're breathing is shallow, not deep and even the way it was a few minutes ago. I'm making you... uncomfortable?"

He laughed, so near that strands of her hair trembled against her cheek. "Not uncomfortable, Shelby. Aroused. You're having an incredible effect on me." With a light stroke of a fingertip, he tucked the hair behind her ear.

She opened her eyes and met his gaze, surprised that his feelings mirrored her own. "I know."

"That surprises you?"

"You look so... hungry."

His gaze burned into her. "I am."

"You don't look very happy about it." She lifted her hand to his cheek, needing to touch him, needing to know that what she felt was real.

"You've shot my professional distance straight to hell."

"I'm glad."

"You feel it, too." It was a statement, not a question.

"I've never felt like this before," she admitted, trying to translate the elusive feeling into words. "I create sensations that I believe are appropriate, but I don't feel, Jason. I act."

The fire in his eyes blazed, and to her amazement, his reaction stoked that ribbon of flame inside her.

"I want to make you feel." His declaration was so simple, yet so potent. When he lifted his hand to her face and traced his fingers along her jaw, she shivered. "Concentrate on the way I make you feel. Describe it to me."

Her eyes drifted close, and she focused on his fingertips, the feathery light brush against her skin.

"The air between your fingers and my face feels heated, electric."

He molded her jaw with the strong warmth of his palm. "Now?"

"Aware. The strength of your touch. Of you."

His hand trembled as he traced the shell of her ear.

"Little tingles are spiraling down my neck. Almost like tickles."

She sensed his nearness, but when his breath puffed hot against her ear, she jumped, the tiny flame inside her flickering wildly. Her mouth opened, but the only sound to escape was a surprised gasp.

Jason chuckled.

"Build on that feeling." He traced the curve of her shoulders, then his hands trailed down her bare arms in a slow silken progression that made her tingle in the wake of his touch.

"Are you committing this sensation to memory?"

Her senses were so heightened that even his voice rippled through her. She whispered a hushed "Yes" before feeling him withdraw.

Suddenly he was in front of her, slipping the sandal from her left foot and tracing the arch, the rise of her ankle, the sweep of her calf.

She hadn't realized her legs were so sensitive, that a simple caress of his hand could be intimate. Even though their only physical connection was his thumb circling the underside of her knee, Shelby felt him everywhere.

His deep, even breathing resonated like music in her ears. His maleness seemed to glow from him, until she was sure she would melt beneath its brilliance.

His mouth.

He pressed a warm kiss to the tender curve below her knee, and pleasure radiated outward. Real pleasure. That's what this was. Somehow she knew. Not from any prior experience, but because this was what she always dreamed it would feel like.

"Jason." She breathed his name on the edge of a sigh. "I feel so…

alive. I'm glowing inside."

"Let it build." His breath gusted against skin moist from his kiss, and a delicious shudder billowed through her body.

His touch was so gentle, so *right*. She didn't resist when he coaxed her knees apart. His fingers tempted, teased, but she sensed his hesitation, knew he waited for some sign to continue.

Shelby opened her eyes. Seeing him wedged between her thighs was a purely sensual experience. She had known this existed, just hadn't experienced it for herself.

Until Jason.

He met her gaze boldly. She recognized the emotion that sharpened his features, hooded his eyes. Her heart fluttered with the knowledge that she was affecting him, too.

"Don't stop," she said simply.

"Tell me how you feel." The command was a caress.

"I feel... connected to you. Filled by you."

He slid the hem of her romper up her leg, and his gaze held hers as he ran his tongue along the inside of her thigh. "Does my touch overwhelm you?"

She shifted uncomfortably in the chair as unfamiliar sensations pooled between her legs. "No. Yes."

A smile lifted the corners of his mouth.

Drawing up on his knees, he leaned so close that her breath ruffled his hair and made it tickle her nose. She felt a rush of such tenderness that she couldn't resist pressing a kiss to the top of his head.

Emotion played across his face, so fleeting that she couldn't pinpoint his mood. Had she offended him? Her breath caught. Her whole being filled with waiting, until his nostrils flared, and she recognized what she saw in his face.

Need.

Jason struggled, his battle to calm the desire that lurked in his expression plain for Shelby to see.

Raising her hand, she stroked the tense curve of his jaw. Burnished stubble rasped her fingertips, an odd, yet visceral, sensation, and she watched while he tamed his hunger.

Jason had to be the consummate actor. His chest rose and fell sharply, but within seconds, he had leveled his breathing.

And Shelby recognized what else she had seen in his face.

Loneliness.

She knew that feeling intimately.

"You're doing the most incredible things to me." He fixed her with a crooked smile that made her pulse jump.

"Ditto."

He stood and held out his hand. "Come, *student.* It's time to continue our studies supine."

She took his hand. Her mouth went dust dry as they stood so close he filled her vision. When his fingers dropped to undo the buttons of her romper, she looked up to study his face. A face that held such a fascinating blend of strength and hunger and isolation.

The buttons popped open, one by one, and the romper parted. He focused on his task as if she was the most important thing in his world. She liked the feeling. She liked Jason.

"Nervous?" His fingers brushed her stomach and her muscles contracted.

"No."

It was the scariest thing she had ever admitted, but this felt right. Jason felt right.

Now if only she could trust herself.

Here was this wonderful man, her very own Max the angel, and she could screw up at any time.

Shelby drew a deep breath. Doubt would get her nowhere. Clearing her mind of negativity, she focused on the stimuli Jason presented her— the tingle that shimmered through her when his hand brushed her hip, the strange sensations that stole the strength from her legs.

He pushed the romper from her shoulders, and it slid down her body in a whisper, leaving her standing in only her bra and French-cut panties. His burning gaze raked her boldly. The vein in his temple throbbed. The muscles in his throat worked as he swallowed hard.

Shelby had never felt so beautiful in her life.

There was wonder in his expression as he traced the arch of her shoulders with warm palms, barely touching her, yet scorching her skin with his heat. His hands trembled as he skimmed her arms, her breasts, her waist, her hips. And even as she marveled at the wild ache that pulsed low in her belly, she let the sensation wash through her, not needing to draw upon the wealth of emotions she kept stored in her actor's memory. Not needing to act.

She *felt.*

For the first time in memory, she felt.

Jason guided her onto the bed with a tender touch, his smile encouraging her to lie down, to trust him.

She did.

"Concentrate on what you're feeling, Shelby. Just tell me to stop if you're uncomfortable."

She smiled at him, gifted by the eager light that flared in those beautiful black eyes. Closing her own, Shelby cleared her mind, sharpened her focus to the way her insides trembled.

The bed dipped when Jason sat beside her. "How do you feel?"

"Excited."

"Good."

He slid the pillow from beneath her head so she lay flat, and she heard it fall to the floor with a thump. With light strokes, he brushed the hair from her face and smoothed it around her.

She must look decadent, like an innocent maiden on the sacrificial altar. She had played a similar role once, but then she had evoked angst and fear. Now all she felt was anticipation. Hope.

She sensed Jason's gaze. When his fingertip trailed from her chin down the arch of her neck, a stream of tiny embers ignited inside her. A hot ache grew in her throat, made it impossible to swallow, to speak, to do anything but let him guide her along this path of arousal.

He outlined the straps of her bra with his finger, his touch gentle, teasing, as he dipped beneath the lace to trace the curve of her breast.

As he followed the contours of her stomach, her abdomen, the womanly pillow of her sex, she quivered.

"Oh!" Had she really uttered that heartfelt sigh?

When his mouth grazed her ear and his hot breath gusted across her skin, Shelby knew without a doubt that she had. Sparks lit inside her like fireworks, tiny flames sparkling to life as he circled his tongue in that sensitive place behind her ear, then sprinkled gentle kisses along her neck.

Her eyes shot open when he stretched out beside her. He gathered her into his arms. Shelby could only gasp as her body fit against his in all the right places.

His wide shoulders created a haven, the perfect place to lay her head.

His pulse beat steadily beneath her cheek, and she marveled as her own pulse quickened.

His earthy male essence filled her senses, heightening her awareness. The strong arms that held her close protected her, cherished her, as she and Jason lay together in a haze of sensation. Slipping her arms around his waist, she marveled at the trim hardness that hinted he enjoyed physical activity, another clue to the only man who had made her *feel.*

Shelby *felt* his clothing rasp her bare skin. She *felt* his muscled thighs buttress hers, pulling her close until she could feel the hardness of his desire against her.

He explored the contours of her back, trailing his hands upward along her spine, his touch gentle, knowledgeable.

Jason knew how to stoke the fire inside her, and when he unfastened the hooks of her bra, she experienced no uncertainty, no panic. Only the swell of her breasts as they grew heavy with expectation.

He cupped her bare breast with a strong hand, his thumb circling her nipple, until the ache inside became a pull of desire between her legs.

She arched against him.

"Do you like this?" The hunger in his whisky voice was no act. He wanted her, and his hard body radiated his need, a palpable force.

"And this?" Knowing fingers tugged at her nipple until it hardened into a tight pearl.

Tendrils of sensation rippled through her. Exquisite.

"Tell me what you feel."

"I feel... I *want.*"

More.

She wasn't sure what more was, but she quickly figured out what would further their quest for fulfillment.

"I want to feel *you.*" She slipped her hands into the waistband of his jeans and tugged at his shirt.

Needing no further urging, Jason kicked off his shoes while Shelby slid the shirt up, revealing a wealth of bronzed skin, the smattering of burnished curls.

He ripped the shirt over his head and tossed it aside. The breath hitched in her throat at the sight of his wide chest, all strength and sinew. All man. All desire.

Eagerly, she lifted her arms to him.

Jason sank into her embrace. She could feel the urgency he held in check as her breasts crushed the hot wall of his chest, rasping the crisp curls until her skin tingled with the need to feel him touch her.

Somehow he must have sensed her need. Cupping her breasts, he dipped his head, and his hot mouth fastened onto a nipple. Shelby moaned. Nothing in her experience had ever prepared her for the intensity of this sensation. She had heard, had dreamed, but, God, she had never *known*.

He created magic. In her body. In her mind.

The fire blazed.

He laved her nipples with a swirling tongue. She moaned. She wanted. *He knew.*

His hands drifted down. He rolled the panties over her hips, and with his foot slid them between her legs until they joined the rest of the clothes on the floor.

With a flash of white teeth, he tugged on her nipple, and the exquisite sensation that followed robbed her of speech. She could only stare at him in wonder, not knowing anything except that she didn't want him to stop.

Jason apparently had no intention of stopping.

Placing a hand over her abdomen, he began a leisurely descent toward her most intimate place. He parted the tuft of hair between her legs, rounded the soft swell of her sex with deliberate slowness and dipped his fingers between her thighs. He fondled that tiny pearl of her womanhood until the fire inside her blazed into hot sensation.

Her thighs parted, and she pressed upward into his touch.

A ragged groan escaped him, and he captured her mouth with his, sharing his arousal with the hot sweep of his tongue.

Her mouth burned, her senses spun, and she met his kiss with a demand of her own.

Don't stop.

He didn't.

He stroked the tiny pearl of her desire, his fingertips testing the moist heat between her legs until she gasped at the wildness of the sensation, cried out her urgency against his lips.

He slid his finger inside.

The fire between her legs became a pulsing beat that thrummed through her entire body. Her sex throbbed around his finger as he massaged her with sizzling strokes, forced the flames higher with every sensual thrust.

Suddenly Shelby understood. An explosion waited just beyond the fire inside. Just a few more strokes. She could *feel* it.

The flames blazed hotter. Heat scorched every inch of her, singed the edges of her hope to experience this ultimate joining.

She writhed against him, drew upon his lips, urged him to take her beyond the flame.

Jason did.

He stormed her with touch until she could see the fire just ahead in the distance, feel the heat burn. Need flared so bright she thought she might explode.

Her senses reeled.

The flame was so close she could almost touch it.

Almost.

Then the breath clogged in her chest. Her heart pounded too hard. And Shelby tumbled into the black tunnel of fear.

The Ironic Farce

He had lost her.

Even though he'd been anticipating it, Jason almost missed the signs that it had happened. Her ragged breathing. Her trembling muscles. Her clammy skin. For an instant he had thought she was climaxing, but the deathlike paleness of her face quickly snuffed out that hope.

Her emerald eyes stared at him—unfocused, glazed with her own private terror. She pushed at him with shaking hands, tried to sit up. As he spun onto his knees, lifting her, trying to coax her back with soft words, he could feel her panic.

"It's all right, Shelby. Breathe with me."

Her lips parted. She tried. God, how she tried, but he could tell from her strangled gasps that she wasn't succeeding.

Her chest rose and fell rapidly. Tears suddenly trembled in her eyes, spiking black lashes into star-points before they spilled over pale cheeks.

His heart throbbed so hard in his chest it hurt, because of her fear. His helplessness.

Locking one arm around her, he stroked damp hairs from her cheek. "Breathe with me, honey." Puffing his cheeks in example, he wiped his expression clean, refusing to let her see his concern, realizing that in all his years of acting he had never had to struggle harder.

White lines ringed her mouth. Each gasp failed.

"Come on." He could hear the edge of alarm in his voice and struggled to hide it. "Exhale with me. One. Two. Three. One. Two. Three. Now take a deep breath."

A wheeze.

"There you go. Let's try again."

Holding her tight, as if he could chase away her fear by strength alone,

Jason counted and breathed, again and again, until her trembling lessened and her eyes began to focus.

He smiled at her, relieved when she drew her first real breath. "It's all right, honey. You're going to be all right." He wiped the tears from her cheeks.

Shelby met his gaze with eyes that sparkled like jewels. Her expression crumbled. A sob, aching and terrible to hear, tore from her lips. He eased her back onto the bed while deep racking sobs shook her slender body and clawed at his heart.

When Jason cradled her against him, cheek to cheek, he realized her face was not the only one wet with tears.

This was his fault. He was supposed to be coaching her, not making love to her. But she had been so responsive. And so completely thrilled.

He had wanted to bring her to climax. She'd been so close. He still ached with need, but that no longer mattered. The sound of her pain chased away everything else from his mind.

With her face buried in the crook of his neck, Shelby cried her heart out. Lifting the corner of the comforter, Jason pulled it over her, feeling an unfamiliar need to protect, to offer a safe shelter against the storm that raged within her.

She clung to him, her trembling lessening by slow degrees, and he felt relief, far more than he ever believed possible. The way tears moistened her hair into a dark frame around her face touched him, and the way she bit her lower lip to stop its quivering tugged at his heart.

Helping Shelby face her demons suddenly seemed more important than anything he had ever done in his life.

It was an awesome feeling.

"I'm sorry," she whispered, her voice muffled against his skin.

He almost smiled. Raising himself onto an elbow, he peered down into her face. "Why's that?"

"I freaked you out."

His cheeks still felt sticky from tears, so to deny her claim would have been ridiculous. "I knew this might happen when I signed on. That's why I'm here, remember?"

She gave him a tight smile and sniffled loudly.

"Give me some of the credit, honey." With a finger on her chin, he lifted her face. "I wasn't doing my job. I was making love to you."

"You gave me what I wanted. You were so gentle." Hurt and longing flashed naked in her gaze. "And I was *feeling*, Jason. Really feeling."

Her shoulders slumped. She looked so defeated that he could only watch her grimly as he thought desperately for some way to make her smile.

"Come on. It's not so bad. We've only just started." He tweaked her nose the way an adult might do to a child, and when her tear-spangled eyes widened, he felt like a fool.

He rolled to the side of the bed. "I'll get you a tissue. Want something to drink?"

Sitting up in a graceful motion, she gathered the comforter around her. "I'm some kind of hostess. I dragged you into bed before I even offered you a drink."

Now he had made her feel self-conscious, too. What the hell was wrong with him?

"I won't hold it against you." Jason beat a hasty retreat.

After retrieving a box of tissues from the bathroom and giving it to Shelby, he made his way to the kitchen. A water cooler held a place of honor in the corner, hinting at Shelby's predilection for healthy drinking, but Jason headed toward a wine rack he spotted on the wall opposite the refrigerator.

He could use a glass.

Selecting a decent merlot, he searched through the cabinets for glasses, hoping Shelby hadn't been saving this bottle for anything special.

The uniform neatness of her kitchen hinted that no special event was forthcoming. Life on location left little time for anything else, and Shelby's immaculate home indicated that she didn't make time for much besides work. The delicate furnishings and design revealed no trace of a male in her life. He found himself pleased to an absurd degree.

This coaching session was turning out to be full of surprises. His reaction to Shelby was the most incredible of them. His taste in women had never run in any specific direction, but Shelby was about ten years too young for him and definitely in the wrong business.

Jason made his way back toward the guest bedroom, reflecting on all the twists his emotions were taking. He found Shelby wrapped in the comforter, perched on the window seat with moonlight silvering her hair. The sight of her brought a lump to his throat. She was so beautiful. She struck some primitive inner chord in him. He belonged here. No matter what bizarre events had brought them together, Jason was meant to be in this room with her.

He had never been more sure of anything in his life.

"I brought wine." Silently crossing the room, he sat beside her.

She accepted a glass and sipped without looking up.

"Do you still think you can help me?" Her question ended with a plaintive sigh.

"I can help you act," he replied honestly. "But I don't know enough about what's bothering you to do much beyond that."

Her gaze locked onto his, and he could almost feel her determination flare between them. "I'll settle."

"But will you be content?"

That elicited a smile. She shook her head. "Probably not now that I know what I'm missing. Beggars can't be choosers."

He wanted to tell her she wasn't a beggar, shouldn't have to settle, but he held back his opinion. Only Shelby knew how much effort she was willing to put into her recovery. Jason couldn't force her, no matter how much he wanted to.

Perhaps his coaching could facilitate changes in other areas, though. He had a theory. "I think the key is affective memory. If you want to act through your anxiety attacks, you're going to have to draw stimuli that gets you out of the trauma mode and into a sensual one."

"What happens if I haven't had any sexual experiences that are... well, *pleasant*?"

He anticipated her question, if not her blush. "We create them."

She sipped her wine thoughtfully, then held the glass out in a silent salute. "That works for me." Her fine black brows drew tight in a frown, but she held his gaze steadily. "You're sure you don't mind? This could get messy."

He admired the courage it took for her to admit that. "I don't mind."

"Why?"

It was a simple question, but Jason didn't have a simple answer. "You touch me."

"Pity?"

"No."

"What then?"

"I don't know," he replied truthfully, not at all sure that revealing his emotions was prudent. But his professional distance had bailed on him already, and he just didn't feel like acting right now.

"I think I know what you mean." The smile that softened her exquisite features encouraged him.

Taking a sip of wine, she set her glass on a low table beside the window. Her slender fingers grazed his when she plucked the glass from his hand and placed it next to her own. "You're a nice man, Jason."

He couldn't suppress a snort of laughter. "I've been called a lot of things. Nice generally isn't one of them."

"I can't imagine how anyone could miss it," she said, shifting in her seat. The sight of her long shapely legs stretching out from beneath the comforter drew his full attention. "Unless no one knows the real Jason Gage. Do you keep him hidden away and play a role for the world?"

Her question struck so close to home, he could only stare at her in wonder. *Yes.*

The answer filled his mind, and even though he could not actually admit it, Shelby must have seen it clearly on his face.

She swept a light touch across his cheek. "Then I am flattered you let me glimpse the real Jason Gage. It's easy to think of you as Max Brandauer, but I think the man far surpasses the angel." She rose in a fluid motion that nearly took his breath away.

"You're also a very attractive man, and I suddenly find myself wanting you very much. Unless you have something else planned for the night." Her voice lowered to a throaty growl. "I'd like to rehearse again now."

Jason blinked. It took him a moment to realize she had slipped into character. Right before his eyes. Effortlessly.

Letting the comforter fall to the floor in a whisper of satin, Shelby stood before him naked, the willowy curves of her body gilded in the golden spray from the lamp.

"Will you make love to me, Jason?"

The First of Many Retakes

Every drop of blood in Jason's veins plummeted to his cock.

Apparently his voice had gone along for the ride, because he couldn't seem to form a coherent reply. His mouth opened, he felt the muscles in his throat work, but only a ragged gasp came out.

He had the vague thought that an accomplished actor should do better, but quickly cut himself a break. He was a man, after all—a man sitting a mere foot away from a naked Shelby Moran. If that in itself wasn't enough to leave him speechless, all the feelings she was stirring inside him were.

"Here, let me." She slipped to her knees, and her breasts jingled suggestively with the motion. When she gazed up at him, summer eyes hooded with desire, Jason realized her face was level with his crotch.

Oh, God.

Pale fingers flashed in the lamp light as she unbuttoned his fly and slid the jeans down his legs. Her every movement was slow motion, designed to entice, and though he knew this was the Shelby he had seen many times on the screen, in character, *believable*, he was helpless to resist her.

With her direction, he stepped out of his pants and stood before her in his briefs and socks. She leaned back on her haunches and inspected him boldly.

"Oh my." She maneuvered the briefs over his thickening erection. "You are gorgeous all over."

His cock accepted the compliment graciously by rising to full attention.

Shelby chuckled, a full-throated sound that ruffled through him like a shiver. Her breath gusted across his skin, hot and sweet, and he braced his legs apart to control the effects of her assault on his senses.

The fresh, faintly floral scent of her hair wafted through his awareness. Sooty strands of her hair fluttered over her ruby nipples in an enticing game of Peek-A-Boo. The seductive strokes of her hands scorched his flesh as she explored his thighs. Her fingers dipped and teased the sensitive skin between his legs, making his cock jump toward her hand like a heat-seeking missile.

Shelby slid her fingers in a sinuous glide around his hips, cupping his buttocks with both hands and urging him toward her. He could sense the hint of her breath on his skin, imagine the moisture of those lush lips.

A sound of satisfaction emerged from someplace deep within, some hidden place that echoed through his body only when his beast awoke. A sound that burst forth as a groan.

She responded to his need. Her body arched sinuously toward him, and her dark head dipped low. The breath solidified in his throat when her tongue glided along the length of his shaft in a slow wet spiral.

His hips thrust forward of their own accord. He balled his fists and fought the urge to pull her toward him, to demand an act that should only be a gift.

With smooth fingers she caressed his buttocks, urging him closer as she drew him into her mouth, sucked on him with long blissful pulls. A shudder ripped through him. His legs shook. He wondered how long he could stand.

Forever.

His body surged. The pleasure, so pure and explosive. It had been so long. Too long. The hot velvet walls of her mouth drew his arousal to life, worked his body into a sweet frenzy. His world spun out of control, and he speared his fingers into her hair to guide her rhythm, unable to stop himself, craving what she so lavishly offered.

Black silk swayed down the trim lines of her back as she worked his cock with generous strokes. She cupped his balls with a gentle hand. But it was the sight of her slender waist flaring into the gentle curve of her hips that undid him.

Without fully willing himself to, Jason pulled her into his arms and staggered back toward the bed like a drunk. She landed full length on top of him, her graceful body draped over his in all her naked glory. Every feminine inch branded him, fused reason and pleasure together in violent turmoil.

He could only groan when her mouth captured his in a kiss. Her tongue darted into his mouth, demanding, sending currents of erotic need coursing through him. He joined the game, and suddenly his world narrowed into tongues that dueled in hot abandon, seeking, searching, warm breaths coming together as one.

Her hair cloaked them in shadow. Like a sooty waterfall it brushed his shoulders, snagged the rough skin along his jaw, threaded into their mouths. Cool silk when everything else between them raged out of control.

Her fingers seared trails of fire along his neck, shoulders. Her breasts crushed against his chest, pebble tips grazed his skin, shattered him with sensation.

He could feel her heart throb in time with his. Bodies in sync. The sensation was unfamiliar, yet it filled him with longing to become a part of her. He *needed* to plunge deep inside her, to ride together on this tide of desire.

With shaking hands, he traced the furrow of her spine. Blindly he met her kisses. His body blazed with unfulfilled desire, but though she lifted him on the crest of a breaker, a tiny voice in his head reminded him that her lovemaking was all a performance.

She was acting.

He wanted to be more than her co-star. He wanted to be her lover.

He shouldn't push her.

But couldn't stop himself.

Wedging his erection between her thighs, he teased her soft opening, finding her dry as a scattering of fallen leaves.

A sober reminder that he was here to help.

He had to slow down. Had to make her feel… *something.*

His erection was a white-hot ache between his legs. Every inch of his body pounded, strained for release.

Arching his hips, he pressed into her softness, trying to ease the ache, control it. No one had ever actually died from unfulfilled desire. At least no one had ever documented it.

Slipping his hands between them to fondle her breasts, he brushed her nipples in slow circles while he tasted her mouth with his tongue and drank of her sweetness. Shelby gasped, her breath catching in her throat like a sob. She trembled in his arms.

He recognized her struggle for concentration and cheered her on with a reassuring touch.

"Remember how good it felt when I kissed you here." He demonstrated with a light brush of his lips across her ear.

"And here." He pressed feathery kisses down the graceful column of her neck.

She didn't pull away, and encouraged, he caressed the curve of her waist with a light stroke.

She shivered.

Poised on the brink. He could see it in her heavy-lidded gaze when he lifted his mouth to hers. He traced her lower lip with his tongue, sensuously, and when a sigh slipped between her parted lips, a sound of pure pleasure, Jason knew she was winning the battle to combine her feelings with her ability to act.

Unable to resist, he fondled the curve of her buttock, pressing into her softness, the satin warmth of her thighs molding his erection, a bittersweet agony.

Her teeth caught his bottom lip in a light nip. Jason tilted his head back and stared into her face.

Her eyes sparkled.

"You're a nice man, Jason Gage." Her breathy voice quickened the need inside him. "A nice man with a problem."

She caught the length of his erection in slim fingers and gave a knowing tug.

He groaned.

"Need a hand?"

Another slow pull with those long fingers saw him bucking unceremoniously.

Shelby laughed, the twinkle in her eyes telling him she was back in character. The swelling ache in his crotch threatened to engulf him. Jason struggled for control.

But when she bent over him, rosy lips parting to take him inside, she proved his control was all an illusion. With erotic strokes of her swirling tongue, Shelby lifted his desire to the edge, until his body only knew sensation. His concern that her lovemaking was a performance disappeared like smoke into the night.

She bobbed over his cock, her tongue laving the bursting head in slow, wet strokes that coaxed waves of sensation outward from her touch. Fighting the urge to spear his fingers into her hair and guide her strokes, he sank his fingers into the sheets, buffeted by sensation. Struggling for control.

But thought vanished completely when Shelby rose above him like a goddess of Venus, ivory shoulders thrust back, ruby-tipped breasts temptingly displayed under the fall of smoky hair.

His heart stuttered in his chest.

Stroking his wet cock against the folds of her sex, she took him in inch by glorious inch.

He had died and gone to heaven.

With her eyelids partially closed and a secret smile curving her erotic mouth, she welcomed him into her body until he hilted. Heat bound them together as surely as if they were one.

The shapely beauty of her body and the sleek caress of her skin taunted him. She dipped low, breasts rasping his chest, mouth caressing his cheek, then arched back as she rode him.

His legs shook, and with a strangled groan, Jason clasped her buttocks, lifted her off him, then plunged back inside as he crested, and wave after wave of ecstasy crashed though him.

But sanity returned with Shelby's triumphant smile. She sparkled, fresh as the grass after a summer rain, lifting his spirits even though he felt like a cad.

She had performed. He had come.

She was thrilled.

"I did it, Jason." She smiled ecstatically at him as though he had actually done something. "I really did it."

He sucked in another deep breath. Closing his eyes, he was dismayed, but not surprised, to find the sight of her beaming face burned into his eyelids. No help there.

He opened his eyes again. "Honey, you've got some work to do on your climax."

"Ha!" She laughed and eyed him imperiously down her slender nose. "I was great."

His legs still vibrated with the intensity of his orgasm. "No doubt there."

He still tingled from the effects of her greatness warring with the heaviness of satiation that weighted his body. Christ, he was too old for this. He wanted to roll over and die.

But Shelby did the rolling. Right off of him, eliciting his groan when the cool air hit his skin. Retrieving the comforter from the floor, she covered them and molded herself into the contours of his body as if she belonged there.

Her cheek rested in the curve between his shoulder and neck, her long legs threaded through his, and he couldn't have resisted stroking her smooth skin even if he had the energy to try.

"Are you okay?"

"Takes us old guys longer to recover."

Her disbelieving laughter rippled through the air. She ran slim fingers through the mat of fur on his chest. "Not my angel. He's beyond such a mortal concept."

"Trust me." At the moment, Jason felt the fifteen years between them like a century.

Shelby only smiled and snuggled closer. He sensed her elation, her joy, and wouldn't dream of spoiling her victory. He held her, resting his cheek on the warm silk of her hair.

She had accomplished something wonderful tonight. She had worked through an anxiety attack and seemed to have created a pleasant sensual experience for her memory scrapbook.

Jason supposed he should feel some sense of satisfaction that he had done his job. He didn't.

His ego was bruised. He knew she couldn't overcome her trauma in one session, but… Jason inhaled sharply as the truth struck him—his *head* knew.

Apparently rational thought had nothing to do with Shelby.

He traced the curve of her shoulder in wonder, and when she sighed softly, he realized she had fallen asleep.

A smile tugged at his lips. She felt so right wrapped in his arms. She belonged with him.

And then he understood.

Rational thought had no place around Shelby because his heart was calling the shots.

How in hell had this happened?

Special Effects

"Someone named Paige called while you were in the shower," Jason told her when she appeared on the balcony. "I let the recorder pick it up."

Nodding, Shelby half-sat on the balcony railing, close enough to Jason for polite conversation, but far enough not to get sucked in by his magnetic presence.

Her jitters were back in force this morning. Just the sight of him—tall, masculine, gorgeous—and the memory of his hands on her body stole the words right out of her mouth.

"I hope it wasn't a call you were waiting for."

"A friend," she explained. "I'll call her back later."

Much later. Like after the sun went down, so Paige wouldn't realize she hadn't been on the set all day and get on the next flight out of Washington. As welcome as her presence would be, Shelby had Jason and his request for privacy to consider at the moment.

She sipped her coffee and tried to alleviate a pang of guilt for blowing off her dearest friend in the world.

Paige and her husband Christopher knew about the return of her anxiety attacks, and they had been calling every few days just to say hello. They were worried about her. Shelby didn't know what she had done in a past life to deserve Paige and Christopher Sharp, but it certainly hadn't been anything she had done in this one. They were gifts from heaven personified.

"Is she a close friend?" Jason asked, peering at her through gold-rimmed eyeglasses.

"Like a sister."

"Wes didn't mention anything about your family, and I don't recall ever reading that you had any."

"I don't." Shelby smiled warmly, charmed that he was interested in her. How gentlemanly. How *Max the angel.* "My parents died when I was young. I lived in foster homes until I went to live with Paige in college."

Instead of offering the well-intentioned, yet unnecessary, sympathetic remarks she had come to expect whenever mentioning her upbringing in the foster care system, Jason asked, "Did you meet her in school?"

Shelby shook her head. "Through a volunteer program when I was about eight. She's been 'family-by-love' ever since."

"Are you a loner, Shelby?"

"Seems that way, doesn't it? Maybe that's why I'm such a control nut." She chuckled softly, then something he'd said earlier came to mind. "So you think my problem is a control thing?"

"Control is definitely a part of you," he said with a knowing smile. "You seemed much more comfortable in control last night."

Damn. Heat seared a path straight to her cheeks. Shelby averted her gaze to the silvery shoals barely visible beneath the breakers as the tide shifted.

The sight helped calm her, helped her focus. Dawn broke in ribbons of blush and gray just beyond the horizon, awesome and uplifting.

Humbling.

She was lucky to be alive. Ten years ago she had traveled a different path, a path that had almost killed her. But with lots of luck and wonderful people like Paige and Christopher, she had turned her life around and made something of herself.

She could get over this problem.

With Jason's help.

"Have I said thanks for last night?"

He glanced up from the laptop computer open on the table and laughed. "Honey, I should be the one saying thanks. My knees are still weak."

Heat bloomed in her cheeks again. She liked the way he called her honey. "I was good, wasn't I?"

"I'm going to kiss Wes the next time I see him."

He was teasing, she knew, but she was flattered all the same. Jason appeared different this morning. And it wasn't just the wire-framed glasses that made him seem like the height of academic masculinity. Like the time he played August St. Germain in *Conversations With Godfrey.* She had loved him in that film, with his sexy European accent.

"Hmm."

Her gaze trailed over him appreciatively. This morning he seemed content, drinking his coffee and working on his laptop. His laughter came easily. He looked at her with an almost tender expression. Perhaps sex did that to him.

Sipping her cooling coffee, Shelby remembered what sex did to her.

Her previous experiences had been such busts that she rarely made the effort anymore.

Awkward.

That one word summed up her entire sex life in a nutshell. Usually so worried about doing it right, she could never relax, let alone feel.

But she had felt last night with Jason. Exquisite new sensations that she had no names for, but somehow knew only he could make her feel. And when she remembered all the delicious tinglings and flutterings that had made her sigh aloud, Shelby knew she would not be content until she experienced them again.

What was happening here?

She had expected to *act* with her coach, not *feel*. But Jason had done the impossible, and now her emotions were getting all tangled up. Her heart went all soft and mushy whenever she looked at him.

She was playing with fire.

That's what was happening. Jason Gage had no use for Hollywood—a well-documented fact. She lived and breathed Tinsel Town. This situation was a disaster in the making.

She eyed him curiously, but he seemed oblivious to her scrutiny as he scowled at the computer monitor, then bashed out a rush of words on the keyboard.

A frown drew his brows together and compressed his lips into a straight line. She had explored the heat of his mouth with her kiss, had tasted the strong angle of his jaw with her touch. Her fingers tingled when she remembered caressing the muscular hollows of his chest, and how his broad shoulders blocked everything from her vision except for him.

He wore a robe now, loosely belted at the waist, and a tempting length of hard thigh was exposed, reminding her of how his hairy legs had twined between hers. How the pulsing shaft of his erection had felt inside her.

Hot. Thick. Swollen.

The sensitive place between her thighs prickled with memory.

Setting her coffee cup on the table, Shelby recognized this as the same feeling she had experienced last night when Jason had touched her. A budding ache that spread outward like the petals of a flower.

Shifting her bottom on the railing, she found that pressure only increased the sensation. Swirling tendrils of warmth spiraled into her belly and down her thighs. She held back a gasp of surprise at the tiny pinpoint of desire that just begged to be touched.

Casting a surreptitious glance at Jason, she found him engrossed in his work. She considered retiring to her room to investigate her newfound sensuality, but was afraid of losing the fragile sensation.

Propping a knee on the railing, Shelby stood in a relaxed stance that left her legs parted just enough to explore. She pretended to adjust her robe and slipped a hand inside. Her fingers felt cool as they skimmed her abdomen, her touch curiously decadent as she sought that secret place.

She zeroed in on the tiny bud with a light touch, and her sex seemed to gather in a pleasurable squeeze. Increasing the pressure slightly, she rolled her fingertip around the hard pearl until a shimmer of pure sensation rippled through her.

Oh.

Another stroke of her finger. Another wave of pleasure. Her breasts swelled. Her nipples grew hard until they peaked through her robe like pebbles.

This was what she had been missing, what she hadn't allowed herself to feel.

Until Jason.

Every sense heightened until she could smell the breath of the ocean on a breeze and sense the summer heat that lingered just beyond dawn. The way the chenille robe lay against her bare skin like a tickle.

The sensation blossomed. She shifted on the railing, pleasure building inside her, as delicate as spun sand, yet as steady as the tide. Her whole body felt languid, dreamy, carried away on a wave of warm sensation.

When the robe slipped from her shoulder, exposing her breast to the ocean breeze, she couldn't bear the thought of moving a muscle to cover herself.

Until she heard Jason suck in his breath.

Shelby glanced up to find him watching her. The raw hunger on his face sent a ripple of excitement through her.

"I'm onto something here." She barely recognized the sultry voice as her own.

"I'll say." He grinned the most crooked, crazy grin, and her gaze traveled down to his lap, where his erection jutted from between the parted folds of his robe.

Instead of feeling awkward or ashamed, his reaction only enhanced her arousal. Emboldened, Shelby indulged the sensation.

One tug on the belt, and her robe fell open.

Jason's eyes widened.

She smiled at him, encouraged, then dipped her finger into the soft folds of her womanhood.

Wet.

Like the petals of a flower after a spring rain. Pleasure unfurled, blooming inside her, urging her to nurture the feeling. Instinctively she rocked her hips, seeking, amazed by her response. So simple, yet so irresistible.

She fondled herself with long strokes, inspired by the way his gaze slid over her, slowly and seductively, by the yearning in his hooded eyes, by the erotic fullness of his mouth.

A sensual current passed between them. Her breath quivered on the edge of expectation. Her gaze slid down to his thick shaft, swollen, *ready*, gleaming with the tight sheen of arousal as it surged in response to her attention.

Jason slipped his hand around it, fingered the wide head in a slow teasing glide in time with the rhythm of her own heated caresses. She felt the sexual connection between them like a magnet, and the breath caught in her throat at the intimacy. The pleasure inside her mounted.

She sighed.

He stood and silently closed the distance between them.

Her heart smiled at the hunger in his gaze. Carried her even higher on the crest of elation.

Lifting a lock of her hair from her breast, he wound it around his finger, the wonder in his expression dazzling, the simplicity of touch not enough.

She arched toward him, needing, uncertain.

Jason knew.

He caught her nipple between a thumb and forefinger and squeezed. Need spiraled through her body and pooled between her legs, a long melting pull that made her heart beat faster and her insides tremble.

He slid his hand down the length of her arm until his palm covered hers and gently pressed against her sex. She writhed against the pressure as the glow inside swelled and mounted.

A low murmur of erotic wonder slipped from her lips. Her breath came in a long surrendering moan as the ultimate pleasure burst upon her, sprinkling through her like a sweet summer shower. Barely able to stand, Shelby clung to him.

Holding her within the circle of his arms, Jason rained soft kisses along her brow, rocking her tenderly against him until her heartbeat slowed to normal and she could breathe in more than a ragged gasp.

His throaty whisper echoed in her ear. "My, my, you have made progress."

"What about you?" His hot erection branded her.

With a finger hooked beneath her chin, he lifted her face toward his. "Watching you find satisfaction means a great deal to me."

His sweet words humbled her. Searching his face, Shelby saw the truth in his tender gaze, the contentment of his expression. Laying her cheek on his shoulder, she blinked back a teary smile.

This was more than she had ever dreamed possible. Held against the broad chest of a wonderful, caring man, her body drowsy while the ocean breezes bathed them in a balmy warmth. He was Max the angel, and this could have been a scene from a movie.

Except she wasn't acting.

She had experienced real pleasure, and her heart brimmed with Jason's touch.

Not the actor who had drifted into her life like an angel, but the man.

Her hand slipped between them to fondle him. "Let me watch you."

It was neither a question, nor a demand, but Jason lifted his head in obvious surprise, a quirky half-smile curving his lips.

She thought for an instant he might refuse, but suddenly his strong hand surrounded hers, and with quick, sharp strokes, he guided her in the method of his fulfillment.

His hot sex jumped in her hand, and she could feel the blood surging, feel the power of his arousal. Excitement rushed through her. The feeling amazed her.

Jason amazed her.

His glasses rested crookedly over eyes half-closed with desire. The chiseled planes of his face relaxed, and his mouth melted to kissable softness. She couldn't resist raising on tiptoe to press a kiss on those lips.

His arm banded her close, and he returned her kiss with abandon.

Her heart turned over.

And as their mouths met and their bold strokes lifted him toward fulfillment, Shelby understood the gift Jason had bestowed upon her. He was vulnerable in his passion, yet he was willing to share that vulnerability with her.

Suddenly she knew that Jason was right. All along her problem had been a control thing—she had never allowed herself to be out of control. He had seen so quickly what had taken her ten years to understand.

But that wasn't so surprising. Jason Gage was an incredible man.

And never more so than at the moment of climax. He bucked sharply, once, twice, and then, as a growl tore from his throat, he spurted his passion over her stomach.

With a delighted laugh, Shelby leaned into him, sealing their naked bodies together with his love juices, just as she hoped to make her newfound ability to *feel* a constant part of her life.

Fade-In

Shelby learned something else about Jason Gage that the tabloids had never reported. He was a wonderful cook. As they sat in her bed, naked, feeding each other like lovers, she decided she liked a man who was full of surprises.

"Open up." He speared a bite-size portion of crepe with his fork and held it to her lips.

"I shouldn't." She shook her head. "Wes will kill me if I gain an ounce."

Jason set the fork on the plate, and in one very graceful, very unexpected motion, pushed her onto her back. He raised himself on his elbows and gazed down at her, his powerful lower body pressing her into the mattress. "Do you always worry about what your director wants?"

Shelby sighed. "Wes is a tyrant. You know that."

"*I'm* a tyrant, and you have to keep up your strength because I plan to work you hard today."

"Is that so?" she challenged, laughing at the way his brows knitted together in a threatening frown.

He swooped down to catch her mouth in a kiss. A sweet kiss that tasted of coffee and syrup and horny male.

His kiss challenged her. Rewarded her. Only Jason had ever kissed her this way, a long easy joining of souls that felt so right. Charmed, Shelby melted into his embrace.

He took her face and held it gently as he explored her mouth with a dreamy intimacy. Her immediate, automatic response surprised her—she wanted to touch him.

And when Jason broke the kiss and gazed at her with a tender promise in his gaze, Shelby knew he had found the key to unlock her heart.

The realization filled her with sudden fear.

Rolling to her side, she retrieved her coffee cup from the night table, averting her gaze under the pretense of thirst.

"Better get in my quota of caffeine if you're expecting much from me today." She sounded nervous to her own ears and wondered if he noticed.

He did.

Lying beside her, he caressed the tense muscles in her shoulders with comforting gentleness, not asking, not speaking. Just being.

It was so simple. She had been shielding her emotions behind an impenetrable wall, never leaving herself unprotected for an instant.

That's why acting suited her so well. She had all the control. But *feeling* wasn't about summoning up emotions from her memory bank, it was about trusting her heart. Whether the result was pleasure or pain.

She had been afraid.

Even though ten years had passed, she was still afraid.

"It's about being vulnerable, isn't it?"

His brows shot upward. "A revelation. When did this take place?"

"When you were at the brink of orgasm."

He grimaced. "Guess I'll have to work on my performance. I wasn't trying to provoke deep thought."

"I don't want you to act. Your responses were what made the moment so powerful."

"Did they now?" His words hung in the air between them.

Something in his oddly wry expression made her wonder if... "Does my acting during sex bother you?"

His slight nod and ironic chuckle made her admonish gently, "It really shouldn't, you know."

His gaze never wavered. "I know."

Propping herself up on an elbow to face him, Shelby took his hand, determined to make him understand. "You're a wonderful coach, Jason. Please don't take my troubles personally."

"I don't." He lifted their joined hands to his heart, and her spirits soared. "This isn't about coaching. I can coach you just fine when I'm not thinking about making love to you. Tell me you don't think about it, too."

"I do."

"I'm glad." The smile that brightened his face stole her breath.

Or was it panic?

"You really shouldn't be." She squeezed his hands wistfully, then pulled away.

"Why's that?" He rolled into a sitting position in one graceful burst of muscle and sinew that she couldn't help but admire, then leaned back against the headboard and folded his arms across his chest, waiting.

"I make notoriously poor choices in men. You're no exception. You're here to coach me. Then you'll have to go."

"What if I don't want to?"

"Then we've got a problem."

"Which is?"

She exhaled in growing exasperation. "The most obvious is that all the years you've spent getting out of Hollywood, I've spent getting in."

"Quite true." He chuckled, although she didn't see anything to laugh about.

"You don't see that as a problem?"

"Not really." He fixed his gaze on her legs and caressed the length of her thigh with his toe. "We're back to control again, Shelby. If I'd wanted an *easy* scenario, I wouldn't have chosen you, but I must confess it was the last thing on my mind when I knocked on your door."

Chosen?

"I'll bet it was," she muttered, desperately trying to ignore an admission she just wasn't ready to deal with. "You really didn't look happy to be here."

"And you're skirting the issue." He faced her, affection glowing in his eyes. "I don't expect it to be easy, but I'm willing to make a few sacrifices to be with you."

"Sacrifices?"

He shrugged. "Maybe sacrifice isn't the right word. Letting go of some previously held misconceptions might be better."

Shelby shook her head to indicate that she didn't understand. But she desperately needed to. Her heart was fluttering wildly out of control and her mouth felt as dry as dust.

"I haven't been happy, Shelby. Not for a long time. I thought it was my lifestyle—acting, coaching, the lack of privacy in Hollywood—but the truth is, I'm just lonely." He slipped his foot between her knees and nudged her legs apart with a seductive grin. "I just didn't realize how lonely until I met you."

She had guessed, had seen glimpses in his handsome face. Amazed as she was that someone of Jason Gage's status could be lonely, his admission also broke her heart. She knew the feeling intimately. But instead of running from acting, she had buried herself in it.

That was the *real* problem. Not the logistics of where they lived and worked, but the reason she felt all alone.

Her deep dark secret.

Somehow it always came back to that.

"You don't know anything about me, Jason. Not really."

"I know how I feel. Nothing else really matters."

Other things did matter, and the thought alone sent a shudder through her.

"Everything I feel for you is so new," she blurted. "I don't know if I can have a relationship, Jason. I don't know if I can *love*."

His smile was so tender that her heart turned over. "I'm willing to take the chance."

He took her hand and pulled her into his arms. "I'm not asking for anything, Shelby. Just a chance to explore these feelings with you. Given the dynamics of the way we met, I thought it best to be up front with you about how I feel."

An unfamiliar contentment warred with some very familiar doubts. Shelby ran her fingers through his hair, savoring the rich texture. She enjoyed so many things about him. The raspy feel of her bare breasts against his chest. The muscular heaviness of his legs draped across hers. But most of all she treasured the tenderness that softened his expression when he looked at her, as if he cherished her beyond anything else in the world and wasn't afraid to show it.

Could she ever share her past with him?

She had no ready answer. But risk was the key here, and Shelby decided she would risk anything to feel the way Jason made her feel. Tilting her mouth toward his, she gazed deep into his eyes and traced the curve of his neck with gentle fingers. "I'm game, Jason. Let's explore."

Fade-Out

Shelby had been game, all right. All afternoon Jason had coached while Shelby performed. He tested and she improvised. He loved her and she felt. They had explored their passion until they literally dropped from exhaustion.

And now after waking content in her arms, Jason knew what he felt for Shelby was real.

Love?

Did he know how to love? Shelby had voiced exactly the same concern earlier, but the truth was, he hadn't had much experience with that emotion in his own life. His parents had loved him, but their love had been all tied up with ambition and control. He had been the son to follow in their images, the shining example of what brilliant performers and wonderful parents they were.

Jason had no complaints, though. Chase and Elena had loved him to a fault, and they had always welcomed him back from his rebellious forays with forgiving arms. He was fairly certain that Shelby had never known that sort of unconditional love.

Lifting a strand of hair that had fallen into her face while she slept, Jason considered Shelby's emotional scars.

What sort of tragedy could have made such a vibrant young woman so terrified of intimacy?

Rape? Molestation?

Grief, like the sharp edge of a blade, stabbed his heart when he thought about the possibilities.

He sheltered her within the tight circle of his arms, feeling the steady beat of her heart. She nestled against him as though she belonged there.

She did.

Jason had never known such an inspired need to protect, to nurture.

To love.

Like Shelby, he had shielded himself from this emotion, scorned the very idea. Why?

Her gentle breathing rippled through the stillness. He held her close, mulling the question. An ocean breeze sailed through the balcony doors, and goose-bumps sprinkled the slender length of her arms. Jason tugged at the sheet until her gorgeous body became a tempting vision of shapely curves swathed in pale yellow satin.

He exhaled a long sigh of satisfaction. Peaceful. That's how he felt. For the first time ever, that familiar restlessness didn't gnaw at him. He felt mercifully content.

For the life of him, Jason couldn't figure out why. He had experienced a lifetime of admiration from his fans, his parents' fans, but it had never been enough.

Why?

When the answer struck, so simple and clear, he almost laughed aloud. He hadn't met Shelby.

The people in his life had needed Jason Gage the actor—needed his fame, his connections, his talent. Shelby needed none of those things. She needed *him*.

All along his quest for fulfillment had been a quest for love. Now he had found it. In a beautiful slip of a woman who doubted she even knew how to accept or return it.

Jason pressed a soft kiss to her silk-straight hair and felt a little thrill when she stirred in response.

He loved her. He wanted to wake up to the sound of her voice, the naturally bright way she spoke that matched the energetic way she moved. He wanted to experience her humor, test her anger, explore her intellect.

Share the secrets that haunted her.

The shrill bell of the telephone rang out, and he snatched the receiver from the night table before it screeched a second time and disturbed her.

"Hello," he rasped, trying to keep his voice down.

"Good afternoon," came the pleasant response. "This is Doctor Pich's office calling to confirm Shelby's appointment in the morning."

He recognized the name of a respected psychoanalyst who had offices in LA. Shelby was in good hands.

"I'll give her the message." Jason hung up the phone.

Glancing at the bedside clock, he slipped from the tangle of Shelby's arms and grabbed his robe from the floor. Unless he missed his guess, she would awaken soon, hungry. He was starving.

With a parting glance at the beautiful woman who had captured his heart, Jason made his way to the kitchen.

The phone rang again.

"Hello." Wedging the portable between his ear and shoulder, he returned to his task at the sink, drying leaves of romaine for a salad.

"Do I have the right number?" a feminine voice asked in apparent surprise.

"Depends on whom you're calling." He glanced down at the Caller ID where the area code read: 202. Washington DC.

"Shelby."

"You've got the right number, but Shelby can't come to the phone right now. I'll take a message."

Jason met complete silence on the other end.

"Who am I speaking with?" the voice demanded suddenly, and he couldn't help but notice the no-nonsense strength in an otherwise silky voice.

"A friend," he said, unwilling to give his name.

"Well, *friend*," she said, and Jason knew he hadn't made a friend with his evasion. "You tell Shelby that Paige called."

Oh, hell! "I'll tell her."

He returned the portable to the base with a groan. Paige from DC. Damn. Shelby was right—he didn't know enough about her.

But as he peered absently at the telephone, he noticed something interesting. She liked cutting edge. Caller ID. Portables and cell phones with all the buttons and bows. An elaborate answering machine. A state-of-the-art security system.

Another piece fitted into the puzzle about the woman he loved, and when she woke up, he'd tell her about Paige's call.

But when Shelby's anguished moan had sent him running toward her bedroom, questions were the farthest thing from Jason's mind.

He found her tangled in a sheet, drenched in sweat. A chill glazed the full length of his spine when he saw her deathly pale face, the tears that squeezed through tightly-closed eyelids. She was still asleep.

Two long strides saw him beside her. "It's okay, Shelby. Wake up."

Jason knelt on the edge of the bed. "Wake up," he commanded, shaking her shoulder to rouse her.

Her eyes flew open, unfocused. Frightened.

He lay a reassuring hand over her heart to find it beating frantically beneath his palm.

A nightmare. Fear etched tight lines around her mouth. His own heart breaking, he gathered her into his arms, and she clung to him, her slender body trembling.

He lay back on the bed, stroking wet hair from her face as she came back from the horror trip she'd been on.

Anxiety attacks and nightmares.

He was tempted to call Doctor Pich. But just as quickly, he dismissed the idea. He wanted answers, but he wanted them from Shelby. Until she was ready to trust him….

"I'm not really an emotional wreck, Jason." Her voice was ragged from slumber and tears. She looked up at him with a soul-melting gaze. "Except for a few quirks, I'm perfectly normal."

He squeezed her tight. "I know, honey."

"I feel like such a jerk."

"Helluva nightmare, hmm?"

"A doozy." A shadow clouded her brilliant gaze.

"Want to talk about it?"

He could feel her conflict in the way she tensed, and he wondered what bothered her more: reliving her nightmare or sharing it with him.

"Will it help?"

"Usually does."

She sighed, and her frown deepened. With his thumb he caressed the tiny crease between her brows, pleased that she hadn't refused outright, hopeful that she might open up.

"They frighten me," she said, trailing a finger along the nape of his neck. "I hadn't had a nightmare in years, and then all of a sudden—boom!—I'm having one every few weeks." She sighed again, sounded tired.

"What do you think triggered them?"

Nervously, she moistened dry lips, and her mouth dipped into an even deeper frown. He sensed her uncertainty, sensed her retreat.

She shrugged.

Disappointment rushed through him. She wasn't ready to trust him yet.

"Doctor Pich's office called to confirm your appointment in the morning," he said, hoping to engage her in the conversation a little longer.

"I was going to blow it off. I know your schedule's tight."

"Do you think that's a good idea?"

Shelby tossed her hair over her shoulder and sent it tumbling down her back like a sooty waterfall. "Probably not," she admitted with a roll of her eyes. "But I don't want to waste any of our time together. Wes expects me back on the set Monday."

"I'll wait." Jason reached out and grabbed her hand. "Wes can, too."

She brushed her lips across his knuckles, sending his nerve endings skittering in rapid response, but she still looked troubled. "I won't take too long. Promise."

"I'll wait." Not only would he be here after her therapist's appointment, he'd be here until she was ready to trust him. However long it took, and it definitely looked like it might take a while, since she seemed so committed to steering the conversation elsewhere.

"Hungry?" She rolled to the edge of the bed and slid fluidly to her feet.

The sight of her silhouetted in the natural light of the open French doors was like a blast of fresh air.

"Read my mind," he said, not sure which was stronger: the hunger in his stomach or the hunger in his crotch. Propping a pillow behind his head so he could watch Shelby as she brushed her hair, he pondered the question.

Her hair tumbled in a glossy fall down her back, outlining the neat lines of her ribs and ending just short of where her waist curved inward.

Her long shapely legs and the graceful way she moved hinted at a natural athletic ability, and he wondered if she would bike along the coast with him or prefer to take long walks along the beach. Maybe he would luck out and she'd enjoy both.

God, he wanted her.

Setting the brush on the dresser, Shelby caught his gaze in the mirror. "I'm starved."

That answered the question of which hunger he'd satisfy first. "I'm working on dinner."

"You're a talented man, Jason Gage." She smiled and slipped into a light robe.

He hoped talent would be enough to win her, because she was so obviously comfortable being alone.

And then it hit him.

That aura of... something about her. It had been nagging at him since they met, but he hadn't known Shelby well enough to pinpoint what it was until now.

Guilt.

She wore it like a shroud. Whatever had happened all those years ago still haunted her in more ways than she seemed to realize. Despite all her years of therapy and hard work. Despite her protests of having resolved all her issues, Shelby had missed one very important thing.

She had never forgiven herself.

It was Jason's best guess, and it fit. Her avoidance of intimacy. Her willingness to settle for acting instead of feeling.

What the hell had happened to her?

The question gnawed his soul, urged him to his feet. Taking her in his arms, he buried his face in her hair and inhaled deeply of her moist feminine scent, staving off his own rising panic. Shelby could never love him unless she learned to love herself.

These Names Weren't on the Playbill

"Ding! Ding-a-ling!"

The doorbell chimed. Jason cursed aloud at the interruption, at the computer monitor, and at his own inability to concentrate on this lecture when his thoughts kept steering back to Shelby—just like an old trail horse kept heading back to the stable.

How was she making out at her therapy session?

He attacked the keyboard with renewed vigor.

"Ding! Ding-a-ling!"

The damned bell kept ringing. Jason resolutely ignored it, determined Hell would freeze over before he answered the door. Finally there was silence again, and he breathed a sigh of relief.

Until he heard the unmistakable sound of footsteps tapping on the wood plank floor in the foyer.

"Shelby, are you home? Your system isn't on." A feminine voice called out, and if Jason wasn't mistaken, this was a voice he recognized. "I saw a car in the garage and used my key."

With a groan, he shoved the chair back and stood.

Moving quickly through the house, he turned the corner and came face-to-face with a stunning woman who stood just inside the open doorway as if hesitant to enter. He ground to a dead halt, unable to stop staring.

Dressed in a stylish silk jumpsuit, a sapphire shade remarkably similar to her eyes, she was tall and slender and strikingly beautiful. A halo of wild red curls framed a delicate oval face, and Jason suddenly felt very undressed as her deprecating gaze swept over him in return, taking in every inch of his bare chest and feet.

"You must be the *friend*," she said dryly. Raising a finely-arched copper brow, she stared him down in a silent command to explain.

"Paige from DC?"

He didn't need her short nod to tell him he was right. He recognized both her voice and her tone, and he also sensed that Paige from DC was a woman used to getting whatever answers she wanted.

"I thought you had retired from show business, Mr. Gage."

She had recognized him, and to Jason's surprise he felt only a mild sense of amusement. Whether anyone discovered he was here no longer mattered. The idea of the media chewing over his love for Shelby didn't really bother him. Not as long as he had Shelby. "I have."

"Since Shelby hasn't mentioned word one about you, perhaps you can fill me in on the details. *Friend* doesn't really tell me much." She jingled her keys impatiently, gaze dropping deliberately to his chest. "Are you here in a professional or personal capacity?"

"Both."

"I've read about your new profession, Mr. Gage. Should I be concerned about her health?"

There was no mistaking the worry she tried to hide behind carefully controlled features. Paige from DC cared for Shelby very much.

Jason felt the first connection click into place between them. His defenses dwindled. "Call me Jason, please. I'm here in both capacities, and, no, you don't need to be concerned about Shelby."

"Where is she?"

"She had an appointment this morning. I expect her back shortly." He motioned toward the living room. "You're welcome to wait."

Paige didn't move from the doorway, though, and when a tall man suddenly appeared beside her, Jason understood why.

"Christopher, this is Jason Gage. The *friend*." She met the man's gaze with a wry grin. "My husband, Christopher Sharp."

Jason made the first move, crossing the foyer and extending his hand. The Sharps were important to Shelby, and he suspected he had some making up to do to remedy his first impression.

A *lot* of remedying if Christopher Sharp's scowl was any indication.

He was a huge man with a firm grip and an all-business stare. There was something naggingly familiar about him, too, but Jason couldn't place it.

What he could place, however, was that Paige and Christopher Sharp were a power couple. Definitely physical people, they seemed to flow together as if they had been cast from the same mold. Where one ended, the other began.

"Please come in and make yourselves comfortable," he said.

The Sharps followed him into the living room. Paige took a seat on the settee, while her husband loosened the tie around his throat with studied movements. Getting down to business.

"Shelby hasn't mentioned you as a friend," Christopher said, resting a large hand on his wife's shoulder.

She leaned into his touch so naturally that Jason felt a twinge of envy for the kind of closeness these two apparently shared.

He wanted a place in Shelby's world, and to earn one, he would have to make friends with the Sharps. The fact that Christopher believed he knew all Shelby's friends was revealing.

"I love her," he said simply.

Might as well play his hand. He'd shoot straight with them and see what happened.

Paige quirked a copper brow. Christopher glowered. Their combined scrutiny was so intense that he could only surmise they found him seriously lacking as a partner.

"Does she share your sentiment?" Paige asked, elegantly and to the point.

Clasping his hands over his knees, Jason leaned forward and faced her with a smile, deciding in that instant he liked Paige Sharp very much. "Poised on the brink, I believe. I'm hopeful."

"Don't get too hopeful, Gage," Christopher challenged. "I'm not convinced you have anything to offer her."

Paige patted her husband's hand as he glared down from his lofty height. Some silent communication passed between them, before he said, "Shelby doesn't need a rogue."

"I agree." Even though Christopher was justified in his opinion, although news of his decadent youth had been greatly exaggerated by the media, Jason would not back down. "She's held herself back from love for a long time, and to be frank with you, I'm glad. It's given me the opportunity to meet her."

"When exactly did you meet her, Jason?" Paige asked.

"Two days ago."

Christopher snorted. "In which time I suppose you've formed 'an eternal bond with the woman of your dreams'."

"Touché." Jason leaned back and folded his arms across his chest, unable to suppress a smile at Christopher's performance of a line from one of his early movies. "But, yes, it's something like that."

"She's not the woman to scratch your itch."

"No, she's not," he agreed, and the silence swelled between them.

"What Christopher is trying to say," Paige began delicately, "is that Shelby is a woman who has… a woman who needs…"

"What I assume you're trying to say is that she still has some issues to work out." Watching the two of them try to make their point without revealing anything was becoming almost painful.

"She's told you?"

He didn't miss the catch in Paige's voice, and Jason didn't hesitate. "She hasn't confided in me—yet. I hope in time she will."

"What difference would it make?" Christopher braced his hands on either side of his wife and stared Jason down.

He was being interrogated. No getting around it. All that was missing was a light and an observation window.

"I think trusting someone might help."

"Is that a professional opinion?" Paige asked.

"Not really. It's hard to assess her situation when I don't know what's troubling her. It's almost irrelevant, though, since I don't have any professional distance." He shrugged, smiling when he met Paige's sympathetic gaze. "Shelby deserves to know love. I intend to be the man she discovers it with. My gut tells me she blames herself for something that happened to her a long time ago, and I'm able to distance myself enough to know she can't love me until she lets that go."

Christopher thumped his hands down on the back of the settee in apparent frustration. "You talk good, Gage. But knowing what an actor you are, how are we supposed to believe you?"

Jason met the man's dark gaze steadily. "I'm not interested in whether you believe me. I'm interested in Shelby."

The front door opened, and he heard Shelby call out, "I'm home. Jason, do you have company?"

"You do." He stood as she appeared in the doorway, her eyes widening in amusement as they flicked over his bare chest. She glanced at her visitors.

A smile of genuine delight wreathed her features, and she literally did a little hop-skip as she sailed into the room, arms spread. "Paige! Christopher! What are you doing here?"

"Business." Christopher caught her in an enthusiastic bear hug and lifted her off her feet. "Paige tried calling you."

"I know. I'm sorry I haven't returned your calls. I've been—busy." She cast a sheepish glance at Jason before Paige wrapped her in an embrace that brought on a round of teary laughter.

Jason retreated to the doorway, intent upon leaving them to their greetings and taking the opportunity to get dressed. Christopher observed him warily while shrugging out of his Italian suit jacket. When he draped it over the back of the settee, Jason noticed a semi-automatic pistol in the shoulder holster strapped around his back.

And he remembered where he had seen Christopher Sharp before.

The Denouement

As her "family by love" sat down to a brunch that she and Jason had prepared, Shelby had never felt so content. Paige and Christopher behaved like protective parents, grilling Jason all during the preparation of the meal and looking as if they planned to continue between bites. She found their concern endearing.

Given their combined years in law enforcement, and elevated positions with the FBI, Shelby understood they were only interested in her welfare. They always had been.

In addition to a thousand kindnesses, Paige and Christopher had offered her the gifts of friendship and love.

And loyalty.

She owed them her life.

Except Christopher swore *he* owed *her* because if it hadn't been for Shelby, he never would have won Paige's heart.

The three of them were a family.

And as Shelby listened to them cross-examine Jason, she wondered if the time had come to add someone else into the equation.

Paige and Christopher were professional interrogators, but Jason was holding his own. He had a dry sense of humor that smoothly deflected Christopher's attempts to intimidate him. Paige was tough but kind, and Shelby guessed that Jason had already won her over.

He was charming and pleasant and confident, as though he had every right in the world to be sitting in her kitchen. He did. Because she wanted him there. Her heart fluttered every time their gazes met across the table.

Jason belonged with them. She could envision them together on the holidays like a real family. The only problem now was turning the image in her head into a reality.

She could never have *any* kind of relationship unless she opened her heart and shared her past—and let the pieces fall where they may. Her conversation this morning with Doctor Pich had left her thinking that perhaps putting the past behind her wasn't all she had to do—that she still had to make peace with the young girl who had gotten into so much trouble ten years ago.

"*Simple, but not easy*," Doctor Pich had told her, and Shelby agreed.

Dredging up her past would be a risk. But, Shelby decided while gazing across the table at Jason who was laughing at some lame joke Paige had just told, Jason Gage was worth it.

"You *are* a marvelous actor." Paige caught Shelby's gaze and winked. "I *almost* believed you liked my joke."

"She can't tell a joke to save her soul," Shelby explained, delighted Jason had made the effort to be nice. "Yet for some bizarre reason that Christopher and I still haven't figured out, she humbles herself by trying."

"It's an exercise in humility," Paige quipped.

Jason stared at her over the champagne flute. Shelby rolled her eyes while Christopher massaged his temples as though pained.

Paige pursed her lips in a disgruntled moue. "Ignore them, Jason. I don't have a shred of humility in me. I have to work at it."

"I'll deliver a more convincing performance next time."

"Oh, you were wonderful," Paige assured him. "But I wouldn't believe God, Himself. I really can't tell a joke."

"No one's perfect, my dear." Christopher cast her a loving glance that made Shelby believe in soulmates. Then he patted Shelby's hand and said, "There'd be no living with her if she didn't have at least one imperfection."

"Humph." Paige tossed her napkin onto her plate in a fit of mock pique.

"Be careful," Shelby warned Christopher. "She'll get you as soon as you walk out the door."

"Not to worry. We'll be in meetings for the rest of the day. She has no choice but to be on her best behavior."

Paige nudged Shelby with an elbow and sighed. "He'll want me to be respectful, too, I bet."

Christopher nodded. "I'm the boss."

"Are you sure you can't stay?" Shelby took Paige's hand, felt her slim fingers squeeze tight.

"I'm sorry. I don't see how we can leave the hotel. We've just got so many meetings." She cast an accusing glance at Christopher. "He's going to work us to death. But we'll squeeze out for dinner once or twice. He promised."

"Just call. I'll make myself available."

Paige patted her hand, then faced Jason. "Perhaps you'll join us."

"I will."

Shelby's heart soared. He expected to be here a few more days. Hopping to her feet before anyone caught her blush, she began clearing the table. Before she even got the dishes in the sink, Jason appeared by her side and whispered, "Go say your good-byes. I'll get this stuff in the dishwasher."

She smiled. He smiled back.

"Sorry we have to run and leave you with the mess." Paige intruded upon their moment with a knowing grin.

"No problem," Shelby said. "Come on. I'll walk you out."

Sandwiched between the two people dearest to her in all the world, she led them to the door, sorry, as always, to see them go. "Make sure you leave time for dinner. We can come to the hotel if it's more convenient. I'll be back on the set Monday, and it will be at least another eight weeks before I can get to DC."

"Promise." Paige's eyes misted, and Christopher, always sensitive to their need for long farewells, took his cue.

Enveloping Shelby in those strong, loving arms, he rocked her against his chest. "You call if you need anything."

Shelby couldn't miss the concern in his voice. He was worried about her. Smoothing her fingers over his graying blonde hair, she stood on tiptoes and kissed his cheek. "I promise."

He gave her a squeeze, then let her go. "I'll get the car."

Paige faced Shelby with misty eyes. It had always been like this between them. Tears prickled the backs of her lids. She took Paige's hands. "Promise me you'll take care. No dangerous undercover assignments, okay?"

Paige laughed through her tears. "Ever since Christopher was promoted, he refuses to let me do anything that's fun. I've spent more time at Quantico this past year than I have in my entire career."

"Good. I worry about you."

"Ditto." Paige wrapped her arms around Shelby.

Paige radiated the same sense of security and contentment Shelby had always felt with her. "You're too good to me."

"Never!" Paige replied vehemently and gave her a tight squeeze. "Do you love him?"

Shelby nodded, unable to form the words past the swell of emotion in her throat.

"Then trust him, sweetie. I've never seen you sparkle the way you do when you look at Jason. He's a good man, and he loves you."

"You're so sure, are you?"

Paige rolled her eyes. "It's all over him. Besides, he told me."

"He did?" Her heart filled with hope.

"He did, and I believe him." She wiped the tears from Shelby's cheeks. "Just be happy, and call me if you want to talk."

"I will."

The sound of a car horn beeped, and Christopher pulled a rented Lexus up to the portico. The driver's door swung open and he appeared. "Come on, ladies, before we end up swimming out of here."

Shelby laughed and shooed Paige off. "Go on. I'll see you before you leave L.A."

She gave Shelby a parting kiss and headed down the stairs to where Christopher was holding the door for her.

He beeped one last time before driving through the front gate, and Shelby waved, distracted from her bittersweet thoughts by Paige's parting advice.

Trust him.

Her whole world had changed overnight. Literally. She was falling in love with Jason Gage. She finally had a chance for happiness.

But would Jason still love her when he knew what she had done?

"Hey. You okay?"

She hadn't heard his approach and spun around at the sound of his voice. His smile flowed through her like sunshine, chasing the doubt from her mind. His arm came around her, and she rested her head against his chest.

"I'm always sad when they leave."

"It's wonderful to have people you love so much."

There it was, that loneliness again. She snuggled against him. "They're my family."

They could be yours, too.

"What did you think of them?"

"Paige is lovely. The verdict is still out on Christopher. He thinks I'm too old for you."

Surprised, she glanced up into his face. Apparently he was serious. "Whatever makes you think that?"

"It's a guy thing. He looks at you like his beautiful young daughter, then he looks at me like some nasty old pervert."

Shelby blinked back her tears with a laugh. "Christopher is just protective. Besides, *I* don't think you're too old."

"Good thing. I had no idea you hung with such powerful people."

"I knew them when they were nobodies," she said in mock disdain. "Paige, at least. Christopher was already important when I met him."

"Tell me about them."

The afternoon sun bathed them in its warmth, and Shelby felt the glow melt the chill around her heart.

She told Jason how she had met Paige through a volunteer program. Paige's father had recently died, so she had no family living. She sort of adopted Shelby, and they had become friends. Sisters.

"When did Christopher come into the picture?"

"Oooh! A love story." She sighed, long and dramatic, eliciting Jason's laughter. "Christopher had been Paige's instructor at Quantico. He swears he fell in love with her there, but Paige wouldn't give him the time of day. He chased her around for eight years... until this one assignment." Shelby swallowed back the lump in her throat. "He trapped her on an island where she couldn't get away, and then he stole her heart."

She shivered, and Jason's arms tightened around her. As much as she adored Paige and Christopher's love story, she hated the reason they had been on that assignment.

It had been because of *her*.

They had never shared the gory details. They hadn't needed to. Shelby already knew what kind of crimes took place on that island.

"That is quite a love story. So why don't you look caught up in the romance?"

Shelby rested her chin on his shoulder and stared out at the English rose bushes she had planted last spring.

They had grown untended in recent weeks, lovely in their wildness, and she marveled at their freedom to bloom, to grow unfettered by anything other than the need to reach the sun. She wanted to experience that freedom, too.

Taking a deep breath, she forced the words out. "I hated that Paige even went to that island. She was undercover for two years. It was terrible. A really ugly case."

Jason's finger locked beneath her chin, and he lifted her face toward his. The sun cast his features in sharp relief, the hint of burnished stubble outlining the clench of his jaw. His sable gaze seared into hers. "I read about the case, Shelby. I recognized Christopher from photographs of the trial."

Shelby's heart missed a beat.

Jason knew.

Her mind raced. She didn't know what to say. Retreat? Confess? The blood seemed to drain to her toes, and she felt light-headed, dizzy.

The moment of truth had finally arrived.

Break a Leg

Jason thought she would bolt, but Shelby pressed her eyes tightly shut and said, "Christopher should never have been so visible. Paige, either. *They* absorbed all the media attention to…to protect…"

He had never loved her more than in that instant. Somewhere within herself, she had found the strength to share her past. "Who, Shelby?"

"*Me.*"

Tears slipped between her closed eyelids. Jason leaned back against the balustrade, taking her with him, cradling her against his chest. "Want to talk about it?"

Shelby wiped tears on his shirt. "Paige and Christopher were protecting me," she finally said.

"From what?"

"The sordid facts." She blinked her eyes open, her expression one of profound sadness. "I was the witness."

As soon as he had placed Christopher, Jason had guessed she was involved, but as he recalled the details of that shocking trial, he called upon all his years of acting experience to keep his expression blank. "I see."

The silence lengthened, but he held Shelby's gaze steadily, even as a range of emotions flashed across her face. "That's it? No shock? No hightailing it out of here?"

"You want a performance?" He couldn't help but smile, feeling some of his own tension fade. "I'm not surprised, Shelby. I told you I recognized Christopher. Knowing what I know about you, it wasn't hard to draw my own conclusions."

"You already know?"

"Well, I don't really *know* anything except what you told me, but I *guessed* enough not to be surprised." He dropped his arms so they rested lightly around her waist, and they stood, facing each other in the warm afternoon sun. "Honey, we all have shadows. I have more than I care to admit. Point is, I put them behind me and moved on."

"I thought I had."

He knew she had conquered her demon now. His throat constricted when he asked, "And then the nightmares started?"

She nodded.

"What triggered them?"

"Lewis Goddard was murdered in prison."

Jason exhaled heavily and rested his chin on the top of her head, feeling the weight of her statement like an anchor. He had read all about Lewis Goddard, the leader of a crime ring that produced custom porn films. He had been convicted of murdering his actors and sentenced to life in prison.

"I thought I had put the past behind me, Jason." The pain in her voice burdened the anchor a little more. "Life wasn't perfect, but it was good enough to content me. I had my family, my work, and if I was a little lonely sometimes…well, it just seemed an awfully small price to pay."

"Why should you pay at all?" It was such a simple question, yet she seemed surprised.

"I've made choices. I have to live with them."

"You're being hard, honey."

Her beautiful green eyes grew flinty. "I made some hard choices."

Guilt.

Therein lay her true problem, and he was determined to help her see it. "How did you get mixed up with a crime lord like Lewis Goddard?"

"One of his talent scouts."

"Where did he find you?"

"My high school drama club. It was the only reason I was still in school. I loved to act." She laughed, a short unforgiving sound that quickly became a sob. "Paige used to bribe me. If I passed all my other classes, she footed the bill for acting lessons."

"Sounds like she had you figured out."

"She did. Until I met Goddard's scout and saw a shortcut."

Tilting her head back, she stared at him, and he saw regret. "It was a whole new world, Jason. An exciting one. Goddard's clubs. Premieres. Expensive hotels. Foster homes and high school just couldn't compete."

"You must have been so young."

"Barely fifteen."

His struggle with control slipped a notch, his hand trembling as he brushed an errant strand of hair from her cheek. He didn't trust himself to speak.

"Goddard was casting a film," she explained. "I auditioned and won the lead. I knew the whole situation was wrong. He might have been professional. He had the production company, the people, the credentials—but he wouldn't discuss the script with me."

"You never told Paige?"

She shook her head. "I already knew what she'd say. Everything I didn't want to hear."

Of course not. Most fifteen-year-olds weren't big on hearing the world wasn't everything they thought it should be. Perhaps Shelby didn't realize that. Massaging her shoulders, Jason kneaded away the tension knotted there, and she let her eyes drift close with a sigh.

"Lewis Goddard owned an island where we were scheduled to film, and it wasn't until I was there that I finally understood what he wanted me to do."

"Pornography?" The question tore from his throat in a growl, despite his best efforts to keep his emotions below the surface.

She seemed to have expected his reaction and pressed shaking fingers gently against his lips. Her eyes misted. "He had this really elaborate set-up for rehearsing. A 'method' he called it. A technique he used with all his actors to get them comfortable with each other." Her voice cracked. "He wanted me to practice the sex scenes with my co-star."

Jason held her close, offered his strength, even when her words seared through him like acid.

"He scared me, Jason. His people scared me. They had guns, but they were as terrified of him as I was. There was no way off the island. My co-star... Bobby," her voice broke, and he sensed she was remembering. "He tried to protect me, didn't want me to feel ashamed by what we were doing. He was a year older than I was, and he tried to act tough. He was just as scared. We figured if we just did what Lewis Goddard wanted, we could go home."

Jason stroked her hair, her shoulders, her back, as she choked out every word with the horror of a fifteen year old. "But we didn't go home. Even though we did everything he said. Even when we found out that the entire wing where we rehearsed was wired and he was watching—"

His body jerked in stunned surprise. He hadn't known. Certain details must not have been released to the media. He tried, God, how he tried, but no amount of acting skill could help Jason hide his reaction. He vibrated with a helpless fury unlike anything he had experienced before.

His fists clenched when he thought of Shelby, so young and scared, all alone except for her brave boy hero who was no match against a monster like Goddard.

Shelby clung to him, trembling hands stroking, offering comfort, as if he was the one about to break. He grabbed her hands, knowing what he had to do. Goddard was already dead. Paige and Christopher had helped Shelby find justice. He would help her find peace.

"There's more, isn't there, honey?" He could see it in her face. He had to make her understand that these were Goddard's crimes, not *hers*.

"It was a snuff film." The words spilled from her lips as if her torment ate at her from the inside, and he braced himself against the truth she needed to share, the truth that jeopardized his control.

"We had shot almost the whole movie. We thought we were almost finished, but then...during the last sex scene...someone *murdered* Bobby. Staged it so...so it looked as if *I* had killed him. I was there, on top of him, and suddenly there was all this blood and he was gagging..." Shelby began to shake.

"Jesus!" Jason exploded and scooped her into his arms. Carrying her into the house, he sat on the settee with her curled in his lap like a child, rocking her, while her sobs tore at him.

"Come on, honey. Breathe. It's okay." His own throat was raw, choked with tears as he fought back the image of a terrified Shelby, in trouble and alone.

And when she lifted her gaze to his, Jason thought his heart would break.

"Don't," she whispered, kissing the tears from his cheeks.

Cupping her face between his hands, he closed his eyes, unable to face her anguish. "I feel your pain."

"You shouldn't."

"I do." He pressed a tremulous kiss to her lips. "I love you."

Her tears flowed, and she tried to pull away.

He held her. "Don't turn away from me, Shelby. Share yourself. I want to understand."

And she told him. Huddled in a wretched ball on his lap, she told him how she had hidden in an elevator shaft for two days, stolen a personal watercraft and escaped to the mainland in the dead of night.

She told him how she had hitchhiked to Paige, cross-country from California to Virginia, with nothing more than the clothes on her back and the terror that Lewis Goddard would be after her.

He had been.

Paige had set Shelby up in the Witness Protection Program until she built a case strong enough to convict Goddard. Jason thanked God for Paige, who had cared for a young girl all alone in the world.

He held Shelby, their mingled tears streaming over his lips, a vision of her in the middle of a pitch black ocean, so desperately frightened, seared into his brain. Resting his brow against hers, he couldn't resist the urge to touch her, to kiss her and feel her warmth pulsing beneath his lips. She was so alive. Even in her grief, she made him feel alive.

And she had trusted him enough to share her past.

"Bobby's death still haunts you."

A shadow of despair clouded her features. "I met his mother at the trial, Jason. She... she *thanked* me."

The contempt in her voice fitted another piece of the puzzle in place. "Why does that surprise you? Your testimony convicted her son's killer."

"You make it sound so... *noble*." She spit the word from between clenched teeth. "There was nothing noble about it. I did the only thing I could, and I was just fortunate enough to have Paige and Christopher on my side."

"You're being too hard on yourself." Yet he understood, with all his heart and soul, he understood. She had found the courage to seek justice, no matter what the cost, but she still didn't think it was enough. "The right thing wasn't the easy thing. You gave up your life to see justice done. Lewis Goddard went to prison. *Died* in prison. Haven't you suffered enough?"

He saw the answer gather in her eyes like a summer storm.

No.

"Bobby died. He was so sweet, Jason. He tried so hard to be brave so that I wouldn't be scared." Tears spilled down her cheeks, her voice ragged, grief-stricken. "He didn't deserve to die."

He kissed the tears away, tried to reassure her, to absorb some of her anguish. She sobbed harder.

"I dragged Paige and Christopher into this...this mess. They went to that island. They lived with those...criminals. All because of me. Whatever I've suffered just doesn't quite compare."

He had to make her understand. His heart depended on it. "Forgive yourself, Shelby, because until you do, you can't love me." Jason ran his hands along her neck, her jaw, her cheeks. "The way I love you."

Relief broke from his lips in a sigh when she answered his plea with one of her own. "Help me, Jason. Show me how."

It's a Wrap

Shelby slanted her mouth over his. She wanted him more than she had ever wanted anything before, *needed* him to help her feel something beyond this despair. He hadn't turned away. He knew everything, understood her demons, and he still loved her.

Jason.

She ran her fingers through his hair, kissing the tears from his lips, laughing, crying, drowning in a swirl of emotion that she *felt* inside.

A low growl tore from his throat, and he plunged his tongue into her mouth. He knew what she needed. He took what he wanted.

His kiss awakened her senses. Need roiled inside like a maelstrom. Desire forged a fevered ache low in her belly. Running her hands along his neck, she outlined the corded muscles with eager fingers.

Jason dragged her off the settee, protecting her within the circle of his arms as they rolled to the floor. She gasped as their hips locked, and his erection pressed into her softness like a command.

Running her hands along his waist, hips, buttocks, she rocked against that maleness, showing him boldly what she needed. No longer afraid. "I want you."

She had trusted him with her past. Now she would trust him with her heart. "Love me, Jason."

His look of bold desire made her heart swell and her body ache. He braced himself above her, and Shelby gasped at the savage beauty of him, at the fury of a passion that etched stark lines on his beloved face, at the glaze of need that burned in the depths of his sable gaze.

Tugging the shirt from the waistband of her jeans with jerky motions, he tore it open with rough hands, buttons popping in all directions as the fabric parted. He dragged her bra from her body with the shreds of her shirt and stripped the jeans down her legs in impatient strokes. She lay naked before him. His gaze scorched her, and she saw the fire in his eyes, recognized the need that drew his muscles tight. His chest heaved with ragged breaths. She felt his hunger. She felt his love.

All along he had coached her, caressed her, coddled her, always putting her pleasure first.

Not anymore.

His urgency fed her own, whipped through her until she understood in the vaguely-functioning portion of her brain just how masterful his control had been.

"I love you, Shelby." His voice was rough gravel, awakening such primitive excitement inside her, Shelby thought she might explode.

She held her arms to him. Eager. Ready.

Suddenly his hands were all over her, searing across her thighs, molding the feminine mound between her legs, sweeping upward along her ribs, plucking at her nipples, until she cried out in abandon.

She arched against him as a current surged across her breasts, tightening the tips into eager crests. Sliding her hand between them, she stroked his male hardness through his jeans, wanting him to lose control and tumble with her into this whirl of erotic sensation.

He grabbed her with a wild strength, rolling her beneath him suddenly, stealing her breath with his kiss. Blood surged from her fingertips to her toes. Desire pounded like thunder between her legs. She would die unless he satisfied this ache inside, this urgency he had created.

He knew. Spearing his hand into her hair, his lips came down hard, and she met each thrust of his tongue, wanting to give him everything. Her body, her past, her heart.

Her trust.

A gift as precious as any she could give. But did she know how to be vulnerable?

The tenderness in his face as he gazed upon her, the love in his eyes, filled her with such hope that she felt the answer straight to her soul.

Yes.

She had known it since the moment they met. He would never hurt her. With a half-sob, half-gasp, she held onto him as he lifted her to her knees, bodies pressed together, hearts racing. He broke their kiss only to yank the shirt over his head, and together they fumbled with the button at his waist, hands tangled as they slid the jeans down his hips. His sex sprang free. Hot. Hard. Shelby resisted the urge to touch him while he kicked off his clothes.

Powerful muscles played beneath the dark sweep of his skin. Burnished curls nestled in the ridges of his chest, veeing downward along the muscled lines of his stomach, circling the base of that splendid erection.

He was magnificent.

And he was *hers*.

Jason sat back on his haunches, taking her with him, and with a grateful sigh, Shelby let him pull her into his arms, awed by the feel of him against her. Her nails raked the muscles along his back in excitement as he thrust into her in one bold stroke, need unleashed, desire raging like a storm around them.

"Trust me, Shelby."

"I do."

He filled her. A moan slipped from her lips, a low, throaty sound that surrounded them. Her body trembled.

His hands locked onto her hips, lifting her off his thick shaft, then driving her back down. Sweat slicked their skin together. Passion built like a tempest, and Jason knew, oh, yes, he knew exactly what to do to push her into the midst of the storm.

He drew her into his rhythm, pounded into her with exquisite fury. She soared. Grinding out a sound of the purest male triumph, he watched her, knowing, as her ecstasy mounted. Exploded. She cried out, her sex clenching his in violent bursts, as the most incredible sensation of rapture whipped through her.

Driving into her one last time, he poured out his own pleasure while she clung to him, gasping, laughing aloud for the sheer joy of it.

She had never imagined climax could be so sweet. Even the delightful sensations she had coaxed from her own body did not compare with this heart-melting bliss, the languid glow that pulsed through her with the rhythm of her racing heartbeat.

Draping his arms around her hips, Jason leaned back against the settee and closed his eyes. "God, I'm too old for this."

She could feel his heart throb in time with hers when she rested her cheek on his shoulder. She had never known such contentment. Such peace.

"Marry me, Jason," she whispered into his ear. "Be my husband and make lots of babies with me."

He cracked an eyelid. "I'm *really* too old for this."

Shelby arched backward to gaze into his face. "I love you. I'm prepared to give up acting. You have another life now, and I want to be a part of it."

He rolled her off and under him with an agility that belied his earlier claim. "Never. You have a gift and I'll push you to use it until we're old and gray and performing for dinner theaters."

"*We're?*" she asked, not sure she heard him right. "You're retired."

"I think I could be persuaded into accepting a role or two. I'm having a helluva hard time envisioning you performing sex scenes with other actors." He nipped at her shoulder with a growl. "You'll be my leading lady, won't you?"

She gazed into his burning black eyes, suddenly unsure. "I thought you only wanted privacy?"

"I want a lot more now. I want love. I want you." He stretched out, wedging a leg between hers until her sex nestled warmly against his thigh. "I think we can come up with a compromise that lets us both do what we love. If you'll relocate north with me, I think after the initial shock, the media won't hound us too much. Some press will be good for your career."

The breath caught in her throat. "Are you saying yes, Jason?"

"Yes, Shelby. I'll marry you." His eyes sparkled.

"Are you sure?"

"I thought my life was making me lonely, and Hollywood was my life. I left. I was still lonely. Until now."

His tender expression warmed her straight to her soul, and her heart sang with the knowledge that she was living, not acting. She *felt* this swell of joy inside. "The babies, too?"

"At least six." He smiled a roguish smile. "I have to show Christopher I'm not too old to do you justice."

Laughter bubbled from her lips, and Shelby closed her eyes, savoring this moment of shared love. She had wasted so much time punishing herself over mistakes made long ago. Mistakes she had paid dearly for, had done everything possible to correct.

She *would* learn to forgive herself. With Jason's help.

"What about my past? There's always the possibility that it leaks out.

Will I embarrass you?"

"Bad press, honey?" He quirked the bronzed slash of his brow. "I'm immune." Ruffling her hair back from her face with a tender touch, he said, "Besides, I've got a blue movie in my own credits. I'm sure Wes will be happy to tell you all about it."

Shelby wondered if that movie was what Wes had used to blackmail Jason into coaching her. She rested her head against his arm, basking in the warm glow of his love, not really interested. Right now all she could think about was how dashing he would look in a tux.

Even more handsome than Max Brandauer had looked when he gave away the bride in *Heaven's Traveler*.

And as Shelby envisioned Jason playing the role of groom before an altar, another thought occurred to her. "Should we invite Wes to the wedding, do you think?"

"Invite, hell." Jason laughed and pulled her into his arms. "We'll blackmail him into paying for it."

It was a grand plan.

About the Author:

Jeanie Cesarini is a multi-published author who lives with her very own romance hero and their two beautiful daughters in the South. A transplanted Yankee, she particularly enjoys stretching out beneath moss-draped oaks and indulging in her favorite pastime: reading thrilling crime novels then soothing her jitters with a wonderful romance. **The Spy Who Loved Me** *and* **An Act Of Love** *allowed her to triumph over evil, to create love from the harsh reality of crime and create a happily ever after from a past mistake. She loves believing that, at least in fiction, good always triumphs over evil and hopes Secrets' readers enjoy believing, too.*

Enslaved

by Desirée Lindsey

To My Reader:

Everyone loves a good, angst-filled love story and adore a tender, provocative hero. Here's to vulnerable alpha heroes—to a sensate adventure with Nicholas and Crystal, their undying love, fierce passion, and all things as brilliant as his gift to her...

I give you award-winning seduction—may your hearts be *Enslaved*.

Chapter One

Lady Crystal Halverton stood gazing out the massive wall of windows with her back to the man she knew so well—the man her husband hadn't spoken to in weeks. Not since they'd parted ways out-of-sorts with each other.

Nicholas Summer had come like she knew he would.

And she desperately needed his cooperation.

With her fingers, Crystal cleared a spot where her breath fogged the glass pane. The rains had stopped their battering ram of sound on the roof. Despite the warmth from the blazing hearth at her back, the sky above the rear courtyard looked utterly despondent and sent an involuntary shiver through her. The winds felt colder this year, she thought, as she watched the approach of winter whip leaves across the rolling lawn of Halverton Hall's vast gardens.

Where once the house had been filled with laughter and happiness, it felt empty now—more like a prison of failures each day her husband stayed away. The gloomy and dreary weather matched her ever increasing despair and she wondered how Nicholas would feel when he learned the reason behind her hastily penned summons.

"I was so afraid you'd left London," she told him. "Thank you for coming, Nick."

"The dispatch sounded urgent," the deep voice answered behind her from the gold-braided settee. "Are you all right?"

"Freddy really does feel badly," she said feebly, avoiding the concern lacing his question, "about the disagreement over the hounds. I know he'll come around soon…it's just his pride is so delicate."

"So you called me here today to smooth things over?"

That would be a whole lot easier than what she intended. "I needed to speak with you in private…about another matter."

Interrupting them, the liveried footman in green and gold entered the drawing room with a tray of petit fours and a fine, black Darjeeling tea reserved for those occasions when Lord Summer came to call.

Crystal nodded at the table, her guest was familiar enough to the family to dispense with formality. "Please, Nick, help yourself." Her heart started an erratic dance the minute the door closed behind her footman.

"It's obvious you didn't call me here to discuss how Fred thinks his hounds are superior to the ones I acquired in France." His gaze was on her profile, his voice low, intimate. "You look pale. Have you eaten today?"

"No," she told him softly, "and please don't press me, not today."

"All right. I'll talk about the weather until you're sufficiently bored."

She shook her head. "I suppose you indulge your paramours in the same way. I should be jealous if I were not your friend."

"Neglect shows on you, puss."

His endearment touched her. Made her heart clench. "I'm not sure I like being read so well."

"Don't be angry, darling. Remember we practically grew up together. Knowing what you're feeling isn't difficult."

She sighed. "You've always been better at reading people than most men. I shouldn't wonder it comes in handy with overwrought women."

"With you I take special pains. It gives me great pleasure to find I've not lost my touch." The deep timbre of his voice was teasing and caressing in turns.

No, she thought, *you haven't lost your touch.*

From the drawing room window the courtyard looked deserted and gray. Dark snow clouds edged the wintery sky. A handful of birds clung to branches, their little bodies fluffed against the cold. She felt a pang of pity for the poor creatures, who not unlike man, sought warmth and protection where they could from the harshness of life.

"I'm a friend, Crystal. You know I won't spread your secrets around for gossip. Tell me what's wrong and I'll try to help."

She rested her forehead against the window, felt the cool glass panes startling cold against her skin. *That's why I chose you.*

"I won't be leaving for Edinburgh until tonight." His cup clanked onto the table. "Come, let me take you out for a walk, and you can tell me how married life is beginning to bore you."

It was a joke with them, of course, her marriage to Freddy Halverton anything but boring. "I already went for a walk before you arrived." She knew he was only trying to pull her out of her melancholy shell.

"Then a carriage ride? I'll bundle you up and we'll race around the estate—see how many tongues we can set to wagging. We used to do that well, you and I."

His devil-may-care tone reminded her of the days when she would have thrown convention to the wind. Could she really have been so careless all those years ago? So young?

Contemplating the changes in her life, she turned from the window. Her gaze rested on her childhood friend with a fond appreciation of his disarming good looks. At thirty, the wealthy man of a thriving merchant-line, Nicholas Summer was the model of virility. A paragon of masculine grace that took her breath away. His hair was thick as sable, still a rich, dark brown. To her, Nicholas looked every bit the young blood she'd loved as a girl—back when he and Freddy Halverton had taken London by storm. Time had changed many things, but not Nicholas.

Nick was five years her senior and still possessed an air of danger, dark passions, and irresistible charm. In the circles she belonged to, his name purred from the lips of breathless wives. And here, in her drawing room, the incorrigible Lord Summer was lounged in a sanguine sprawl on her settee. Typical, she mused, how he tied his white cravat as if to proclaim a rakish disregard for convention, while Freddy on the other hand took great pains to affect perfection.

She closed her heart to that painful thought.

"I'm losing him, Nick," she whispered weakly, her stomach knotting in anguish as if voicing the words made final the acceptance of losing her husband's love.

The silent sympathy in Nick's vivid green gaze told her he had not missed the nuances, the long weeks Freddy spent away, presumably hunting at their cottage near Dover.

"For what it's worth, he's alone, Crystal. I know he doesn't keep another woman."

"Oh, and I guess that should make me feel better. They're all in your bed—is that what you're telling me?"

"I'm sorry, puss."

His sympathy was almost more than she could bear—her empty bed becoming a stark contrast to his. "I don't think there's ever been any question about *your* ability to sire, has there? Aren't you glad now you're not saddled with a wife who has trouble breeding?"

"I would still love you, puss," he said with mild seriousness.

She slanted him a disgruntled look. "But you wouldn't have made me happy, isn't that what you said?"

"Fred was the better man."

"Really? I wonder on whose authority you arrived at that falsehood."

"Fred hasn't stopped loving you, Crystal."

"Not yet." There was no animosity in her voice, only a strained tiredness. "But neither have I been able to give him an heir."

"Don't blame yourself. Have you thought it might be Fred with the problem and not you?"

For a man who'd probably sired half of England, Nick's announcement seemed a mockery of her pathetic handicap. She had pondered over everything until her brain ached. Pointing fingers, she had decided, did nothing to lessen the burden—the stark longing in her husband's eyes. Nor did it lessen the yearning in her own heart, when their friends had hoards of children they only casually acknowledged.

The *problem* was, regardless of who was at fault, the result of their inability to have children had slowly erected a wedge between them. Which was why she had desperately agreed to go along with Freddy's outrageous request.

"I will do anything to keep my marriage from falling apart, Nick, anything."

Then because she'd held it bottled up all week, the misery and sorrow gave way to hot tears. One by one they trickled down her cheeks.

Nick came out of his chair and closed the short distance between them. He drew her tight in genuine concern. "Don't cry, darling."

He held her closer, murmuring soft praises against her hair that made her throat burn with self-pity. In her weakened state, Crystal gladly accepted his charity. She leaned on his strength, reveled in his warmth, when she had for many weeks been bereft of warmth, of hope. She let Nick be her rock, let him comfort her. She was too weary to worry about convention, about ruining his fine linen shirt with tears. Grateful for what scraps of attention he gave her, she pressed her lips to his chest. In Nick's embrace she could forget the world, her troubles—the affection they shared for one another brought her no shame.

She drew in a ragged breath, felt his hand soothing the tightness from her neck. His fingers were strong, caressing. After going so long without a simple touch, being held by him felt close to heaven. Just like old times. At first she had worried about feeling nervous—but now it was as if all the years since their last kiss had been washed away. He smelled of rainsoaked forests and leather. Under her cheek, his chest was solid. He was the same way she remembered him at seventeen, yet different in remarkable ways. Muscles honed by action rippled beneath his shirt. He towered above her. Tall, powerful, infallible.

She sniffled against him, felt his arms tighten, his compassion reach out to her. "I don't know if I could bear your rejection, too," she whispered, clinging to him in a manner she knew was desperate.

"Shh, darling, I'd never do that to you."

"You don't know yet why I asked you here." She knew him. He'd probably never speak to her again, never hold her like he held her now as though he cherished her. Like Freddy used to cherish her. But then she'd already spent the night crying over Freddy. Worrying about the future. Its complications. Now was not the time to have qualms about her promise.

"Tell me what I can do for you," Nicholas prompted reverently, "and I'll do it."

So trusting, so irresistible, and so gallant. "I want you," she murmured softly, "to give me a child."

The slight stiffening of Nick's body told her she'd been right. He was shocked.

His chin was resting on her head, the noticeable change in his breathing curiously touching.

"Are you serious?" Though he sounded calm, his heart was racing against her cheek.

She nodded against his chest and sniffled. "Very serious."

At least he hadn't said no.

"In fact, Freddy is staying away," she explained in a breathless rush, "until I send him word you're going home. The staff is leaving tonight. It will be only you and I alone in the house."

"Fred gave his consent?"

Another shock, she knew. One he hadn't expected.

"His blessing really. Freddy said if anyone could get me with child it would be you. He wanted me to approach you." Remembering her husband's anguished expression and not understanding it had upset her horribly. The despair in his voice had scared her. He hadn't explained why he was suddenly adamant about having an heir, just that it was imperative she talk to Nicholas. When she had balked, Freddy had begged her in a strangely hoarse voice that had cut straight to her heart. She'd set her fears aside, assured him she still loved him, and agreed to do as he requested. "Nick, I know what you must be thinking. God help me, but I want to please Freddy so badly I agreed."

His hand smoothed her hair. "Good Lord, Crystal. How could a man live with himself after sending his wife to seduce his best friend?"

Overwhelmed by the same uncertainties, wanting only to be done with fulfilling her husband's wish, she bit her lip to staunch the flow of misgivings.

"Really, it isn't all as insane as it sounds," she defended softly, "I think Freddy's plan makes perfect sense." She had to believe that—she must. "We've tried everything—the countless potions, the doctors who had no answers. You're our last hope."

"Are you sure?" he asked gravely.

Heartened by what sounded like his acceptance, she looked up at him, praying he wouldn't disappoint her. "I've thought about this long and hard. Quite honestly, I don't want to talk about it all night. I don't want to hear all the reasons why we shouldn't. I want you to carry me upstairs and make love to me."

"Just like that?"

Certainly she sounded like a stranger even to herself. A woman driven by fear of failure to the point of desperation. But it didn't matter. Everything important to her was slowly deteriorating before her very eyes. She'd failed Freddy in the most elemental way as a wife, but she would not fail him in this.

"Perhaps not *just* like that." Blushing, she admitted, "It may take a couple of days."

"And if it takes longer?"

Her heart twisted with sorrow. "I have no choice. You should have seen him, Nick, the way he kept looking at me as though he was leaving and never coming back. I can't fail. He won't come home until I'm with child," she told him plaintively. "In which case I'm prepared for it to take as long as a month." She'd gone over the details in her mind into the wee hours of the morning. "I'll need you to cancel all your engagements. That way you can stay in bed with me until I'm certain—"

"Slow down." His arms dropped to his sides. "I didn't agree to anything."

Desperation clutched at her belly. "I know what I'm asking sounds absurd, but please don't say no. Can't you just imagine I'm one of your many paramours? I'll even keep the room dark—"

"I can't."

The statement rang out with deafening clarity. No margin for maybe. Just resounding denial.

Reeling with dread, Crystal pulled away from him. Her throat filled with a suffocating desolation. She kept her face averted, tried to draw on the strength of her resolve while the ruined remains of her future flashed before her eyes.

"You mean you won't," she clarified softly.

She watched his expression in the window's reflection where they stood in uncomfortable silence. She could feel his pity reach out to her, sense his struggle—while beyond the perfectly manicured lawn, the grounds of Halverton Hall looked as bleak as her childless marriage.

Swallowing hard at the tight knot, she turned abruptly away and blindly made her way to the table. She forced herself to drink her tea slowly as panic rose up her throat to suffocate her. Her husband's parting words rang in her ears, impaling her heart. "I'm not getting any younger, Crystal. I need an heir—a son to entail Halverton Hall to."

When she had told Freddy he was scaring her with his morbid talk, his lips had thinned into a stubborn line. "You care for Nick, don't you?"

All she'd been capable of was nodding.

"Then I must have your word that you will talk to Nick tomorrow before he leaves for Edinburgh."

The way he'd pressed her for a promise frightened her. She'd sensed something had claimed the husband she loved, something had happened that she couldn't fight, something horribly wrong that he wouldn't talk about. "All right, I'll speak to Nicholas," she had said at last, giving in. "I promise you."

"Thank God. I'm counting on you, Crystal."

Freddy had finished packing and left her standing in the middle of his bedchamber. No goodbye kiss this time. No sweet parting hug. Crystal had run to the window, sobbing silently as she watched him ride away. The way he'd withdrawn from her frightened and confused her. It was as if he'd, for some reason, locked her out of his heart.

Determined not to let this one small failure panic her, Crystal turned to Nicholas. "If you won't help me, I will just have to find someone who will," she told him convincingly, her head held high, her voice shaking with emotion.

Across the twenty feet that separated them, Nicholas stood rigid, a muscle clenching in his jaw.

"Don't you think this has gone far enough?"

"Not near as far as I intend to go."

Nicholas drew a deep breath to battle his fury, not caring to rationalize why her blithe statement twisted his insides.

"Then an advertisement in *The Whoremonger's Guide* should do the job," he remarked dryly, "or if you really can't wait, you could stand on Half Moon Street near the Strand and peddle your wares." He let his gaze rake her slender curves in a bold assessment while the image of her giving herself to a stranger ignited all the demons he'd thought conquered. "With a body like yours, you should do well," he went on heedless of her crushed expression. "Put some red on your lips, wear a halo, and your clients will be calling you an angel. After a month you might even start looking forward to their generosity, you won't need the pin money Fred gives you. Hell, in time, your husband may even find your broadened knowledge in bed enjoyable."

"Stop it," she cried, covering her ears. "Don't you say another word! And don't you dare take airs with me, Nicholas. If you really cared, then I wouldn't have to resort to whoring."

"Good God, listen to yourself. You're not making sense." Nor could he leave her like this, feeling alone and rejected. "Why would making love with me be different than with another?"

Afraid she'd break down in front of him, Crystal clutched her teacup. Already her fingers were trembling so badly she feared she'd look down to find the skirt of her simple blue frock speckled with tea stains. Dear God, to voice her innermost feelings now would be the absolute humiliation.

The obvious reasons came easier. "The difference is simple. With you, I wouldn't have to suffer the shame afterwards. No one would have to know how desperate my husband is besides you and me."

"Then again," she said softly over the cup's rim, "I was so hopeful you would not mind so much. That you might even look forward to bedding me." She sounded like a petulant child, and hated it, but he'd wounded her gravely. "Obviously things have changed between us without my being aware. Freddy was right when he said you would be difficult."

In the numbing silence that followed, the air filled with a breathless kind of expectation.

His gaze burned with green fire. "My God, Crystal, surely you know how hard it is for any man to deny you?"

"I don't know what I believe anymore." Her voice vibrated with sadness.

"You don't have to do this. You could approach the orphanage—I could help you with the arrangements if Fred won't."

She smiled weakly. "Then everyone would know something was wrong with us."

"Don't you mean Fred's pride wouldn't survive their pity?"

"The orphanage is out of the question." Her tone was implacable.

"Damn Fred. You shouldn't have to do this alone."

"If things go as planned, I won't *be* alone."

"Any man will do, is that it?"

Her bottom lip quivered. "We wanted you."

"Well I'm not for hire."

She took a deep breath as the last of her hopes dwindled. "We would have made a beautiful child," she said thickly, her throat convulsing. "If you had only consented."

He didn't move, didn't breathe.

For a briefest moment, something in those emerald eyes touched her with warmth. She thought he might change his mind. Then the moment turned, again.

Frustration pulled his mouth into a grim line. "What you really want is some fool. Preferably two. One to service you through the day, while the night shift sleeps. Preferably someone with blue blood. Perhaps you'd like me to help you search?"

His cool tone made her feel sordid and cheap. "Don't do me any favors. I shall flounder along quite well on my own."

He laughed harshly. "Floundering hardly begins to describe your inexperience with men. Do you even know what a courtesan wears to seduce her clients?"

"I'm not an ignorant school girl," she reminded him tartly. "And what I don't know, I'll learn. I have *friends* who'll help me. Women with experience who have always been eager to share their secrets." Her husband's anguished expression—her promise to him—stiffened her resolve. She slid her gaze to the clock over the mantle. Already having decided on a reckless new course, she approximated how long it might take to pen a missive to Sarah Brown—how long before the dispatch made its way to the Theatre Royal on Catherine Street. "My only regret is that I have wasted my time. Had I known you would be so difficult," she went on, "I'd have paid closer attention to them."

He smiled tightly. "I should have married you, puss. I'd have given you a house full of children and put you out of your misery."

"Don't be ridiculous. I was seventeen and naive. I would have made you miserable." Hoping she sounded calmer, she moved to stand beside him at the window. "You shouldn't worry that I hold it against you. Freddy was, after all, a very dear and persuasive young man."

"Like a bulldog with a one track mind," Nicholas said sardonically.

"I like bulldogs, they're a dependable breed."

"And I'm not, I suppose."

"Poor, Nick. You're the wolf all dogs dream about."

His gaze bore into her. "Wolves understand boundaries, Crystal. If you were *my* wife, I'd never allow another man to touch you."

The implied message warmed the barren regions of her soul. "Fidelity? Coming from you?" She searched his face, saw he was serious. "Somehow I find that hard to believe."

"There was a time your husband felt the same way. Have things changed so much in eight years?"

She looked away from him, gazing out the window in a dreamlike way a wistful child might. "Freddy wants an heir very badly. Have you never wanted something so much it hurts?"

When after a moment he said nothing, she looked up to find those intense eyes of his watching her. For one incredibly brief moment, some fierce and almost tangible emotion flickered within their emerald depths. Then, elusive as a whisper, that emotion burned away.

"You really don't have to answer." She had always thought it a terrible waste for a man as extraordinary as Nicholas Summer to have found no one to love, no one equal to his passion.

Sighing, she turned from the window and gracefully made her way to her writing table. "Please feel free to stay and finish your tea." Pushing aside a delicate china saucer, she picked up the heavy, lead inkwell before heading for the door. "I'm sorry to have troubled you—we needn't speak of this matter again."

"Crystal—"

"Thank you for coming. I hope your trip to Edinburgh is safe. Give my regards to your mother."

Chapter Two

A week passed before Crystal received word from her husband. He had changed his mind—his letter said he would be coming home the end of next week. His message implied he'd forgotten to settle an important matter with their solicitor. What she read between those lines was he wanted to know if she'd been successful with Nicholas.

That nervous gnawing in her stomach churned into nausea. She couldn't face her husband's disappointment, his anguish.

Crystal rubbed her eyes and pushed herself up in bed. She'd already wasted a week being desperately lonely and feeling inadequate. And her husband's dispatch had sent her into a bout of melancholy that had her servants tiptoeing down the hall past her bedchamber. Even her maid was afraid to disturb to her, her groom hesitant to bring her news.

This morning, she noticed bleakly, her able-looking butler waited like always. Thin as a reed and solemn-faced, he stood a discreet distance just outside her door, his eyes downcast. "It's all right, Graves, I know my husband isn't coming home." Her voice sounded raspy, tired. Her hair was a tangled mess, her nightrail wrinkled like her composure. She no longer cared what they thought.

"I beg your pardon, my lady," Graves muttered, wringing his hands together. "It's not Lord Halverton I came to see you about. It's your gentleman friend, my lady. Lord Summer seems awful worried about you. He's come to take you for a ride, he wants us to have you ready right away. Said he won't take no for an answer."

"Was he furious when you handed him his unopened letters?" She'd heard the commotion Nicholas made in her foyer.

"Yes, I was," came the deep voice from the doorway. Startling them, Nicholas stepped around Graves and approached the bed. Crystal's heart skipped erratically. Devastatingly handsome, Nick gave her no time to compose herself. She glimpsed the tight buff breeches hugging his long muscled legs. How the royal blue riding jacket cut in the height of fashion gave an added touch of arrogance to his impossibly wide shoulders.

The calmness in his voice was deceptive. Nicholas' fierce scowl had Crystal squirming.

"Sorry, my lady, I could not stop him," Graves apologized with red-faced embarrassment. "Lord Summer insisted on seeing you."

Coming out of shock by degrees, Crystal clamored to still her thundering heart. "It's all right, Graves. I will deal with Lord Summer myself." She sent Nick a fierce scowl of her own.

Graves hurriedly shut the door leaving Crystal alone with her testy visitor.

Before she could move, Nick bent down and gathered her into his arms. Still reeling from one surprise, she hardly had time to recover her wits before he was wrapping the counterpane around her transparent night-dress, pulling her onto his lap. They sat in silence. For all his glowering, he held her like a fragile china doll, his embrace curiously compassionate.

"I ordered you a bath," Nick told her softly, his hands unsteady. Coming in to find her looking pale and broken had instantly lanced his heart wide open. "Your maid told me you haven't been out of the house in days. After you have bathed we're going for a ride."

"A ride?" she parroted in a rush of trepidation.

"What did you think? That you could keep me away by simply barring your door to me?"

Her mind, now fully recovered from the shock, started working frantically for answers. "You ordered me a bath?" she asked nervously, aware he was watching her with a diabolical glint in his eyes. "Surely you don't intend—"

"To watch?" He could hardly stay angry with her looking so pitiful. "I thought that was what you wanted."

She averted her eyes. "I've changed my mind about your staying." He'd just barged in without a welcome and ordered her a bath. As if he hadn't wounded her pride not two days past. "You must leave immediately." Her hands lay fisted in her nightdress. "Now, before the servants start talking."

"A smart staff knows they will be dismissed without references should they talk."

Her gaze met his. "You brute, if you are bullying them—"

He put his finger to her lips to shush her. "They don't like what's happening any more than I do."

Because he was touching her, she tried not to respond, but the imploring tenderness in his voice breached her barriers. Something was passing between them...something fragile and warm. Comforting. Vital.

Knowing he shouldn't, but damned if he could stop it, Nicholas' finger searched the smooth texture of her lips. Her defenses were crumbling, the stiffness of her spine melting away under his touch. With a soft little moan that stroked his senses, she opened her lips to him, parting sweetly, giving him license to ravish.

"After your bath, I'm taking you away for a while." He abruptly shifted her from his lap just as the bath water arrived.

Because she knew he would, in fact, assist her if she didn't do as he wished, Crystal quickly disrobed behind a screen upon which graceful white swans were painstakingly painted. Some minutes later when she emerged from her bath all squeaky clean and smelling of gardenias, she found Nicholas holding a towel for her, his gaze averted.

"This is all very mysterious." Standing on tiptoe, she frowned at him over the top of the modest shield and snatched the towel. "Where is it we're going? Or is that a secret?"

"You will see." He chose a slate-colored riding habit with black braiding which he laid out on the bed with a fashionable little headdress and limerick gloves. Lastly, he retrieved from the bottom of her wardrobe the leather boots of the same morose shade.

In the courtyard, Crystal's pretty bay mare tossed her head while dancing a tight circle around Nicholas' huge black stallion. The horses sensed the excitement, flicking their tails and snorting their disdain for being patient. Nicholas leaned from his saddle, made a last minute check of the mare's girth and then they whirled around and were off down the drive at a fast trot that whisked Crystal's demure little hat from her head. She left it where it fell, knowing she could retrieve it later and far too giddy with excitement to care. Riding in the morning was something she'd missed dearly. Up until a month ago Freddy had always ridden with her. Now, when he was home, he preferred staying behind, content to read his newspapers and debate the importance of rotating crops with his land manager.

Just to be out of the house was exhilarating. Nick knew her weakness for horses and wild gallops and as angry as she'd been at him, she couldn't stay mad. Not on a glorious morning like this. Color bloomed in her cheeks. The mists were just clearing, the air crisp. Her hair, soon free of its pins and tousled by the horses' fast pace through the countryside, clung in damp tendrils to her neck. Going for a ride with Nicholas was exactly what she needed, she realized, her spirits rising in spite of her misgivings about her husband's return. And when those thoughts would have darkened her day, she quietly pushed them away.

The horses raced around a bend in the road and came upon that all-too-familiar secluded glen where naive love had nearly been Crystal's undoing a decade ago.

Nicholas reined alongside her, his smile ready, his keen gaze on her face. "You remember where we are?" he asked, nudging his high-strung stallion next to the prancing mare. "You remember what we did here?"

She shot him a blushing grin and suddenly looked shy. Like all those years ago, he thought her as captivating as the first rays of sunshine peering over the horizon. He'd watched her transform from a vibrant young tease into the woman the ton claimed breathtaking. Their claims merely brushed the surface. To him, Crystal was as passionate and infuriating as any woman he'd ever taken to his bed.

Stimulated by that image, the burning flame in his gut twisted lower through his groin.

They dismounted in silence, his hands at her waist to assist her to the ground. Standing close to her, layers of consciousness registered upon his senses. She smelled exotic. Ravishable. Redolent of everything sweet. A sweet temptation belonging to another man. Best he remember that, should he start to lose his mind.

When Nick would have dropped his hands and turned away, she caught him around the waist and snuggled her head against his chest like a trusting child. Nick's heart thumped hard against his ribs. Lower, there was another part of him swiftly turning just as hard. "Come," he told her when he couldn't trust himself a moment longer, "I want to show you something."

Leaving the horses tied to a tree, he walked ahead of her through the knee-deep grass.

In the middle of a vast lush valley stood a lonely sentinel of young love, a huge overhanging oak dominating the view. Its massive branches were draped like heavy arms over a verdant glen, just as it had when Crystal and Nicholas discovered it over a decade earlier.

"Oh, Nick!" Crystal broke into a run, lifting her skirt over the tall grass, her hair flowing out behind her in brilliant golden waves. He stood for a moment and watched her, his chest constricting with emotion.

Crystal reached out her hand and captured his as he stopped near her under the cover of branches. With her other hand, she traced the deep grooves in the tree bark, the symbol of all her young dreams and fantasies. The jagged lines felt rough and smooth—much the same as the tempestuous fondling between inexperienced lovers. Surrounded by a perfect heart carved deep enough to last all eternity, her fingers lingered on their initials.

Crystal turned to him, her eyes misting with emotion. "I remember the day you carved this. You were wild and full of yourself and you told me you were eloping with me, that I didn't have any choice but to succumb to slavery. We were both laughing, because you kneeled in the grass like a beseeching knight pretending to kiss my hem and got grass stains on your breeches." She paused when the memory of what followed made her breath hitch. "That was the same day Freddy proposed to me...and the same day you later sailed for Italy." Still a painful memory after all these years, she lifted her hand to run her fingers over his name. "So why did you bring me here? Why now?"

He drew her into his arms. Gently at first, until she pressed closer. Then he held her as if the world would fall out beneath him. He held her without reserve, like he had all those years ago when he touched her in ways only a husband touched his bride. When he'd been out of his mind to have her and yet told her he wouldn't marry her. When she offered him what no gentleman of honor took. And he had regretted it every day since...denying himself that brief glimpse of heaven.

"I brought you here"—he swallowed—"to show you that things haven't changed. That it won't work." His lips brushed her hair. "You accused me of not caring. You're dead wrong, puss. It's because I care, I can't have you. Because if I bed you, I'll only end up hurting you."

Her pitiful little sounds of anguish made him feel like a insensitive bastard. He feared she'd break down. And perverse as it was, he almost hoped she would...so he could go on believing she was suffering as much as he had suffered these last eight years. Seeing her humbled should have made him feel better, but the exact opposite was happening, her utter unhappiness was shattering his soul.

"I don't know what to do any more, Nick. Nothing makes sense. I'm so afraid, so alone," she whispered at last. "If you would just hold me like you used to." So soft was her voice, he had to strain to hear her. "If you won't seduce me, then leave me a memory to hold onto. Please, Nick, just touch me."

What she asked of him made his heart hammer madly in his chest. "If I touch you that way, it won't be enough. We'll want more. You know how it was between us."

"I promise not to ask for more...please, Nick, I'm so empty, I feel so cold. I don't want to be alone—"

"Shh, puss." He kissed her hair and knew exactly how vulnerable she felt. "Come with me."

He led her away from their hiding until they found themselves in a lushly secluded area just large enough to turn around—where the shadows embraced them in a circle of intimacy. This time Crystal was no innocent, she was as knowledgeable about seduction as he was. Nick leaned his back against the rough tree trunk, feet braced on either side of hers, his head telling him to go slow, his heart ignoring rationale. For a brief moment of insanity, he damned to hell the consequences and crushing the skirt of her demure riding habit drew her tightly into his groin.

His head swam, his blood pumped furiously through his body. Her hands slid down his back, then lower to frantically draw him closer. The sounds of the meadow faded into a blood rushing beat pulsing loudly in his head. Wanting nothing more than to fill her ache, waiting for what seemed half his life to bring her to climax, he hadn't realized how that blazing need had taken its toll. He captured her wrists to slow her exploration, slow the tempo of their impassioned madness to a more bear-able level of burning desire. What control he'd managed to hold onto was fading.

Her writhing body pressed hotly against his became a searing torture. So perilously close to release, the powerful urge to drive into her was so hot, so potent, his sex stiffened in painful need. Nick's last shred of thought, as he lowered his mouth to conquer, was he wanted her more than life, wanted to penetrate her every way imaginable. Penetrate her heart.

Crystal opened her lips to his mastery, felt him invading, tasting, demanding, making her swoon with cresting waves. Then their kiss went beyond carnal exploration and flared into a voracious flame of mating that burned brighter and hotter than either of them anticipated. Unconsciously, his hand slipped between her thighs in an attempt to seek the lush wetness his body craved. She quivered uncontrollably as he explored the folds of her skirt, the fabric a frustrating barrier hindering deeper penetration. His hands clenched in her skirt, his agony peaking, desire flaring, every nerve in his body preparing for the blazing moment when he touched bare skin.

Crystal cried out, sagging against Nick, panting for air, her weight supported solely by his thrusts...each exquisite penetration of material and mastery filling her womb with searing sweet friction.

Little moans of hot need brazed his skin where her breath burned, as she pulled the buttons free on his shirt to press her lips to his chest. A deep groan rumbled in his throat as her assault moved lower.

Her hands cupped his groin, groping impatiently, shamelessly asking for more...when the high shrill pitch of a horse's scream dragged them abruptly back to reality.

Heart pumping in his ears, his body corded and tight, Nick held his breath and listened.

Crystal stirred from her rapturous delirium, her breathing strained. "Hounds! Do you hear them?"

"Christ!" Nicholas drew a rasp of air, took one last look at her disheveled state, her luminous eyes, the flushed glow of passion brightening her cheeks, and decided there was no time to waste righting her tousled coiffure. Being interrupted by a pack of hounds in hot pursuit, and discovered by the riders not far behind the chase, would be damaging enough to a woman of social rank, but should that woman be another man's wife, the deed would be unforgivable. Crystal's reputation would suffer. And before Nick would see her destroyed, he'd vow to celibacy.

They emerged from the cover of the trees at a run.

Despite her skirt tangling her legs, Crystal tried to stay up with Nicholas as he pulled her along behind at a breathless pace. The horses danced in frenzied circles a few yards ahead. By the time Nicholas and Crystal reached the giant oak where the horses were straining their tethered bonds, the hounds burst from the brush. Out in the lead, a flash of red fur zigzagged across the open field less than fifty yards away.

The beautiful fox ran for its life.

"Poor thing," Crystal cried, doubling over with an effort to drag air into her lungs. They were both out of breath, their sides heaving, when Nicholas lifted her off the ground and onto her agitated mount.

"Ride for town," Nick shouted over the baying of ravenous dogs. "I'll circle around the forest and meet up with you later." When she hesitated, looking down on him with a crestfallen expression clearly laced with regret, he met her gaze for one dangerous moment longer, then smacked her horse on the rump.

"Why can't I stay with you—" Her words were lost in brisk departure, her horse already bolting off. Crystal's full concentration turned immediately to the task of keeping her seat.

Glancing briefly over her shoulder as her mount sprinted ahead of the snarling pack, Crystal's last glimpse of Nick was him racing in the opposite direction. Her heart pounding, her lips tingling and her body still trembling from her devastating encounter with blatant sensuality, Crystal rode hard and swift for home.

All the way back to London, the emptiness in her belly grew. It festered into a craven longing that she knew no relief from without Nicholas. When he'd looked at her with lust-darkened eyes just before they parted, she'd seen it in his gaze, realized in that fleeting moment before their intimacy had been shattered that Nicholas had been just as powerless as she to hide it. Damn the hounds! Damn their ill-timing!

Chapter Three

Like an anxious child awaiting the first glimpse of a fairy, Crystal sat perched restlessly near the window that evening, her gaze searching the shadowy landscape for a flash of black—for that instant man and beast would come into view. What could be wrong? Why hadn't he come?

She waited there the next day as well, determined more than ever to assure herself that Nick was coming.

It wasn't until the third day when her spirits started to flag, when her nerves were strung out, that her tryst with Nick in the forest started to feel more like a dream than a reality. She wouldn't yet accept that he was purposely staying away. She tried to tell herself his absence was only temporary, that he'd been just as carried away as she had, but the truth was, the more she grieved over what could have happened, the more foolish she felt. Nicholas had, after all, been quite clearly resisting. In fact, he had expressly told her he wouldn't bed her.

When, on the morning of the fourth day, Nick rode up to Halverton Hall, Crystal wasn't receiving him. That she decided quite out of self-preservation. She'd put that whole heart-wrenching scene in the forest behind her, she wanted nothing to do with that memory or those feelings.

Nick came back that noon only to be turned away again. He persisted a second time that evening and was told the same story. Lady Halverton wasn't accepting callers.

"He has threatened to climb the trellis outside your window, my lady." Graves gave reports on Nick's visits. "I think we should take it down right away."

"I'm sorry, Graves. Do you mind?"

"Not at all, my lady."

Crystal had kept her door locked every time she heard Nick arrive, she wasn't taking any chances of being caught off guard again. He'd not sweep into her bedroom and set her heart soaring with any more well-intended gestures that would end in disaster for her.

He'd sent her notes that she left untouched, sent her flowers she gave to the housekeeper. She could hardly keep up with the onslaught.

Yet in all fairness, if she were honest with herself, Crystal found Nick's persistence comforting. Even if it intensified those vulnerable feelings she was trying to ignore.

She swallowed against a lump of pain. In time, Nick would go away, stop trying to wear her resistance down. Leave her to her self-destruction.

Graves entered her room with another armful of wild white orchids. Nicholas knew they were her favorite.

"Lord Summer is not to be trusted anymore, Graves." She stared un-flinching, the shadows of evening falling across her bed where she sat dragging her fingers through her snarled hair. "Tell the footman to shoot him on sight."

To his credit, the man's face gave only a hint of a smile. "If that's your wish, my lady, I'll see to it your orders are carried out."

"Have there been any dispatches for me besides his?" she asked dis-passionately.

Graves' brows drew together in thought. "A letter arrived earlier this evening from Lady Sutherland, her footman delivered her apologies. Seems she has been visiting her sister in the country and didn't get your missive until morning last." He pulled two envelopes from his pocket and slid them onto the table just inside her door. "The other, I can't say who it's from, my lady. I was otherwise engaged with Lord Summer when the woman arrived. She didn't give her name to the footman."

Heartened by the news, her first time in what seemed days, Crystal glanced at the scant moonlight filtering between the drapes. "What time is it, Graves?"

"Just past ten, my lady."

Not too late. "I think I'll manage dinner now."

"Yes, madam," he replied with a beaming smile, "I'll bring a tray directly."

After he shut the door behind him, she slid from bed. A ray of hope bloomed in her dismal world as she reached for the letters.

An hour before midnight, Nicholas rode up to the Halverton's door-step and handed the reins to a sleepy lackey. The response he received, however, from Crystal's young footman was not the one he expected.

"Sorry, sir, I have orders to shoot you on sight."

The dim light afforded by the street lantern gave the lad's boyish features a yellow tinge. Nicholas' brows slanted at opposing angles, his gaze fastened on the pistol pointed at his chest. "Orders from Lady Halverton?" he ground out.

"Yes, sir."

Patience gone, Nick contemplated the younger man's unrelenting stance, wondered if the insolent pup would like having the gun's steel barrel wrapped around his neck. Though it might make him feel better, he knew injuring Crystal's young footman would only make matters worse between them. "Is the Lady at home?" he said with forced civility.

"I can't say, sir."

Which meant in layman's terms, she had already slipped out. After a week of lying in bed, eating hardly enough to sustain a pulse, speaking to no one according to her maid, she had miraculously recovered. To elude him it seemed.

He should have found that knowledge encouraging, but dread of another sort wormed into his conscience. He'd grievously hurt her, now she was making his life hell. Hell he could manage, it was Crystal's sudden return of spirit that worried him.

Damn her, she'd not changed her mind.

Knowing he'd get nowhere with the footman, Nicholas visited Lady Halverton's stable. It was there he gleaned from a worried and reluctant groom that the Lady had taken a carriage to the Sutherland's soiree, that she hadn't said when she expected to return.

Nicholas didn't find Crystal at Sutherland's either. In fact, the Duchess hadn't seen her good friend for over three weeks and had only just sent a dispatch to Halverton Hall that morning inviting Lady Halverton to her social.

It was long after midnight by the time Nick approached the outer edges of civilized Town. London's East district was a mass of dark shapes, the streets a twisted maze of faceless shadows watching for prey—unsuspecting women like Crystal. A sense of urgency pushed at his weary brain. Nicholas turned his horse down a narrow alley, breathing in the stench of rot and filth. He followed behind a figure in a threadbare coat who was leaning heavily on the arm of some unfortunate woman in equally frayed clothes. Her lusterless eyes held a wariness, lines of fatigue and hard years were twisted upon her bony features. He dug into his pocket as he passed. "Bless you, your lord-ship, bless you," the woman rasped, her fingers clasping his like frozen branches to the gold piece.

He trudged on, towering brick walls flanking his sides. Flakes of snow started to fall, coming down in blurry chunks. February's chill settled in his bones like an icy hand gripping his heart. He'd already stormed the brothels along Covent Garden. The only establishment Nicholas hadn't searched loomed ahead, a fuzzy outline barely recognizable beyond the heavy fall of snow. Fear of finding Crystal there knotted his gut. He prayed he wasn't too late.

A thick layer of cigar smoke hovered over the opulent parlor where Madame Lucina entertained her guests. It stung Crystal's eyes, burned her nose. All around her, clients lay sprawled over plush-cushioned divans and their red satin counterparts. Chairs were arranged around the parlor filled with couples engaged in various forms of foreplay, some already advanced to positions that made Crystal's cheeks flame. She'd heard of wild orgies, she'd tried once to imagine them in her mind. But never in her wildest dreams had she expected this.

"You like watching, Countess?"

The foreign, wine-slurred voice in her ear sounded so far away. Her mind felt foggy, her mouth so dry. The hot breath on her neck sent a shiver of trepidation down Crystal's spine, the cold hand sliding up her arm star-tling her out of her daze.

Countess? Was that the alias she'd chosen? "Please, sir"—she looked around for her fur wrap— "I've made a mistake. I need to leave." The strap of her green gown slipped off one shoulder.

Smiling, her escort drew her closer. "Relax, Countess, you paid hand-somely for my services. You want a child, I can give you what you want." His soft hypnotic voice drummed against her groggy mind. With his arm curled around her bare shoulder, he coaxed her up a flight of winding stairs to the private rooms preferred by the more prudent clientele. "Let me help you, *cara*, let me give you a baby."

"Yes, a baby," she whispered. Her tongue felt thick, sluggish. She was leaning heavily against him as he led her down a carpeted corridor. He opened one of the doors. She stumbled against him as he drew her into a dimly lit room with gaudy, red satin walls. "It's so hot," she stammered. "I can't think."

On the sideboard sat a decanter exactly like the one her escort had poured from downstairs. He carefully held onto her with one arm while filling a glass with ruby nectar. He offered her a taste. "Drink, Countess, the wine will help."

"Yes…the wine." Sipping the sweet potion, she stared straight ahead, the garish trappings wavering in and out of her vision. "You must tell me what I should do," she said stonily.

"Don't worry, *cara*." He reached up, traced his finger over her brow with slow mesmerizing care. "I will go slow."

Some minutes later, she roused from a groggy daze and found herself resting atop her handsome escort on a gold satin settee. He was smiling at her, the smile of an angel. A dark, mysterious, angel. Her thoughts returned, as if in some other dream, to the way he'd walked, the way he'd pulled her along by the hand up the stairs. "I chose you…did I tell you…because your smile"— she tried to focus— "reminded me of someone."

The raised voices of lurid laughter sounding from the other side of the door faded in and out of her consciousness.

"Then close your eyes, *cara*, let me kiss you like he kisses you." His lips grazed her bare shoulder. "Remember his hands…how they felt…let me touch you where he touched you."

Crystal was losing herself, helpless to do anything but follow him. The effect of his entreaty made her breathless, the vision he painted for her stroked a chord of longing in her that left her defenseless. He was caressing her shoulder, his skillful fingers tingling over her heated skin. Her head rolled back on the cushion, her eyes too heavy to open.

"Drink, *cara*, the wine is for you." He poured her more. "It works quickly, I promise." He curled his fingers around hers, lifted her hand with her glass to her lips. Crystal felt the liquid slide down her throat, felt the answering wetness hot between her thighs. Burning, she thought numbly. Between her legs she felt on fire.

"That's it, Countess, relax. I'll help that burning, I'll make it go away."

"Yes," she murmured, her body shaking with splintery spirals of need. She felt something cool—air—on her legs, his hand—she thought—pulling her skirt aside. Her throat made whimpering sounds. Then the growing heat between her thighs spread up, devouring her, arching her back— it pulsed in her womb, opening her to his coaxing. Muffled laughter came from somewhere, a woman moaning. But nothing mattered, not the dark stranger, nor the piquant odor of sin. "Help me, please…"

A draft chilled her bare legs, followed by the sound of decisive footsteps. "Move your hand any higher and I'll kill you."

In a cold, black rage, Nicholas stood over them, bearing down on Crystal and her lover like a fierce dark knight, snow still clinging to his cloak. The man on the divan stiffened. His hand had halted bare inches away from entering her, his head snapped around, eyes slitted, assessing his challenger. "She's not going to appreciate your interference."

Crystal moaned, tried to open her eyes.

Nicholas leaned over, gripped the man's throat. "What have you given her?" he growled inches from the foreigner's handsome face.

"Let him go," a woman behind Nicholas demanded, her voice one of authority, her heavy bosom heaving from the pace with which she'd hurried after the angry man thundering into her parlor. Lucina made an impressive figure in shear black silk, her lush breasts bared, hands on her hips. "The Lady consented to using an aphrodisiac." She paused for a deep breath. "I didn't know how familiar she was with them so I used a mild one. She should be fine by morning."

Crystal reached up, clutching for the angry visage of her savior when the fingery sensations gripping her body peaked. "Nicholas…help me." She cried out his name, panting, writhing.

Nicholas's gaze darted from Lucina to Crystal.

"Listen, I don't want any trouble with you, Lord Summer," the robust madame offered quickly. "If you want her, take her. We'll settle finances later."

Nicholas slowly loosened his grip on the foreigner's neck. The younger man made a hasty retreat, brushing past the curious onlookers filling the doorway who'd gathered for a glimpse of what promised to be a roiling battle.

"Back to your business, everyone," Lucina called out, clapping her hands. "There's champagne for all downstairs."

In the time it took the sheepish-looking footman to call for Crystal's carriage, Nicholas had gathered her in his arms. He took care with the folds of her cape, making sure they were wrapped tightly around her writhing body. Then he bent and brushed his lips along her temple. Whispered something in her ear that seemed to soothe her.

The concern evident in Lord Summer's ministrations for the beautiful

Countess was readily noted by Lucina. In all the years she'd known the infamous seducer, not once had his actions shown such devotion to a woman. It was a brief thing, a moment of unguarded affection she might expect of a lover. This woman obviously meant something to him.

Chapter Four

In the carriage, Nicholas held Crystal in his arms. Her hair had come loose, waves of pale honey lay like a blanket of silk falling about her waist. Her breathing erratic, in her disheveled state, her beauty was devastating, the green shimmer of fabric against flawless skin drawing his gaze. But then she would have been captivating in a wool sack. A particular memory of a grey riding habit had haunted him mercilessly.

This time her fashionable gown, what there was of it, hung off one shoulder in a way meant to entice.

He was furious with her—with himself.

He felt his control slipping, he watched her agony peak. His need, despite his best efforts, swelled with every excruciating twist of her bottom against his lap.

Nicholas gritted his teeth. If she were his wife, he'd have pulled aside her skirt miles back, buried himself in her silken heat. But she wasn't his wife, he thought furiously. She wasn't even able to speak to him.

"Give me your hand, puss," he coaxed, her whimpering driving his body to madness. "Let me show you how to ride this out."

Her fingers clasping his hand were ice cold. He rubbed them between his own, then slowly drew them to the heart of her wanting. He pushed them under her skirt, between her thighs. She was hot, and wet, and the instant he touched her pouty cleft his shaft turned brick hard. The air left his lungs in a rush. Fighting back blinding carnal urges, he guided her fingers, pushing them slowly into her pulsing flesh...and heard the first piercing cry of her orgasm start low in her throat. His body responded, desire burned deep in his groin. Her weight setting atop him made his torture acute, the filmy layer of gown separating them unable to hide his raring arousal. For the second time in a mere week, he lived hell on earth, rational mind useless against a straining libido.

The aphrodisiac promised a slow initiation. Crystal's lingering ascent to impassioned madness, his abstinence a gradual death taking all night. The cantharides familiar to him sometimes lasted through morning.

She was panting, wanting more, her body arching against her hand. He turned his gaze beyond the window, tried to block out her begging. She would bring herself to climax without him.

By the time they reached Halverton Hall her exhaustion was acute. He knew she was at the limit of her strength, resting heavily against him now, waiting for the next soul-robbing orgasm. And he might have felt sorry for her, had she not scared ten years off his life.

"If you want my help, puss, you have to call off your watchdogs."

"Anything," she breathed tightly.

The carriage stopped with a jolt. "I'm going to get you into bed as quick as I can."

Carrying her past the gaping footman whose pistol was now tucked away, Nicholas met Graves at the door. "Lady Halverton would like the servants to leave as quickly as possible. My town house is empty, go there. Tell Burnes I'm staying here."

"But—"

"Please, Graves, just do it," Crystal bit out.

At the top of the stairs, Nicholas kicked her bedchamber door open, waited until he laid her down on her bed. "Dammit, Crystal," he said, pulling her stockings down. "You little fool. What possessed you to go to Lucina's? What did you think you were going to find?"

"He wanted to help me," she rasped as shame washed over her. She lay helpless, utterly weary. Then her body bucked against his arm, cresting need splitting her in two. Broken gasps punctuated her whimpering. Her throat felt raw, her head throbbing. "He wanted to give me a baby. And you ruined it."

The words were barely a whisper, but he heard them. Grabbing the hem of her gown, he yanked the transparent green tulle over her head. "Turn over." He didn't wait for her to comply, he pushed her over onto her stomach. His hands worked quickly, peeling off her chemise. "That boy you wanted likes to work over his clients with broom handles." His hands were harsh, his actions driven by anger. "I was there when his last victim nearly hemorrhaged to death. She was twice your age and old enough to know what to expect."

He rolled her onto her back. "If I have to, I'll put a leash on you until Fred returns. You won't go anywhere without my permission." He tugged the coverlet over her legs.

She laid on her back, clenching her eyes shut, batting his hands away. "I don't need a keeper—get out." She would have railed at him, but her body convulsed, she started to climb again.

Gently, Nick guided her hand where she ached. "I'm staying the night. I'll be here if you need me." And shamelessly, her hand moved of its own accord.

Nick straightened, and watched, his breathing unsteady.

Candlelight from across the room, flickered over her face, the pain mingled with pleasure there, over the perfection of her slender curves, over rouged nipples distended and thrusting with each arch of her back. Light blended with shadows, contouring her full breasts, the valley leading down her abdomen. She was a temptress, pale as white silk. She drew her legs up, let her knees fall apart, her eyes begging him.

Mentally flogging himself for weakening, he swiftly approached the limits of his threshold. Christ, he even had her husband's consent. His release an arm's length away. He could smell her need. He'd seduced women with no remorse, less scruple.

"It's all right if you don't want to be my lover," she whispered fitfully, her eyes already drooping shut. "I'll settle for friendship."

"What happened the other day was a mistake." He heard himself say the unforgivable, felt the falsehood stick in his throat. "Go to sleep, puss."

Then dying inside, Nicholas turned abruptly and walked over to the window. He drew the drapes aside, stood looking out into a dreary sky.

His hands burned hot on her flesh, caressing her lovingly, sliding down her stomach. Her nerves came alive, tingling under the brush of Nick's lips against the soft curls of her woman's place, dragging strangled whimpers from her throat. He was all she imagined he would be, fierce, gentle, capable of rending her every screaming nerve with provocative sensation. She was drowning in a searing pool of bliss so deep and keen she cried aloud, its licking heat devouring her until she could fight it no more. Teasing her, tasting her and tormenting her, Nick carried her higher. Higher

until her world quivered, until she thought she would die. His every move
designed to make her shatter rushed upon her body in unmerciful waves of
utter sweetness so poignant she wanted nothing but to surrender, giving in
to the wild rapture of fire consuming her body and soul.

'Nick, now," she keened passionately, his weight pinning her to the
bed, his body readied for entry. His eyes blazed down at her with a tender-
ness borne of devotion before he commanded her to behold the evidence
of his madness. Gleaming in the candlelight, taut, straining, his beautiful
arousal all flared glory and dominate power flexed under her very rapt
gaze. All that glory was for her, pulsing with need, with a life giving potion
her body ached to receive. He drew her nipple between his teeth, and they
came together in a wild rapturous melding of flesh and bone and hot-
blooded passion. She cried his name, beseeching, thrashing, wanting him
deeper, seeking complete domination, and he gave her more than she ever
dreamed possible, lifting her with each powerful thrust until at last she
shattered in half upon a cliff of sweet hot rapture.

Slowly the sensation brought Crystal awake, her body still hot and
splintering, her mind instantly rejecting the brutal truth that her impassioned encounter was nothing more than a dream.

The heart-wrenching sickness that came with reality, following those
first intense moments of loss, made her want to scream out in denial. Close
on the heels of frustration came the events of last night to fill her heart
with shame. Staring at a fragment of daylight streaking the ceiling, her
mind still drowsy, she made the mistake of trying to move. Her involuntary cry brought Nick's head around. Her body felt terrifyingly heavy, her
legs and arms weak.

"Feel better?"

Soreness forgotten, Crystal pulled the coverlet up under her chin. She
couldn't meet his gaze. "I have a feeling I behaved very badly last night."

He smiled reassuringly. "You had an excuse." Hands at the middle of
his back, he stretched.

From her view in the bed, Nicholas looked tired, his face drawn into a
mask of polite regard, revealing none of the condemnation she'd expected.
He said not one harsh word to make her feel foolish. "I'm sorry. I can't
seem to get anything right. I failed miserably last night, didn't I?"

"No, you didn't fail. If I hadn't interfered you would have had what you wanted."

The weariness in his voice shamed her, brought a hot flush creeping into her face. He'd cared enough to come looking for her, and she would hug that solace to her heart in the empty days ahead. "Please don't tell Freddy, I don't know if I can face his disappointment."

Nicholas was looking out the window, the pale dawn light reflected in his eyes. He didn't speak. The tension in his body, the way he avoided looking at her, spoke of the tortures he'd lived last night. He'd wanted her, she'd seen it in his bold gaze when he'd peeled her clothes away, when he'd stared down at her before stalking away. No matter how hard he tried to hide it, the tiger lurking beneath the surface, eyes shining with heated lust craved her. His need to mate was riding him hard. Her scent had him prowling, primed.

Her cheeks flamed hotter, her brazen thoughts running wild. The image of him coming to her, kneeling between her legs, sent a shiver of latent thrills down her limbs. She was still tingling from her dream. If he touched her, she would melt. Only she knew he wasn't going to give in to the hunger.

Crystal sighed. She must be overwrought, she decided. In reality, she was merely missing her husband. Nicholas was an infatuation, the things she'd imagined him doing to her, her way of preparing for the ultimate seduction. Preparing her body to accept his child.

"You told me last night the woman nearly died. You know her, don't you?"

He stood there stonily quiet, as if not sure he wanted to answer.

"I know her, yes." His sigh seemed dragged from the depths of his soul. "She came to me because she thought I could help her get over her fear." He raked his hand through his hair. "I started out slow. I would spend the first hour doing menial things that required minimal contact. We spent many hours just playing faro. The progress has been slow, and she still flinches from my touch."

Sadness filled her heart. "He must have beat her very badly."

Nick looked over his shoulder at her, saw she didn't understand. "I didn't say he beat her, Crystal."

"I don't understand. I thought you said he used a broom handle on her?"

"Not in the way you are thinking." He waited for the impact to set in. Slowly she shook her head, her eyes round, confused.

Taking pity on her, he told her gently, "What you did for yourself last night, he used a broom handle to intensify."

Her face turned pale as dawning horror filled her eyes, her shocked expression giving way to nausea.

"If he had hurt you, Crystal, I would have killed him."

She pressed her hand to her mouth afraid the churning in her stomach would come up. "I didn't know," she managed, gulping air. "I'm sorry."

"I can't go through another night like last night." His voice was raw, stark with emotion.

"Oh, Nick, I'm so sorry. So ashamed."

"But you haven't changed your mind?"

She dropped her gaze to her lap, slowly shook her head.

Chapter Five

During the next few days, her houseguest took great care to see to it that her spirits improved. Nicholas lavished her with tenderness. When she cried, he rocked her in his arms. When she refused food, he would ply her lips open and feed her with his fingers. She blushed with tingling awareness whenever he touched her. Last night, when he'd brushed her hair by the fire, she'd thought he might give in. She'd caught him looking at her—she'd seen that raw hunger in his eyes. Something had changed between them. How, she wasn't certain, but she felt it. Nick's devotion brought back memories, reminded her of how wonderful it used to be between her and Freddy. It brought pain, too. Reminded her of her inadequacies. Her failures.

When she was with Nick, she felt...well she felt whole.

While she loved her husband dearly, she imagined a very different relationship with Nicholas. A wild, impetuous one, like the one in her dream. Imagined herself giving him her body, his eagerness to show her all the things she'd heard about his wild excesses. Show her the passion absent from her life. She'd started imagining shameful visions where she ran naked through the halls, a lust-crazed Nicholas stalking her, growling her name in frustration. He was always fierce, lavishing her with caresses...with his mouth. Other times they had played like lovers, throwing pillows, laughing at each other, crazily and breathlessly in lust. In her daydreams his hands encoded unruly havoc on her senses. He'd whispered outrageous things in her ear, looked at her with stormy green eyes, plunged into her in fits of passion until she wailed his name to the rafters. But those visions ended up being wistful wanderings of the mind. Frustrating dreams.

Feeling more a failure than ever, Crystal hugged her arms around herself, barely aware of where her feet carried her through the house. Her emptiness was torture. It brought a lump of self-pity to her throat. God, she missed Freddy.

Damn him, why couldn't he just love her again? Like he used to?

One thing was certain, she couldn't go on like this.

Despite Nicholas' efforts to turn her interests away from her problem, the heart of her sorrow was ever cropping up in her mind. She was tired of walking on eggshells, skirting the issues. Nick's patience seemed endless, while her frustrations mounted. The closer the day came for Freddy to return, the more agitated and snappish she grew.

Upstairs in her room, she'd read the note from her friend, Sarah Brown, inviting her to the Theatre Royal for tea. The note was an urgent reply to Crystal's plea.

She heard a noise coming from the kitchen and found Nicholas rummaging through the pantry, flour smeared on his face. Pans clanged noisily together, the homey smell of dough made her stomach grumble. He didn't notice her right away, intent as he was on finding whatever he sought.

It was during their conversation at breakfast he'd promised her fresh-baked bread, said she'd needed someone to look after her. That was when she'd told him what she needed was his precious manhood inside her. They'd argued then, and because she'd had a particularly restless night and hadn't slept, she'd been unusually sensitive. Shaming herself, she'd broken down and cried like a baby, and he had stalked from the room.

She noticed Nicholas had shaved and changed since breakfast. He'd shed formal dress for casual and the effect left her breathless. This afternoon, a sable lock of hair hung over one eye, his pale linen shirt was open at the neck, his sleeves rolled up. A picture of a perfectly domesticated rogue. Her gaze drank in his masculine perfection—his breeches hugging the tight lines of his buttocks, encasing his powerful thighs. The perfect man for the father of her child, she thought pragmatically. Only he didn't want her.

Nicholas found what he was looking for—was turning toward the table when he caught sight of her. His expression turned wary, as if weighing her mood.

"Hungry?" he asked, his gaze burning into her.

Crystal shrugged, tried not to notice how utterly appealing he looked all powdered with flour, his broad shoulders filling her kitchen. "I don't know why you insist on doing everything for me. I'm not an invalid—nor do I want to be pampered. Tomorrow I'm sending word that the servants are to return."

He scowled, let his gaze drag over her from head to foot. "You're dressed? Did you change your mind about going for a walk?"

Crystal felt his displeasure, heard that unrelenting tone in his voice. Her heart plummeted. She had hoped he would notice the extra effort she'd taken with her hair, the way she let it fall in unruly wisps about her face. Hoped he'd find her new jonquil day dress scandalous, notice how it molded her curves like a lover's caress. Her ploy only seemed to anger him.

"Aren't you tired of playing my keeper?" she shot back.

"Don't you like my cooking?" Brows drawn sharply, he concentrated on his task.

His cooking was divine, the way he fed her shamelessly erotic. "No," she lied, blushing. "You're only being nice because you feel obligated to protect me until my husband comes home."

His gaze pinned her, heat flaring into his eyes. For a moment he looked as if he might beat her. Vent all the frustrations she'd heaped on him. They both knew the part about obligation was only partly true. He was doing it because he cared about her, because he couldn't abandon her even pushed to the limit of his control.

"I'm sorry, I shouldn't have said that."

He angrily wiped his brow with a sleeve, left a flour smudge along his hairline before jabbing the dough with his fist. Every line in his body was taut, sprung to breaking point. Her shame deepened. "Please, Nick," she whispered, "forgive me." It was a plea from her heart—she felt it breaking. If he left and never came back she'd fall apart and never recover.

"Christ, this is killing me, Crystal." His voice shook with emotion, his gazed fixed on the table. "I can't leave you here alone. I can't seduce you and I can't go home. We're both going to go insane before Fred returns."

She wasn't sure which upset her more, the way he made her feel foolish and vulnerable or his attempt to make amends for having refused to seduce her. The part she couldn't bear any longer was his pity.

"That's why I'm going out. You'll have the house all to yourself."

His head came up, his expression grave. "You haven't had lunch."

Unable to endure another intimate meal with him, she turned and walked to the door. "I'm sorry I have no appetite for food." She paused to look over her shoulder at him. "I think I'll skip lunch—I'm rather anxious to escape my dungeon."

Then, before he could protest, she slipped out and ran down the hall. In the foyer she stopped only long enough to grab her cloak before hurrying out the door.

Crystal heard her name being shouted as a cold gust hit her in the face. She gasped, her breath coming in foggy puffs before her eyes. Shuddering from the dip in temperature, she stood on the step and quickly swung her cloak about her shoulders. Already a light blanket of snow covered the street, flakes melted on her cheeks. The icy chill bit her toes. Clutching her cloak tightly, she took a fortifying breath and fled down the street as if the hounds of death were stalking her heels.

Nicholas squinted into the cold gust whipping his hair. Turning his head one way then the other, he searched the streets for Crystal's dark shape. She couldn't be far ahead.

Without the protection of a coat, the icy chill quickly seeped through the thin linen of his shirt. Flakes of snow drifted into his face, clung to his lashes. He pushed on, heedless of his own discomfort. He had to find her.

Prodded by desperation, he almost turned the wrong way when a flash of color on the opposite side of the street caught his eye. No mistaking the yellow hem showing beneath her cloak.

He recognized the back entrance to the Theatre Royal.

A clandestine meeting, no doubt, with someone she couldn't invite to the house. Perhaps someone to fill her requisite needs. It would explain her rash behavior, her need to flee his protection.

Glowering, he started across the street.

Chapter Six

Crystal's mad flight came to an abrupt halt on the steps of the Theatre Royal where she'd intended to approach Sarah Brown with her dilemma. To her utter humiliation, Nicholas had caught up with her and despite all her squirming and kicking, he none too gently escorted her home.

They stood in the foyer out of the cold, both of them breathing heavily from the fast pace forced by his angry stride. "How dare you drag me through town!" she railed, trembling with fury, her humiliation making her cheeks hot.

"If you had come quietly," he lashed out in anger, his grip punishing her wrist, "I wouldn't have had to resort to force."

Wishing she was big enough to do him damage, she shoved her elbow into his rib, but he swiftly blocked her pitiful attempt.

Eyes shining murder, she glared up at him. "You have no right to tell me when and where I can go!" she panted angrily. "And if you don't like it, you are perfectly free to leave." Trying to ward off an intense feeling of loss should he go, she waited for him to stalk away.

To her surprise, he pulled her roughly against him. The intensity of his gold-sparked gaze filled with fierce possession sent thrills racing down her spine. "I've had enough. I can no longer stand by and permit another man to touch you. Nor will I let you bear a stranger's child. You leave me no choice."

His sudden words and their meaning stunned Crystal speechless, took all the fight out of her. The tension between them grew palpable. Dare she hope? She narrowed her gaze on him and in a small voice asked, "What are you saying?"

"I can't let you bed another man." His breath fanned her face, his thumb circled the tender skin of her wrist. She was painfully aware of his closeness, the flare of heat under his touch that burned up her arm and blossomed into her heart. She sensed his struggle with an inner demon—his defenses being hacked away. Then his grip loosened and he reached up to unclasp her cloak. It floated to the floor in a pool of velvet. His eyes simmered with emotion, his voice calm. "If you send me away I can't get you with child."

This time there was no mistaking his intent. Wings fluttered uncontrollably in her stomach. "You mean it?" she asked breathlessly, her heart soaring.

One minute they were squared off in opposing corners, the next, his arm went around her waist.

He buried his hands in the heavy spill of her hair, his fingers flexing helplessly. "My God, Crystal," he rasped against her temple, "you make me mad."

The heat in his voice ignited her blood. Instantly her arms encircled his lean hips. She smiled with rapturous delight and pressed her breasts against him, nuzzling her face into the curve between his arm and shoulder. His heart thundered against her ear. He smelled heady and wickedly male. "Oh, Nick, you don't know how divine you feel. I have dreamed of you like this—you pulling me into your arms—taking me right here on the floor." The image pulsed through her brain.

On a groan he bent his head and nipped her earlobe, drew it into his mouth. She sucked in her breath as he impatiently ran his palm down her buttocks and pressed her snug against his virile length. Her heart accelerated. He fisted a handful of her skirt—pulled it up and clasped her waist. When he pressed against her, thrust his thigh between her legs, liquid heat melted through her limbs, sensation dancing over her body. His hands grew impatient, he wanted her as fiercely as she wanted him. She wanted to weep with gratitude…with tears of joy. Her throat clogged with emotion, anticipation making her tremble as she lifted her leg to accommodate him. Looking up at him with a wild hunger that threatened to eat her alive, she arched her back in wanton submission—to give him reign over her body.

Supporting her head with his palm, Nicholas's mouth came down on hers, his vivid hunger stark in his eyes, his tongue thrusting into her sweetness. He devoured her like a man starved for love.

Her body responded on its own. Suddenly she was straddling his leg, the friction of material and muscle devastating between her legs, her heat soaking his breeches.

"Are you sure," he groaned tightly against her mouth, "you still want me?" He sounded in pain, his hoarse whisper tingling over her flesh. God love him, he was letting her know she could stop.

She closed her eyes, knew it was too late, knew she'd crossed over that fine line where nothing mattered besides Nicholas and his devastating mastery. His kisses, his caresses, his glorious shaft thrusting against her womb. "I've wanted you in my dreams. I've wanted you, it seems, for weeks." Her long bout of solitude, now ended, called forth vague visions of Freddy. They momentarily poked at her conscience before she pushed his stark face from her thoughts. She needed desperately to be touched. Loved. "I'll want you day and night…every hour we have together I'll cherish." She shivered in his embrace, her intense yearning singing through her veins.

"Dear God, I want you, Nick…" Her voice shook with emotion, with deep longing, with desperation. "At last we can pretend we are lovers…that you're going to give me a beautiful child."

Nicholas felt her fear, her pain and knew he'd never be able to just walk away when the time came. He'd wanted her years ago when he'd not thought himself worthy. Lusted after her even now with a fierceness that scared him. Miraculously, she was his to plunder, his to cherish because her husband wanted an heir. Fool that Fred was, the man had no idea how rare a gift he'd given Nicholas, the precious woman in his arms was his…even if for a few weeks. Weeks that would end too soon, he feared. Dear God, he was doomed. He would regret making love to her, already hated the bleakness of his life without her once Fred came back. Growling an oath, Nicholas swiftly curled his arm under her leg to hold her against him as he moved with her to the hall table. With a sweep of his hand, he brushed the table's contents aside, gently edged her onto the top.

Under her bare bottom the hard polished surface felt cool and contrasted with the warmth emanating from his rigid shaft straining against her need. Heat swirled her woman's core. Her breathing grew ragged. When she thought she'd scream if he didn't take her, his hand moved between them. In an instant she gasped, his skin was hot, his palm massaging her mons. The shock vibrated to her soul. He touched her with a reverence she craved—with the skill that made her life seem so bereft. Before she could wonder at his tender regard, his finger spread her open, penetrated her velvety folds, made her cry out. She sagged against him. Writhing. Her keening cries echoing off the walls.

He waited with diabolical care while she came down from her climax, then skillfully plunged his hand deeper. Until she was careening. Panting his name.

Dragging in sharp breaths, she arched into him, heard his strangled groan rumble against her ear. Frantic for him, her nails tore at his shirt. While he stroked her, she anxiously fumbled at his waist, yanking buttons, rending fabric. She let out an exasperated sigh, her movements too slow for the escalating sensations flooding her body. He helped her then, his movements swift, practiced. When his heated shaft brushed her cleft, she whimpered. The feeling was giddy, the searing need in Nicholas' eyes wonderfully erotic. Wild abandon sang through her body and she opened her legs while he slid his arms under her knees—drew her to the table's edge.

Then with a wicked gleam in his eyes, he smiled down at her with wolfish possession and thrust into her. The exquisite pressure—his largeness stretching her, plunging into her body—raised her bottom off the table. Took her to the edge of ecstacy. Then he was drawing out, ramming in…and her world shattered.

As her climax clenched around him, Nicholas knew a moment of blinding passion, felt himself slipping into a vortex of intense sensation. He'd never felt so close to losing himself, so close to losing control. The shock bludgeoning his soul vibrated like lashes of a whip through his body. With Crystal he'd expected to be swept away—never so blatantly close to utter destruction.

His body sheened with sweat—her legs clamped around his waist in exquisite orgasm—Nicholas used his weight, pulled her luscious bottom tight and again drove himself into her. Her piercing cry mingled with his strangled groan as his body convulsed, his release exploding down his nerves, his seed pumping into her sweet body.

It was several long minutes later before he felt strong enough to move. His body still shaking from a tempest of passion, Nicholas held Crystal gently against his chest, his chin resting on her head. He breathed deeply, tried to steady his legs. Their impassioned union left him light-headed. He was still trying to recover when he felt her withdraw. Instantaneous regret assailed him. A sharp pain of dread twisted his heart. Now having gotten what she wanted, Crystal would realize her mistake. Being a loyal wife, she'd feel ashamed for coercing him, devastated by her abandon. As damning as that knowledge was, he spent a wholly irrational moment wanting to murder Fred for his selfishness. Then came the calm voice of reason tempering rash thoughts. While they'd both put him in this accursed situation, it was as much his fault as theirs. There was no excuse for his lack of resistance. For lusting after another man's wife.

No less inexcusable, he reflected harshly, was the fact that Fred wasn't around to ease Crystal's pain and soften her burden. "If I haven't just given you a child, Crystal...then the timing could be wrong," he told her gently, his voice gravelly and strained. "Would you like me to leave?"

She slid her arms around his waist and held tight, shook her head. "Just hold me, please," she uttered with a raspy voice. "I'm so frightened of being alone."

His own fear kept him silent.

"I didn't expect...I mean...I didn't know I'd feel so wonderful with you," she told him in a small voice.

Wonderful, he reflected, hardly began to describe the plush softness of her slick heat clamped around his sex.

"This wasn't supposed to happen." She trembled against him. "Lord, what have I done?"

As he expected, her recriminations and guilt weighed heavy on her conscience. She fell silent, dropped her head. Her neck was bared to him, her creamy skin flushed with passion against the daffodil gold of her gown. A gown he suspected she'd donned to torture him.

He brushed a kiss along her temple, willed his body not to move. Though she was no virgin to seduction, her inexperience beyond her husband marked her an innocent pawn. He still pulsed inside her, already wanted to whisk her upstairs for a long, intense initiation where they'd stay until they collapsed. With great effort, he fought down the urge. Christ, she was baring her soul to him and all he wanted to do was ravish her again. "Stop beating yourself up. I had a hand in this, I should have had better sense."

She stirred against him, the tiny pulse along her neck still beating erratically. "What we just shared was so beautiful," she said in awe, "it changes everything between us. Oh, Nick, you tried to warn me and I wouldn't listen. Now I'm going to lose you, too...." Her voice broke.

"Shh, darling." He kept her impaled—afraid she might misunderstand if he withdrew. Slowly, he reached up with his hands and cradled her face between his palms, brushed her cheeks with his thumb. "I'm not leaving you, Crystal. I've already changed all my plans, I'm at your disposal for as long as you need me."

His tenderness made her want to wail to the heavens for the unfairness. She'd thought all her problems solved. She wondered now, with a dreadful ache, if she'd ever be able to return to her old life. To her husband. Then a sudden thought panicked her. "My God, what day is it?" She twisted in his arms, her face turning pale.

Nicholas felt a keen loss as she pulled away, her warm sheath withdrawing, their bodies no longer connected. In an instant he'd lost her and their fragile intimacy. "It's all right, puss." He willed his hands to be still while her absence caused havoc on his senses. "It's only Tuesday. The servants won't come back until I send for them."

She looked white as a sheet. "It's not the servants, it's Freddy! Oh God, Nick, he's due home today." She anxiously bit her lip. "I've got to warn him— get a dispatch to him. He can't come back now. Not until I'm sure."

Her words struck him in the gut, his reaction to the news sparking irrational jealousy. Damn Fred to hell, his week wasn't up. He didn't care to analyze why, he just needed more time with her. "If Fred were coming home"—he glanced at the window, saw it was growing dark— "wouldn't he have been here by now?"

She shook her skirt out and moved to the window, conscious that behind her he was fastening his breeches. "You're right, of course." She nervously peered both directions down the street. "I'm probably worrying over nothing." She lapsed into silence, her gaze searching the avenue below.

Her inattention gave him time to recover. For a moment he stood watching her, drinking in her slender beauty, the curve of her breasts—the curves engraved on his mind, those now hidden under the folds of her skirt. For some reason, her preoccupation at the window irritated him. Her agitation over Fred clearly put him in his place. What had he expected? She loved her husband, for Christsakes.

"I'll be in the kitchen—I'll see if I can't find us something to eat." There would be wine and cheese left over from the night before.

Distracted, she nodded. "We could picnic in my bedchamber and you could brush my hair 'til it shines."

He stiffened. "You want me to seduce you in your husband's bed?" His voice was hard, cold as steel.

She turned from the window to stare at him. It was the first time he'd given her any hint of his feelings, the first sign Nicholas showed that he resented her husband's presence. It was a profoundly disturbing thought.

"Freddy sleeps in the master chamber." A sadness weighted her words, there was no longer a need to hide her shame from Nicholas. "I sleep alone in my bed."

He paused by the door. "Then we'll dine in your chamber."

Chapter Seven

At the top of the stairs, the bedchamber door stood open to Nicholas. He noted the room was comfortably heated, in the hearth a fire blazed. Crystal sat at her writing desk, immersed in thought, her head bent over a parchment. The rich gold hue of her waist-long tresses picked up the glow of the firelight, shimmered with warm russets cast by the flames. The plush, white robe exposed an expanse of shapely calf, her delicate profile giving a glimpse of the seductive curve of her lips, the elegant tilt of her nose. If Crystal were his wife she'd be enslaved in his bed. She damn sure wouldn't be neglected.

His bare feet made no noise as he crossed the floor. She'd used an oak log, instead of coal, for the fire. The blaze heated his skin, the log crackled and hissed, sent sparks fluttering up the chimney. A woodsy smell filled the chamber. She had taken the heavy brocade counterpane from the bed and spread it on the floor in front of the fire.

Wordlessly, Nicholas kneeled and arranged their feast on the royal blue fabric fashioned as a table. In the larder he'd found wine, a brick of cheese and a tray of finger cakes.

Next to twin wine glasses, he set a bottle of port. Then he withdrew a small velvet pouch from the pocket of his silk robe and dropped it near the glasses.

Facing her, Nicholas stretched out on his side, hand propped under his head where he waited for her to finish the missive.

Crystal had heard Nick preparing their meal. She was keenly aware of his gaze fastened on her with those intense green eyes. He knew her well. Intimately now. As a lover did. In the foyer he'd given her a most cherished gift, lavished her with sensual warmth. In return she'd unwittingly hurt him by mentioning Freddy. She would have to guard her tongue until they came to an understanding about her husband.

Pondering her blessings, Crystal smiled to herself. In a week's time, if her monthly didn't come, she'd know she was carrying his child. The thought that she might already be pregnant was a heady one. It made her feel wondrously decadent, and horribly wanton. Nicholas, her gallant knight, had given her all that in a single afternoon.

What he had in store for them tonight, God only knew. But the prospect had her heart throbbing. Warm excitement skittered down her spine, spread between her legs in wet gushes of heat. Her body, now attuned to him, craved more. The yearning between her thighs dampened her robe, her body seeking its mate, reaching toward a fire that threatened to consume her.

Afraid she'd fling herself into his arms and beg to be ravished, she kept her face averted. Over the last hour she'd fought down the overwhelming urge to flee the room, run for her sanity. Throw herself at Freddy's mercy. Her fear, she tried to tell herself, was silly.

Her heart, though, nagged her.

When she'd exhausted all her reasons for delaying the inevitable, she rose to her feet. Nicholas' musky smell still clung to her skin, tremors still raced over her flesh where his hands had caressed her body a mere hour earlier. Swallowing hard, she forced her feet to move. When she came to the edge of the counterpane, she halted and let her gaze wander over him. Like her, he had changed clothes. His chest, she noticed, was bare under his robe, his skin gleaming like bronze in the fire's glow. He looked every bit the prodigal libertine. His robe of crimson silk heightened his aura of seduction, drew her gaze to the blatantly raised bulge straining against its silk sheath in randy display. Because she was watching, he moved his powerful body to give her a better view until his splendid erection lay bared for her pleasure. Her reaction to him was instant, sensation shot to her core. Liquid heat slid down her thigh, and her cheeks burned with shame while she stared in amazement. How she'd managed to accommodate his size, she didn't know. He looked enormous—his beautifully swollen head curved into a flat stomach lined with hard muscle. She noticed with awe the maze of veins running along his engorged length.

Blushing, her gaze flew to his face and riveted there. His eyes burned hungrily, his nostrils flared.

The letter she held in her trembling fingers floated to the floor near the counterpane.

Nicholas extended his hand to her. "Are you hungry?" he asked softly, subdued amusement dancing in his eyes.

She laid her fingers in his…felt the warmth of his skin, his vital strength. She melted to her knees beside his head. "Nick…I…" She wet her lips with her tongue. "We must talk first."

He swiftly curled into a sitting position and crossed his legs. "We'll talk later. Come…sit in my lap." He guided her bottom until her back leaned into his chest. Her hair spilled like waves of blonde silk over his arms—over his hands where they rested on her stomach. "I have something for you." He scooped up the pouch and dropped it in the folds of her robe between her legs. "Open it."

"You didn't—"

"Just open it," he persisted.

She bit her lip anxiously, her curiosity mounting. She shouldn't accept a gift from him. Yet fascinated by his persistence, she stared a moment at the black velvet pouch. It was heavy—she guessed the weight of a gold guinea. The soft velvet against her fingers felt warm as she slowly pulled at the drawstrings. Then her fingers dug into the bag…hit something that felt like a glass sphere. He'd given her a glass egg?

Puzzled, she held the glittering object up to the fire and inspected it closely. Firelight danced over the sphere. Prisms of color ricocheted off the many faceted edges. A beautiful crystal of some kind, she mused. Then her wedding ring caught her eye, sparkling with glittering fragments of light, its colors joining the rainbows on the walls. Her heart caught in her throat as dawning realization took her breath away. Diamonds this size didn't exist, or if they did they were worth a king's ransom. "My God, this can't be…tell me you didn't just give me a diamond."

He smiled warmly. "The mines I purchased in Africa have produced some amazing results. This one arrived a fortnight ago."

"Good heavens, I can't accept this." She turned to give it back when his hand closed over hers. Stanching her protest, he nuzzled his mouth along her neck, his tongue flicking over her sensitive skin, the smooth curve of her ear. Sensations ripped through her pulsing center, her vision blurred. "I want you to wear it, puss," he said softly near her ear.

She shuddered against him. Her nipples tightened against her robe, the swollen weight of her breasts tingling. It took all her will to whisper, "Wear it how? There's no clasp and no hooks."

"If you'll pour the wine, I'll show you," he lazily drawled.

The pulsing between her legs was spreading a carnal heat upward. She couldn't think, much less grasp the importance of his generous gift. Already aching for him, Crystal obediently did as Nicholas asked, while he shifted against her back and shrugged out of his robe.

When she'd accomplished the task, he carefully dropped the diamond into the wine of one glass. It clanked like a rock to the bottom. He slid his arms under hers and pulled her tight against him. Trembling violently, she became painfully aware of his splendid arousal pressing against her back. Her pulse raced out of control. His naked heat burned through her robe.

He fed her then with erotic languor, with his fingers, then gave her wine to wet her parched throat. Beside her, the glass with the diamond sat untouched, its presence a reminder of something mysterious to come. Nicholas was lavishing her, she knew, tantalizing her with his special sorcery. Soon the warmth of the fire, combined with her alarming consumption of wine, blended all the harsh edges of the room into a glowing flush on her cheeks.

When her robe slipped down her arms, a heady frisson of anticipation thrummed through her ravenous body. Nicholas rained kisses along her neck, murmured, "I've wanted to hold you like this...for a very long time." His voice was a rumble of heat against her neck. "Your husband will have his heir...though what I do now is not for him...it is for you." Slowly his hand reached for the untouched wine glass. "For all the long nights you slept alone in your bed. For all the nights I could have held you in my arms." With slow mesmerizing care, his other hand drew aside her robe, burned a path down her belly. She writhed against him, her near climax arching her back along his arousal. Driven to craving madness, she shamelessly drew her knees apart for him. The fire's heat warmed her bottom, her pouty cleft beautifully displayed with glossy wetness.

He nudged the wine glass against the luscious juncture. "Open your eyes, darling, watch me touch you." He dipped his fingers into the wine, let them trail wetness over her stomach—lower over the soft mound of darker blonde curls. He hooked his middle finger over the rim of the glass, tipped it into her vagina. Her fingers dug into his thighs as sweet wetness trickled between her legs. "Easy, darling...now feel the pressure." With infinite care, he pressed the cool diamond against her pouty folds, held it snug, heard her sharp cry of pleasure. "How much do you want, Crystal?"

he asked, pushing the slender end half-way into her.

She wanted more with a mindless desire, an insatiable craving. "Desperately," she whimpered, her throaty moan heady with need. She tried arching against his hand, tried to drive the jewel deeper. He moved his hand away, left the diamond lodged, watched her hips seek his assistance. "Hold still for me, darling. Watch my hand…" A paroxysm of shudders converged on her as he slid his flat palm down her stomach, cupped his fingers over the diamond and eased it into her. Her wetness poured into his hand, her panting cries brought him close to losing control. "You want it deeper?"

"Please, Nick…" she gasped, opening to him, rocking into his hand. "I ache…"

On the verge of wasting himself against her writhing hot bottom, he leaned her forward, shifted to his knees. Her bottom angled against him. He pulled her robe over her hips. The luscious sight of her sweet cleft engorged with a diamond made his pulse thunder. And because he could wait no longer, he nudged his head against the jewel, penetrated her, drove the egg into her pulsing wetness. A trickle of sweat snaked down his neck. Crystal's head was thrown back, hair wildly tossed around her slender beauty. His hands gripped her hips, he pushed in—felt her tight spasm, her keening cry—then pulled out with agonizing friction. He watched a climax shudder through her, saw the flame-light dance over her blissful features. And then the tempo changed as he slipped into her with his fingers—deftly withdrew the diamond and adjusted his grip on her with a restless, hot-blooded urgency.

This time when he drove into her, he reached the depths of blinding need. He pulled back then pushed deeper, craving her—gorging on rapturous sensations, wanting to put his mark on her, each plunging stroke merciless, fierce, unchecked. Their bodies grew hot and sweat-sheened. And she cried for him, helplessly enslaved, wanting to be covered and penetrated, wanting him to fill her with his seed.

His knees forced hers further apart as he thrust into her, his hands clamped hard on her waist so she couldn't move, couldn't evade him, so he could conquer her, make her crave what he had for so long wanted to give her.

There was no rational thought, no remorse, only need and sensation and ravenous mastery. She invited him into her body, clenching around him as he penetrated her to the hilt and ground against her womb.

When he felt her coming, his own orgasm begin to crest, he tightened his grip. She gasped.

Thrust deep against her womb, he wondered in a flash of insanity if she'd love his child, if he'd be permitted to visit, if it would be a girl or boy. Then his breath caught as she careened over the edge…and his back arched, his eyes shut, and he released sweet life into her body.

The log in the fire had long since smoldered to ashes when Nicholas was jolted awake by a noise. His gaze darted around the room, his brain trying frantically to locate something familiar, some clue to where he was. In the next instant he became aware of Crystal's nude form lying snug against him, her breathing steady, her head resting on his arm. Still groggy from sleep, he wondered if he was dreaming. He closed his eyes, remained motionless, and listened. There. Hollow sounding footsteps. Coming from the stairway outside the bedchamber.

A voice in the hall shouted for Crystal.

Heart thumping in his ears, Nicholas came instantly alert, his reflexes automatic as he clutched the counterpane and hastily covered Crystal as a shadow filled the doorway.

Crystal stirred against him. "What is it—?"

Nicholas had no time for a response.

Chapter Eight

"Crystal, where the blazes are you?" The voice coming from the shadow carried a distinct slur, the candlelight held aloft swaying in his grasp. When the intruder's eyes adjusted to the dark to find Crystal wasn't alone, he cursed.

In a heartbeat, her husband's gaze turned from shock into cold appraisal, his lips pressed together in a hurt expression.

Heart pounding, Crystal clasped the blanket to her bosom and tried to sit. "I'm sorry, Freddy, I wanted to warn you"—she pointed a trembling finger to the letter still lying where she'd dropped it— "I even remembered to use the special code we agreed upon." Shame strained her voice, and she desperately searched her mind for something to say to soothe his pride.

Nicholas got to his feet and hovered protectively over her, his face implacably calm. "I'll leave."

"No," she cried, then quickly realized the error of her outburst. "I mean..."—she fought for a calming breath— "I think as long as we're all together maybe we should talk."

Nicholas' face grew uncompromising, while her husband's grew fiercely for-bidding. Why did she feel so wretched? As if she'd willingly cuckold her husband?

Nicholas bent to scoop up his robe and whispered close to her, "He's been drinking—now is not the time to discuss colors for the nursery. I'll leave." He swiftly tied his robe around his waist and walked toward his anguished friend.

Eyes curiously bright, Halverton barred his path. "Did you enjoy my wife?"

Nicholas' shoulder brushed against Freddy's in the narrow doorway. "Christ, Fred, isn't this what you wanted? Get a hold of yourself."

Halverton reached out and grabbed his arm. "Don't forget Crystal is my wife—"

"Freddy, don't." Crystal stumbled to her feet. She'd once thought her husband's disappointment unbearable, but his jealously was a thousand times worse. "Please. Nick's your friend."

The coverlet trailed across the floor behind her as she hurried to her husband's side. "Please, let's not argue tonight," she pleaded, looking up at Freddy's crestfallen face. The smell of sour ale almost overwhelmed her. The thought of him riding in his condition, the possibility of something happening to him, deeply frightened her. "You must be exhausted." She tugged on his arm. "Let Nick leave if he wants to." She slid a glance at Nicholas and hoped he understood she wasn't trying to evict him.

Fred looked down at her, his gaze momentarily softening. "I shouldn't have just walked in like this," he admitted at last in a strained voice. His pain was almost palpable. "I just didn't expect you to succeed, that's all." His eyes held a fatalistic glimmer. "I'm proud of you, Crystal, you've done exactly what I wished."

Giving her hand a squeeze, he turned to Nicholas. "What do you think, old friend? Another time, we could have made a stunning *menage a trois*?"

Blanching, Crystal's heart faltered. "Freddy, please you've been drinking—"

"Yes, I've been drinking." He laughed dryly, looked pointedly at the empty wine bottles strewn over the floor behind her. "But then so have you."

Crystal shuddered as the coolness of his tone sank into her heart. Nicholas kept dangerously silent.

Her gaze traveled to the hearth and guilt pierced her wavering courage. The evidence of their mating lay in disarray over the floor. Wine glasses. Trays of leftover food. Her robe. Amidst the clutter sparkled a fire evoked by the candlelight. Dear God—her diamond. An exquisite reminder of intoxication of another kind. She prayed Freddy wouldn't notice it.

That thought froze, when to her horror he staggered toward the clutter.

Crystal held her breath as he bent on unsteady legs and retrieved her missive from the floor. Her heart pounded in her throat as she looked at Nicholas. In that endlessly tense moment, their gazes meshed. No words needed. This was where their glorious union ended, their last night together. There would be no one there in the morning to feed her with gentle persuasion, no one there to soften her loneliness once Freddy returned to the country.

Her husband took the missive with him as he walked to the connecting door between their bedchambers. He was abandoning her again, she thought, disspiritedly.

"I'm meeting with a solicitor in the morning," he told them, "I'll be leaving early." The door opened with a whisper. "If you have a boy I'd like to name him after my father." Then he paused in the open doorway to look over his shoulder. "Stay as long as you like, Nick. She'll need you."

Crystal stared unblinking as the emotionless announcement of her husband's blow crushed her last hope. After she'd carried out his wishes, after she'd prayed he'd be happy, for reasons beyond her comprehension, he still chose to abandon her and all their hopes of happiness. She'd been so gullible, tried so hard to please him. While the only thing that mattered to him seemed his heir.

Feeling utterly bereft and alone, an old despair surged into her heart. For the innocent babe she could be carrying. For the love she tried to hold onto. And for Nicholas, who must be as confused as she was.

"I'm leaving for France at the end of the week," Nick said gently, "I'll call on you before I sail to see how you're feeling."

Nick's words jarred her out of her melancholy. She turned to stare at him in numb misery. God, no. "You're leaving?" she whispered, sounding pathetically close to tears. Her throat worked convulsively for air as she fought against the insane desire to cling to him—beg him to stay.

His hungry gaze devoured her for a breathless moment—then he told her very quietly, "The diamond is yours, Crystal. When you're alone you can wear it for me…and remember tonight."

The intimacy of his words hung between them like a caress. His regrets strained his features. Both of them felt the pain. The pull of something deeper. Something forbidden. Then because there was nothing either of them dare do about it, he turned and walked away.

By the following afternoon, Crystal's house was returned to its usual grim order. Freddy had left early as he'd promised and she'd awakened with a deplorable headache. Her lady's maid resumed her post, carried out all the mundane tasks that Nicholas had done for her with lavish seduction. She tried telling herself she was merely overwrought, it was her husband's love she longed for, that he would return, explain his rash behavior and once again restore to her her faith. Then she would remember last night and Nicholas invaded her thoughts. The way he'd looked at her in that unguarded moment before he left haunted her. After the precious time she'd spent with him, her emptiness seemed all the more keen. The diamond in her pocket was all she had left of him. A diamond and, she prayed, a child.

That week passed with agonizing swiftness. Nicholas stood at the bow of his yacht—early morning dawn peeking over the horizon on the Thames— and stared at the bustling dock as he pulled away from shore. He thought over the past night's agony. He'd walked the street outside Crystal's house last evening, and later watched the glow of the hearth illuminating the window from his obscure post in a closed carriage. He'd kept a vigil there for hours— until the light faded and her room grew dark. He'd spent the night trying to relegate her to the place she belonged—out of his thoughts—but had failed.

He regretted, now, telling her he would call on her. She was the wife of his friend. A temptation. The precious taste of her was imprinted on his jaded soul, her passion flaring like flames searing an image on his memory. To have gone to her under the pretense of inquiring about her health would have been his utter destruction. It would have been dangerous to see her again. Torture to abstain from dragging her into the nearest corner and impaling her until he rid himself of the insane desire to keep her.

No. It would be better for them both this way. She'd receive his letter, find it sufficiently circumspect and be saved the burden of embarrassing goodbyes.

Paris offered an escape, her beauty unlike any Nicholas could remember in London. Trees sprouting new blossoms scented the air with their flowery fragrance, while the feminine crowd in their spring-colored walking gowns made a rainbow of swishing color along the sidewalks. Emerged from their cocoons after the harshness of winter, they chatted animatedly about the Paris *Season*, and which guests to add to their parties.

He approached a milliner's shop on the Rue Saint-Honore, his focus fixed on the opposite side of the street.

One woman in particular stood out from the rest, her wide smile curved up with feline pleasure as she caught sight of him coming in her direction.

Evette Collier was looking exceedingly beautiful, her pale violet gown molding voluptuous curves of a woman practiced in luring men into bed. A riot of dark curls cascaded down her back, her jaunty little hat with its enormous plume gave her a decided edge of sophistication. Her face was shaded by a matching violet parasol trimmed in the same lace that flattered her heavy bosom. Since she rarely emerged from her boudoir before noon, it was his fortune to have found her out and about.

They met under the canopy of a small pastry shop.

"Dear God, Nicholas, I thought I must be fantasizing about you again." She gracefully extended her hand, eating him up with her hungry brown eyes. "You look so edible...*mon Deiu*, I've been missing you," she purred with sultry sweetness.

Because she expected it, he took her slender fingers in his and brought them to his lips—let his fingers tighten perceptibly in a blatant caress of possession. He remembered their last encounter well—the cream eclair adorning his arousal —her tongue licking sweet confection from his shaft while she searched his face like a greedy child looking for praise.

She would do, he decided somewhat cynically. "If you're not busy, I would like to take you sailing on the Seine."

Her almond-shaped eyes sparkled with promises. "For you, I just canceled all my engagements. Perhaps you won't mind if I bring along lunch." She held up her recent purchase. "I've been famished for eclairs."

His smile lacked the characteristic enthusiasm. A year ago he'd have looked forward to rendering his body for her pleasure. Evette was amiable and extremely well versed in his tastes. She was everything another man might desire in a wife, while to him she represented everything that contrasted with the one woman he couldn't have. In that regard she was perfect.

An hour later as their carriage rolled to a stop at her doorstep, Nicholas helped her alight and escorted her into the house. When he'd not accommodated her in bed aboard his yacht she had been disappointed, but patient. She'd even been tolerant when he'd declined lunch.

It wasn't until they entered her drawing room where she firmly shut the door behind her and turned to face him that her composure shattered.

"All right. I've been throwing myself at you all afternoon and nothing seems to move you. What have I done to displease you?" she asked in pouty tones, her bosom heaving with each breath.

Nicholas settled into a chair as he tugged his cravat loose and tossed it over the back of the elegant blue settee. "Don't worry, sweetheart, it's not what you've done—it's what I'm about to do."

At the seriousness of his tone, she came to stand over him, looking down at him with avid regard. "And just what is it"—she dropped to her knees between his legs— "you're about to do?"

Time to sever ties with his heart. "I came to propose marriage." There he'd done the unspeakable—put an end to his torture.

Evette's gurgle of happiness made him feel like a cad. She climbed into his lap and kissed him hard on the mouth. "My God, Nicholas, of all your conquests, why me?"

His brows drew together. "Why not?"

She drew back to look at him and smiled. "You're not exactly thrilled about this, for one."

He shifted her off his lap and rose to his feet.

She was looking up at him with calm reproach. "You already have a string of devoted bed partners, for two. And three, you could have any woman you wanted eating out of your hand."

Crystal's lips sucking sweetmeats from his fingers flashed into his thoughts. The searing sensation was like fire hitting his groin. God help him, he knew of no other way to cut her from his life.

"If you want a declaration of love, I can't give it."

The dark beauty tilted her head and studied him. "You'll find I can be very practical when I need to be. And a practical woman would be a fool to decline your offer." She smiled complacently. "Under the circumstance, I guess I'll have to content myself with your wealth. When will our wedding take place?"

He recklessly tossed aside the voice of caution. Already set on a course of self-destruction, at this point he didn't much care whether he lived or died.

Eager to be done with it, he said, "Just as soon as we dispatch a message to London and the banns can be posted." The same recklessness that drove him from London, drove him to carelessness. "In the meantime, you're free to make any purchases you need at my expense. I'll go tomorrow and make arrangements with the bank to extend you funds." He watched her eyes go soft with some emotion and experienced an uneasy feeling in the pit of his stomach, but he heedlessly pushed on. "After lunch we'll visit a jeweler to select suitable rings."

Chapter Nine

Crystal clutched the badly crumpled note in her fist as she curled into a tight ball of misery in her empty bed and gave into despair.

Forgive me for leaving without saying good-bye.

Your devoted servant, Nicholas

No regrets. No tender teasing. Just cool, emotionless words. And she'd read those words at least a hundred times since the message arrived yesterday morning. She'd cried after the footman left. Silently wept in misery when she'd drug herself up the steps and locked herself in her room.

He'd left her. He had told her he was going to France—still she thought he might stay. The cruel pain of reality hurt.

She'd never expected to miss him so much. What a fool she'd been to think she could make love to him, have his child, and resume her life as if they'd never shared soul-binding intimacy.

The maid banging on the door roused but a flicker of notice. "Go away," Crystal croaked, her throat hoarse, her head throbbing. Alone in her cold bed, she lay robbed of her will to fight. She had no strength left.

"Please, milady, open the door," the woman cried in earnest. "'Tis four days since you ate last."

A scuffle of feet and voices penetrated her dim consciousness—sounded like Graves and her young footman—their voices muffled with concern.

God, why can't they just let me die?

The thunder against the door this time resounded around the room, hinges creaked under the assault. Weakly, Crystal pulled the pillow over her head to shut out the noise and the raspy sound of her breathing as she gasped for life....

Minutes later, the door crashed in with a shuddering, wood-splitting boom. Butler, maid, and footman poured through the opening, rushing toward the bed with fear on their faces.

Graves reached her first. "Draw back the drapes"—he shot over his shoulder to the footman— "open the window, quickly." He swiftly drug the pillow away from his mistress' face, dreading he might not be in time to save her.

Lady Halverton looked asleep. Deathly pale. He quickly leaned over her, put his cheek near her mouth. Faint breathing whispered over his face. Relief brought dampness to his eyes.

Wasting no time, Graves knelt and pulled his poor sweet mistress against his chest. She sagged over his arm like a limp rag doll.

Beside him, the lady's maid shrieked at the sight. "Is she dead?"

Graves shot her a quelling look that would have sent a lesser woman fleeing for cover. "Get yourself downstairs and fetch us a doctor."

For the next three days the doctor came and administered laudanum, bled Lady Halverton, and left. Graves had issued orders that all visitors were to be turned away with an understanding that his employer wasn't feeling well. It was the staff's duty to protect their grieving mistress.

On the fourth day, when their mistress didn't awaken, a sealed message was sent to Lord Summer's residence. It was Lord Summer she called for in her delirium. Graves hoped Lady Halverton's close friend might wish to be there to help her in some way.

Several days went by while Graves waited for a reply. Implicit directions issued by Lord Halverton before he left clearly indicated he didn't want to be disturbed, that if his wife needed anything the staff was to contact Lord Summer.

In Paris, Nicholas threw himself with a reckless kind of numbness into the farce of his engagement, while the exhausting hours of civility he'd been forced to maintain for the sake of his fiancée took their toll. He lived his own private hell, going through the motions of pretense. Most days he kept his misery tightly contained. But today his torment felt more acute, the knife blade pressed against his heart plunging deeper with each passing hour. All the eclairs in France—all Evette's seductive wiles—couldn't keep thoughts of Crystal from haunting his memory.

God...Crystal. She was scarred upon his soul. He craved her with a fierceness that knotted his gut. Like a man craves death when he finds his life at an end. Every time he plunged into Evette's willing body he saw Crystal's wanton beauty. Crystal opening to him...writhing against him...beckoning him to his doom with sultry blue eyes.

Today, he and his intended were traveling back to London. Back to face the music—where the pain of being near Crystal would drive him mad.

"You look like a man who's lost his only friend," Evette said reflectively as she joined him in the drawing room.

Not just a friend, he thought grimly, someone infinitely precious.

"I have no friends," he said moodily, starring out the window. "You must be thinking of someone else."

Patient as always, she gave him a sympathetic smile as she reached up and brushed a lock of hair from his forehead. "Shall we go then?"

Smiling tightly, Nicholas followed Evette out of the room. In the foyer they paused at the mirror for her to adjust her hat. He then waited while she slipped her fingers into the soft, kid gloves that she'd purchased with his money. Lastly, came the meaningless emerald engagement ring.

She smiled happily up at him and slid it onto her third finger.

Though innocent, the proprietary gesture seemed a particular favorite of hers...one that annoyed the hell out of him.

Two weeks after her ordeal, as early morning light filtered over the floor, Crystal was roused from her deathbed out of a dreamless slumber. A sickly feeling made her mouth water. A horrible rumble tightened her stomach. Her hand flew to her mouth in a panic as bile surged up her throat.

Stumbling from bed, she collapsed on the floor and grasped the chamber pot to her chest when her insides erupted.

She heaved and coughed. Then retched again.

Retched until her sides ached.

Several minutes passed before she felt the cold floorboards beneath her. Now wide awake and trembling, she weakly laid her head back against the bed for support and wondered if she was dying. Her mouth tasted vile. Sweat soaked her nightrail. Vague memories of Graves' face close to hers— his muffled voice speaking to her—stirred her recall. The doctor's face, she remembered, had been there, too.

Beyond that she couldn't remember.

My God. How long had she been in bed?

She'd no sooner set the chamber pot aside, when the door burst open, followed by the doctor. His face registered shock when he spotted her sitting on the floor.

"I'm pregnant," she whispered weakly, remembering now the joy of discovering she'd missed her monthly courses just minutes before her utter desolation surrounding Nicholas' ill-timed note.

The doctor knelt beside her and helped her back into bed. He regarded her with open concern and smiled kindly. "Yes, you are with child, Mrs. Halverton. Don't worry, in time the sickness will go away." He indicated a bowl of broth. "Though I didn't mind feeding you, it's good to see you up and about. How are you feeling?"

Her ears were still ringing. "Death would be preferable."

"Yes, well, you must eat if your baby is going to be healthy."

The memories of the last few weeks came back to her then with horrifying vengeance. Freddy's cold words. His anguish. "Does my husband know?" she asked anxiously. "Has he come home?"

The doctor reached for the bowl of soup, his face blank, his eyes avoiding hers. "Eat first, then we will talk."

Crystal did as he asked. And Doc Phillips entertained her with stories of a patient who'd delivered a fine baby boy. How the mother had lost several babies. How she'd lost all hope. He told her how happy the parents were now, how brave they were to keep trying.

Although Crystal's first two spoonfuls of beef broth had rumbled her stomach, by sheer determination for the baby's sake, she kept them down this time. Her baby would be all right. He must be all right.

Feeling decidedly stronger after a couple of mouthfuls, she finished her broth and set the bowl aside. The doctor's solemn calm worried her—something about the way he avoided her gaze sent a tingle of premonition down her spine. "What aren't you telling me?"

Surprising her, he reached for her hand, took it between his cool palms. His skin felt leathery soft against hers—the wrinkled-lines around his kind, brown eyes bore into her with pity.

Her heart fluttered erratically. "What's wrong?" she whispered, her throat closing tight with fear. Dear God, not the baby. "Is it the baby?"

"My dear woman, your baby will be just fine." He patted her hand, squeezed it tightly. "It's you I'm worried about, you've lost weight, you're still very weak…" His voice faded as he traced his finger over the blue veins of one delicate white hand.

"Dear God, what is it? Just tell me!"

Heaving a deep sigh, he said, "Lady Halverton, it pains me to see you like this. Your distress is a grave concern. I want you to know that this has not been an easy decision for me, that your health is a priority. But"—he regarded her closely— "I knew you would want to know that there has been…well…a death in the family."

She paled. "A death?"

"Yes, your husband asked that I not say anything about his illness, he didn't want you worrying. He died peacefully—"

To Crystal's panicked brain the words hammered like blows of death along her shattered nerves—and she heard nothing beyond the word "died." Tears flooded her eyes, rolled down her cheeks in warm streams. Not Freddy, she cried. Not now.

With a sickening clarity that clogged her throat, she realized now part of why he had withdrawn from her, why he seemed so insistent she approach Nicholas. He wanted an heir because he was dying. He wanted Nicholas to be the father.

Nicholas to be the father….

Blood pumped the litany though her veins, throbbed like drum beats against her temples—made her head spin.

Plunged into grief, she shivered uncontrollably while her future swam before her eyes with painful clarity. Dear God, Freddy wasn't coming back—the anguish she hadn't understood when he looked at her was because he loved and wanted her taken care of. While she'd been feeling sorry for herself, scared and lonely, he had spent his last days alone.

Oh, Freddy, I'm so sorry, I didn't understand.

She could imagine it so well, how Freddy had planned ahead, planned on Nicholas being there for her. But Nicholas had left. She was completely alone—her life suddenly turned inside out. She was a widow carrying a love child created out of passion with a man whom she'd coerced into seducing her.

The bleakness and pain of her loss rippled through her body.

She gasped for air, fought off encroaching darkness. The doctor's voice faded in and out, muffled by the surging black numbness dragging at her subconscious.

With a vague awareness, she felt Doc Phillips lifting her shoulders—then something foul smelling—a liquid tasting like laudanum was being poured between her lips.

A few ragged breaths later she felt no more pain.

"Has Lord Summer returned from France?" Crystal asked in a small voice the next morning as her lady's maid entered with a breakfast tray. "He should be notified"—she took a deep breath— "of my husband's…" She swallowed hard, and fought a new rush of tears.

The woman nodded sympathetically. "Yes, my lady, Lord Summer has just returned from Paris. A note was delivered to him this very morning." She plopped the heavy tray on the bedside table. "Incidently, Lord Summer has announced his engagement to a Miss Collier. The banns have been posted, and the wedding is scheduled for the end of this week. 'Course, knowing how fond you are of him, Mr. Graves took the liberty of sending your congratulations."

Crystal felt the blood draining from her face.

From the doorway, Graves cleared his throat. "That will be all, Miss Jones."

Mumbling an apology, the lady's maid scurried out of the room.

Still reeling, Crystal stared round-eyed at Graves, her chin trembling. "Exactly when were you planning to tell me? After the wedding?"

Looking justifiably contrite, he dropped his gaze to the floor. "Forgive me, my lady. After all that's happened, the doctor said it was best we didn't add to your distress."

Utterly devastated by the news, she turned from him and rolled onto her side. Her heart pounding in her throat swiftly brought back the sick churning in her stomach. To describe her intense feeling of loneliness as distress was achingly inadequate. Her husband was gone. Their last moments together were etched on her mind with images of his fatalistic sorrow. In a few days time, she would be laying him to rest along with her future happiness. Her emotions this morning felt shredded beyond repair.

Now, the shock of Nicholas marrying tore her heart wide open in a wholly irrational way. The pain of it mixed with a searing, illogical jealousy. Envy toward this other woman clutched her chest, while she struggled with the burden of her guilt.

Dear God forgive her, her husband's body wasn't even two days cold. While she knew now what Freddy intended—that she turn to Nicholas—it still felt like she was betraying him. And Freddy, he must have known all along she was in love with Nicholas. Hopelessly, recklessly, and shamefully in love.

She wrapped her arm protectively over her abdomen, the precious life growing there. The love she felt for Nicholas burned like blazing coals.

Her heart twisted with pain. With her newfound love came the gut-wrenching realization that while she loved Nicholas with every fiber of her traitorous heart, he had been looking for a wife.

Nicholas had helped her out of kindness—given her the child she wanted—nothing more.

She heard the shuffle of footsteps as Graves left the room. She wouldn't cry, she told herself sternly. She had the new life within her to get her through the days ahead, she would survive this, dammit. But being in a breeding way had a way of making even her sternest intentions buckle.

Turning her face to her pillow, she gave into overwhelming grief, silently sobbing for Freddy…and only after her tears exhausted themselves, did she curl into a tight ball, whimpering Nick's name.

Chapter Ten

In Summer's London town house, Evette dropped her bundle of hat boxes and extravagant purchases in the hall before entering the drawing room where her soon-to-be husband sat brooding over a glass of brandy.

She kissed his cheek affectionately and plopped down beside him. "Oh, my toes are aching with a vengeance." She kicked off her shoes and propped her feet up on the nearest cushioned footstool. "I must have visited every shop in the city."

He stared into the empty hearth without comment, the dispatch from Halverton Hall balled tightly in his fist.

"Tell me, darling, who is this Halverton woman I'm hearing about?"

Nicholas' attention swung to his fiancée as he tried to remember what it was he had decided to tell her when the time came. His thinking moved slowly, thanks to the effects of good brandy. "Why do you ask?" he queried darkly, his head throbbing with a passion.

"No reason, I suppose. It's just she has recently lost her husband—"

"So I've just learned." His vision blurring, he set his glass aside.

Taking pity on him, Evette closed her eyes, rested her head against the cushioned settee. "I'm sorry, darling, about your friend. I found out about it from Her Grace, the Duchess of Sutherland. She just happened by the same shop I was in and I overheard her talking about the poor widow and how the doctor found her near death in grief."

Nicholas abruptly rose to his feet, his heart hammering.

When he didn't speak, she opened her eyes to find him restlessly prowling the floor like a caged cat. So, he was in love with the woman—the rumors she'd heard were true. "I heard that you know Lady Halverton quite intimately."

His gaze turned on her with a fierceness that burned with animal wildness. "Why don't you just ask me if I fucked her?"

She grimaced. "It's all right, darling, I understand now where your
preoccupation comes from." As composed as she looked her voice held a
distinct quiver. "Don't worry, I told you before I'm a practical woman.
And a practical woman doesn't expect fidelity. I just wish you weren't in
love with her."

Evette's blithe statement left Nicholas momentarily stunned. Was it
love? This feeling tearing him apart? Christ, only a complete fool would
fall in love with a married woman. A widow, he amended, haphazardly.

"I knew you really didn't want to marry me, not when you were obviously pining over another woman. The hell of it is, I am going to regret
losing you. No man has ever given me pleasure the way you have."

That tremor of emotion she'd tried hiding from him, had he recognized it for what it was months ago, apparently ran deeper than he thought.

Because she was being brave, because he suspected he'd just broken
her heart, he offered her what he offered no other mistress. "Whatever you
want, Evette, it's yours. I'll see that you receive it."

Sighing, she pulled the engagement ring from her finger, and resolutely handed it to him. "Since I shall have to live without you, I should
like a place of my own. I've always thought how nice it would be to live in
some exotic heathen desert—maybe have my own ship, so I could sail
about like you have, maybe retire and live in a harem of some handsome
young sheik. Perhaps I shall even marry one of those rugged buccaneers
from America, who knows? Surely with enough gold I could choose the
life I wanted, and not be left destitute by every man who falls in love."

Closing her eyes on a deep sigh, she wiggled her toes. "Now please be
a dear, won't you, and send Bessy down to rub my feet. I really am having
a wretched day."

Nick gave her a parting kiss for old time's sake, and hoped he didn't
appear as eager to bolt from the room as he felt. "By the way, this town
house is yours. Tomorrow I'll have the yacht transferred into your name."
Feeling expressly generous in his present state of inexplicable joy, he
stopped at the door and added, "You'll find an account in your name as
well with enough to buy your own harem of young men, should you decide on that. We've shared good times, Evette, and I wish you sincere
happiness. God knows, you have just given me mine."

Evette waved him off, bravely staunching the flow of tears until after he left the room.

Nicholas walked until he was reasonably certain no one would notice, then he ran, his long strides taking him the rest of the way to Crystal's front doorstep.

When he knocked, he never expected her to answer the door.

It seemed they were both incapable of speech while for a fleeting moment time stood still.

The misery he saw in her face deepened the dark circles beneath her eyes. She'd lost weight, her face pale, thin. Her ethereal beauty, so fragile, so easily destroyed, twisted his gut into a knot of guilt.

"You're back?" she whispered raggedly, her eyes suddenly bright with tears.

He should offer his condolences, but he didn't. "France held no interest for me. All I thought about was you."

Her bottom lip quivered. "Is that why you're engaged now?"

The misery in her voice clamped around his heart with a force that left him reeling. "I'm not leaving here until we talk. If you want me to beg you, I will."

She pulled him into the foyer then, shut and locked the door. When she raised her eyes to his, all the suffering she'd endured glimmered in their depths. "I wanted to die when you left. If you think I'm going to give you up, I won't."

He slowly reached for her hand, drew it to his lips. "Let me hold you," he whispered roughly, pressing his mouth to the soft flesh of her palm. "God, let me love you, puss."

And because Crystal loved him to distraction, she couldn't deny him. Suddenly, the other woman didn't matter. Uttering a soft moan, she went into his arms. She shuddered in his embrace. Ravenous with need, he nuzzled her neck, his breathing searing her flesh as he devoured her with his hot mouth, nipping and suckling her ear. His hand cupped her bottom impatiently.

Heat emanated from his body, sank into her bones, and Crystal weakly clung to his solid length in desperation. The pain, when he left this time, would be worse than cutting out her heart, but she wanted him. Fiercely. Completely. Filling her with his engorged desire, with the liquid fire burning between her legs. For a time he was hers, for now that had to be enough.

With his other hand, Nicholas clasped her hard against his chest, the supple feel of her pressed along his length, the faint smell of gardenias unique to the woman he'd never thought to see again becoming an ache in his heart that wouldn't go away. He wanted to carry her upstairs, lay her down before a blazing fire and ravish her until he collapsed. Yet he held back, trying to tell himself she was recently widowed and understandably grieving.

He tried telling himself he could live without her should she no longer need him. But deep in his heart he knew he couldn't let her go. Crystal was his, she should have been his eight years ago.

She was pressing her breasts against his chest, her hand greedily massaging his erection through his breeches. Alas, in the space of a heartbeat, nothing in the past mattered. He wouldn't worry about the future, somehow the future would take care of itself. But Crystal...Christ, he needed her in irrational ways.

As her hand slipped down the front of his breeches, his spine stiffened. When she clasped her warm fingers around his shaft, he thought his heart would stop. Bludgeoned by the hot-spurred urge to rut against her hand, he came near to ravishing her right there on the floor like a randy youth. But he wanted her begging...wanted to hear her crying out his name like she had in his dreams.

His fingers locked around her wrist. "You'll waste me," he rasped hoarsely, "if you touch me like that. Give me your hand."

He heard her muffled protest against his chest as she tried to twist her hand free of his grip. "It's your choice, puss," he whispered softly, "either we wait until Graves finds us like this or you wrap your legs around me right now and let me carry you to bed."

He waited for what seemed an eternity, then his willful little puss lifted her leg to his waist. As soon as her wetness seeped through the fabric stretched taut over his erection, he knew there was no evading what was destined to be his utter surrender. Hell and heaven vied for dominance over his soul, and with a mindless urgency he lifted his hips into her...seeking that which was his. Just as restless, Crystal's hands drew him in tightly, her cleft grinding against him. Aware that she hovered near climax, he glanced at the hall table, remembered the afternoon when they had the house to themselves.

"No, puss, this time I want you in bed." He took her hand then, lifted it to his lips, drew her finger into his mouth. Crystal sagged against him, whimpering, writhing. His tongue flicked over her finger, tasted her, wet her and an answering throb pulsed through her veins. "I can't wait," she moaned, her nails digging into his back.

The smell of her heat clenched his groin. Mutual lust burned between them. Victim of the same pained pleasure she felt, he slid her finger from his mouth…then remembering a dark night in a certain carriage, he slowly drew a ragged breath and guided her hand between her legs. She was drenched, her labia pulsing for him…his already straining erection lengthened a painful minuscule more. He swallowed his groan. Like an impassioned fool on the brink of spilling his seed, he gritted his teeth, pushed his fingers and hers between her swollen folds, deeper into her silken passage. "Stay with me, puss," he breathed tightly. Gently holding her hand in place, he felt her shuddering near orgasm. "Hold on, darling. I'm going to carry you now very carefully up the stairs. Don't move your hand…wait for me…and I'll show you how much we've missed you." *I'll love you like you wanted me to years ago.*

Fingers laced, he cupped her bottom and lifted her, let her weight settle against his hips where he held her hand trapped between them. "Hurry, Nick," she whimpered, resting heavily against him. "Please hurry."

Taking great care, he managed the stairs, having to stop but once when Crystal's body tensed against a climax at the top of the landing.

In her bedchamber, he lowered her onto the counterpane and followed her down. His brain quickly registered the fire someone had started in the hearth, the medicinal smell clinging to the room, at the edge of his vision an empty bowl setting on the side table. Stark reminders of Crystal's fragile health, of the missive from Graves awaiting him upon his return from France.

Fool that he was, he might have lost her and never been given the chance to tell her what it was that took him so long to come to terms with.

Pinned beneath him, she writhed. And he lowered his head, ran his tongue over her parted lips, tasted the sweetness of her breath. Her nails clawed at his back. Impatient. Frantic. "Please," she gasped, ripping his shirt from his breeches. "I need you inside me."

Sweat trickled down his back. His heartbeat thrummed through his veins. Braced above her on one arm, he grabbed her shoulder, half lifted her from the bed, bent his head to suckle her bottom lip, his mouth harsh, his fingers biting into her flesh. Working quickly with his other hand to pull the barrier of her skirt out of the way, he crushed her hard against his chest, forced her mouth open with his, plunged his tongue deep into her throat, the need to possess eating at his brain. He couldn't stand the thought of her lying like this with another man. She belonged to him…somehow he would have her.

Or at least that was how he imagined it, his cool reasoning responded, as he roughly raised her hips to admit his pounding thrust.

He took her with a fierceness of wild abandon, he kept her wanting him all night, wooing her, tasting her, spilling his seed into her luscious body, neither of them wanting to break the intensity of their rapture, neither of them talking of tomorrow. They made love with tender caresses, with exquisite slowness, and long into the morning when dawn spread over the floor, when at last he poured his soul into her with the gentleness of a man sealing his vow upon her heart.

Nick stood naked at the window, peering through the drapes at the tangle of late afternoon traffic, of carriages blocking the street below. Crystal lay sprawled over the counterpane, wondrously displayed for him in her big bed, her pale beauty bared to his scrutiny, tendrils of tangled gold encircling her shoulders. He ached for her with raw need, wanted her with a recklessness that would very likely kill him. Was it love? Or madness?

Evette had called it love.

He'd been a fool to think Evette could make him forget his little puss. Crystal's every graceful gesture was engraved on his memory. The way she smiled at him with that engulfing heat in her eyes when he touched her, the way she glared like a mutinous child when he insisted she eat. Sated now, her eyes closed in slumber, her lips curled in repleted aftermath, he imagined what it might be like to have her like this in his bed, in his life. More than anything he wanted to be the one at her side when she woke in the morning, the one to bring her to shuddering climax in the middle of the night.

Already he wanted her again. The heat from their mating filled his nostrils, the faint essence of her scent lingered on his dampened skin. His hungry gaze devoured. Her alabaster beauty stood out in stark contrast to the passion flushed pearls of her nipples. Lower, wavy blonde curls nestled between her legs—its silken wetness a greedy sheath for his rampant sex.

He pulled his gaze away from her, looked out the window. The thought of taking another mistress made him see how ludicrous were his plans of putting Crystal out of his mind.

"You're not going back to her, are you?" a small voice rose in the solitude.

Nicholas started, swung his gaze toward the bed again. Sitting cross-legged in the middle of the mattress, her hair spilling over her nakedness in golden dishabille, sat his precious reason for living. So pale. So fragile, he thought. Utterly vulnerable in her sultry pose. Utterly desirable. The anguish in her eyes gave his heart a painful tug. "I thought Evette would help me forget you. The marriage I sought was to drive a wedge between us."

Her gaze went to his erection, and the way her eyes devoured him made it difficult to concentrate. He knew what she was thinking. "When I laid with her, it was you I saw, Crystal. When I fucked her, it was your body I wanted. Christ...you have tortured me."

Her gaze rose to his, shimmering with hope.

He heaved a deep, soulful sigh. "In response to your question, the answer is no."

"Oh, Nick," she cried happily, launching herself off the bed at him. With a wolfish grin on his lips, he easily caught her in his arms while the impact knocked the air from his lungs.

She was mewling with delight, raining joyful kisses to the hollow of his throat, his chin, her smile more radiant than any sunrise he'd ever seen.

"Crystal, I'm not going to lie to you," he murmured against her hair, "and tell you there aren't going to be consequences to my rash actions—"

"I know." She pressed her cheek to his heart and the vital warmth there. "The banns have been posted," she murmured, "the entire city of London knows. What will we do?"

"That depends on you."

"On me?"

With slow deliberation, he drew her chin up with gentle fingers until he was looking into her soul. She held his fate in the palm of her hands. "Tell me what you want me to do." He was letting her decide. He was walking the edge of a blade.

She blushed under his heated scrutiny, the trust there. "I want your love," she said simply, as if her entire existence weren't held in the balance by his response.

"Is that all you want, puss?" His voice was silky deep, his words bringing flags of crimson to her already flushed face. Biting her bottom lip, she dropped her gaze.

Finding her maidenly embarrassment charming, he didn't wait for an answer, but lifted her into his arms and carried her back to the bed. He perched on the edge with her in his lap, held her nakedness nestled against his broad chest. "Maybe you still need reassurance." His fingers were kneading the tension from her spine.

Crystal's body shook with the intensity of her joy, overwhelming happiness making her vision go blurry. Within Nick's embrace, she felt warm and safe...protected. What he gave her was so incredibly wonderful, his tenderness a balm to her deprived soul. She tingled where their bodies touched.

Groaning, he bent his head and captured her mouth, drove his tongue between her teeth and plunged into her sweetness.

The fire blazing through his body evoked a yearning in Crystal that shuddered like lightning upon her soul. She clung to Nick in glorious abandon, felt his heated desire nudging against her bare bottom. His sensuality left her giddy, breathless. "I prayed you would come back to me," she rasped.

"Did you?" His hand on her back grew unsteady. "Perhaps you were feeling just a trifle guilty?"

She drew back to look at him, her lashes spiked with joyous tears. "How do you mean?"

"How long were you going to keep me in the dark before you told me you were carrying my child?"

Her cheeks flamed anew under his heated gaze. "That was my secret," she told him. "Besides, I didn't think you would appreciate the burden when you were to be married. Who told you? Was it Graves?"

"Graves had nothing to do with it." He moved his hand up, cupped the heavy weight of her breast, grazed the swell of alabaster beauty with his finger. "Rather a simple observation on my part. You see, I notice every little change in your body."

While wanting desperately to hold onto him, to have him say the words she needed to hear, she still couldn't ignore the fact that he'd gone to Paris to look for a wife. "If this woman loves you like I do, she won't let you go."

His smile flashed white against dark features. "So you admit you love me?"

She twisted her hands together. "I have for some time—I just didn't know how much until you announced your engagement." She swallowed against the lump of pain at the thought. "Oh, God, Nick, I'd rather die than watch the two of you together—"

"Shh," he soothed, running his fingers through her hair, knowing he would move heaven and earth to keep Crystal now that his child grew deep within her womb. Now that their love was out in the open. "Don't worry, puss, the engagement to Evette is off. You're the one I'm in love with." He crushed her tight. "No other woman has ever driven me to madness the way you have." His body was trembling with the fierce need to penetrate her, his voice husky, possessive. "Is that what you wanted to hear?"

Glancing away, she nodded against his chest.

He tenderly ran his finger along her jaw, brought her chin around so he could peer into her liquid blue eyes. "Marry me, Crystal—put me out of my misery."

Her lips parted on a gasp. Thinking she was dreaming, Crystal warily scanned his face for what she sought as dizzy elation left her fighting for breath. There was no denying the devotion in his eyes was a sweet murmur of the love she needed. That love made her go weepy, her acceptance shining in her eyes.

He brushed a tear away. "I really should let you sleep—"

She shook her head. "I'll sleep later." With trembling fingers, she boldly reached for what she wanted more than sleep. More than nourishment.

His smile strained, his shaft responding to her feather-like strokes, he shifted with her in the bed and covered her with his body. "Are you certain you want more?"

"Mmmm." Eyes shimmering, she snuggled her breasts against his softly-pelted chest, reveling in the roughness of hair braising her skin. The hard length pulsing in her palm. "Remember, you promised me a house full of children"—she quivered where his fingers invaded— "and I shall explode if you lick me there again."

"Then open to me, puss," he murmured against her neck, "I want to feel you wet and climaxing around me." Nuzzling her breast with his lips, he captured a lush coral nipple between his teeth and drew on the tight nub with gentle tugs. His one hand penetrating, invading, his tongue lathing one tender peak, then the other, he took her over crest after blissful crest. Until she arched in hot abandon, parting her pale thighs to accept him, her fitful pleas whispering against his ear.

Still, he held back until she was drenched and thrashing beneath him—then guiding himself into her love-swollen sheath, he tipped her bottom up to take all his engorged desire...and heart pumping, plunged into her with all the driving fire of possession. She was all the woman he needed...the mother of his child...the only woman he had ever loved. And he thoroughly branded her his with each ravishing thrust....

About the Author:

When Desirée Lindsey isn't writing romantic passages, she's taking care of the farm, the menagerie of animals her husband added to her chore list, and reading what she loves best –historical romance. To her, elegant gowns, horse-drawn carriages and gallant knights are the embodiment of everything romantic and dashing. She gave up the city life and her RN degree to pursue writing romance while enduring freezing temperatures, tornados and coyotes on the eastern plains of Colorado where she, her husband of many years, and their two children reside. She secretly admits to thriving on the outrageous and sultry, and loves weaving her stories with sinful splendor. In her opinion, there is nothing more captivating than a hero whose speech is wickedly masculine, his voice a velvet rumble...

My fondest regards to those who stood by me during the making of this sensual journey; my heartfelt thanks to my own alpha hero, Jeff—you're the magic in my life; to my son, Jeffrey, and daughter, Demi—Mom adores you both. To my mother, sisters and brothers for your never-ending faith and love. To my cherished friend Laura Altom and our writing journey together. Warmest of thanks to cohorts Amy Sandrin, Lynda Cooper, Maggi Landry, Terri Clark, Joyce Farrell, Audra Harders, Chelley Kitzmiller and the dozens who have believed in *Enslaved*. To my gracious editor and mentor, who patiently stood by me and nurtured with praise. You women are the stuff our heroines are made of.

Lastly, but certainly not least, my very humble gratitude to the Divine presence in my life whose love for us all makes faith possible, dreams come true and miracles happen.

Out of which *Enslaved* was born. Enjoy!

The Bodyguard

by Betsy Morgan
and Susan Paul

To My Reader:

Alana Manley's drug of choice is men. Kaki York's last assignment was Desert Storm. What happens when this female bodyguard is hired to protect the Oscar-winning actress from a stalker, and herself? Put on your jammies, crawl in bed, and read on...

Chapter One

P.S. I think you should know, Alana Manley's drug of choice is men…Ka-say-yo! Lee!

Eyes wide, Kaki York read the last line of the fax for the third time. Her eyebrows knit together. She sat in nothing but an old oversized T-shirt with her shapely legs curled beneath her on the couch in her rented beach house in Savannah, Georgia.

For God's sake, what kind of statement was that? It sounded as if Master Lee was trying to tell her this woman was a nymphomaniac. Surely not. The Seoul-born martial art expert was no doubt just having his usual problems with English.

The summer moon hung low in the sky casting a million sparkles on the water, and the evening air smelled sea-fresh coming through the open window. A scent of magnolia blossoms came to her from beyond a weathered white-picket fence. Down the road, lighted shop windows offered an endless variety of treasures that would have fascinated her at another time. But what had arrived earlier today—the request—was all that concerned her now. It was also the reason for her earlier video store run.

So much for a quiet three-month vacation, Kaki thought, as she pointed the remote control at the VCR and pushed play.

The previews of upcoming attractions ran. She took a handful of hot buttered popcorn from the bowl and popped several pieces into her mouth. Only the faintest trace of a smile hovered on her lips as she savored the salty delight.

She watched with interest as Alana Manley's latest box office hit began on the television screen. Still, she could not imagine why Master Lee wanted her to be this woman's bodyguard. If someone was stalking Ms. Manley, it seemed to her that a team of security professionals was in order—not just one black belt.

Taking a deep breath, she stretched. Her thoughts on the matter were unimportant. The man who had taken her in when she was orphaned at seven years old, loved her as his own daughter and taught her everything he knew about Korean Karate, had asked her to come to New York. And she would. It was as simple as that.

Kaki knew of Alana Manley, of course. Who didn't? She had flirted with the camera for most of her twenty-nine years. When the actress received an unprecedented thirteen million dollars for the meaty role in her latest feature film, it had made head-lines across the globe. But Kaki had never seen one of her movies. Until now.

There was a quick flash of Alana's face; the rich auburn hair, the sensual long lashed, chocolate colored eyes, the natural pout of her full red lips as she sat in a straight-backed chair and adjusted herself to a more comfortable position. Kaki shook her head. Alana Manley really was lovely. If only she had looks like—

The camera closed in on the stunning star, who sat with her legs spread wide apart. Kaki could clearly see that she wore no underwear. When Alana rested her fingers on her naked sex, Kaki choked on her popcorn, spewing more than a few pieces across the room. Grabbing the bottle of pop she took a long swig, hoping to quell the spasm in her esophagus. It didn't work. She choked again. Then coughed, which sent a stream of the carbonated liquid up the back of her nose.

Jesus, Kaki thought, shooting to her feet. Had she survived the officer's candidate school at the Great Lakes Naval Academy and Desert Storm only to die, drowning in a river of Coke?

With a groan, she snatched a tissue from the box on the coffee table and flipped off the tape. After blowing her nose several times, washing her face, and taking a few moments to regain her composure, she took a seat again. Head in her hands, Kaki thought few things ever surprised her. She had seen a great deal in her thirty years, but this was definitely something that had taken her by surprise.

The next afternoon, in her luxurious penthouse in New York's elite Central Park West where she spent most of each summer, Alana Manley, not surprisingly, was perfectly groomed. She knew what a man wanted and just how to give it to him.

Unlike most women who had used sex to gain opportunities and open doors that would have otherwise been closed to a struggling actress, she was not ashamed of the fact. Why should she be? She had not only enjoyed the ride, but was now one of the highest paid leading ladies in the motion picture industry. And though her morals were in constant question, her talent as an actress never had been.

As her gaze drifted to the golden statue on top of the white and gold marble mantel, Alana realized accepting the Oscar for Best Actress had been the most orgasmic experience of her life. With a smile, her thoughts spiraled to the evening ahead. There was always hope.

One of the biggest secrets to her success with men was focus—undiluted, undivided attention to the man she was in bed with. She concentrated totally and completely on him. She made him feel he was the only man in the world, that he was the sexiest, most desirable, most wonderful lover she could possibly have.

"Nothing is a bigger turn-on," Alana said turning to Jenna Tucker, her assistant, "than knowing you are the object of someone's desire and that you are the sole center of attention. Surely the best way to make love to a man is to let him know that you are truly carried away by desire."

Alana was in a hurry, but she took a few extra minutes to explain the reasons why she was such a success, on screen and off. "Now, scoot…or I will be late," she said, tapping the crystal of her gold Cartier watch with a perfect, red varnished fingernail that would match her evening heels. "And I am never late."

Jenna nodded knowingly. "Would you like me to run the errands for you, Ms. Manley? When Mr. Lee phoned this morning he said that under no circumstances should you go out until your new bodyguard arrives."

Alana waved a hand dismissively. "Mr. Lee was a dear friend of my father's when he was alive, and because of that he worries far too much about me. If every well-known person went into seclusion because of a few crank phone calls, there would hardly be anyone on the streets of New York. Besides, this will not take very long, and you know I really like to do these things myself."

"I know," Jenna said. "But I still do not think this date tonight is a good idea, Ms. Manley. You don't even know this man. Maybe you should cancel—"

"Not on your life!" Alana cut in with a musical laugh.

Jenna's reply was an expansive sigh.

Alana shook her head and gave her assistant a sweet smile over one shoulder. "For heaven's sake, stop worrying. James has been my driver for years. He is perfectly capable of handling any situation that might arise, he's an ex-marine. He is also very devoted."

"He is in love with you," Jenna corrected with a raise of her eyebrows.

"Nonsense," Alana said shrugging into her jacket. "He is just lonely, that's all, and enjoys the attention I give him."

Jenna started toward the door. "If you say so, Ms. Manley," she said. But mumbled under her breath, "There is a big difference between being lonely, and being lonely for much too long."

Two minutes later, Alana Manley secured the last huge ruby and diamond earring to her dainty lobe, put on her Foster Grants, and hurried out of her suite.

As she went into the warm July day, she thought it really was a shame that she never stepped more than halfway out onto her balcony overlooking the park, but she was afraid of heights. She had chosen this suite because it was the best. Had she been able to find a penthouse on the first floor, she would have gladly leased it.

James had the limo waiting. "You look stunning, Ms. Manley," he said as he opened the door and waited for her to get in.

"Thank you, James," she said genuinely pleased by the compliment, but not surprised.

Once he had pulled the black limo away from the curb, Alana instructed him to head uptown to a special French bakery. She smoothed a nonexistent wrinkle in her classic DKNY suit and thought about the man she was to meet at the Opera later this evening.

In the handwritten missive delivered yesterday, by a very good looking and impeccably dressed young man who had awaited her reply, Hunter Morgan had simply requested the presence of her company the following evening. And should she accept, he would like her to wear a red velvet gown and wait for him in the small main vestibule of the Metropolitan. They were seeing Verdi's Aida.

Hunter Morgan.

They had never met. Ironic, Alana thought, that he had picked her favorite color as the means by which to recognize her in a veritable sea of fashion.

Alana might not know Hunter Morgan personally, but she knew him by reputation and that was enough for her. In the ruthless world of acquisitions and mergers, he was notorious. A financial genius. A legend. Insatiable womanizer. He was heterosexual, totally. Alana also knew that the Metropolitan Opera House, which opened in 1883, was paid for, in part, by his great-great grandfather who was one of New York's most famous, and infamous, nouveau riche. Today, Hunter was considered one of the most eligible bachelors in the world, if not the most eligible. He lived moment to moment, "The public be damned."

Only one fact emerged consistently from the tabloids.

No one woman had ever captured his heart. Or, his attention for long.

Alana smiled. We'll see who's the hunter and who's the game. I may not be as civilized as you think.

She was, she suddenly realized, looking forward to the possibilities, and only woke from her daze when James brought the limo to a halt. She stepped out and entered the shop. The fragrance of freshly baked brioches was so overpowering that she could not restrain from buying her favorite white-raisin beignet and eating one on the spot. Then, she asked the clerk for two babas su rhums, the ultimate pastry, before directing James to the next destination.

The limo approached the block-long restaurant from the Broadway side, where the cafe was, then turned left at Twenty-sixth Street, pulling up to the main entrance. She stepped through the door and once inside, was immediately greeted by the owner, Charlie Magaddino.

"Ms. Manley," Charlie said as she approached. He took her hands and smiled handsomely. "Always a pleasure, especially when you are alone."

Alana returned his smile. "Kind, as ever," she said. "You are very sweet."

Charlie gazed at her appreciatively. "Your paté de foie gras will be ready in just a moment. If you will excuse me, I will get the bottle of Chambertin you wanted."

Jenna Tucker greeted Alana at the door and took her packages. "I will take care of the food and put the wine to chill. Is there anything else you would like me to do?"

"Yes," Alana said. "Please arrange the jasmine scented candles around the bedroom and turn down the sheets. Oh…and do not forget to slip that little something under the pillow."

"No ma'am."

From a seat by the window on wings of steel, John Pierpont "Hunter" Morgan glanced at the lights over the city as his pilot circled, waiting for clearance to land at LaGuardia.

A half-smile formed around the corners of his mouth as he picked up the remote control and fast-forwarded the videotape until he reached his favorite part. To him, Alana Manley was "sex on a stick," and he would pass the time enjoying the spectacle.

Silently, sipping Dom Perignon, Hunter wondered what she would think if she knew that he had had a video camera installed behind the mirror in her bedroom. That her every movement for the past two months had been secretly recorded. He almost laughed aloud as he recalled how easy it had been to buy the cooperation of the hotel's head of security.

Sometimes the couplings he watched were rough, almost brutal, the men seeming to thrust into her before she was ready, as careless of her pleasure as they would be a whore. But, he thought with satisfaction, those men never returned to her bed.

This one, however, whom Alana called Damian, a tall, muscular man with American Indian features and long dark hair, bound in a meticulous ponytail, had been in her bed several times this month alone. There had been some straight sex, of course, but there had been some interesting variations, too. All of which Hunter was eager to try himself.

The swarthy skinned man was now shirtless and shoeless. Hunter could see his manhood, still restrained by his tight fitting and faded jeans, was hard with erotic desire. When Damian held out his arms to Alana, Hunter could see her nipples were already pointing through the thin silk of her chemise. He immediately felt the corresponding hardness in his member and unzipped the fly of his tuxedo pants to release it.

Smiling to himself, Hunter took one more sip of champagne from the Waterford Crystal flute and watched them undressing each other, deep in the throes of lust. Within seconds they were both naked, and Alana was in her lover's arms.

Her body engrossed Hunter, the lovely skin and the graceful legs, the beautiful face with its full chestnut waves flowing around her shoulders like Renaissance paintings of angels.

When Hunter watched Damian go down on his knees before the dainty auburn V of tight curls that concealed Alana's pink lips that he had no doubt were moist and swollen with readiness, he wrapped his hand around the hard length of his distended cock and stroked until the size surged almost painfully. His eyes shone as he watched Damian lift his head to Alana's breast and let his tongue curl around one nipple and heard her gasp.

Damian then drew his head back at once and Alana groaned with the loss. Her body squirming and crying with the injustice of it all. Damian's white grin was wide and wicked. "I did not hurt you, did I?"

"No," Alana whispered in frustration, breathlessly. "You did not hurt me."

She uttered a sigh as Damian lifted her to the bed and knelt over her. Alana opened her legs wide, but remained passively on her back and quiescent, as he licked her nipple, running his tongue over the hard point until she grasped her breast in her hand and held it to his mouth like an offering and begged for his teeth.

Hunter continued to watch as Damian slowly nipped at Alana's flesh, teeth just grazing the sensitive skin of her areola, but deliberately avoided the jutting peaks of her nipples that were hardened in obvious anticipation of his mouth; her body, arching, and stiffening with its fever. While his tongue tormented her, his skilled fingers worked on her other breast, gently rolling the hard swollen flesh, until she reached between their bodies and found his thick hard sex with her hand.

Damian immediately stiffened and moaned. Reaching down farther, Alana touched his taut sac, softly caressed it with her fingers, his breathing harsh and ragged, and Hunter's body stiffened with hunger. He tugged hard on his sex.

Damn her, he thought furiously, watching Alana lay down on her belly, drawing Damian on top of her. She had everything he wanted, beauty, variety and intensity…and her appetite was insatiable. Tonight he would have her, make her plead with him, more than she had ever pleaded with any man for what she craved.

What Hunter saw was stimulating beyond control, and his right hand worked instinctively on his own erection, bringing himself closer and closer to the brink. His breathing turned ragged as he watched Damian draw up and look at Alana's small tight buttocks under him, caress her, then slide his hand under her smooth belly, between her legs, and place that thick hard erection deep into her.

Hunter immediately became engulfed by his own need of Alana's slick opening, her rough little mouth and the warmth inside her. As he watched Damian ride her with one vicious thrust after another, and heard Alana moan against the silk sheets of the bed, Hunter's right hand tightened on his cock, worked the member, abusing his shaft as if he meant to break it off. When he saw Damian jerk in the throws of climax and Alana shudder beneath him, Hunter stiffened and gasped.

The opera house was jammed with congenial noise when Hunter Morgan arrived. A good many people were there whom he recognized immediately, and so was Alana Manley. Her eyes enormous, dark and clear, as she sipped her wine, waiting.

Hunter could see the woman he would be fucking tonight, and for as long as he wanted, was perfectly at ease. He walked forward through the crowd, getting the usual stares from several available women who were none too happy to see him heading for the Hollywood star.

Alana turned at the soft touch on her shoulder and found Hunter Morgan's eyes burning as blue as the heart of a red-hot flame. With a slight movement, and no effort, he pulled her close, against the hard length of him.

Alana's eyes widened and her breath caught in her throat. "Hunter?"

"And so...our evening at last begins," he whispered as he kissed her cheek almost nonchalantly, and his fingertips descended to her breasts.

"B-but..." Alana protested.

A quick hard kiss instantly silenced her. Then he took her by the elbow and led her up the tight angular main staircase at a good pace.

With her heart pounding she hastened to keep up with him. Hunter Morgan certainly was an appealing figure in his evening clothes, and the thought crossed her mind that they made an attractive pair. But there had been something in the depths of his eyes that she found disturbing. Her feelings for this mysterious and forceful man were definitely mixed. How could she be excited, yet frightened at the same time?

They were among the last people to enter the auditorium and they hurried to their seats in Hunter's private box on the second tier. Alana remained silent, not knowing what to say. He came close then, and kissed her. She did not embrace him as she wanted, but she did slip her tongue between his lips, and for a few seconds their kiss deepened. Then he drew away.

"You're dazzling in red," Hunter said.

"Red is my signature color," she replied with a sensual smile.

Just as they settled in, the houselights faded, and he pulled out a set of foldable glasses and handed them to Alana. She immediately checked out the other boxes around and across from them for familiar faces.

She was looking forward to hearing the beautiful and powerful Leontyne Price sing; her performances were always such a rare treat. But unfortunately she knew that Mayor Rudolph Giuliani's bratty kid—who had been on David Letterman more times than she—would be giving Ms. Price a run for her money tonight. He was already screaming and rolling wildly all over his father's lap.

With a sigh, Alana shifted her gaze to the boxes across from them. She saw Donald and the strumpet from Dalton, Georgia in deep conversation. Then she caught a quick glimpse of a cherry-faced man with red hair sitting in the shadows and realized it was the rather robust Senator Pat Moynahan, whom she liked very much. Just as Luciano Pavarotti, the great tenor, became visible in the wings, the house went black.

When Hunter moved his chair closer to her, Alana received a shock. But, a pleasant shock. When he reached out and cupped the back of her neck in his hand, drawing her face close to his, she was lost. In an instant the atmosphere in the private enclosure was transformed.

Hunter brushed his lips over hers in a slow sensuous way. She wanted to taste him and responded immediately by opening her lips. He kissed her slowly and surely. His warmth flowed through her body; he did not let his lips rest for long. She wanted more. So much more. She shivered and tiny tendrils of excitement snaked their way through her lower stomach. When he moved to the cleavage between her breasts, her nipples hardened and ached. She breathed hard and fast.

Abruptly, he stopped.

"Well," she said, and forced her breathing to slow.

"Do not talk," he said as he pulled the velvet of her gown up over her left knee, over her thigh, and placed his hand beneath it. Reaching between her legs, he brushed his fingers over her garters before sliding them into the crotch of her silk panties. Her clitoris hardened and throbbed sharply.

After a minute Alana obeyed, feeling hopelessly vulnerable as Hunter arranged her gown with his free hand so that to a casual onlooker nothing would seem the least bit out of the ordinary. Then, she finally felt the pads of his surprisingly cool fingers touching her soft lips and a thrill ran through her as she inhaled sharply.

With a crooked grin, Hunter said quietly, "Next time we are together I would prefer that you do not wear panties."

She nodded, but stayed still, holding her breath. Hunter turned and said something cordial to the elderly woman in the box to his left. At the same time he slid a single finger between her wet lips and caressed the swollen bud within at the same time.

Beyond caring, lost in her own lascivious dream world, Alana's sex throbbed and her thighs tightened. When Hunter continued to brush his fingers quickly and cleverly over her opening, slick with desire, it was so tantalizing she almost moaned aloud. The movements of his fingers began to drive her crazy and Alana could do nothing but bite her lower lip to keep from crying out.

She finally gave in and leaned back, closing her eyes. "Just relax," she heard him say.

How could she? Hunter's fingers were flying across her inflamed sex. First rubbing furiously, then flicking and pinching. From a great distance Alana could hear the insistent music of the orchestra as it accompanied a moving soprano and tenor duet, but was fully aware of Hunter's blue gaze intently staring at her. In a slow movement that was almost imperious, she raised her hips against him in an effort to increase the pressure against his hand, but he moved his hand gently away.

Instantly, her gaze met his.

"Not yet," Hunter murmured softly.

"B-But I—" whispered Alana, beseeching him with her eyes.

"I will bring you to climax, but when I decide. And that will not be until much later this evening," he said very softly, but clearly, then lowered his mouth onto Alana's open one.

At Alana Manley's penthouse suite, her chauffeur was not happy. He had wanted to wait for Alana at the opera but she had sent him on his way.

Exactly two seconds after the bell chimed James snatched open the front door. The woman standing in the hall promptly stated her reason for being there and his jaw dropped open. After a moment he placed both hands on either side of the doorjamb and leaned forward as if wanting a closer look.

"You are Ms. Manley's what?"

Kaki looked him in the eye. "Her bodyguard," she said for the second time.

James stared incredulously. "This is a joke, right?"

"No," she said clearly. "This is not a joke. I was hired by Mr. Lee to serve as Ms. Manley's bodyguard. I assumed my arrival was expected."

"Your arrival?" James laughed. "Hardly!"

Forcibly, she kept her temper under control. "My name is Kaki York."

He laughed again. "Khaki? As in the pants?"

"Sort of," she said, irritated. "The spelling is different. And before you ask…no, I'm not joking about that either."

James continued to stare as the strawberry blond beauty with the dancing green eyes. She stood in front of him with all the pomp of a seasoned Marine.

The big man shook his head. "Mr. Lee must have lost his mind."

Kaki's face flushed hotly. "I believe you will find Mr. Lee to be in full possession of all his faculties."

James immediately straightened to his full height, which was impressive. "That is a matter of opinion."

She clasped her hands in front of her and took a deep breath. "May I come in?"

He boldly swept her sleek figure with the keen gaze of a connoisseur. "Only if you are here to apply for a job as a secretary."

Kaki smiled indulgently at him, as if she were preparing to speak to a slow child. "I hold a black belt in Taekwondo, Korean Karate," she said easily. "And I served five years as a captain in the United States Navy."

The ex-marine placed his hands on his hips. His glance was piercing. "I am sure that qualifies you to be a very well rounded person, Ms. York. But I do not believe Ms. Manley needs someone who can tie knots and just happens to look good in bell-bottoms. She needs a professional bodyguard."

Kaki stood stiffly; her every muscle tensed. Already exhausted from lack of sleep, the last thing she needed was this big jerk giving her a hard time.

"If necessary, I am prepared to demonstrate my expertise," she said with pleasure.

"Oh, this I have to see," James said with a chuckle. He stepped aside and gestured for her to enter. "Please."

Once inside, Kaki turned to face him. "Now?"

James grinned smugly. "Of course."

In a split second he was on the floor with his face pressed firmly against the cool marble, and his left arm jacked up behind his back in an inescapable hold. Kaki's knee rested firmly against his spine, just between the shoulder blades, and she was pressing a Heckler and Köch 9mm calmly to his right temple.

Having no other choice, James spoke through his teeth to the floor. "I hope that damn thing is not loaded."

Kaki could not help it. She smiled. "I am afraid it is, but I assure you that I have the safety firmly in place."

James made a low sound in his throat. "Thank God for small favors," he mumbled. Then erupted, "Now let me up!"

Kaki's response was immediate. She released her hold on him and with a catlike swiftness. Calmly, she sheathed the 9mm in the holster at her back.

He stood abruptly and faced her. They stared steadily into each other's eye, until James turned his attention to Mr. Lee who was just coming through the front door.

Tommy Lee had witnessed the whole humiliating display. "I see you two have met," he said casually. His gaze shifted to Kaki and he bowed gallantly.

She smiled, widely. "Master Lee...Yo-bo-say-yo," she said, respectfully returning his bow before moving forward to give him a big hug.

"Oh joy, you are friends," James said as he righted his clothes. "And she speaks Korean, too." He pinned Lee with an unpleasant look. "You cannot be serious about hiring a woman to guard Ms. Manley," he snapped, looking more than a little insulted.

Lee remained an undaunted figure in his black silk suit. "She handled you quite well."

"I am not the stalker," James grumbled.

Lee's hooded eyes smiled. "True. If you had been, this unpleasant business would be concluded."

James stiffened.

Lee ignored his reaction and returned his attention to Kaki. He gazed proudly at the slender figure in a navy blazer and jeans. "Kaki was one of my best students. She is a third degree black belt and an ex-Navy Seal. She also spent time stationed in Kuwait during Desert Storm, and served as one of General Norman Swartzkopf's personal bodyguards—"

"I'll just bet," James interrupted, smiling at Kaki wickedly. "A man in Swartzkopf's position no doubt has his perks. And she is definitely a pleasure to look at."

Kaki swallowed her need to tell this man to jump up her ass. "Master Lee, since Ms. Manley does not appear to be in at the moment, I will go and check into my room now."

Tommy Lee sighed. "I am sorry to say that against my advice, Ms. Manley has gone out for the evening, but I would like you to stay for a moment. There are some things the three of us need to go over." He paused to run splayed fingers through his ink-black hair. "You and James will be working closely together. It is important that you establish a good working relationship."

Kaki nodded and the two shook hands guardedly.

Lee focused on James. "I realize that you have been in Ms. Manley's employ a long time and that you care about her a great deal, but who I hire as her personal bodyguard is really none of your business. You are her chauffeur."

The chauffeur? Kaki almost laughed, but suppressed it when she saw James narrow his eyes at her. She would need his cooperation to protect Ms. Manley and she did not need to alienate him any further.

Lee continued, "After threatening phone calls, and the dead cat you found in the limo last week, Ms. Manley needs a personal bodyguard. A good one. Kaki is one of the best in the business. She is also one of the few who have the unique qualifications needed for this assignment."

"Does Ms. Manley know her new bodyguard is female?" James asked.

"She does. And she is quite pleased with my decision," Lee said.

James paced back and forth. Lee stood stolidly. "The dead cat signals the stalker has psychotic aberrations."

James stopped then, leaned against the wall and crossed his arms. "And I suppose she is an expert in that area, too?"

Kaki stood still, her temper simmering. How many times had she gone through this scenario? She was beyond tired of it, but this time refusing to take the position was not an option. She owed Master Lee much. She loved him like a father. No, this obstinate man could give her considerable problems, but she would not refuse to guard Ms. Manley because of him.

She couldn't.

Kaki tensed as she remembered the day she and her sister, Nikki, became orphaned.

"I am here to take you to the county home," the woman from social services had said matter-of-factly, just after the funeral of their parents.

Kaki felt tears rising as she thought about how the cruel fates had left two little girls alone in the world. Her sister and she had been inconsolable, and uncontrollable. No one could handle them. They were shuffled from one foster home to the other, until finally, a judge had ordered them taken to Master Lee. To be taught discipline.

She smiled thinly. They had learned discipline and respect, yes. More importantly, this gentle warrior had taught two little girls to believe in love again. Now grown, both experts in the martial arts, they were secure in the knowledge that as long as Tommy Lee lived, they would never again be alone in the world. She had traded in her ribbons and bows for a karate uniform and learned how to persevere and excel, and even become one of the best of the best. All because of Master Lee. She would not disappoint him now.

"James," Lee said interrupting Kaki's thoughts. "Kaki has experience dealing with this type stalker. What better cover for a bodyguard than posing as Ms. Manley's assistant? A male could hardly do that and go unnoticed."

James reluctantly agreed with a raise of an eyebrow. "Jenna is her assistant."

Tommy Lee did not miss a beat. "And she will continue to be. To any outsiders, Kaki will appear as nothing more than a newly hired employee. In my opinion, if the stalker believes Ms. Manley is unguarded, he...or she, for that matter, is more likely to make careless mistakes that could lead to a quick apprehension."

James seemed to hesitate, but nodded.

Kaki closed her eyes briefly, relieved.

Chapter Two

At the Metropolitan, Act III was underway but Alana Manley sat nearly oblivious to the ominous opening. Seconds later as everyone leaned forward to see the stage she only felt the thrill of anticipation. Still aroused by Hunter's bold onslaught, she wiggled in her chair and unconsciously adjusted herself into the best position for stimulating the sensitive area of her ripe flesh.

"You are enjoying yourself I see," Hunter said with the raise of a dark eyebrow, his amusement of her present situation evident by his derisive expression.

He casually leaned back in his chair with a look on his face in which Alana was positive she saw a tinge of devilment. She said nothing in reply and quickly shifted her gaze back to the stage. Much to her surprise he made no further comments, and she was able to put the world aside and enjoy Price and Pavarotti's final duet.

When the lights went up for the last time everyone stood and bellowed bravos, getting a small wave from the performers in return.

At precisely fifteen minutes before midnight Alana and Hunter entered the lobby of her apartment building on Central Park West.

The elevator attendant, with his immaculate white gloves, pressed a button and within seconds they exited on the top floor. Without a word Alana removed a single key on a silken cord from her evening bag. In the dim light, she turned the key in the latch and the scent of jasmine assailed her senses as she preceded Hunter into her penthouse suite.

With a firm grasp on her hand, he stopped her. "I think I have found

Paradise."

Alana tilted her head and looked directly at his handsome face, the slightest shadow of facial hair on his jaw. She kept still as her lips curved into a smile. "I have arranged a surprise for you...come inside."

Hunter's hand slid up the pale silkiness of her bare shoulder, drifted lightly over her throat, and gently cupped her face. "I would be delighted," he said, then lifted his gaze to the specially set table in the middle of the living room.

Easing her hand free of his hold, Alana lifted her chin so that her gaze softly commanded his. "The food comes much later."

His mouth brushed hers with a light caress, twice. His sweet breath was warm on her face. A moment later they made their way across the marble-tiled foyer. The slow, driving beat of Ravel's Bolero enveloped them as their eyes adjusted to the light. Shimmering candles lit the entire suite and Alana was pleased with the effect.

Following the path that the music set Alana led Hunter into her bedroom. Silently they moved past the turned down bed that was sprinkled with rose petals and into the large bathroom, where long-stemmed white roses in a crystal vase shone through the flickering light.

Alana turned to face him. "Wait here for just a moment and do not undress; I want to do that for you."

"You've planned ahead." Looking intrigued, Hunter smiled and leaned casually against the counter to wait.

"Being prepared saves time," she said in a caressing tone and left him to enter a small dressing room with mirrored walls, though she made certain to leave the door open so that he could have a good view of the show. And he would watch with pleasure, she thought, if the expression on his face was any indication.

She undressed, slipping out of her formal gown without haste. Nude, except for her garter belt and stockings, she slipped her pedicured feet into a pair of high-heeled slippers and wrapped a red silk kimono around her. Without speaking, she went into his arms.

"You are so beautiful," he breathed, rubbing his cheek against hers. He kissed her deeply and pulled the pins, one by one, from her hair until it fell like a fragrant curtain over her shoulders.

"So are you," Alana said, slowly kneeling at his feet and then sliding her hands up Hunter's tuxedo trousers until her fingers closed on the zipper. "Relax," she whispered, opening his fly, smiling up at him as she eased the black material over his lean hips and peeled away his pants. The swish of fabric sliding down his legs was distinct, as was the slap of his trousers hitting the tile of the bathroom wall when he kicked them away.

The white silk of his briefs revealed his erection and Alana smiled to herself.

His gaze from under the fringe of dark lashes was unmoving. Gently grasping his erection through the silky fabric, he ran a practiced hand down its length, and she sucked in a breath as its sized surged on demand. "Then do so, darling," Hunter said in invitation. "I want you to undress me and pleasure me while I watch. I enjoy that," he whispered, then released his gentle grip on his sex and waited.

Alana stared at him, her eyes glazed with sharp desire. "Oh, I will," she assured him. And she was starving for him. The pulsing in her vagina was already spreading a carnal heat upward; her nipples hardened against the cool silk of her wrap, the swollen weight of her breasts tingling.

She began by opening her robe, just a little, to expose the deep cleavage of her full breasts, and then she raised her head and kissed the sensitive flesh of his inner thigh. He unbuttoned his jacket. She held his gaze intently, focused on the deep cleft in his strong chin, the full pout of his lips, his sky-blue eyes, the shiny blackness of his hair—the tanned, sculpted muscles of his torso. Shrugging out of his satin-lapeled jacket, he tossed it aside.

When he pulled his tie loose at the collar and reached for the pearl buttons on his white silk shirt, Alana touched his hand. "I want to do the rest." Her voice was velvet soft.

Hunter exhaled softly and nodded. Again, he rested his hands on either side of himself and gripped the edge of cool marble.

"Good," she murmured with a faint smile, opening the front of her robe fully and releasing her breasts. The cool scented air in the room immediately caused the darker area around her nipples to tighten and wrinkle.

"I like what I see," he said softly.

Alana smiled and lifted her hands to cup her breasts and hold them up, as if offering them to him; the tips of her fingers traced and toyed with her nipples until they were stiff jutting peaks.

Hunter's breathing became labored. He raised a hand to run his palm across the rosy hardness with a feather-light touch. He inhaled deeply.

Alana moaned. And seeing the storm that raged in his eyes, she knew then that they would ride the heat of passion like a comet burning both ends of the night. She could hardly wait to feel the hunger of his strong arms, the magnificent hardness of him plundering her intimate feminine flesh. She yearned for him, heated, damp and swollen, was ready for him. But she refused to give into the baser need to expose her soft opening and beg him to take her—no. Hunter Morgan would be the one to beg.

Now Alana moved with conscious effort, slowly running a single finger just inside, and along, the elastic waistband of his briefs. The thick muscles of his hard well-defined thighs tensed, the lean hips too. She gazed blatantly at his splendid erection, long and thick as it strained against his briefs. Touched it, felt its heat radiating through the soft material.

Hunter sucked in a breath; his head fell back. Her long, cool fingers freed the velvety hardness from its constraints and gently cupped the hanging sac behind, teasingly played with him as she might roll Chinese balls in her hand to relieve the tensions of the day. His body radiated with unreleased passion and it pleased her. She wanted to torture him. Exquisite torture. She knew she had succeeded when he groaned breathlessly, his sex jerked with the intensity of its throbbing blood flow, and he spread his legs wide. The soft tender parts of her swelled unbearably and the inner walls contracted.

With eager anticipation she caressed the taut-capped vermilion head; the supple softness of his firm shaft. Taking the warm hardness in her hand, she wrapped her fingers around its thick width and squeezed—just a little. She raised his strong member then, and pressed her face to the hard, smooth flatness of his lower abdomen, nuzzled the thicket of soft curling dark hair that spread from the root all around his thighs and up in a decreasingly thin line to the navel.

God, he was magnificent, she thought, and devoured his naked charms with her gaze, inhaled his sweet manly scent, laved greedily the sweet bag of nature's sweets beneath with her warm wet tongue. He moaned and closed his eyes. The long muscles of his thighs trembled with anticipation. He shoved his fingers deeply into the soft chestnut waves of her hair.

Alana continued to torment him, her hands making endless movements to caress and stimulate his genitals. When his hanging sac became taut between his thighs, drawn up in pleasing wrinkles, her lips nipped, kissed, and traced it as her fingers ran lightly up the sensitive branched vein and down the full length of him until his hips were inching up toward the warmth of her mouth.

He reached down and took a breast in each hand, rolled the nipples simultaneously between thumb and forefingers, and an answering pull tugged deep within her stomach. Her sex instantly filled with a rush of hot moisture; she inhaled deeply of the scent of their mingled arousal heavy in the air. Knowing she did not want to go further now, she forced herself to move away and took a deep cleansing breath.

"Are you not as hot for me as I am for you?" he demanded as he dragged her up from her knees and into his strong embrace.

She sucked in a quick breath at the jarring sensations he evoked within her being. "Oh, yes," she said instantly. "But first...I want to bathe you."

He ran his warm palm up her neck and cupped the back of her head. "Do you?"

Straightening, she stood before him, and raised her emerald gaze to meet his so far above. "Very much so," she said, and without protest Hunter allowed her to remove the rest of his clothing, kissing every inch of him as she did.

"I've never had a lover bathe me," Hunter said. "You intrigue me, Alana Manley, in many ways." Bending his head low, his lips touched hers lightly before gently sliding his tongue over them, which sent a shocking bolt of lightning deep down inside her. So hot was the strike that Alana moved away from him. Abruptly his hand tightened on her back and pulled her close again with an authority that left her with no doubt who was in command, and it remained firmly pressed against the base of her spine.

"Do with me as you will, darling," Hunter said, reaching out to slide the pad of one finger across the tops of her breasts. "But please, take your time."

Then, in the flickering candlelight, Alana saw his tattoo. She blinked. It was fascinating—a small Bengal tiger expertly depicted in full color and waiting to pounce on his left shoulder. Oddly, she had never made love to a man with a tattoo before and it was wildly arousing. She traced its outline with a sculpted nail, kissed it wetly and ran her tongue across the length of it.

He placed a finger beneath her delicate chin and lifted her face to his. "I am, after all, the hunter," he said cutting into her thoughts.

Alana's wide eyes gazed up at him. "I guess so." The words rode on a breathless whisper.

She left him then to run his bath, adding rose petals and a foamy azure liquid from an antique frosted glass decanter. She picked up the champagne bottle from the iced bucket nearby, leaned over and poured him an icy glass of wine. "You will enjoy this much more after a few glasses of champagne." Handing it to him, she patted the water.

With the raise of a dark eyebrow, he stepped into the scented bath and relaxed in the tub. "Won't you join me?" he gently queried.

"No...not this time. I have some other things I need to do."

"Ah, more surprises," he said, smiling at her across the candlelit space. "Then I won't keep you." he finished in a low whisper.

Turning, she headed for the door, and then, looking back over her shoulder, quietly said, "Don't start anything without me."

He laughed. "I wouldn't think of it. Besides, it might be frustrating for you to watch."

Alana agreed.

She returned a few minutes later carrying a small sterling silver serving tray filled with white mushroom caps that were stuffed with glistening caviar. And as Hunter lay back and soaked in the soothing warmth, she finger-fed him the appetizer.

Later, after she had soaped his body and shampooed his hair, she wrapped his naked body in the cleanest, softest white terry-cloth robe. Reaching up on tiptoe, she kissed him. His searing blue gaze scanned her face and his arms pulled her tightly against him.

"Not yet," she said and wiggled out of his embrace.

Hunter's dark brows rose slightly. She poured him another glass of champagne. Slipping her hand in his free one, she led him into the living area where they would eat a late supper and gestured toward the finely set table. "There is room at my table. Why don't you pull up a chair?"

His eyes lit up and his expression was one of pleasure. His brushed her cheek with his fingers. "I would be delighted." Taking a seat, he set the crystal glass aside. "My appetite is both voracious and wholesome."

She laughed musically. "I would not want it any other way."

As Alana bent to light the single candle in the delicate holder there was no mistaking the look in his eyes. Then with a wink she disappeared into the kitchen.

Expelling a pleasant sigh, she thought that all men, if they were truthful with themselves, wanted a woman to be a lady in the living room and a whore in the bedroom. And she intended this night to be a perfect blend of ecstasy and lust.

Five minutes later, she returned with the petits de foie gras and Chambertin from Charlie Maggadino's restaurant. Placing them before Hunter, she took her seat and gazed out at the summer night, with its magic moon, through the sliding glass doors that led to the balcony.

She was about to shift her gaze back to him when she caught a definite glimpse of a shadow cutting the bright moonbeam's path in two. Someone was out on the patio. She froze, then the wind howled. She shook her head. How silly she thought—her suite was the penthouse, her balcony over a hundred feet straight up—it had only been the clouds riding on the wind. Suddenly thunder rumbled in the distance and she stared at Hunter. "It looks as if a summer storm is coming."

"I believe it is already here," he said, "and I intend to try in every way to make it roll out of control." His wicked grin caused them both to smile.

For the next hour, they ate and laughed and kissed across the table. When they were finished, Alana slowly and deliberately glided over to the CD player on the other side of the room and changed the disk. To the seductive tune of Kenny G's saxophone, she padded her way across the wool carpet and back to Hunter. She slipped out of her kimono, and let it fall. Leaving it in a lovely heap on the floor, she drew him by the hand and into the bedroom.

Motioning for him to join her in bed, Alana slid her hand under the pillow and pulled out two silk scarves. Hunter did not hesitate. He removed his robe and tossed it on a gilded chair. Lying next to her now, he clasped his hands behind his head and settled his back comfortably against the satin covered feather pillows.

Reaching over to finger the long lengths of red silk she held loosely in her grasp, he asked, "Are those for me or you, my darling?"

She looked back at him, her emerald glance direct in his heated gaze, and saw a blaze of desire as blue as the center of a hot flame smoldering in his eyes.

"Which would you prefer?"

He hesitated for a moment, as if undecided. "I think, sweet Alana," he said, tuning on his side to face her and sliding his foot between her legs, "this time I will let you decide and set the pace..."

She arched a finely shaped auburn brow and scooted forward, which enabled her to apply more pressure to the top of his foot and her swollen clitoris at the same time. "I told you that red was my signature color," she purred as she trailed the silk scarves along the inside of his muscular thighs and over his enormous erection.

Hunter shifted his gaze to her pale pink garters. "Every shade, I see."

His insistent arousal was hard and huge like his body. She kept her gaze riveted to the ostentatious display as she placed her hands on his shoulders and urged him to lie on his back again. Then she straddled him. Supporting herself on her knees, she placed a scarf in each hand and knelt above his rigid length. Heat radiated between their bodies. His strong hands spanned her waist; he lifted her, guided his erection toward her drenched vulva. When she locked her elbows and held her bottom fast in its raised position, stopping him short of penetration, his fingers dug into her buttocks. "Now what are you up to?"

"Wait and see," she whispered. She bent down to nip his lower lip with her teeth. "I want to play a little game," she said. "You are up for it, aren't you?"

Hunter's stiff instrument remained pointed to the opening of her slick sex as surely as a divining rod to water. He first gave his searing member an intent perusal, then directed his attention to the succulent double pout between her legs and jammed his fingers inside her, hooked them on her pelvic bone and pulled her up so she was almost raised off her knees. "What do you think?"

She glanced downward and grinned. "Is this going to be my choice, or not?"

He pulled his fingers out so abruptly she almost lost her balance and impaled herself on his erection. "I'm willing…this time, but there is something you need to know." His eyes were an icy-blue, hovering for a moment as he raised his drenched fingers and touched them to her lips. "If I'm not pleased—fully—I will punish you. And enjoy every minute."

Alana opened her mouth, snatched his fingers between her teeth and sucked her essence from them. When she released them, she smiled fully, then ran the tip of her tongue across her white even teeth. "Agreed," she said without a single reservation. "I choose that I am now the hunter…and you are the game. You must do as I say and obey my every command, but I promise I will not hurt you," she said with a mischievous grim on her full red lips.

Hunter threw back his head and laughed.

But he stopped when she took his wrist and quickly and efficiently tied one of the scarves around it, then brought it up to thread the red silk through the brass headboard before securing his other wrist to it. Once she had him tied securely to the headboard and was certain that he was propped up nicely against the pillows, she unstraddled him and left the bed.

"Where are you going?" he demanded.

Alana stood next to the bed gazing down at his full, straining arousal and then shifted to his face. "Wouldn't you like me to entertain you?"

"In this bed," he said without amusement.

Alana shook her head and smiled back over her shoulder as she walked away. "Not yet."

First she picked up her vanity stool and positioned it at the end of the big bed and in front of a full-length wall mirror. She placed one foot on it allowing Hunter a clear view of both her backside and her front in the flickering candlelight as she removed the high-heeled slipper, unhooked her stocking from the pink lace garter, and slowly rolled it down one shapely leg. Then she took the transparent ribbon of silk and tossed it at his feet.

Hunter tensed on the bed. His sex was so firm, sculpted like his body, and she felt like jumping on top of him and riding him, but it was too soon. He had not begged her yet. But he will, she thought with pleasure.

"Enough of this game, Alana, come here," he said in a not-to-be-denied tone.

"Not yet," she said again softly and placed her other foot on the stool and went on to repeat the same motions as before, removing her other stocking. Unhooking her garter belt she sighed and allowed it to slip slowly from her waist to the floor.

Hunter groaned and instinctively tried to sit up, but was held fast to the headboard by the thin silk bindings. He jerked the bindings again in frustration but did not say a thing.

Alana gave him a seductive smile and placed her palms on the seat cushion, thrusting her bottom high in the air. Her full breasts dangled beneath her. His gaze immediately focused on the arousingly inviting refection in the mirror of her firm buttocks and the plump moist slit down the center.

Leaving one hand on the stool for support, she slowly slid the other up the inside of one thigh before threading it between her legs, allowing it to rest only after she had slipped her middle finger deep inside her. She groaned and her head lulled a little to the side, her nipples hardened visibly.

She looked at Hunter through huge eyes glazed with desire. For a moment the throbbing heartbeat of Hunter's stiff member entranced Alana.

"You agreed this night was my choice." She paused for a short time to move her finger slowly in and then out of herself; she arched her back at the pleasure it brought. "I only wish to give you pleasure. Surely you agree that the greater the desire, the greater the pleasure."

Hunter's muscular hips involuntarily jerked, seeming to search for what she was intentionally denying him as he watched her fingers in the mirror, glistening wetly, again slip out of the heated entrance to his paradise and begin to pluck and play with the swollen bud of her pleasure.

Alana did not stop pleasuring herself when she asked, in a breathless whisper, "Do you truly want me to stop? Would you go back on your word now?"

"I never go back on my word," he ground out through clenched teeth.

She smiled in a wickedly seductive way. "I thought not. If I come to you…will you let me do as I like with you—however I like—and without protest?"

He said no more, only nodded.

Alana had known he would, and she could see from the state of his arousal he wasn't at all opposed to the idea.

She moved then to the end of the bed and climbed his hard body like a tree. This time she not only heard, but also felt his deep muffled cry of frustration.

In the rented suite just across the hall that evening, Kaki York could not watch the monitor one more second. She flipped it off, and the other four too. Raking a hand through her hair, she seriously wondered if she could handle this assignment after all. Twenty-four-hour surveillance had suddenly taken on a whole new meaning.

At first she had been thrilled to find Master Lee had installed a high-tech security system that enabled them to monitor Alana Manley's movements by way of hidden cameras strategically placed throughout her penthouse. She had agreed that they would have a much better chance of catching this psychopath if she was not seen as being joined to Ms. Manley by the hip day and night, dogging her every move. But now, she would have preferred to be sleeping on the hall floor outside her front door to watching her sexual escapades...more to the point, that man's...on a full color screen.

So, she thought, this was what Tommy Lee had meant when he had said that Alana Manley's drug of choice was men. Dear God, she hoped this would not go on every night—she would never survive.

Kaki was so lost in thought that she never noticed Jenna Tucker ease in the room, only to walk away in disgust—or heard James Kulick come into the room to relieve her.

At the sound of James' voice, she nearly jumped out of her skin. He looked so different from the way he had looked in his chauffeur's uniform. Propped against the door jam with his arms crossed over the wide expanse of his chest, he was dressed in faded jeans, a black denim shirt and cowboy boots. He looked rumpled and windblown, but handsome.

"Some bodyguard," he said with dripping sarcasm. "The monitors are off and you did not even hear me come in."

Kaki bristled. "Maybe you enjoy voyeurism, but I do not," she said with enough force to cause James to arch a dark eyebrow. "Nevertheless, I will try to do better in the future." She nervously wiped her palms on the seat of her jeans. "I am a bit overtired at the moment. Are you here to take over the watch?"

He nodded. "That's what I'm being paid for."

Kaki stood with a brief sigh and a yawn. She picked up her nine-millimeter off the desktop and returned it to her shoulder holster. "Wake me at six. We need to check Ms. Manley's suite for security leaks before meeting with Tommy Lee to discuss what else needs to be done," she said and brushed quickly past him, heading straight for a cold shower and bed. Over her shoulder, she said, "Enjoy." Her voice held the smallest hint of huskiness.

James yelled after her, "Pleasant dreams." His deep voice held a derisive tone.

She absolutely refused to respond.

"Are you still hot for me?" Alana asked as she pressed her pelvis hard against Hunter's already painfully distended erection.

His eyes were heated, restless. "Yes."

She slid her hand between them and pressed her fingers to her pulsing labia. Shifting beneath her, he groaned as the back of her hand touched the heavy weight of his testicles. She moved from her position and slid her legs between his outspread legs, kneeling above him. "Do you want me to touch you?"

"Only immediately," he said with a grin.

His perfectly formed penis stood rigidly upright. She touched him delicately, tentatively, as if he were a rare jewel that held the secrets to her unquenchable thirst for the rare hard stone before her. She ran the tip of her finger up and down the bulging veins, the moist, glistening slit at the tip, the swollen hard taut globes drawn up tightly against the root.

Lifting his hips, he made a sound in his throat, a low growl, as she lifted the shaft to better stoke the velvety skin. With him bound and unable to respond in kind, it gave her a sense of power to see him strain for her touch. She watched his erection swell even more, the dark pink peak stretch its skin to what looked like the breaking point, his pulse quickened and forced out the transparent droplets of arousal.

He sucked in a harsh breath when her tongue flicked over the tip, then curled into her mouth as she tasted his salty essence with leisurely decadence. Her mouth hovered the merest breath away from the little ridge of skin where the shiny red head was joined to the shaft. "Are you in a hurry to be inside me?" she whispered, then enveloped his penis with her mouth and held it, not moving, but hugging it like a snug vagina.

He could barely think. It took him a moment to catch his breath, to speak. "I don't want to wait much longer."

Thumb and forefinger encircled his sex, and she moved her hand up and down the shaft in the same rhythm as she sucked the tip of his sensitive head. With the other hand she used mild finger movements over his testicles. When she stopped, he groaned in frustration.

She rose up then and kneaded his strong chest muscles with her hands, her fingers rolled and tugged the small hard nipples—her lips kissed and sucked. "Do you want to be inside my mouth...or plumb the depths of my inner passage?"

He opened his mouth to speak, but she quickly pressed the pad of her index finger to his lips, stopping him. "You may choose either place, but I won't let you come in my mouth."

"Do me," he said huskily.

"But what do you want me to do?" she asked.

"Anything you want. Everything you want."

"What if I want you to do me first?"

"Come here then," he said to her.

Instantly she moved over his chest until positioned just a few inches above his face, with her knees planted on either side of his head. Almost ready to burst, she moved herself down so that she was directly over his mouth, so close that she could feel the warmth of his labored breath on her clitoris.

She moaned and gazed down at his handsome face; she used her fingers to open herself wide for him. "Open your mouth and lick me...suck me."

"With pleasure" he said, and then his tongue, long and pointed, snaked out and lashed the sensitive area of skin that marked the pathway to her pleasure. She reveled in the rough wetness of his tongue skimming across her clitoris repeatedly, his teeth nipping, she rotated her hips and groaned loudly. The faster he licked, the harder her fingers dug into his hard muscled shoulders. When he took her fully into his mouth and sucked the hardened and protruding nub as if milking her passions—from far inside her a guttural cry escaped, a desperate whimper of passion and she was off his face and scrambling down his body to reach his thick, throbbing member.

Quickly straddling his hips, she roughly shoved his stiff sex inside her, slid down the full length of him, stopping only when her groin met his. He cried out in savage grunts from the searing pleasure.

She drew air into her labored lungs, sweat beaded on her forehead, between her breasts. Wanting him beyond the power to comprehend, she began to ride his hardness and his erection quickened with the first pumps of pre-orgasm.

"No! Slow down," he growled, his body barely in check. He held his breath, closed his eyes, and focused his mind on everything but the carnal urgency that had taken control.

She stopped her movement. "I want to come now," she said on a suffocated breath and leaned forward to brush sensitive nipples across his wet lips. He responded by sucking first one then the other greedily. Licked and bit them until she could stand it no longer and pulled her breasts away. "I want you now, right now," she said and threw her head back. As she did so she gripped him, feeling his ribs under her palms, and rotated her pelvis shamelessly against his groin, controlling his penis to such a degree that she flipped the head against her cervix, amplifying the pleasurable sensations to the extreme.

His gaze pinned hers. "Now then, hurry." he growled raggedly, already beginning to ejaculate. "Damn you!"

She gripped his rigid sex with her interior muscles and began sliding back and forth toward his shoulders, faster and faster, with an almost rough, brutal vengeance until she climaxed, her scream echoing in the sumptuous candlelit room. He cried out from the pleasurable pain and eagerly thrust his pelvis to meet her desperate movements until his back arched, his eyes shut and he gushed into her.

Alana's body was aglow with sensual heat when she released Hunter's wrists from their silk bindings and fell into his strong embrace.

Lying in a cocoon of pillow and satin sheets, he shook his head and smiled. He tightened his arms around her. He said, "Next time, darling, you will suffer the torments of the damned before I allow you release."

She snuggled more deeply into the crook of his arm. "I look forward to it."

Chapter Three

Four hours, and a cold shower later, James Kulick was still as eager and edgy as a tomcat on the prowl. And, if that was not enough to put him in a foul mood, his hand still hurt like hell from when he had punched the wall.

He pressed his fingers to tired eyes. Alana's way of life with her constant parade of lovers had always irritated him, but until now, he had never had to see it so…up close and personal. He could, of course, just tell her how he felt. And he'd be wasting his breath. He wondered how much more it would take to make her stop. Now eyeing the fresh set of scraped and bruised knuckles, he swore. Alana Manley was going to drive him over the proverbial edge.

Kulick shook his head. He was relieved Alana's assistant had arrived at work on time this morning, and that keeping an eye on Alana was now her responsibility for a while. He was a bundle of raw nerves; he needed a break. After glancing at his wristwatch, he turned and stepped out of the bathroom.

Drying his wet head with a towel, he went into the living room. Past the kitchen, and down the hall he found Kaki's bedroom. He knew she had picked this one before he saw the suitcase on the floor. He'd smelled her, as a predator does his prey.

Maybe it wouldn't be so bad working with her after all.

The door was not shut, so he pushed it all the way open and plowed in to wake her—at least that had been his intention. Instead, he froze just on the other side of the doorjamb.

As stunned as if he had been hit with a two-fisted punch, he scanned the enticing buffet of femininity laid out before him on top of crisp white sheets. There was hardly any resemblance to the woman he had seen just a few hours ago. This woman was one of slender, voluptuous grace; he was awed by the unexpected and sumptuous display.

A spiking surge of lust ripped through his senses. A droplet of sweat slid down his temple and his still semi-aroused member shot as hard as a woodpecker's lips. He touched the throbbing ache at his groin. He wanted her. All of her.

Just as instantly, he realized what he had been thinking was crazy. He told himself that he would have been able to set his thoughts aside if…if Kaki York had not been lying on her stomach with only a short slip of a gown to hide her curves, which also happened to leave her long slender legs completely bare. His mouth tightened.

James stood for a long time and watched her sleeping in the mellow light of early morning, struck suddenly by the reality of her beauty, noting her soft, metered breathing; that her right cheek rested on the white cased pillow her arms were tucked beneath. She was an arresting sight with her red-gold waves starkly flowing in casual disarray on her pale shoulders and her shapely little rearend in clear view.

Weary and frustrated, he groaned inwardly and then shook it off, forcibly took back control of his wandering mind. He smiled a little—just a quirk at the corner of his mouth. His careful steps muffled by heavy carpet, he approached the bed and stopped at the edge.

Taking one end of the damp towel in each hand, he spun it tight, and took aim. When he let it fly, snapping the terrycloth in a "crack the whip" fashion at just the right moment, the homemade weapon hit right on target.

"Bull's-eye."

Kaki shrieked in pain from the solid whack to her bottom and sprang to her feet with amazing speed for a person who had been deeply asleep just seconds ago. But having already witnessed just how fast she could react, James was not too surprised. Still, he was shocked that she had cocked her automatic weapon and aimed at his head in the same amount of time.

She must have been sleeping with the damn thing. Okay, so he was impressed—a little.

Under the circumstances he dropped the offending weapon at once and raised both hands high in the air in mock surrender.

"All right, I'm sorry. Now you can put the gun down." He stared directly down the cold steel barrel of her nine-millimeter.

Kaki murmured something he could not quite make out before she eased the hammer back in place, flipped on the safety, and lowered the weapon. Not unaware, but certainly unconcerned that James was a man of considerable size, she advanced on him with determination. When she reached the object of her wrath, she stood on tiptoe so that she could look him directly in the eye.

Then she jabbed a finger in the middle of his wide chest.

"Ow!" He feigned injury.

She poked him in the chest again—harder—and he gave her an I-can't-believe-you-did-that-look.

"Let me tell you one damn thing, you giant flaming jackass. . . If you so much as even think of doing that to me ever again, I swear to God that I will shoot you dead without a second thought."

James almost laughed but thought better of it, then his gaze shifted from her face and slowly drifted to her heaving milky-white cleavage. When he saw a red flush spread up her slender neck and flame on her high-boned cheeks, he lifted a brow. "You, blushing?"

She said nothing. Slowly she breathed deeply, as if trying to gain some semblance of composure, but her gaze remained steady. He liked that—a whole lot. Because, for some reason, he was positive only a privileged few had ever seen Kaki York flustered.

He raised a hand and fingered his chin thoughtfully for a moment. "Well, I have to say that you don't exactly look like a natural born killer, sweetheart."

Despite her state of undress, her gaze stayed cool and level. "Neither did Lizzy Borden," she said. "So don't push your luck, big guy."

He laughed this time and shot her a look that said he was not all that intimidated by her threat. Folding his arms, he ran an appreciative gaze over her compact figure that was barely hidden by the thin layer of silk.

She sighed. Men were so predictable.

Kaki held up her hand like a stop sign. As an ex-naval officer with five years' experience as a member of an otherwise all-male special forces' unit, she had learned to recognize the signs, confront the problem before it got out of control, so all involved could return to the business at hand.

"Wait, don't tell me," she said with an absent wave of her hand. "The wet hair—the towel. I've got it. You've just had a cold shower and it didn't work. You're still hot and bothered from viewing Ms. Manley's Sexual Olympics. And—" she crossed her arms and tapped a finger on her lips "you want to go to bed with me."

James stepped forward and slipped his arms around her. "That about sums it up."

She had to tilt her head back to meet his dark gaze. "You don't even like me and yet you want to screw me."

He shrugged and flicked a finger down her hair. "One has nothing to do with the other. I want you, Kaki, and I want you bad. Now, why don't you admit that you want me, too."

Her eyes narrowed as she stared at him. "With you?" Kaki snorted. "In your dreams, Kulick."

She broke free, turned, and shoved splayed fingers through her tumbledown hair. Irritation scored deep between her finely shaped brows as she placed her weapon on the nightstand.

With resolve, she went over to the chair, yanked on her robe, nearly cutting off her breathing in belting the sash too tight, and watched James advance. She glared at him. An attractive man in a rugged sort of way, she thought objectively. Nicely built, and definitely not unappealing, even if he was a bit rough around the edges. A pity he was such a horse's ass.

"Sorry, James. I am not interested. Besides, we have work to do. I'm taking a shower. When I'm finished we can go over every inch of Ms. Manley's apartment for security leaks. I'm sure there are only about a million and one." Kaki's voice was flat as she turned and headed toward the bathroom.

But he was not giving up that easily. He was hard with lust.

He followed her across the room and took her in his arms again. "Alana won't be out of bed until way past noon. Believe me, I know. And Jenna's with her now. We have plenty of time to finish what we started."

"We haven't started anything, James." She slapped his hands and shoved his arms away. "I have no intention of having anything to do with you sexually. All I have to do is work with you."

She only sighed when he placed a hand on her shoulder, preventing her from putting any distance between them.

"Come on, Kaki, you didn't wear a nightie like that to bed for no reason. You knew I would be turned on after watching that little scene in Alana's bedroom. And seeing you like this makes me hotter," he lowered his head and murmured against her ear. "

His warm breath sent a shiver down her spine, and she could feel him stiff and rigid against her bottom, which caused a passionate fluttering deep in her stomach. Appalled at her reaction to the feel of his body against hers, her mood took a decided turn for the worse. Now, she was no longer mildly irritated—she was pissed.

Keeping her back to him, she said, "I did not wear this gown in the hopes that a longshoreman wanna-be would feel me up while I was asleep."

Anger glinted in her voice, and…something else that she did not care to identify. But the quick elbow to his ribs had him coughing up a breath and allowed her to break free. She tossed her hair back and walked over to the nightstand to retrieve her weapon. Without hesitation she turned to face him, took steady aim, and calmly pulled back the hammer.

She took a step closer. "Keep it up, and the question of whether or not I will continue to work with you and not mention this unfortunate incident to Master Lee will be the least of your worries. I will shoot your dick off."

"For God's sake, Kaki, calm down."

"Funny, that's exactly what I was going to suggest to you."

James set his massive shoulders. "Fine."

Saying nothing, Kaki watched him lean against the chest of drawers and cross his arms over the wide expanse of his chest. She hadn't expected him to give up that easily, but she was so relieved that she didn't think to question his motives. Lowering the revolver she sat heavily on the edge of the bed.

James Kulick. A dangerous man for her to be alone with, she thought. She hadn't simply felt anger when he had snapped her rearend with a wet towel and then taken her in his arms. She hadn't felt anything she could remotely describe as simple. And then, when he had pressed the hard length of his erection to her, what she'd experienced was nothing short of a primal soul-searing arousal.

What in the world was the matter with her? This kind of thing did not happen to her. Gut-deep, red-hot arousal for a man she hardly knew and was positive she didn't like? This was insane, she told herself. The entire situation was insane—that was the problem—and her involvement with these people had only just begun.

Suddenly, she had the distinct feeling that if she didn't get the hell-out-of-Dodge, and fast, she'd be sucked into this…this…decadent world of sexual debauchery in which Alana Manley obviously reigned as queen—with all the mesmerizing force that Alice was drawn through the looking glass by the White Rabbit.

With a groan she fell back on the mattress and covered her eyes with a forearm. When she removed it two seconds later to see if James had left the room, he was just pushing off the dresser. And his state of arousal was undeniably evident. She would have had to be blind not to see his erection, hard and straining against his denim jeans.

She could have gotten up, used her gun—used any one of the defensive, or offensive moves that were as much second nature to her as breathing. Even if she was feeling a small surge of curiosity, even of lust, she could ignore it. She'd done it before. But as she watched him approach her with fascination, she didn't want to fight the clouding of her senses. But why?

Kaki had no idea.

"Why don't we start over?" James drawled.

Blood pounded hotly in her temples. She didn't answer, but she didn't say no either. That surprised them both.

If she had, he might have stopped. Maybe. Maybe...she didn't want him to.

His gaze drifted from her face to her breasts. One glance like that from him, and her insides began to melt. She could feel the sudden rise of her chest as she began breathing just a bit more quickly. Damn him! she thought. Why didn't he just go away? Her nipples hardened against her negligée. His gaze on her like a caress while the cool silk clung to her body. Her face hardened.

Wearing this gown had been a mistake. A big mistake. Huge.

She immediately jackknifed into a sitting position and he came to stand in front of her. Though her gaze was focused on something other than his face, she could feel him gazing down at her. Assessingly. Lasciviously. She tilted her head back to look into his eyes. He was just kneeling.

"Enjoy the view?" she taunted him, desperately trying not to let him see how his nearness affected her.

There was a tawny glint in his deep brown eyes and dimples appeared in his tanned cheeks. "Love the view," he said in a new and almost silky voice. Then took the gun out of her hand and set it aside.

She did not protest; she was more concerned with the feel of blood rushing to her face. Why was her body doing this to her?

James gave her no time to think. He reached out and cupped the back of Kaki's neck in his hand, drawing her face close to his. She gasped at the surge of heat that rushed through her traitorous body, touching parts of her she had forgotten existed.

He pulled her to him, brushed his lips over hers in a slow, sensuous way, and what was left of her control vanished. She responded almost immediately by lifting her cheek to his. He kissed her again, slowly and surely. When he eased her back on the bed and stretched his long length out beside her, Kaki began breathing hard and fast.

A tremulous silence hung between them. James was pressing against her. He caught her confused, frightened glance and held it.

"J-James, no…stop…let me up—"

"Don't talk."

She tried to get up. Ignoring her wishes, he caught her shoulders, pushed her down on the bed and slipped the thin straps of silk from her shoulders, exposing her, and kissing the soft pink skin of her breast. She half-closed her eyes and her head lulled to one side. He touched a nipple and it came erect and hard; he pinched it, rolled it between his fingers. Her lips parted and a sigh escaped, her breath came unevenly, her body trembled with lust under his touch. He cupped her other breast in his hand and squeezed. Her stomach jolted.

It was as if her body had an existence—needs all its own and she had no control over how she responded. Reason no longer existed. She could only focus on wanting him, needing him, feeling the long hard length of him inside her.

"I want you," he said plainly, as if there was ever a doubt in her mind.

"I-I shouldn't. We—"

"But you do—and we will," he said.

He bent his head and kissed her breasts, kneaded her nipples, took them into his mouth. He sucked gently at first, and then with forceful pleasure until they swelled into distended rigid jewels…until, she could stand it no longer and arched her back like a cat in heat.

"Don't you?" he asked as his mouth trailed over her breasts, then her stomach. He slipped his hand between her thighs and lightly skimmed her moist opening with his knuckles.

Kaki cried out, her back arched. Her legs fell open, but when she lifted her hips in an unconscious attempt to increase the pleasurable pressure with his hand, he removed it. She groaned and her hips jerked at the loss.

"Don't you?" he asked again, with more force this time. She squeezed his arm.

"Say it," he demanded.

When she still didn't respond quickly enough, he snaked a hand slowly up the sensitive skin of her inner thigh until he reached the apex of her need. She bit her lip in anticipation of the pleasure of his touch, breathing in the scent of her own arousal. It didn't come. His fingers barely brushed the soft, damp curls around and above her intimate flesh.

Her green eyes opened wide and she forced herself not to squirm. "Why are you doing this?".

"If you want me, say so," he demanded in a husky tone.

"I want you. I can't bear it any longer."

He probed at her entry, cupped her, making tiny caressing circles with the callused pad of a finger over her erect clitoris. A mist of perspiration broke out on her brow. He took his hand away. A tremor rocked her slender frame. Her lips parted in a gasp. She peered at him intently, her emerald eyes ablaze with unfulfilled passion.

"Where do you want me?" He grazed a hard jutting nipple with his teeth. She moaned; he bit down and sucked. Fire surged through her.

"Inside me," she gasped.

Only then did he release the hard pink tip abruptly and lick it, once. "No, not yet," he said.

Her clitoris throbbed in protest, her vagina contracted. Then, she felt his hands moving down to her waist, her hips, removing her gown altogether. In seconds, she lay completely naked on the bed, the air cool around her. She smelled the sandalwood from his heated body and her nudity was suddenly exciting to her under his gaze. He rose to his knees and placed a pillow under the small of her back so that her breast and belly and thighs formed a smooth slanting line.

"Stay," he murmured in a deep low voice. She did, and an undisguised desire met his eyes.

He stood up, turned his shirt over his head with one hand and tossed it on the floor. His sable gaze caressed hers, promising to fulfill her every dream as he removed his socks and boots, ripped open his jeans, stripped them and his briefs down to his feet. She rose up, braced herself on her elbows, and through the haze of her growing excitement she gazed at his dark handsomeness, his brooding, moody eyes, that held her captive.

Straightening before her, James was uncaring of his nudity and her gaze was inexorably drawn to his rampant erection. His engorged penis stood proud and taut, the ridged head broad and swollen, reaching almost waist high. She had never wanted anything so badly in her life. Her vagina shot heat upward and a rush of liquid heat skimmed downward through her inner walls that opened. She swallowed, opened her mouth to speak, shut it again.

"Do you want me?"

She didn't answer, but he waited, stroking the softness of her inner thighs. Moments later she breathed, "Yes." She had to have him now. Passion and a hot-blooded need overrode her doubts, nothing mattered but putting out the fire he had ignited in her very soul.

Gently grasping his erection, he ran a practiced hand down its length. "You are sure you want me," he said placing his legs on the inside of hers. She thought she would die. When he gently pushed her thighs farther apart, she lifted her hips, tentatively seeking relief from the burning desire.

He didn't come to her; he arched a dark eyebrow in question.

"Yes, I want you," she whispered, then his fingers touched her heated entrance and dipped softly into her lush wetness, aching and swollen for him. She gasped, shivered, her skin rising up in goosebumps.

His lips curled into a seductive smile. "You are so hot," he said softly, stroking gently, sliding his expert fingers inside her.

She gasped, her head fell back. In a second he was on top of her, his impossible hardness resting smooth and hot against the wet mouth of her sex, with a hand braced on either side of her head. Her fingers wound their way into his thick hair. She moaned, her hips rose. His mouth came down on hers roughly, his tongue powerful in its onslaught. She devoured the taste of him.

"I can't wait," he said in a husky rasp as he reached down and eased her apart with expert fingers. Her breath caught in her throat. "Are you ready for me?"

"Umm," she breathed, her lips quivering softly.

He gave her a crooked, rueful smile. Spreading her legs wide with his knees, he fitted the tip of his penis to her. With control he slipped in and out, moved the swollen head of his erection over her hard slippery crest, teasing her repeatedly until she too whimpered and moaned, rotating her hips, lifting them, trying to draw him deep inside her.

Her body was so near orgasm it was rigid under his, and he could no longer control himself. He thrust solidly into her, as deeply as he could possibly go. She cried out at the tight heat that flared all the way to the pit of her stomach; her arms twined around his strong solid neck desperately and pulled him tightly to her. He penetrated her in an increasingly deepening rhythm until she became feverish beneath him, thrusting her hips up to meet each new, driving invasion of her body. Clinging to him, she cried out his name and he moaned. Her fingers tangled in his hair, he drove in deeper and deeper still, sending her spiraling along the waves of passion.

Whimpering breathlessly she clung to him; she was hot around him and he was shuddering on the brink. Her panting cries of release sent him over the edge. His back arched and the powerful rhythm of his lower body plunged into her, out of control, until he felt hot desire pumped uncontrollably down the length of his engorged shaft. His hands harshly gripped her hips like a man possessed and he lifted her, pulled her hard into his last violent penetrating thrust. Holding her with firm hands, his chest heaved and his body shook as he ground himself against her until the madness finally ceased.

Sapped of every last ounce of strength, he collapsed on her, gulping in air as she did the same beneath him.

As soon as Kaki drifted back from the idyllic depths of pleasure, the enormity of her acquiescence hit her. What had she done? She was a trained professional in the middle of an assignment and she had totally forgotten about the client she was supposed to be guarding…And just to indulge herself in a wild bout of mindless, lustful sex! Good God, she had lost her mind.

When she stirred beneath him, James lifted his head and trailed a finger down her throat. "You're stunning. Absolutely stunning. Do you know that?"

She grabbed his hand to keep from losing her mind again. "Get off me!" Her voice was harsh with self-disgust.

James' eyes glinted when they met hers. "What?"

She gave him a razor-sharp glance. "Get off me!"

When he didn't move, she grabbed his thumb and bent it back until he did.

"Dammit all to hell, Kaki!" he said, shooting to his feet and checking to make certain his thumb wasn't broken.

When James whirled, the raw fury in his face was staggering, but she didn't see it. She was halfway to the bathroom. "Come back here!"

She didn't.

He swore and went after her. But just as he caught up with her, she slammed the door in his face and locked it. "The next time I see you, Kulick, it had better be in Alana Manley's suite!"

"Fine!" he shot back at the pain-in-the-butt behind the closed door.

"You'll want it again, Kaki York," James muttered to himself as he snatched up his clothes and moved quickly out of the room. "Sex with me is like country music—you try not to listen, but you just can't help yourself."

Chapter Four

Kaki had to admit that she did not feel any better after her quick shower. This was clearly the beginning of a very bad day. She glanced at her watch. It read 8:30. Thirty-minutes until she was to meet Tommy Lee in Alana Manley's suite. With a sigh she finished dressing in a loosely fitting banana-yellow silk shirt and her favorite pair of Guess jeans. After tying her hair back into a ponytail, she pulled on her high-top sneakers.

She was deep in thought when several hard knocks on the door broke the silence. With a loud groan she went to answer it. Expecting to see James Kulick, she snatched the door open with considerable force. The young man she faced instead, started.

"Sorry," Kaki said and gave him an apologetic smile. "I thought you were someone else."

He shoved a manila envelope at her. "Ah. . . sorry to disturb you, Ms. York, b-but this is for you."

Before Kaki could thank the messenger, he was gone. With a shrug, she closed the door and made her way across the room to sit at the table. Examining the outside of the large envelope she saw it was from Tommy Lee, which she thought odd considering she would see him in just a few minutes. She shoved aside the light breakfast she had ordered from room service and opened the envelope. Dumping the contents out on the table, she read the note first.

Dear Kaki,

I am sorry, but I have been called out of town on urgent business. Ms. Manley is expecting you, so do not worry. You can handle this assignment without me.

James is a stubborn man, but he can be a great help to you. He is not just a chauffeur; he is also a very good bodyguard when he has to be. Not as good as you, of course. But then I didn't train him. Do not underestimate his abilities, Kaki. He spent ten years in the Marines as an explosive expert and he handles a gun with expertise. Let James cover your back; he is a good man. I have already spoken with him and he has agreed to help.

Enclosed are the threatening letters Alana has received. I had them dusted for prints, of course. Nothing. Go over them and see what you can come up with. I will be in touch.

Lee

P.S. Keep a close eye on Alana. She is not taking these threats nearly as seriously as she should.

"Damn." Kaki's voice was flat as she stared out the window.

Tommy Lee knew she preferred to work alone. Why, she wondered, did he insist she needed James' help? Well, there was no way to ask Lee. So she might as well just accept that she had a partner.

Kaki leaned back in the chair with an expansive sigh.

Now she had to spend a whole lot of time with James Kulick. And she would have to share information with him. And she had the distinct feeling she would have to fight him off every five minutes.

She shook her head. Smart move—having sex with him, she told herself. And she knew it was not just anger she felt because of that. There was a lot more emotion mixed up with the anger.

But she was not going to think about him now. No, she would think about him later.

Alana Manley would have slept until noon, if the ringing telephone had not jarred her to consciousness. Still, she lay in bed for a moment, unwilling to surrender the comforting darkness, fighting the fact that she had to answer the phone.

She groaned in protest. Mornings were always a bad time for her because she rarely went to bed until several hours past midnight. But this morning, she had had even less sleep than usual. Because it had been close to dawn before Hunter Morgan left her bed—almost five o'clock.

The ringing persisted. Alana reluctantly pushed her sleep-mask up onto her forehead with one hand, while she groped blindly to pick up the telephone's receiver with the other. Only because she had to. If she didn't, it would just keep on ringing.

"Hello."

Heavy breathing.

Anger shot her upright. "Who is this?"

"Whenever I see you touching someone else, my headaches begin. I don't like headaches," said the rather cryptic and oddly asexual voice on the other end of the line.

Alana's stomach lurched and she shot to a sitting position. "Who is this?"

Icy laughter. Click.

The caller I.D. displayed 'unknown'. A chill ran down her spine. She braced herself.

Obscene caller.

Yes, the statement was one that could have frightened anyone and her name had not been used. It was just some pervert dialing random numbers.

Suddenly she wished Hunter Morgan had not gone to Los Angeles for a business meeting this afternoon. Quickly she slammed the receiver back into its cradle and unconsciously wiped the palm of her hand on the bed sheets as if she had touched something dirty. She drew a deep, steadying breath to chase away her nervousness. After all, this wasn't the first obscene call she'd ever received. There was no reason to be afraid.

It was only when she stood that her legs buckled and she had to sit on the bed to recover.

Kaki knocked on Alana Manley's door at precisely 9:00 a.m., and if it had not been for her nervousness about meeting the movie star for the first time, and seeing James Kulick again, she would have paid closer attention to the telephone repairman who stood waiting, a little too patiently, for the elevator.

Jenna Tucker opened the door and let Kaki in with apparent reluctance. Then when she'd introduced herself, Jenna said, "I know who you are."

Kaki ignored her and instinctively looked at the doorjamb, studying the lock's strike plate. As she examined the brass plate in the door, she found that the jamb was set improperly. With a sigh, she thought one swift kick or shoulder roll to the door and she could break right through. The penthouse suite might be the priciest, but she could already tell that the security here was cheap.

"Something I can help you find?" Jenna asked, eyeing her with a frown.

Kaki's face was blank. "No, thanks. But would you please tell Ms. Manley that I would like to see her?"

The younger woman looked at her as if she had lost her mind. "At this hour?"

"Yes," Kaki said without hesitation.

Jenna shook her head. "If you'll wait here, Ms. York, I will see if Ms. Manley is awake."

"Thank you."

Taking a seat on the nearest chair, she wondered where James was—she'd thought he would be here when she arrived. She was glad he wasn't. She was unsettled enough without having to deal with him, too.

Five minutes later, Alana Manley walked into the room and Kaki stood.

Alana wore a deep red silk kimono. The rich, vibrant chestnut waves that fell in disarray about her cameo face and continued well past her shoulders, shimmered under the morning sunlight that shone through the floor-to-ceiling windows. Obviously she had just gotten out of bed. And Kaki thought she had never seen a lovelier woman. Much more attractive than she appeared on screen. Even her toes, the nails expertly manicured and painted a British red, were pretty as they peeked out from under the floor-length swish of material as she walked. Deep sable eyes dominated her thin, fine-boned face.

Kaki shook her head. Nobody had pretty toes.

Yes, Alana Manley did. No wonder, she thought, that the men came looking for her.

Then Alana smiled, and Kaki saw warmth and friendliness, and she gave a small sigh of relief.

"Thank you for coming," she said softly. "I'm Alana Manley."

"Kaki York."

Alana nodded. "I'm glad you agreed to take the position as my personal bodyguard."

Kaki looked at her in surprise. "May I ask why?"

Alana laughed as she crossed the room and took a seat on the sofa. She motioned for Kaki to do the same. "Because I have seen you in action and I was impressed. That's why."

Stunned disbelief spread over her face as she sat next to Alana. "Me? When?"

Alana didn't answer at first because Jenna came into the room and poured coffee for them both.

"Thank you," Kaki said, taking the dainty china cup.

Jenna inclined her head and left.

Alana cradled her own cup in her hands. "Mr. Lee is very proud of you. Did you know that?"

Kaki nodded, the telltale flush of embarrassment heating her cheeks. "Sometimes more than he should be."

"I have seen what you can do, remember?"

Kaki nodded again. "But where? I can't imagine."

Alana took a sip of her coffee, then lifted her gaze to meet Kaki's. "My father and Mr. Lee served together during the Korean War. Though my father was a Marine, and Lee, a Special Forces instructor in the South Korean Army, they were assigned to a joint unit and became close friends. When my father died, Mr. Lee kept in touch. He somehow felt it was his duty." She paused then to place her cup on the coffee table in front of them. After tucking her legs beneath her and adjusting the red kimono, she clasped her long-fingered hands in her lap. "Anyway...when I started receiving these crank phone calls I contacted him and asked his advice. He knew I'd already hired James and that he was my bodyguard/driver so to speak; that he was very capable. Still, Mr. Lee did not feel James alone was sufficient protection for me under the circumstances and strongly suggested that I hire you. He also sent me your resume, along with a tape of your win at the 1995 National Taekwondo Championships. And, as I said before, I was impressed. With everything." She smiled then. "Someday, Kaki, you must tell me about being the only female member of the Navy Seals. It must have been delicious having those hard-bodied and dangerous men all to yourself."

Kaki discreetly rolled her eyes. After what she had seen last night, she was sure Alana Manley would have thought so. She cleared her throat and took another sip of coffee. "I have to admit, Ms. Manley, I never thought of my expertise in quite that light before."

"That's too bad," Alana said in a tsk-tsk fashion. "Obviously you need someone who can teach you to appreciate the joys in life. And I am just the one to do it, too." She smiled devilishly. "And please, call me Alana. For heaven's sake, we are going to spend nearly every waking moment together until this...this person is caught. We certainly can't stand on formalities the entire time."

"Yes, ma'am. I mean, no, ma'am," she said, flustered.

Alana shook her head emphatically and took Kaki's hand in hers. "No, ma'ams—no, Ms. Manleys—just Alana, okay?

Kaki smiled. "Then Alana it is."

"Good!" She stood then. "If you'll excuse me now I will go and get cleaned up."

Just as she turned to leave, Kaki said, "Ms...ah, Alana." she corrected quickly. "If you don't mind, I need to check the apartment for security leaks."

Alana smiled over her shoulder. "Do whatever you like, my dear. As of right now, you are in charge."

With that, she exited the room as gracefully as she had entered.

Kaki immediately got to work. She checked the locks, then the windows and door alarm. Within thirty minutes she knew that she would have to build an entire new security system.

Three hours later, James Kulick sat slumped on the couch in Alana's penthouse suite drinking a cup of coffee. He watched with aggravation as Alana and Kaki talked out on the balcony behind closed French doors.

"What the devil do you think they are talking about?" he asked Jenna as she made her way past him with a light lunch of salad, cheese and wine in her hands.

"How should I know?" she shot back over her shoulder.

James grumbled in response, snatched up the remote and flipped on the local television station.

"And now the national news," the commentator announced just before a picture flashed on the screen, and he almost dropped his coffee cup on the floor.

Without shifting his gaze from the television screen, he shot off the couch and went to the French doors. He rapped hard on a glass pane with his knuckles. "Kaki, Alana, get in here!"

The door opened and the two women came inside. "What the devil is wrong with you?" Alana demanded.

James still did not shift his gaze and pointed to the TV.

Alana immediately sat in the nearest chair before she fell down. "Oh my God!" Alana exclaimed, clamping a hand over her mouth.

"What is it? What's the matter?" Kaki asked, placing a hand on her shoulder.

When Alana did not answer, Kaki's confused gaze shifted to James. He shook his head.

Alana listened intently, not saying a word, her tawny-colored eyes widening with horror as the details unfolded. A successful male model had been found dead in his New York City apartment early that morning. Murdered. Shot in the head. Execution style. With a dead cat left lying on his chest.

A twenty-six-year-old man who had appeared on the covers of hundreds of romance novels. A man simply known as Damian. And now he was dead.

Chapter Five

The phone rang and James answered it. When the short conversation was over, he turned and faced the women.

"Lt. Ballard is waiting for me downstairs in the lobby. I'm going to meet him. Alana, you and Kaki, don't unlock this door. Not for anyone. I'll let myself back in."

Alana and Kaki agreed as James pulled the door to, locking it securely behind him.

When James reached the lobby, he quickly assessed the man standing before him. The lieutenant was a powerful man with a sun-darkened complexion and the hulking presence of someone not to be argued with. He appeared to be in his middle to late thirties, with striking blue eyes and a handsome face with sharp features and a full day's stubble adding to his roughish air. His blonde hair was buzzed short in a no-nonsense style. The man looked as if he would be at home on a Harley, riding at the speed of light, with a Lucky Strike dangling from between his even white teeth.

"What can I do for you?" The lieutenant sat down and tipped back in a chair, nonchalantly surveying the room.

James was not to be fooled. He knew the lieutenant well. "As I said on the phone, I'd like to look at the file on this Damian fellow." Lt. Ballard didn't respond right away, but reached for a crumbled pack of cigarettes resting in his shirt pocket. He took one in his teeth and lit it with a scarred Zippo lighter that had seen its better days. Finally, he said, "What does Damian have to do with this case of yours?"

Now James became irritated. "Do you know that Ms. Manley was one of Damian's lovers, that she has received several threatening letters over the last few months and phone calls, and found a dead cat in her limo."

"A dead cat?" the lieutenant said with a straight face.

James couldn't decide if Lt. Ballard was toying with him or not. His brother had a way of annoying him with practically no effort at all.

"Yes, a dead cat," James shot back. "You have to take this seriously J.T. Someone is terrorizing Alana Manley and we need to know what kind of danger she could be in so that we know how to go about protecting her."

"Who is with her now?" J.T. asked.

Kaki, her bodyguard."

J.T. swallowed. "Kaki?"

"Did I stutter? Kaki is a woman who has a blackbelt and comes highly recommended. Alana is safe for now, but if you don't get off your butt and hand over the Damian files, that might not be for long."

After deliberating a moment, Lt. Ballard pulled a cell phone from his back pocket. When he spoke, James realized he had called the station.

"Could you please bring me the files on the murder investigation of that model, Damian? I'll be waiting at Alana Manley's penthouse in the lobby."

When J.T. ended the conversation, James focused on his brother. "Brother or not, I'd better not hear any of this leaked to the press or I'll have your butt for obstruction of justice, you hear me?"

"I think you have it backward, J.T. We're not trying to interfere with your investigation, but bring justice to whoever committed this murder, while protecting other potential victims. That's all."

"Okay, fine."

At that moment, a uniformed police officer entered the hotel lobby and hurried over to the two men, handing some folders to the lieutenant.

"Thank you." J.T. dismissed the young officer with a nod.

As the man left, J.T. handed the folders to James with a final admonishment, "Be careful."

James nodded. "I will."

Within twenty minutes James and Kaki settled down in the rented suite they used for twenty-four hour surveillance of Alana with the files Lt. Ballard had provided. For the next hour they reviewed them, along with penciled summations of telephone calls, the autopsy report, and photos taken at the crime scene.

They went over the files first. Ballard hadn't been kidding when he'd said Damian was a lady-killer. From the notes it was apparent that his affairs had been extensive. One particularly lengthy memo about an interview conducted with a near swooning and current lover named Bitsy Maxwell, caught Kaki's attention. Though married, Bitsy claimed to have been involved with Damian for the past two years. She also was convinced that he had recently become romantically involved with a "certain unnamed Hollywood Hussy," and only because she wouldn't leave her husband for him, but there was nothing much beyond that.

James was the one to shove reports about a second and third homicide under her nose.

"What the hell?" Kaki asked, scanning the papers.

"The Telex is from the Fort Lauderdale Police Department," he said. "It's about a homicide that took place exactly seven days before Damian Scott's. This guy was also killed at about the same hour of the night." He paused to point to the other. "From the Chicago Police Department about a homicide on the south-side that took place over a month ago—"

"All three have the same MO," Kaki said. "Shot in the head at point-blank range with a 120 grain nine-millimeter bullet, but I still don't understand where the dead cat that Alana found in the limo fits in with all this."

James clasped his fingers behind his head. "Probably just someone trying to throw the investigation off track."

"We'll soon find out. For now, I'm off to bed," Kaki said, trying to yawn and stretch at the same time."

With that, she headed for the door. James stood and followed her. They both stopped in the hall and said goodnight before going into their rooms.

Muffled sounds coming from Alana's suite awakened Kaki. Jumping from the bed, she snatched her jeans from the floor and pulled them on under her T-shirt. Taking her 9mm from the nightstand, she checked the load, tucked the revolver in the back of her jeans and headed for the door.

When Kaki burst into Alana's suite, she started screaming uncontrollably. Just then something was slipped around her neck.

Instantly, she knew it was a piece of rope that was gripped in the man's hands and he was tightening it around her neck.

Her throat burned. Her lungs ached. Darkness stole over her.

Chapter Six

The stranglehold jerked even more firmly around Kaki's throat. Reaching for the gun in the back of her waistband she fought the darkness. She lost her grip and the 9mm fell and hit the floor. Along with it, a good amount of hope. Dammit!

She struggled to get her fingers under the rope, but it was already cutting deeply into her flesh. The assailant twisted it harder.

Kaki knew that she only had seconds to get away before she lapsed into unconsciousness. She lifted her knee and kicked backward with all her strength, but she missed. Her assailant having evaded the blow twisted the rope still tighter.

She tried to cry out, but no sound escaped her throat. Hell, she couldn't even draw a breath. Her face burned like fire, and her eyes felt as if they were popping out of her head.

Desperate, Kaki jammed her elbow into her attacker's stomach. The move caught her attacker offguard and he stumbled for a second, which caused him to loosen his grip on the rope.

That was all Kaki needed. Spinning, she brought up her right knee hard and caught the man between the legs. With a scream, the attacker staggered forward and lunged for the door. Kaki fell to the floor just as the elevator across the hall lurched into motion again. Frantically, she groped for her gun. She had a much better chance if she got to her gun. But she was weak from the attack, and too slow. When the elevator halted and the doors flew open, the attacker shot out into the hallway.

With a sudden burst of strength, Kaki sprang to her feet, and tackled the man. The man threw her off and she staggered backward, her head throbbing from the impact. She looked up in time to see the man pull a gun from inside his jacket. She leapt forward and hit his wrist with a knife-hand strike. The gun popped out of the man's hand before he could fire a shot, and spiraled across the floor. Either she was seeing things or his entire hairline shifted several inches to the right.

At the noise, James ran into the hallway and toward her. Kaki shook her head to clear it. He stopped dead in his tracks as he spotted her gasping for breath.

"You, okay?" He narrowed his eyes, lifted her chin with his forefinger and assessed the damage to her neck.

She nodded the affirmative.

"Hurry, he's getting away," she managed to shout painfully, louder this time.

Kaki rested for a millisecond, drawing a deep breath as she bent with hands on her knees.

"Let's go get the sonofabitch." She gingerly tested the ligature marks with her hand.

James grabbed her elbow and steered her down the hall towards the front door. They exploded onto the sidewalk at full speed. They would have to double-time it to catch up.

They had traveled several yards when James stumbled. He swooped down and lifted something off the pavement and shoved it into Kaki's hand.

She glanced at the object, it was light in color and hairy, and she flipped it over. A wig!

The hunted assailant came into view through the bobbing shoulders of the cops up ahead. A long ponytail danced across his back, bouncing up and down with each step.

James and Kaki gained quickly on him. They rushed past like a hurricane, the perpetrator only a few feet away.

"Stop," James screamed as he reached out desperately and nabbed the flying hem of the baggy jacket between thumb and forefinger. He quickly worked a handful of fabric into his palm, jerking back hard as he dug in his heels, coming to a sudden stop.

The suspect lost his footing and hit the pavement hard. He jumped up immediately and turned on them in a fury.

"Jenna," Kaki whispered, eyes wide in stunned disbelief.

James took Jenna out with one punch.

Epilogue

Kaki leaned back in the rattan chaise and slipped on her shades. James sat, legs outstretched, ankles crossed, in the chair next to her, zinc oxide white on his nose. She suspected that behind his dark sunglasses he was intently surveying the scene. One that included dozens of topless women.

St. Tropez, not a bad place to resume her vacation. Alana had insisted on sending them on the trip after they apprehended Jenna, possibly saving the actress' life.

She shook her head. "James, I still can't believe Jenna was the one. I would have never guessed in a million years that she was a lesbian. Much less an obsessive psychopath."

He stretched and yawned, "Kaki, we have been over this at least a thousand times. Her apartment was practically wallpapered with Alana's image. The diaries spelled it all out. She had been in love with Alana since the first time she laid eyes on her. Over time she just got sicker and sicker, acting on more and more of her twisted fantasies."

"My money would have been on Hunter Morgan," Kaki observed. "That is one twisted bastard."

"Yes, twisted," James turned to face her, "but not twisted, obsessed, psychotic bastard."

Kaki picked up the Pina Colada from the table adjacent to her chair and took a long drink, "I hope Alana won't be too upset with us for declining her offer to stay on as her permanent security team."

He shook his head. "I'm sure Hunter Morgan will protect her quite well until she hires another bodyguard. Besides, I'm looking forward to exploring Savannah. The South and Southern Belles have always fascinated me." He shot Kaki a wicked grin. "I am just dying to eat a Georgia Peach."

Kaki tried to smother a chuckle and failed. "What if I told you that I know where you could find one right here in San Tropez?"

James lifted an eyebrow. "I'd say show me."

"Just walk this way…"

About the Authors:

Although Betsy Morgan and Susan Paul both live in South Georgia, less than ninety-miles apart, they met for the first time at the Romantic Times Convention in Fort Worth, Texas. Kathryn Falk, Lady Barrow, introduced Susan, a multi-published author, and Besty, an aspiring one. She suggested that they keep in touch. As they did just that, Susan and Betsy decided it would be fun to collaborate on a story.

__The Bodyguard__, Susan's second story for __Secrets__ (__Savage Garden__ appears in __Secrets Vol. 2__), and Betsy's first, is the result. Was it fate that the infamous Lady Barrow intervened?

Who knows?

Susan and Betsy certainly think so!

The Love Slave

by Emma Holly

To My Reader:

To me, good erotica is like a glass of wine with dinner, slightly decadent, darkly exciting and—who knows—if it gets my pulse pounding, it might lower my cholesterol! A good romance, however, is dinner. I've gotta have it, no ifs, ands, or buts.

When I saw my first *Secrets* collection, my writer's imagination was sparked. Romance and erotica entwined in a single story? What a yummy idea. I knew I had to try my hand at it. I hope you enjoy my attempt in *The Love Slave*, and I hope you come back for more!

In the days before Empire, the country of Srucia was a collection of loosely affiliated city-states. Chief among these was Ammam. Nations far and wide sent tribute to the Lady of Ammam, whose formidable army had held the scourge of Southland at bay for four generations. Despite local rivalries and the ever present threat of invasion, this was a time of peace. The old ways flourished, especially the tradition of the love guard.

Chapter One

Princess Lily tied the scarlet ribbon beneath her breasts. She was seventeen today. Though her gown blazed the white of maidens, the ribbon declared to all her approaching womanhood. Today she would select her love guard, the trio of slaves who would protect her person and teach her the mastery of men. Thus prepared, in one short year she would choose her official consort.

Not a moment too soon, according to her mother. To Lily's dismay, Lady Fortis liked to call her the Royal Doormat. In front of people.

It was fortunate she could not see her daughter dressing herself. Lily had let her maids leave early for the fair. Her toilette was simple and they were good maids; they never slacked or grumbled and Lyn did have an eye for one of the jugglers. But perhaps this was exactly the sort of thing a doormat would do. She *was* running late, though even her mother could not have predicted that her hem would rip and have to be mended.

Lily bit her lip. Who was she trying to fool? She even looked soft. She hadn't her mother's height, or her spectacular bosom. She supposed she was pretty. Her hair was chestnut brown and hung past the curve of her bottom. Her eyes shone as green as the Indje in flood, and last week the miller's son had assured her that the roses on the chapel were not softer than her lips.

Her mother thought she was sleeping with the miller's son, cutting her teeth on him, as she put it. She would be angry to discover she was not. Lily was saving herself. Nurse had raised her charge on stories of her own homeland, where the king ruled above the queen and women preserved their virginity for their husbands, or at least for their One True Love.

This sounded romantic to Lily, even heroic, considering how strongly the pleasures of the flesh could call to a healthy girl. Fortunately, only a year remained until she married. Unlike her mother, she intended to wed a man she could love, a man too gentle to require mastering. He would also be a powerful prince, of course, one whose alliance would benefit Ammam's people.

Bolstered by her daydream, she leaned out the window of her tower. In honor of her birthday, white and gold pennants had been strung between the six corners of the castle. Though times were peaceful, soldiers patrolled the rose-granite ramparts. *Strength is peace,* Lady Fortis said, and she made sure her men stayed keen. Their armor was polished, their shields bright. Fully a third wore Ka'arkish chainmail, which was neither iron nor steel, but some substance known only to the dour Northern metalsmiths. The mail, which was twice as strong and much lighter than plated steel, was invariably a trophy of war. The Ka'arkastanians would part with but limited quantities and were unmoved by threats or charm, both of which her mother had employed.

As if aware of her attention, one soldier waved from the nearest tower. Lily couldn't remember ever seeing a soldier wave at her mother. Lady Fortis paid them well, deeded land to her officers and sent a sack of gold to any soldier who married a local girl, but she did not encourage familiarity. Lily wished she could fault her mother's iron manner, but the evidence was against her. Ammam's knights fought more fiercely than any except the Yskutians, and everyone knew they were a race of sorcerers who could not fairly be compared.

With a small and all too familiar sigh, she craned her head in the other direction.

She found distraction in plenty there. Stands had been erected in the courtyard so that the townsfolk and nobles could watch their princess select her love guard. The candidates hailed from every corner of the continent. It was considered an honor to serve the Lady of Ammam, the greatest Lady yet, many said. Though Lady Fortis had fought no major battles, she had wrought more changes through treaties and building projects than the last three ladies combined.

Lily despaired of matching her. Who feared Ammam's princess? Who respected her, for that matter? Soldiers waved at her. Maids felt free to run off and play, and never mind she'd told them they could. She shouldn't have told them. On this of all days, she should have been strict!

Oh, cease your puling, she thought, with a disgusted shake of her head.

No one makes you a doormat but you. If you dislike it so much, do something about it.

"I will," she said to the empty chamber. "I will learn to rule and my people will respect me. What's more, I will begin today." The words were almost firm by the time she reached the end of her declaration. Still, she jumped when she heard a rattle at the door.

"There you are," said Nurse, huffing and puffing from her climb up the tower stairs.

Lily beamed. Nurse was a small, round woman. Lily adored her more than anyone in the world except for her mother's lover, the wise and quiet Vizier. The one time she'd defied her mother was for Nurse's sake. Lady Fortis had wished to dismiss her, saying that the woman was encouraging her romantical ways. Lily had to admit she had a point.

Now Nurse looked about the chamber, no doubt searching for a maid to scold. "What have you been doing, child? The scryer has been waiting on you this last hour."

"Oh!" Lily covered her mouth with both hands.

"Oh, indeed," said Nurse, though not unkindly. "Must you be late for everything?"

It seemed worse than pointless to explain about the fair and the juggler and the unexpectedly torn hem. She hung her head. "I'm sorry. I'll try to do better."

"Pshaw," said Nurse. "You know better than to apologize to the likes of me."

Lily released a silent sigh. It seemed changing would be harder than saying the words.

The scryer waited in the shadows on the courtyard's east side. She wore a long grey gown with a cowl. The Jewel of the Third Eye, a coin-sized opal from deep in the southern desert, glimmered above the bridge of her nose. Lily stiffened. The scryer intimidated her as much as Lady Fortis, despite being young and kind. She had been trained by the Yskutians and shared their otherworldly air. Lily feared she would peer into her soul and read her un-princesslike thoughts.

Now the scryer placed long, slim hands on her shoulders. "Just follow my lead, Princess. I'll tell you what I wish you to do. There's no need to be nervous."

Lily tried to heed her but she'd never seen such a crowd at the castle. Thousands thronged the walled courtyard, all waiting for a glimpse of their heir. In a way, this would be her first act of rulership. If she chose unwisely…

"Hush," said the scryer. "Follow your heart. Then all will be well. Although—" She paused. Was it Lily's imagination or did the woman's eyes twinkle? "I would not advise choosing a slave who will not rise to your hand."

Lily nodded. She did not, however, have the faintest idea what the scryer meant.

Lady Fortis opened the festivities by thanking her neighbors for sending the flower of their manhood into Ammam's service. One by one, the representatives of each country filed up the steps and set an offering at her feet. The offering was not grudged. Many love guards went on to hold high posts after their year of service. Vizier himself had been her mother's slave and none save the Lady wielded more power. His native country was guaranteed fair hearing on any issue.

Lily listened to the speeches with half an ear. I will choose the biggest, meanest slaves I can find, she vowed, and I will master them. They will tremble at my air of command. Her face twisted with a grimace. More likely they'd die laughing. Perhaps she'd be better off with a few medium-sized, moderately mean slaves. Surely mastering those would be challenge enough. Squirming in her demi-throne, she gazed around the courtyard in search of likely candidates.

Six gilded cages had been erected on the lawn, each holding a score of slaves. Clearly the cages were more symbol than reality. Any of the young men could have squeezed between the bars, had they chosen to do so. Lily eyed them. They were not the peasants she'd expected. Though clad in kalisaris, the plain white skirts of quarry workers, the sheen of their skin and hair proclaimed them the sons of good homes. It was impossible to tell which ones might be mean, or even moderately mean. To a man, they stood calmly.

She wondered if she could have borne the prospect of slavery so well.

Finally, the flowery speeches ended. The scryer glided up the dais, bowed to her mother and handed Lily a small golden key.

"Come, Princess," she said in a melodious, carrying tone. "Come choose your guard."

Lily followed her graceful figure across the springy coastal grass. She hoped she didn't look as awkward as she felt. This was what came of being late! If she'd met the scryer ahead of time, she'd have been instructed on what was to come.

When they reached the first cage, the scryer directed her to unlock the door, then called a candidate to the entrance. He looked as nervous as Lily felt. She ventured a reassuring smile.

"Hast thou lain with a woman?" asked the scryer.

Lily's eyes widened at the question, but the candidate did not flinch.

"I have not," he said in a voice that barely shook.

"Lift your skirt," ordered the scryer.

The candidate did so. Lily tried not to choke. He was naked beneath the clean white linen. His sex dangled, thick and pink, between strong, hairy thighs.

"Cup him from beneath," said the scryer.

A subtle nudge broke Lily's paralysis. Her mother would be horrified to discover she had never handled a man's naked organ. Hesitantly, she curled her fingers beneath the swaying shaft. It was smooth, like silk.

"The sac as well," corrected the scryer.

As gently as she could, she gathered the joggling bundle and lifted it toward the scryer's view. A sound broke in the candidate's throat. Within her hand his cool, soft flesh began to swell. The candidate flushed, but it seemed he could not curb his body's reaction. When his organ had risen beyond the horizontal, the scryer positioned her hand above it and gazed into the man's eyes. After a moment's silence, she said, "This candidate speaks true. He is worthy of service."

Then she called the next young man to the door. Goodness, Lily thought, anticipation and alarm shivering in unison down her spine. Surely they couldn't mean for her to touch them all?

But they did. She had not imagined such a variety of organs existed. Some were long, some short, some wide, some thin. Some sported fetching cowls which slipped back as their owners' shafts lengthened in her palm. Others were as bare of adornment as a monk's shaven pate. She saw penises as pink as the inside of a shell and as red as a maple in autumn. She saw penises that jerked like hunting dogs and others that rose as gently as a curtain blown by a breeze.

Her skin grew warm and cold by turns. They were lovely, all of them, and so magically responsive. A heavy pulse settled between her legs. Oh, that this entertainment ever had to end!

Only two of the candidates were pronounced "impure" by the scryer, and only one failed to rise in her hand. With so few eliminated, she did not know how she would choose. She could not tell one man from another, having spent precious little time gazing in their faces.

Then, at the fourth cage, one of the candidates set himself apart. He was a comely youth, lean and strong and as fair as any girl. His light brown hair hung to his shoulders in waves. When he stepped to the door, he clutched a handful of daisies over his heart.

"Princess," he said in the deep tones of a man grown.

Lily fought a smile. What a naughty puppy. With a low bow, he held out the humble bouquet, which he'd obviously plucked from the lawn surrounding his cage. She glanced at the scryer, who nodded that she might accept the gift. She, too, seemed to be fighting amusement.

"Hast thou lain—" she began her ritual interrogative.

One of the candidates erupted from the back of the cage.

"Cheeky bastard!" he shouted, and took a flying leap at the first candidate's back.

Lily shrieked and dropped the flowers as the men tumbled onto the lawn and began to scuffle. Stop it, she thought, unconsciously wringing her hands. Oh, please stop it. Then she saw the blood. With that, her fear left her. She grabbed Daisy-boy by the scruff of the neck.

"That's enough," she said in a tone of such ringing authority she barely recognized it.

Daisy-boy was not as impressed as he should have been. Still full of fight, he swung his fist towards her face. The spectators moaned. At the very last second, he checked the blow. Immediately, he fell to his knees. "My lady." He pressed fervent kisses to the hem of her gown. "Queen of my heart. Princess of princesses. Please forgive me. I was overcome by passion."

"Bastard," muttered his attacker, who sat on the grass nursing a bloody nose.

Lily looked at him. His hair was as red as his temper, but his looks rivaled his foe's. Where Daisy-boy's face was clever, however, this man's was painfully honest.

"These two," she said, the words leaving her mouth almost before they'd reached her brain. "I choose these two."

"Very good," said the scryer. "With luck they will fight as valiantly for you as they do against each other."

"They had better," she declared, and impressed herself by administering a playful cuff to Daisy-boy's ear. The crowd roared with laughter. Their approval rushed to her head like wine, but she couldn't afford to lose her wits now. One slave remained to choose.

She found him in the last cage. Even supposing the last two failed to impress her mother, this one surely would. He stood apart, his arms crossed over a powerful chest. He was taller than the others and broader, not a youth verging on manhood but a man in truth. A smoky cross of hair marked his torso. He had the warm, bronzed skin of Ka'arkastan and the slanted eyes of Yskut. A half-breed. Brute strength paired with age-old sophistication.

She shivered, half in fear and half in interest. Did she truly dare choose this slave?

His eyes, as black as his shaggy hair, narrowed when the scryer beckoned him forward. Such a terrible stare, so full of anger. I couldn't, she thought. But then something strange happened. His dark eyes bored into hers, and a hot stab of feeling pierced her heart. *You,* said a voice in her mind, all joy and trembling. *It's you.* His glare intensified. She didn't care. She felt as if she had stumbled across a friend she'd been missing for years and had never hoped to see again. It was almost like one of Nurse's stories where the lover comes back from the dead.

Nonsense, she thought. This glowering fellow was no object of romance. Her nerves must have unbalanced her mind.

"Hast thou lain with a woman?" the scryer asked in her lovely, gentle voice.

Hope tightened the back of Lily's neck. Or was it dread? He couldn't be a virgin, not this towering man with the shadow of a beard and the hot, knowing eyes.

But "Yes," he growled in a voice like rusty iron. He did not sound happy about it.

"Lift your skirt," said the scryer.

Lily bit her lip. Slowly, sullenly, he lifted his brief white wrap. His sex was as big as the rest of him. The shaft hung heavy and thick over the curve of his scrotum. He had one of those cowls that had fascinated her on the other men. She longed to see it slide back over his arousal. No longer shy, she reached out to cup him.

Nothing happened. He did not warm, or twitch, or swell. The only sign
that he knew she touched him was the ticking of a tiny muscle in his jaw.
She suspected he was doing it on purpose. Perhaps he knew some arcane
Yskutian trick for controlling his body. Enough, she thought. She might
not be masterful, but she had learned a thing or two about the male anatomy
today. In this, at least, she would rule. She moved her hand up his heavy
shaft. She felt a quickened pulse, a flicker of movement beneath the smooth
outer skin. She stroked him again.

"Do not do this," he said through gritted teeth. Beads of sweat glistened on his forehead. "This is not my will."

She hesitated. What did he mean? Had he been kidnapped into servi-
tude? If that were true, he should have shouted it to the skies. He would
have been released at once. Perhaps he was reluctant to serve, but that
would make mastering him all the sweeter. Do it, she ordered herself. Don't
be a coward.

She stepped closer and let him feel her quickened breath, and let her
hardened nipples brush his chest. Yes, that was the secret; the evidence of
her arousal woke his own. His manhood stirred in her hand. Encouraged,
she petted the beast until it rose, until it throbbed to each gentle stroke as
to the lash of a whip. Now that he'd come to heel, his sex was harder than
any she'd held before. As red as her own red lips, it curved upward like the
strut of a longbow. A tear of moisture appeared on its naked tip. Lily swept
it away with her thumb, then gasped at the melting-smooth skin his cowl
had revealed. His thighs trembled with strain.

"You had better stop, Princess," he growled. "Unless you want everyone in those stands to see your slave spill his seed."

He said the word as if she truly were a slavemaster, as if she were
going to chain him to an oar and work him into an early grave. But his
scorn did not matter. What mattered was that he had said it. *Your slave.
Yours.* The victory was heady.

"I choose him," she said, releasing the man so abruptly he staggered
back a step.

"Very well," said the scryer. "The choosing is complete."

The candidate's huff of disgust could be clearly heard by all.

Chapter Two

He was every bit as surly as she'd expected, though not as disobedient. He stood quietly behind her chair with the other slaves during the banquet, an interminable affair of speeches and course after course of heavy food. Torches lined the hall, flickering over tapestry and stone. Lily had a table to herself. She wished she dared offer the men some of the food she wasn't eating and the wine she wasn't drinking, but her mother watched her like a hawk. Probably Lily ought to be doing something she wasn't, something masterful, but she honestly couldn't think what.

Of her three slaves, only Daisy-boy was cheerful enough to speak. Ian was his name. He and the redhead had reached a truce. She didn't pretend to understand it, but she'd seen men behave this way before, as if the spilling of blood cemented friendship. The redhead, called Col, was trying to pretend his broken nose didn't pain him. The court physician had taped it but Col refused the crushed ice Lily had obtained for him. Beneath the tape, his nose was swelling like a plum. Finally, the sight grew too much for her.

"Slave," she said. "I— I order you to apply this ice."

Col's spine snapped straight in surprise. 'As you please, Mistress.'

There, she thought, handing him the bowl. That wasn't hard. She'd ordered him to do something he didn't want to do and he'd done it. Her glow of triumph so warmed her she was able to ignore her mother's baleful glare, and the fact that the brooding Ka'arkish hulk was staring stonily into the distance and had missed this demonstration of her power.

Ian said his name was Grae. He was two months younger than her pretty boys, just shy of nineteen. Lily didn't believe it, but Grae confirmed Ian's claim with a curt nod.

"But you look so much older," she said.

She could only imagine what he read into that. His chest rose and fell and his gaze heated. He was staring at her breasts. Lily clutched the jeweled stem of her wine cup, abruptly aware that her nipples were tingling. The effect unnerved her, but she forced herself not to flinch. When Grae looked away, his face was hard.

"I worked with my father," he said.

She eyed his muscular arms. "Was he a blacksmith?" The beast pretended not to hear.

She knew she should force him to answer but her father appeared then, a silent shadow at the end of the hall. He rarely attended public functions, preferring to remain closeted with his books. Lily should have been flattered, but her throat tightened with dread. He glided down the central aisle, oblivious to the whispers. He was tall and straight and wore garments as black as his beard. Eyes turned towards him as he approached the high table. As always, his spirit seemed deeply withdrawn. Only his eyes, the same olive green as Lily's, glittered with secret life.

He climbed the dais where Lady Fortis, his wife, sat shoulder to shoulder with her beloved Vizier. He bent and kissed her cheek, then continued his measured journey to Lily's side. He put his hand on her shoulder. His fingers were heavy and cold. She looked up at him, into the grave, handsome face that seemed to know neither bitterness nor joy.

"Felicitations on your birthday," he said in his husky, seldom used voice.

He left as silently as he had come.

Ian murmured something humorous, but Lily didn't hear it, didn't hear anything until they returned to her tower and Nurse revealed that all her maids had been dismissed.

"These laddies will do for you now," she said with a laughing glance at the slaves. "Dressing and bathing and building up the fire. Two will share your bed each night and one will guard the door."

"Share my bed?" Lily repeated, unable to hide her shock.

"Aye, Princess," Nurse confirmed. "But there'll be no funny business unless you wish it. Their virginity is yours. They cannot give it to you nor any other without your permission."

Grae had been examining each of her six arrow slits. At Nurse's words he snorted, probably his version of a laugh.

"You," Lily said, as imperiously as she could. He turned to face her, arms behind his back, stance wide, like a soldier awaiting orders. Sensing mockery in the pose, she decided then and there that he would not sleep in her bed this night. "You will stand guard."

He smiled, not a nice smile, though his teeth were white and straight. "As you wish, Princess. But it might be more efficient to break the night into watches. Even I need to sleep."

"Watch your tone," Col warned, his fists clenching at his hips. "She is our mistress now."

Lily expected another fight, but Grae inclined his head and took a symbolic step back.

"Forgive me," he said, but it seemed to Lily he apologized to Col rather than to her.

Lily bathed herself behind the painted screen. She knew she would have to overcome her shyness at some point, but tonight she was reluctant to allow the men such intimate access to her person. To make up for the lapse, she ordered Col of the broken nose to brush her hair dry before the fire. That was pleasant, though Grae kept up a constant mutter about the poor security arrangements in the tower.

"You have my permission to see to it," she finally said. "Just leave off your nattering."

He opened his mouth to protest her choice of words, then shut it and strode off to stand watch in the entryway.

"I need a weapon," he barked a minute later. "My belongings are still shipboard."

With Ian's help, Lily tugged open the heavy door to the arms closet. She grabbed the first sword and dagger that met her eye. They were also the finest: Ka'arkish steel with elaborate Laravian hilts. Grae tested the hair-splitting edge on his thumb and grunted.

"These were expensive," he said. It sounded like a complaint.

"So were you," she responded, which silenced him nicely. Her mother would be proud. Lily felt as if she were growing more authoritative by the minute.

When he turned away, however, the sight of his back made her breath catch. He'd been whipped. The firelight turned the faint net of scars to silver threads, too many to count. The marks were old; he must have received them as a youth. But who would whip a child until no unmarred skin remained? Her eyes burned, pity and fury mixing in her breast. Her hand crept out.

The heat shadow must have warned him. He went rigid before her fingers met skin. He said nothing but she knew. He did not want her to see this. He did not want her pity.

The dilemma baffled her. Was showing pity weak, or was obeying his unspoken demand? At a loss, she withdrew just as Ian called her.

"Come, Princess," he said.

Ian, apparently, required little direction. He had pulled back the green brocade hangings of her bed. He had turned down the pink silk sheets and set a carafe of cool water on the side table. Less confident than his partner, Col stood on the opposite side blinking nervously.

Oh, well, she thought. Might as well get it over with. Holding her nightgown out of the way, she climbed the two mahogany steps that abutted the footboard. The frame had been carved to resemble a grape arbor, complete with vines and fruit and delicate birds. All her life this bed had been her sanctuary, witness to her dreams and tears, the imaginary boat for a thousand imaginary journeys. How changed it seemed tonight, how fraught with foreign dangers.

Ian steadied her as she crawled to the pillows. She lay down on her back. Col pulled the covers up to her chest. Then they both climbed in on either side of her. Under the sheets.

Lily ordered herself not to protest. The night was cool and they wore naught but their linen skirts. She simply wished the bed were wider. Two pairs of hairy legs warmed her through her gown. Two broad shoulders. Two sets of inhaling and exhaling lungs. With a grimace, she closed her eyes and pretended to sleep.

For many minutes all was silent. Then, as if a hidden signal had been passed, two long bodies turned to hers and two long arms draped themselves across her belly. Col nuzzled the curve of her neck like a babe, his poor nose hotter than the rest of his face.

Her sex pulsed at the seeking gesture. Were they asleep? Did they think she was?

Col snuggled closer, his leg shifting restlessly against her side. The sheets rustled. Something warm prodded her hip. After the day she'd spent, she could not fail to recognize the throbbing shape. He was aroused. His leg moved again, crossing hers, and the shape flattened against her side.

He rolled his hips forward once, twice, then moaned low in his throat.

"You, too?" Ian whispered.

"God, yes," Col said. "I don't think I can bear it. She's so soft and she smells so nice. And I'm so hard it feels like it's about to fall off."

Ian adjusted his head on the pillow. "You know what the slave trainers said. Your pleasure is hers to dictate. You can't even take yourself in hand except she give you leave."

Col moaned and squirmed again. "I don't need to take myself in hand. If I lie here and smell her for a few more minutes, it'll spill all by itself." Lily felt his toes curl where they were wedged between her feet. "Do you know how long it's been since I came? Six weeks counting the ship's journey. People our age weren't meant to be celibate this long."

Ian laughed but he, too, sounded pained. He reached across her to pat Col's arm.

"It was worth it, Col. We were chosen, both of us. Our families will be proud."

"Our families don't have red hot pokers stabbing them between the legs."

Lily couldn't help it. She snuffled out a laugh.

"Princess!" Ian exclaimed.

"It's all right." She flattened her hand across her chest to calm the laugh. "I was awake."

Col groaned, mortified. She turned and hugged him, which made him groan the louder.

She smoothed her hand down his hard, perspiring chest. "Let me give you ease."

He practically tore the kalisari out of her way.

"Ah," he sighed as she explored his stiffened length. "Ah, yes, Mistress. Softly, softly. Your little fingers are so—"

Her fingers wandered over his swollen sac, stifling whatever he'd meant to say. Lily cocked her head. "You feel different from before. Plumper."

"His balls have drawn up," Ian said, pressing tightly to her back. He'd pulled up his skirt. His hardness was a pulsing rod that pressed and released against the cotton-clad crease of her buttocks. His voice grew huskier. "It means he's about to spill."

Heat swept Lily's body. She wanted to feel him spill. She wanted to make him do it.

She tightened her hand around the thickened shaft. She pulled upwards, then pushed back towards Col's belly. Twice she did this, slowly, reveling in his growing heat, in the tightness of his sexual skin, in his harsh, panting breaths.

"Oh, no," Col moaned. He cursed then and shuddered. A hot burst of moisture jetted against her gown. He shook and grunted with each climactic spasm. He had not quite finished when Ian clutched her hips, cried out and dampened her gown as well.

"Ah," both men sighed, and sagged bonelessly against her.

Happy to have pleased them, she stroked Col's thick red locks.

"Princess," Ian muttered.

Col began to snore.

Her mouth fell open in disbelief. She understood they were tired, but what about her? No doubt her mother would have cuffed the bounders awake. Of course, her mother wouldn't have offered to please them in the first place. Once again, she had done everything wrong. She sighed and squirmed onto her back. One night's frustration wouldn't kill her.

But Grae had his own opinion on the matter.

"Out!" he ordered, grabbing each man by the foot and yanking him down the mattress.

"Wha—" Col said, fighting for balance.

Taking advantage of his confusion, Grae grabbed his arm and pulled him fully out. "Neither of you knows how to treat a lady. Therefore, you will take the first watch."

"It's not their fault," Lily protested. "I didn't ask—"

"You shouldn't have to ask," he roared.

She couldn't suppress a squeak at the volume of his voice. Ian squeezed her shoulder. "He's right, Princess. Col and I behaved abominably and we will do as he says."

But *I'm* supposed to be training you, she wanted to say.

Before she could, Col and Ian disappeared to take up their post in the entryway. Grae remained. He glared at her from the foot of the bed as if she were responsible for putting him in this position. But if he regretted his decision to interfere, that was his concern. She would not sit here trembling like a rabbit at his disapproval.

"Well," she said in as steady a voice as she could muster. "Why don't you show me how a lady should be treated?"

Grae's face tightened, but she knew he wouldn't back down. With a long warrior's breath he grabbed the flint from her bedside table. Though moonlight poured through the room's narrow windows, he lit the brass lanterns that hung from the posts of her bed. When each was burning merrily, he climbed inside and pulled the hangings shut. Immediately she felt as if she were breathing steam instead of air. He was so big, so unyielding and intense. Anticipation shivered through her limbs. What would he do to her?

"Your gown is wet," he said. "Give it to me."

She could not think of a good reason to disobey. Her hands shook as she wriggled the cambric up her legs and pulled it over her head. She held it out to him, crumpled in her hand. He did not take it: he was too caught up in staring at her naked breasts and belly. The silk sheet still covered her lap but he stared at that, too, as if his eyes could burn through the slippery cloth.

To her relief, he was not unmoved by what he saw. His quarry man's skirt stood out as if he'd lodged a club beneath it. Now she must take control, she thought, before she lost the chance.

"Grae," she said. He flinched at the sound of his name. "Grae, take off your skirt."

"Later," he growled.

"Now," she insisted.

Their eyes clashed. His hands moved. In a swift, angry motion, he discarded the kalisari. His sex was beautiful, red and strong. A single blue vein twisted from the deep slash of his navel, through his gleaming black thatch and down his shaft to the big, heart-shaped glans. Fluid glistened on the ruddy tip. She licked her lips.

"Don't," he said, though she hadn't moved. "Don't make me forget what I'm here to do."

"What are you here to do?"

"This," he said, and swooped down on her.

He kissed her temple, her cheek, the tip of her nose, the line of her jaw. The blows were soft and warm, hungry, but fleeting. With a low growl, he nipped the skin of her neck between his teeth, and then finally, finally settled his body and took her mouth. Their tongues met at once, wet and sweet and wonderfully curious. It was a deep kiss, but soft. She'd never been kissed like this before. She felt as if he were opening her entire being through the sinuous seduction of her mouth.

She moaned with pleasure, and tried to kick free of the sheets. As impatient as she, he lifted and stripped them down. Again he stared. She was naked, bare to his gaze. Gently, ever so gently, he ruffled the mink-brown curls between her thighs. The tender gesture brought the sting of tears to her eyes. As it had in the courtyard, a shadow of recognition fluttered across her awareness. Her soul seemed to know this man. She tugged at his arms, wanting him against her.

To her dismay, he sat back on his heels. "I can't," he said, his black eyes shuttered. "Not my skin to yours. I couldn't bear it."

"You can't," she repeated.

"Unless you're offering to let me take you. Completely." His expression gave nothing away. Not slyness. Not longing. Lily wished her own face were as blank but she knew he could see every flicker of hurt, of anger and frustration. She pressed the back of her wrist over her mouth to keep her groan inside.

"Hush," he said, and then his hands were on her: long, delicious strokes that swept her from breast to thigh. "Hush. I'll take care of you."

She wanted to resist but she melted at his touch. He bent closer. His lips captured her nipple, tugging and licking. He kissed a wet trail to her second breast, then down the inside of one arm and onto her belly. He licked her navel and her anger dissolved in a giggle. She felt his answering smile against her skin and thought he might be human after all. Gently, he grasped her thighs in his big, hard hands. She tensed at the pressure.

"Don't worry," he said. "I've done this before. Just not the rest."

"The rest?" she said, though she knew. She knew.

"I've never been inside a woman. Not my cock inside her cunt."

The words sent a shudder through her sex. Moisture overflowed her, warm and creamy.

"Oh, that rest," she said, pretending he hadn't devastated her with those hard, male words.

He smiled and looked up from her belly. His eyes seemed to slant even more in the lamplight. His brows were wings of coal, sardonic, mysterious. "Yes, that rest. How do you think I earned those pretty stripes you were admiring?"

The answer was no clearer than before, but the sudden descent of his mouth erased the question from her mind. In seconds, he'd wrung an anguished cry from her throat. Never had she felt anything so lovely as his tongue moving on her sex.

"Tell me." He paused and applied a different motion. "Did you like that better? Or this?"

She could not answer. Everything he did sent thrills through her secret flesh. He slid two fingers into the first inch of her sheath. She moaned so loudly she heard Col mutter in alarm from across the room.

Grae chuckled. "Like something inside your pretty snatch, do you?"

"Yes," she said. "Yes. Just don't stop. Please don't stop."

She shouldn't have said 'please' but it was too late to take it back. Still chuckling, Grae took her in his mouth again. A heavenly tension coiled inside her.

"Oh," she cried. "Oh, yes."

He pushed her legs wider and worked his shoulders under them. His breath warmed her. His tongue lashed her. His fingers beat a soft tattoo just inside her gate. Her sheath tugged at the intrusion. Her hands tangled in his rough, night-black hair. She was so close.

"Mmn," he hummed into the tiny kernel of her pleasure.

She broke with a low, quavering cry, shattering into a thousand shards of wet sensation, sweet as chocolate, sharp as wine. Like chocolate they melted. Like wine they sang. Her body arched and went limp. Tenderly he kissed her. One last kiss beyond any need for kissing. A chink in his brutal Ka'arkish armor.

An answering tenderness welled up inside her, too powerful to resist. "Grae," she whispered. She sat up to knead the stiff muscles of his neck.

For a moment, he relaxed into the caress, but only a moment. Her face burned with embarrassment as he eased her back and straightened the covers. He blew out the lanterns. But he could not leave. He had ordered the others away and now he must stay. In silence, he stretched out beside her, on top of the covers, with his back to her breast. She heard his heel strike the footboard. The bed was not quite long enough for him. The rhythm of his breathing filled the curtained space. It told her he did not sleep. It told her his need for release had not abated.

She touched his naked hip. He stiffened.

"Hush," she said, and kissed his shoulder. She rubbed a circle around his hip. Her hand crept over his side and into the velvety hollow of his groin. He quivered like a shying horse. His skin felt different from hers, more substantial, but smooth. She reached the edge of his pubic thatch. The heat of his arousal pulsed over her fingers. She combed through the crisp, curly hair.

A callused hand slammed over her wrist. "No," he said.

"But I want to help you. You need it."

"I need it too much, Princess. If you touch me now, I won't stop until we fuck. So unless you want to give up that precious virginity of yours..."

"You wouldn't dare."

"I wouldn't have to dare. I'd make you beg."

She wanted to deny it but she couldn't get the words out. She wriggled her hand free of his grip. "Perhaps," she said in a tone too shaky to impress, "I would make *you* beg."

His laugh was humorless. "When hell freezes over. I may be a slave but I have my pride."

"But how can my pleasuring you injure it?"

He thumped the pillow and resettled himself. "I have my reasons."

"I order you to tell me what they are," she said and this time the words didn't shake at all.

"Order me to mop the floor, Princess. My soul is my own."

"Perhaps I should call the others. They were grateful for my favors."

If she hoped to make him jealous, she failed. "The others don't have what you want."

"You don't know what I want."

"Don't I?" He turned and licked slowly up the side of her face. "You want a strong man you can break, Princess. A man whose spine will make a nice, satisfying crack."

"That is not what I want!" Actually, this was precisely why she had chosen him but he had no right to think so. Certainly not to say so. "Oh, turn around and go to sleep," she snapped.

"As you wish," he said, but so mockingly the victory was hollow.

Chapter Three

He refused to let her pleasure him.

Lily did not understand. Her pretty boys reveled in pleasure. Every night they taught her marvelous things. How to make a man shiver from a single touch. How each man liked to be stroked differently, yet in some ways were the same. She learned to listen for the hitch in the breath, for the moan or whimper that signaled their deepest pleasures. She also learned what pleasured her. The men had taken Grae's scolding to heart. She no longer had to ask, though sometimes she did. *Kiss me here,* she would say and they would quiver with excitement as each competed to fulfill her request. The more daring her demand the better they liked it.

Grae was different. If she made demands of him, he gave her what she asked twice over. He was not satisfied unless he left her weak with pleasure. But he never let her turn the tables.

"I do not understand him," she confessed to Ian one night as they lay in a sweaty tangle, half way to dreamland. "Where is the harm in taking release from my hand? Why does he insist that he will only come inside me?"

Ian stroked her hair. "When a man makes love to a woman they are lost in the madness together. But when a woman makes a man come, by himself, he is utterly in her power, and at his moment of greatest vulnerability. I believe Grae is too proud to put himself in this position."

"If that is true, why are you not too proud?"

"I," said Ian, "am not an idiot."

His explanation obsessed her even as Grae's resistance did. But to force him was not the victory she craved. She must do what he threatened to do to her. She must make him beg.

She ordered him to clothe her each morning, from shift to gown to slipper. He would rise from the task so desirous his hands would shake.

Then she would clothe him. The kalisaris she reserved for her private enjoyment, jealous of the pleasure her slave's bare bodies might give the ladies of the court. For public wear, she ordered fine uniforms from the seamstresses, baby-soft velvet and silk, a caress for them to carry through the day. The cloth was gold and white; her colors for her men.

She loved sliding the hose up Grae's long legs. The muscles of his calves cried to be held in the curve of her palm. The tender skin behind his knee was ticklish, and his thighs were admirably hard. The current fashion in tunics was short, mid-thigh, with a long leather belt to cinch them at the waist. Grae's waist was narrow. She would wrap the leather thrice, then smooth the ends over his bulging groin. He winced every time she did it.

Sometimes she would slip her hand beneath the hem and give his sex a squeeze.

"It would take but a moment," she would say. "A few quick strokes? Perhaps a kiss?"

The answer was always the same. "Only if you are offering yourself to me."

That she would not do. Her virginity belonged to another, to her One True Love.

When Ian and Col shared her bed, she made certain the curtains were open, made certain Grae could hear everything they did.

Alas, when they left to take their watch, he would come to her bed and make a mockery of all she'd learned. The pleasure he showed her obeyed no rules. He was a fire licking over her skin, a storm at sea that made one long to drown. She could not control her response to him and still he refused to relinquish control over himself. A kiss was all the caress he would allow her.

So she kissed him. She kissed him awake in the morning while his sex lifted the sheets in hard, surging throbs. She kissed him in the vestibule at chapel. She kissed him until their lips burned from the friction, until their eyes glazed with hunger and their lungs heaved like bellows.

"Don't," he would say and she would stop. Until the next time.

"Why?" she finally asked. "Are you afraid I'll treat it as a weakness to take advantage of?"

"I know you will," he said.

His words hurt, though she could not deny them. He was only here so that she could master him. But was that so awful? Col and Ian did not suffer under her yoke. Grae would be happy, too. Her determination to prove it grew. Each kiss might be the kiss that broke him, each night *the* night. She began to long for bedtime. Col and Ian did, too. They smiled at the ringing of each evening bell, full of shared anticipation. Only Grae grew surly as the night drew on.

Fortunately, her days were full or the wait would have been intolerable. Her hours with the tutor were increased and twice a week she sat in Audience, once with her mother and once by herself. She preferred judging simple matters on her own, experiencing none of the doubts she felt in Lady Fortis's presence. Common sense unraveled most of the knots her people brought to her. When it didn't, she would set either Ian or Grae to investigate. Ian had a nose for gossip and Grae could stare the truth out of all but the most hardened criminals.

Col was simply a dear. He rubbed her neck if she sat too long at her studies. He organized her appointments and ensured she got everywhere on time. Most importantly, he saw that anyone who came to her was treated well from the moment they arrived to the moment they left. As a result, she had the most even-tempered petitioners of anyone on her mother's staff.

"I do hope you're not planning to go home when your year is up," she said to Col one day. "I don't know how I'd manage without you."

He blushed to the roots of his blazing hair. "It is my honor to serve you."

Touched, Lily took his hand and pressed a kiss to its palm. The flame of adoration that lit his sky-blue eyes embarrassed her.

It disgusted Lady Fortis. She sent Lily a small leather crop with a note. *Infatuation fades,* it said. *Respect does not.* Lily immediately threw both on the fire. To consider whipping a slave for such a reason! Far better to remain a doormat.

In any case, she doubted Col was truly besotted. She had noticed he jumped to do Ian and Grae's bidding as eagerly as her own. She suspected he needed someone to devote himself to. Unlike Ian, who made friends at every turn and Grae, who appeared to need none, Col seemed lonely. No doubt he would have given his heart to any woman who was kind to him.

Would that Grae were as easy to win!

One night she ordered him to bathe her. There was a chamber beneath the Great Hall, where a hot spring had been diverted through the castle. It was a large, echoing room, tiled in flowery blue and gold designs. It smelled of copper and eucalyptus, an earthy scent. She set Col and Ian to guard the door and handed Grae a pot of lavender soap.

"Strip," she ordered as she floated in the shallow end of the steaming bath.

He pulled off his clothes, his eyes never leaving her body. He was hard already. With a caution she suspected had nothing to do with the heat of the water, he descended the steps.

"You must stand," he said hoarsely, "if you wish me to bathe you."

She stood. The water fell to her knees. For a moment, he closed his eyes.

"You've seen me naked many times," she whispered. "Does it still move you?"

"You know it does, Princess. You have only to look at me and my body readies."

She took the pot of soap from him and set it on the marble ledge. She clasped his slender waist and looked into his hot, black eyes. His nostrils flared. His tongue touched his narrow upper lip. He wanted her kiss, she knew, wanted the one pleasure he allowed her to give.

She rose on her toes. She twined her arms behind his corded neck.

"God in heaven," he swore, and swallowed her whole.

She had never known him to be so desperate. He would not end the kiss. He would not let her go. Tighter and tighter he held her, owning her mouth with the avid penetration of his tongue. Twice he lost his breath and broke for air. Twice he clutched her more greedily than before.

Lily stroked the furrow of his spine. His scars tickled her palms and a cry of pity escaped her control. A growl rumbled in his chest. He gripped her bottom and hitched her closer, off her feet, into the angry throb of his groin. She couldn't bear it. She had to touch the part of him he'd denied her. She squirmed her hand between their bodies. She grasped the angled root.

"Don't," he said and shoved her away so hard she almost lost her footing.

"Damn you," she said, her hand on the floor of the bath to steady her. "You are my slave!"

He had just enough shame to look down at the steaming water. "Why must you torture me? I obey you in all things but this. Can you not leave me one scrap of pride?"

"How can this hurt your pride? It is your duty to obey me, as much as it is your duty to mop the floor or stoke the fire."

"I did not choose to be a slave," was all he said.

Lily slapped the surface of the water. "Tell me who forced you then.

I'll have them arrested. I'll set you free if that is what you truly desire."
There. She had thrown the gauntlet between them. His lips narrowed to a
hard white slash. He was shaking with anger.

"If you are protecting someone—"

"No," he said firmly. "No one."

"Then you must fulfill your contract. All of it."

For an instant his eyes held a plea for mercy but they hardened so
quickly she thought she must have imagined it. "I cannot," he said.

"Do you wish me to turn you over to the guards? Do you wish me to
send you home?"

His expression blackened. "Do what you think best."

She did not understand him. He behaved as if he did not want to be sent
home. Surely his freedom was worth the disgrace. As for turning him over to
the guards, he must know she would never do so. She covered her face. Some
slave mistress. No wonder her mother doubted her ability to rule. But there
were at least two men who were willing, even eager, to let her rule them.

She straightened with decision. "Col! Ian!"

Grae gaped at her. Clearly, he hadn't expected this.

"Yes, Mistress?" Ian said, his smile all sidelong charm.

"This slave feels unable to carry out his duties. You and Col may assume them."

"Our pleasure," said Ian, and promptly began to strip.

Grae watched with narrowed eyes as they soaped her body, lingering
over her breasts, her bottom, the plump cushion of pleasure between her
legs. Col washed her hair, kneading her scalp in slow, tingling circles. Her
sighs of pleasure were not feigned.

When they had rinsed her, she walked into deeper water and directed
Ian to hop onto the marble ledge. She put her hands on his knees and eased
them apart. Her head was level with his groin. The heat of the water had
softened him but now, as her breath washed his sex and her hands rubbed
his muscled thighs, he rose to full glory.

"Now," she said. "We will show this man how a slave accepts a gift
from his mistress."

Ian looked at her, his eyes wide. He had told her of this act, but she had
not done it yet. "Are you sure, Mistress?"

Lily smiled and took the very tip of him in her mouth. From the corner of her eye, she saw Grae scowl. You could have had this, she told him silently as she worked the hot, rounded flesh. These groans could have been yours, these shudders of pleasure.

"Mistress," Ian cried, a tight-throated plea for release.

She gathered his sac in one hand and rolled it. She clasped his root in the other and squeezed it. As she drew on him with her cheeks, her tongue laved the magic spot beneath the head. He had shown her this the night before, a sweet gathering of nerves that could wring an explosion from the stubbornest organ. And Ian's was not stubborn at all. His knees tightened around her ribs. His hips contracted, pushing his sex further into her mouth. He spread his fingers wide against her cheek; to feel her suckle him, to feel himself burst.

"Mmn," she hummed, just as Grae had the first time he made her come. She heard him curse and then Ian jerked in climax.

"Ah," Ian said. "Yes-s."

Afterwards, he and Col did not wait for her to ask. They carried her from the pool and lay her on a heap of thick, gold toweling. Amazingly, Ian had not flagged.

"Let me," he said, his shaft rising strong and pink. He pressed it lengthwise between the lips of her mound. "Let me love you, Princess."

He was not a slave then. He was a man asking a man's right from his lover. Lily stroked his long, wavy hair and looked into his portrait-perfect face. He was a good man, fickle perhaps, but kind. He would not hurt her. For a second she thought: It would serve Grae right. But this was not a gift to be given in spite. This was a gift for her One True Love, whoever that might be. She had waited this long. She could wait a little longer.

"No." She cupped Ian's face. "I am not prepared to take that step."

"As you wish," he said, and he and Col brought her to her peak by other means.

Lily watched Grae brush her blue velvet gown by the chamber window. She did not need to oversee the work, but she had no duties for the hour and she had noticed on occasion that his company had the power to calm the turmoil within her, even if he was the one who had caused it. She was certain she was not falling in love; that would have been ridiculous. Assuredly, she only craved his company because he was a wonderfully quiet man.

His hands were sure at the task. She could tell he had consulted her favorite maid, for he was almost as clever now as Lyn. It struck her again that he refused to do anything poorly.

Except obey her. He did not do that very well.

"You should give them leave to take one of the maids," he said as he dabbed a mysterious concoction on a spot of grease.

"Give who leave?" she asked, entranced by the movement of the tendons in his wrist.

"Col and Ian. They were required to be virgins for the choosing ceremony, but it isn't natural for boys their age to remain celibate."

"Boys their age!" She stepped between him and the window, forcing him to look at her. His face was infuriatingly calm. "They're older than you. And they've expressed no interest in 'taking the maids' as you put it."

"Well, they wouldn't express it to you, would they?"

"You think I'm vain, don't you?" She hovered humiliatingly close to tears. "You think I can't imagine them looking at another woman. But for your information, I'm not such an idiot as that. I may be passably pretty for a princess, but I know I'm not the most beautiful woman in the world or the cleverest or, to hear you tell it, the nicest."

"If you're feeling possessive, you could take their virginity yourself."

Ooh, why did he do that? Why did he say the one thing that would hurt her most when it would have been so easy to make her happy? He could not have made it clearer that he cared naught for her virginity himself. She was not used to being disliked, and yet she was not entirely sure he did dislike her. Sometimes, when he touched her in the dark, he seemed almost to cherish her, which made such comments cut all the deeper. Furious with herself, and with him, she swiped her arm across her eyes. She looked out the window. A group of squires were running a mock joust in the courtyard. They didn't have horses so they rumbled along on wheeled trolleys, trying to unseat each other.

It was far easier to picture Grae out there, rather than in here cleaning her gowns.

"I do not think you vain," he said. "And you are more than passably pretty."

She blinked and turned to him. She couldn't believe it. He'd actually given her a compliment. Two, in fact. Of course, being Grae, he spoiled it in the next breath.

"You need to remember that Col and Ian are men, not toys."

"And you need to remember they're slaves." Oh, she hated the way that sounded, even as she said it.

He shook her dress and held it up to the light, his lips pursed, his thick, black lashes shielding his eyes. "You are their mistress," he said, agreeably enough.

But she knew he didn't mean: You are their mistress. Their pleasure is yours to dictate. He meant: You are their mistress. Their happiness is your responsibility. She flushed. Fairness demanded she think on what he'd said, though heaven forbid her mother should ever hear of it.

The three of them lay sprawled across the rumpled shelter of her bed. For once, she had closed the heavy curtains. The lanterns were lit. They cast a golden glow across the green brocade. Ian's silky head lay in her lap and Col was rubbing her feet. Their kindness tore at her conscience. Tradition dictated that she disregard the feelings of a slave. Pride dictated that she do nothing which could be viewed as currying Grae's favor.

What does your heart say, she asked herself, and perdition take the rest.

She cleared her throat. Both men looked up at her and smiled. "I was wondering: would you like to take one of the maids? Assuming you know one who'd be agreeable."

The men exchanged a glance, their brows sporting identical furrows. Ian was the first to speak. "You want to watch us swive, er, make love to one of the maids?"

"Watch you?" Her hand flew to her breast. "Heavens, no! I simply thought it would make you happy to, you know, do as other men."

"Ah," Ian said. "You mean give up the dreaded burden of our virginity." He tapped her heated cheek. "No, Princess, we prefer to wait until you're ready to accept that gift yourself."

Col nodded energetically. "Yes, Princess. We'd rather give that to you."

"But what if it's a long time? What if it's never?"

Ian captured her hand and kissed her fingertips. "Nonetheless. We prefer to wait."

"Besides," Col's face reddened, "it's not as if we aren't enjoying ourselves."

Lily relaxed onto a mound of pillows. "You're right, Col. There's a lot to be said for fun."

To herself, she added: 'Tis a pity it's not enough.

Chapter Four

Lily's mother summoned her to her private office, a small chamber in the heart of the keep. So ornate was the carving on its marble arches and so bright the glow of its stained glass windows that it resembled the inside of a jewel box. Lady Fortis sat writing at her desk, her straight, wheat-colored hair trained back by a golden fillet. Though her pose was informal, she wore her robes of state. The purple velvet was so heavily embroidered with gold it crackled with her movements.

Lily stood on the thick Laravian carpet and waited for her to look up. She clasped her hands behind her back, squeezing them rhythmically to ease her nervous tension.

Finally, her mother set the quill aside and closed her ledger. Her eyes were the color of a winter sky, a pale, clear blue. Her face did not show her age. It was a pretty face. Only the stern set of her mouth hinted at the determination for which she was famed and the dissatisfaction of which she was capable. Her gaze took inventory, skimming over Lily's emerald green gown. Her lips thinned a fraction more.

"You have not taken your slaves. Nor have you disciplined them."

There was only one way she could know this. With difficulty, Lily swallowed her fury at being spied upon. "They are very well-behaved," she pointed out as calmly as she could.

"Yes, I'm sure the experience is valuable, so long as every man you meet is as eager to please as they!" Her mother leaned forward. "You must make them yours completely. You must impress upon them the awareness that you are the source of every pleasure and every pain. That is the way of mastery. Every woman who rules must taste this draught, must know she has this power."

"I— I prefer to master them my way."

"Pray tell, what is your way, Lily? To stuff them with comfits until they beg for mercy?" Her mother's fingertips pressed the surface of her desk as if to force her will through the polished wood. "You are meant to cut your teeth on them, Little Cub. Then when you take a husband, no matter how powerful he may be, you will rule him."

"As you rule Father?" Lily said, the question coming from some hidden depth.

Enraged, her mother slammed both hands on top of her ledger. "I will not have patriarchal ways return to Ammam. You will learn to rule if I have to beat it into you."

Perhaps hysteria put the words in her mouth. Perhaps her slaves truly had increased her confidence. "Ah," she said. "I'm sure being beaten will go far towards teaching me how to rule."

Her mother's lovely face darkened with fury. No sarcasm was allowed but her own. Lily braced for an explosion but a low laugh cut her short. Vizier had entered from the adjoining room. He was neither tall, nor handsome. He bore just enough weight to qualify as corpulent, and his greying hair had been creeping back for years. His nose was large, his teeth crooked. He did, however, have the cleverest eyes and the warmest smile she had ever seen. Now he turned both on Lady Fortis.

"Come, love," he said in his merry way. "Don't be angry when your cub shows her claws."

"Beast!" she spat and flung an ivory bauble at his head.

Experience had quickened his reflexes. The bauble missed him by a foot, hit the chamber door and rolled back across the carpet. It came to rest at Lily's feet. When she picked it up, it snapped in two.

A superstitious shiver crossed her nape. The trinket was a hollowed-out map of the world, a gift from the Yskutian ambassador. Unlike other countries, Yskut did not offer tribute to Ammam, not even in the name of diplomacy. Their reasons for gift-giving ran deeper. They responded neither to wants nor demands but only needs, and those needs were defined according to Yskut's own inscrutable standards.

If the ambassador, for whatever reason, thought her mother needed this trinket, Lily was loath to see it broken. She stared at the two halves lying like eggshells in her palms. Delicate ribs of longitude and latitude connected the continents, on which tiny rivers and mountains had been etched. The piece was a marvel of the miniaturist's art.

"I'll take this to Father," she said. "I've heard he is clever with—"

"You will not." Her mother was breathless, half-standing with anger. "You will not go near that bloodless little man. Throw the thing away. It doesn't matter."

Lily slipped the pieces into her pocket and fought the urge to nod. A nod would have been a lie. She had no intention of throwing the globe away. Instead she waited for her dismissal.

"Yes, yes." Lady Fortis waved her towards the door. "I know you cannot bear my company another moment. But remember what I told you, Lily. I want results."

She'd reached the threshold before resentment overcame caution and made her turn. She ignored the incipient chatter of her teeth. "You will see no results unless you remove your spies, Mother. I will not master these men for the entertainment of servants."

Her mother's eyes narrowed, but Lily stood her ground.

"I will not wait much longer," her mother warned.

Lily sensed this was as close to a concession as she would get.

Vizier caught up to her halfway down the Corridor of Ancestors. He had a quick walk for a stocky man, full of energy.

"Lily, wait," he said. He swung his arm around her shoulders and steered her into a statuary alcove. That she did not resist was a measure of her affection for him. He began precisely as she expected. "Do not be angry with her, Princess. She cannot help what she is."

"How convenient for her."

Vizier hid his smile by rubbing a finger across his upper lip. Then he smoothed her long dark hair behind her shoulder. "Do you know, Lily, it irks your mother no end that your servants are always better-mannered than hers, always more skilled at their tasks. Do you suppose that, on some level, she's aware that she frightens her servants out of countenance and resents your ability to make yours love you?"

Lily scraped her slipper against the base of her grandfather Harry's bust. "She gives me no credit for anything." She sounded, to her dismay, like a petulant child. She cleared her throat and spoke more firmly. "I will master them."

Vizier patted her back. "It seems to me they are mastered already. They leap to do your bidding before you even know what it is. What you choose to do in the privacy of your chamber is your business. Your mother merely wishes to believe that her way is the only way."

Lily nodded, but his words did not lighten her gloom. He lifted her chin on the edge of his hand. "What is it, Little Cub? What troubles you?"

"Grae won't obey me."

Vizier's brows were tufts of grey above his clever eyes. They creased together in confusion. "Grae? Ah, the Ka'arkish lad." Deciding this discussion required more ease, he made himself comfortable on the alcove's small bench, then patted the space beside him. Lily sat and leaned into his big warm chest, just as she had when a child. How often she had prayed he were her parent, her only parent. Now he kissed the top of her head. "Men are led by different things, Princess. Some by fear, some by greed, and some by love. But some will only follow the dictates of their own will. To know which are which is not a bad lesson for a ruler to learn."

"But Mother—"

He smiled and shook his head. "You are one of very few people who has the capacity to set your mother on her heels. She respects you more than you know. More than she knows, in fact."

Lily shook her head. Vizier was, as always, trying to be kind, to mend the ever-growing rift between princess and queen. But Lady Fortis did not respect her. And unless Lily found some way to rule her unruly slave, she very likely never would.

Lily had noticed that, while Grae might think like a soldier, he certainly didn't sleep like one. Nothing short of shouting in his ear would wake him. To her amazement, he'd grown increasingly affectionate in his slumbers. This night, he squirmed over to her side of the bed, took her in his arms and slung his leg over her hip. Her heart squeezed in her chest, even though she knew better than to trust the actions of a sleeping man. How would it be, she wondered, if he turned to her this way when he was awake, not for the sake of giving her pleasure, but for his own comfort, out of his own wish to be loved?

She bit her lip. It was a foolish question. Why should he crave her love? More to the point, why should she crave his? No, she did not. She could not. She craved the pleasure he gave her, as did he; even now his arousal, which had softened in sleep, rose against her hip.

He muttered and pressed closer.

Idiot man, she thought. She raked her fingers through his thick, black hair, then gently stroked her nails down his naked back. His buttocks were so narrow for a man his size, narrow and round and covered in a fine, silky down. They seemed to invite fondling, nay, demanded it. Lily ran her fingers over their contours and they clenched.

She thought back on caresses Col and Ian had enjoyed. Would Grae share their pleasure? She ran her thumb between the two globes. His breath sighed from him. Encouraged, she reached further, further until her fingers nudged the heavy swell of his sac. He uttered a sound of discomfort. She withdrew at once but he shifted closer and higher. His turgid shaft pulsed against the meeting of her thighs, even harder than before. He liked what she'd done. Heat swept her body like the blast from an open bread oven. If she lifted her leg an inch, his sex would snap upward between her thighs. She could rub her hungry bead of pleasure against the shaft. She could pretend they were making love without risking her innocence.

"Grae," she whispered, scratching back up the furrow of his spine.

He moaned and his eyes rolled behind their lids, but he did not wake.

Gathering her courage, she pushed up against the leg that weighted hers. The head of his sex sprang free. She wriggled down until she caught him in a slippery pubic kiss. Gingerly, not wishing to crush him, she lowered her thigh. At once his body tightened around hers. His arms clutched her back and his leg caught hers in a vise-like pressure. Apparently, she need not have worried about hurting him, for he seemed to crave more force and more. He rubbed his cheek against hers like an anxious cat, his beard rough on her tender skin.

She squirmed against his body as best she could. His sex was held almost too tightly to move, but its velvety skin shifted over the rigid interior, as did the skin of her thighs. He moaned, a sound of such longing it brought an answering rush of moisture from her sex. She rolled her hips again and felt teeth grip the muscle between her neck and shoulder.

"Hey," she whispered. The teeth withdrew and were replaced by a tongue. It lapped her, soothed her, a primitive, animal caress.

Satisfied he would not hurt her, she resumed her slow, rocking thrust. After a moment, he joined her, sighing at each motion, and growing warmer and warmer until a fine sheen of perspiration covered his bronzed Ka'arkish skin. Her hands roved, delighted by this unexpected freedom. She measured the breadth of his shoulders. She counted his ribs. She stroked her way down his bent leg to the sole of his foot. His toes curled when she stroked his instep and a new, more emphatic jerk entered the movement of his hips.

He would do this if we were making love, she thought, if he were near the end. The realization inspired a secret thrill. Her own arousal spiraled closer to its edge, but suddenly she didn't care. She wanted his orgasm, his seed bursting hot and strong between her legs.

What matter that she would steal it from him unawares? Whether he admitted it or not, he needed this release. The desperate pounding of his sex told her so, the hitch of his breath, the brazier heat of his skin. He was a healthy young man. If Col had been crazed after six weeks, how much moreso Grae after ten?

She'd be doing him a favor.

Her mind made up, she returned her hands to his bottom, encouraging each thrust to come a little harder, a little faster. His moans turned to pants. His fingers clutched her so hard her muscles tingled. And then he went wild. His speed doubled. His sex seemed to grow still longer between her thighs. His teeth scored her shoulder again. He stiffened and held tight—

"God!" His eyes flew open and he shoved her from him.

A burst of seed hit her belly. He cursed and fumbled between his legs. With the fingers of one hand he pinched the tip of his erection so hard its skin whitened. His other hand did something she couldn't see behind his sac. Whatever it was, it halted his release mid-spurt.

"You," he said. He backed out of the bed, panting and glaring as the hangings tented out behind him. "Have you no honor?"

Despite its recent mistreatment, his cock still pointed heavenward, looking, if possible, even bigger and redder than before. The sight brought a smile to Lily's face, then a giggle.

"Oh." She covered her mouth. "I'm sorry, but it — it just looks so angry."

Grae turned a black look at his sex, then sighed. "Princess. Don't you understand the meaning of the word 'no'?"

"If you hadn't woken you'd be feeling grateful right now."

He sighed again and crawled back into the bed. "That's besides the point. Now, if you don't mind, I'd like to get some sleep."

"At least tell me why," she demanded. "Surely I deserve that much."

He flopped onto his back and crossed his arms. "I'm here for the sake of my family's honor, but I judge slavery no honor myself."

"So you suffer my brutish rule for their sake."

"I never said you were brutish."

Her laugh was thin and bitter. "At least you give me that."

"Princess." He touched her arm in the dark. His breath hitched. For a moment she thought he would pull her against him, but his hand slipped away. "Can you not be satisfied with mastering Col and Ian?"

"No, I cannot," she said, "for, as my mother was kind enough to point out, they require no mastering at all. It is precisely you I must break, because you resist."

"Then we must remain at odds."

He sounded weary, sad even. Was he sorry? Did he wish they could be friends? Oh, damn her stupid heart for caring. She gritted her teeth. "Do not force me to harsher measures."

"You must do as you think best," he said.

Ha. She knew his ways now. He meant to shame her conscience by this and yet, if she did resort to force, he would dismiss her as a brute, perhaps the same sort of brute who had flayed him as a boy. That her pride would not allow. Or her stupid heart.

But how to tread the line between force and persuasion? She despaired of finding a way.

Chapter Five

The answer came to her in the night. Her conscience was not strictly comfortable with the solution, but neither was it uncomfortable. The plan would work, she believed, and more than anything she was weary of the stalemate between her and Grae, weary of her mother's censure and wearier still of her own self-doubt. She told herself she was not too soft to rule. She could make a difficult decision when required.

She thrust back the bed hangings, tired from her sleepless night but filled with resolve. The sun flooded the chamber in long, slanting rays. Grae mumbled something and burrowed into his pillow. If no one disturbed him, he would likely sleep for hours.

Ian smiled as she stepped naked from the bed. "Princess, your beauty outshines the sun."

"Aye," Col agreed. He caught sight of Grae and his mouth twisted in disdain. "Shall I wake the sluggard, Mistress?"

"Nay," she said. "We have business to discuss to which he is not privy."

Ian held a robe for her. "This sounds interesting."

"I hope you continue to find it so once I tell you what I plan. I am depending on your aid."

Col went down on one knee with her slippers. "You may rely on us. Always."

But always was not necessary. Only the length of one night.

She began her day with breakfast, then a bath, then fell asleep as Col and Ian massaged her with scented oil. She woke to find they had wrapped her in a blanket and carried her to a sunny corner of the rose garden. Her head lay in Ian's lap. Col sat nearby, polishing the blade of a dagger she had given him the week before. It was a traditional Ammish weapon, small but dangerous, a weapon a woman could wield. Col treated it like the Crown Jewels.

"Oh, no," she said, rising to her elbow. "My duties—"

Ian pushed her down. "Col has taken the liberty of rescheduling your appointments. You have a bit of a headache, don't you know, and dearly need your rest."

"For tonight," Col said meaningfully.

"You know," said Ian, "I am almost reluctant to help you. That Ka'arkish lunk does not deserve the delightful gift you have planned for him."

Lily snorted through her nose. "I doubt he will view it as a gift."

"The man is an idiot."

Col nodded so hard at his friend's statement that a dragonfly sheered off in fright. On the matter of Grae's idiocy, at least, they could all agree.

The weaving room lay beneath Lily's bedchamber. Like her room, it was girded by six narrow windows, three overlooking the courtyard and three with a view of the land between castle and harbor. A large metal rack was bolted onto one wall. The weavers wound yarn into skeins on its hooks. These hooks were sturdy but not sharp, the space between them large enough for one grown man. One stubborn man, she thought with a nervous smile.

While Grae consulted the metalsmith on the feasibility of installing a porticullus-style door at the base of her tower, she and Col and Ian shoved the looms against the walls and poured fresh oil into the lamps. The men built a fire in the hearth and carried a round table to the center of the room. The utensils with which she set it were pure, polished silver, the cloth a fine white linen. A six-branched candelabra awaited the approach of dusk.

Then they began their search. After much scrutiny, they found one spyhole in the door and another in a chink between two floor stones. She stoppered both with a sense of virtuous rebellion. Her mother had not actually promised to stop spying, and Lily did not wish to lead her into temptation. This was to be a private evening.

Her nerves were aflutter, but she was pleased to see that Grae had bathed before returning and, without being reminded, had changed into his kalisari. Still wet, his black hair was combed behind his ears and caught in a short queue. He looked clean and strong and male.

He was also on his best behavior, neither surly nor silent. His manners were not as fine as her other slaves' but they would suit. She had chosen a simple meal so as not to make him self-conscious, and had succeeded. He ate with gusto. They spoke animatedly on the upcoming harvest, on the prospects for trade between Ammam and the nomads of the Southern desert. Ian displayed the knowledge of a diplomat, Grae the common sense of, well, Grae. By the time she served the fruit course, he was lounging back in his chair and cradling his wine cup to his chest. He seemed to know he had impressed her, and to be enjoying it.

He waved away her offer of candied ginger. "This night is too sweet to spoil with sugar."

He smiled into his cup as he said it, but she knew he meant the words as thanks to her. She almost regretted what she was about to do on this, the friendliest evening they had ever spent.

"Are you comfortable?" she asked, her heart pounding like a jackrabbit's.

"Very." He stretched his legs under the table. His eyes were heavy. The wine was not drugged but deceptively strong. She and the other men had imbibed little.

Wishing to lull him further, she stroked the hard tendons of his forearm. "You do not wish to use the garderobe?"

His brow puckered at the personal nature of the question. "No-o."

"Then I suppose we are ready."

Col and Ian had risen. They grabbed Grae's chair, tilted it back and dragged it on two legs to the yarn winding rack.

"Hey!" he protested, still more confused than angry. By the time he thought to struggle, his arms were stretched above his head and his wrists bound firmly to the hooks. He tried to kick Ian and Col away but was no match for their united efforts. They forced his legs apart and tied those to the rack as well. "What are you doing?" He twisted in his bonds. "Let me go!"

Lily ignored him. Shivers of excitement coursed through her limbs. He was hers now. She could do as she wished and he could not stop her. She turned to Ian. "His kalisari must be removed."

Ian laid one finger along his lean, handsome cheek. "If you don't mind, Princess, I think Col would like to do the honors."

Col bared his teeth and flashed his fine Ammish dagger. He seemed almost as excited as Lily. Her eyes slid down his well-knit body. He was aroused. His white skirt stood out with the thrust of his erection. Awareness shifted inside her. Suddenly she recalled how Col would sometimes touch Ian as he pleasured her. She had thought he was being helpful, but perhaps...

Ian read the suspicion in her eyes. "Yes. We are both flexible that way."

Both! She should have been horrified, but the thought that they would enjoy Grae's subjugation as much as she did aroused her. A quick pulse throbbed between her legs, as if a warm fist were closing round her sex. Unable to speak, she nodded for Col to continue.

Though it would have been easier to unwrap the thing, Col slid the dagger up from the hem of the kalisari, slicing the white linen by inches. The top of Grae's thigh appeared, then his hipbone, and then the short length of cloth fell free.

His sex hung between his legs, soft as yet, but not entirely still. It had lengthened already, and darkened, and was beginning to harden. Before Lily could ask, Ian dragged a thick Laravian prayer rug in front of the rack. Sighing with anticipation, she knelt before her slave.

"Don't," Grae said before she'd even touched him.

"There is no more *don't*," she said. "There is only my will and your pleasure."

His eyes were screwed shut, his body braced for some terrible blow. She leaned forward and blew lightly on the skin of his sex, just that, no more. He rose. Higher. Thicker. Redder. His knees trembled. She had the power now. A rush of dark pleasure suffused her veins. She understood then what her mother felt when servants cowered before her.

Ian handed her the ostrich plume. She began at Grae's feet. She teased them with the feather, then her lips, and finally her tongue. She rose to his calves. She kissed the ticklish spot behind his knees, then proceeded up his thighs. She ran the feather over his sac and up the ridge that girded the underside of his shaft. The rosy head, now bare of all covering, merited one brief swipe of her tongue.

He cursed when she moved away.

"You are not ready yet," she said.

His eyes shot sparks of pure obsidian fury. But he could not say he was ready. That would have meant agreeing to all she did.

She kissed his nipples, searching each from within its whorl of hair. They were tiny but hard and he heaved outwards as she suckled. She kissed her way up his neck, over his Adam's apple to the cleft in his chin. She licked the hollow beneath his lower lip, but she did not kiss his mouth. That he had allowed, so that she would not do.

She descended again, following the line of his breastbone. His ribs expanded and sank. His belly quivered. His sex was so erect she had to pull it from his body.

"Don't," he said one last time, the word a groan more of longing than dread.

She smiled and wet her lips and drew his manhood into her mouth. This time, his groan had no words to it. Like his body, it betrayed him. He thrust forward, straining off the rack, nearly overwhelming her with his length.

"Careful," Ian warned him.

"Tell her to be careful," Grae gasped. "I never asked for this, never— Oh, Lord."

She wrapped her hand around his base and suckled him, slow, deep tugs that drew the skin of his cowl first over and then down. She swirled her tongue around the heart-shaped tip, loving the smoothness of the skin beneath, the power of the flesh it concealed, the vitality.

Grae's moans changed in tenor, growing alarmed.

"Tell them to leave," he begged even as his hips canted towards the descent of her mouth. "I'm tied now. You have me at your mercy. Please. Just tell them to leave."

She let him slip from her lips. She looked at the plea in his eyes, then at Ian.

Ian nodded and smiled. "It is a fair request, Princess. And we have tied him securely."

With their departure, a silence filled the room. The lamps hissed in their oily globes. The rack creaked under Grae's weight. Their breath whispered in synchrony. Still kneeling, she loosened the ribbon that snugged her gown beneath her breasts. His lips parted, eyes locked to the motion of her fingers. She pushed the gown and shift down to her knees, then stood long enough to kick it free. She was glad for the fire they'd lit earlier, though by now it was embers. Her nipples were as sharp from the cold as they were from anticipation.

He wet his mouth as he stared. She knew he wanted to kiss her breasts.

"I make you a promise," she said. Her lips trembled, for this was the moment on which her victory hung. "I will not force you to come unless you beg. I will bring you to the edge and release you...and then I will begin again."

"Lord above," he said, the words hoarse. "You have brought me to the edge already."

Her laugh warmed her throat like wine.

"Princess," he said, smiling in spite of himself at the sound of her joy.

She took him again and there were no more words, only the sweet rise and fall, the smooth hot flesh, the catch in his breathing, the sound like a whimper caught in his throat. He pushed at her, his body begging though he would not. She took him deeper, sucked him harder. Her tongue was a weapon of pleasure. She caught his sac and cradled it in her palm. It felt so heavy, so full. She squeezed it lightly and lashed the pleasure spot beneath the head of his sex.

He cried out as if in pain. His sex swelled in her mouth. His hips jarred forward. One more pull would slay him. She paused, savoring the frantic palpitation on her tongue.

"Please," he said. "I beg you, finish it."

Elation filled her. She closed her eyes and drew on him one last time. Then he came, long months of denial pouring out in a quivering, moaning flood. The taste of him was hot and rich, sweet and strange. He shook, crying out with each pulsing burst. She soothed him with her mouth, with her hands, sucking him gently now and stroking the hard, tremulous flesh of his hips.

At last he sagged, hanging from the rack as if she had drained the last of his strength. Exhaustion overtook her as well, more from the release of tension than from the arduousness of her efforts. She rested her cheek against his belly.

She had done it. She had made him beg.

Then the rack gave a groan as loud as any he had uttered *in extremis*. The hook that had held his left wrist fell to the stone, ringing as it struck. She gasped, speechless with horror. A second hook dropped a moment later, and then it was far too late to call for help. He bore her to the floor with his weight. Covering her mouth with one hand, he stretched her wrists over her head with the other. She heard another clank and knew his feet were free as well.

She screamed her outrage into his palm. He could not do this. He could not steal her victory. But he could.

"Now, Princess," he said, dark and gloating. "We'll see if you know how to beg."

He rubbed his body over hers, chest to chest, legs to legs, and everywhere he rubbed sensation flowed like honey through her limbs. She struggled to squirm away before he discovered how her body betrayed her. It was too late. He already knew. He bent his head and suckled her breasts, drawing her nipples into long aching buds. Removing his hand from her mouth, he swept it between their bodies and curled his fingers over her nether lips.

"Yes, Princess," he said, drawing their tips through her wetness. "Show me how much you want me."

One knee wedged between her thighs, then two. He widened them. He shifted higher. She hadn't imagined he could recover so soon but he was rigid with arousal. His sex slipped against hers, vibrating with lust. He anointed himself in her moisture. He pulled and pushed between her folds, catching her tenderest spots on the smooth, swollen ridge of the head.

"Don't worry," he whispered, hot fire against her ear. "I won't take you unless you beg."

She moaned, resisting and weakening by turns. He moved again, re-aligning himself. The tip of him pressed her gate, entered. Oh, it was sleek and hot. Her body wept for more. He must have been able to feel her tears. They were pouring from her like cream from a jar.

"No," she moaned, but her body pushed up at him, craving all of him, the full, hard length.

"*No* will not get you what you want," he said. He slipped his thumb over the pearl of her pleasure. He pressed it back against the bone, initiating a heart-stopping rhythm that he echoed with his cock. The blunt head pushed against the barrier of her virginity. Her body clenched, willing him to take her with all its strength.

Grae gasped and bit the tender lobe of her ear, but he did not break his word. "A simple 'please' will do," he said, his voice rasping like an iron file.

The sound of it destroyed her. She could not hold firm. She wanted him inside her. Wanted to swallow him utterly. "Please," she said, tears spilling from her eyes. "Please."

"Thank you, Lord," he breathed, and swiftly increased the pressure. He steadied her hips. "Now, Princess. Hold tight."

Her maidenhead gave way with a brief pinching sensation, such a little feeling for such an irrevocable change. He slipped inward. Halfway, no more. His eyes slid shut. He shuddered. And she remembered this was his first time, too.

"Princess." He kissed her temple. "Lift your knees, Princess."

But she was stunned. He was inside her, heat and fullness stretching her secret flesh. Her gift was gone. Her victory was gone. She wanted to cry but her tears had dried. What a miracle this was! She could feel the blood throbbing in his shaft, jittering against the pulse of her sheath.

"Princess." This time he squeezed her captive wrists. "Lift your knees."

She could not resist the urging of her flesh. She lifted her knees and he pressed farther in. Her wonder intensified. So intimate, this locking together of body parts. With a sigh, half resignation, half relief, she crossed her ankles in the small of his back.

He groaned and shoved one more time until he hilted. A long shiver rolled down his powerful body. "Ah, Princess." He turned his face back and forth across the spill of her hair. "I hope you're with me. I'm afraid this isn't going to last very long."

He lifted his head. They stared at each other. Anxiety pinched the corners of his eyes, but she could hardly breathe for the chill-like waves of pleasure sweeping her body. Delicious, intoxicating. All she could think was that she wanted more. She licked her lips. A smile played over his mouth. He ran his hand down her side and cupped her buttocks. "Are you with me?"

She couldn't bring herself to say the words but she dug her heels into his back and levered herself towards him. He pulled back against her strength, then let it ease him in.

"Mm," he said, a sound of profound enjoyment, and let her do it again.

She would not let him go. She could not. He stretched her hands high above her head and all she had to hold him were her thighs and calves. She would not be helpless, though. She made the most of the power she had. He had to fight her for every withdrawal. He began to laugh between his moans.

She was sure her One True Love would not have laughed and yet she could not bring herself to mind. He was making her feel the magic: the soft tingling rise, the ache, the helpless tightening deep inside. Now, her body demanded, but she clenched her teeth against the plea.

"Now," he growled, thrusting faster and changing angles so that he caught her just so, where the ache was deepest. His hand tightened on her wrists. Her heart leapt with an excitement she could not deny. This badly he wanted her. This much. Shoving deep, he ground himself against her.

She cried out. Her back arched. She felt his mouth on her breast, clinging, tugging, and the climax slammed through her. Her sense of her body narrowed to three points: nipples, sex, wrists, all flaming like comets in a velvet darkness. He pinned her, held her by those three glittering points. She would have flown to pieces without him.

Then he flew to pieces himself. His long groan of ecstasy should have been music to her wounded soul. The grateful kiss he pressed to the curve of her breast should have soothed her like a lullaby. But when she came to herself, she remembered. He wasn't her One True Love. He was just a stubborn slave who'd proven once again she was a fool to believe she could master him.

He withdrew carefully, giving her body a chance to relax. He released her wrists and cradled her close. He stroked her back. He urged her head to rest against his shoulder. They might have been long-lost lovers.

But they weren't. When the memory of passion faded, he would return to disliking her as much as ever. And she— She feared she had never disliked him as much as she wished.

"Sorry," he muttered into the tumbled silk of her hair. "Can't keep my eyes open a minute longer."

She waited until he slept, then wriggled free and stood. He curled tighter on the small prayer rug. He looked cold. Vulnerable. Young. She doubled the linen tablecloth and tucked it around him. Then she pulled on her gown.

The aches and pains of her body were nothing to the ache in her heart.

Chapter Six

The tears came as soon as she stepped into the torchlit stairwell.

She could not return to her room. Col and Ian would be there, doing whatever it was they did that she had not suspected them of doing. Despite her curiosity, she did not wish to take them unawares. They would stop at once, in any case. They would ask her what had happened and she would have to share the humiliation she did not want to face, much less recount. She looked down the stairs instead, at the barred wooden door Grae was hoping to fortify against intruders. It led to a passage inside the curtain wall and from thence to the main keep.

She did not know the hour, but Vizier might yet be in his office. She could take her troubles to him.

She shook her head even as the idea formed. Grae had dosed her with her own medicine. While Vizier might not scold, she could not bear to find judgment in his eyes. Sniffing hard, she swiped her sleeve across her eyes. She didn't need disapproval. She could supply that herself. She needed pity. She needed mothering. She needed—

She needed Nurse. Nurse would understand her loss. Nurse would take her side no matter what. Oh, if only she hadn't been sent back to town with the maids. Three slaves, no matter how willing, could never take her place.

But maybe there was a way. She crept to the bottom of the stairs and pressed her ear to the wooden door. All was quiet. There was a gatehouse in this section of the wall which, in this time of peace, was sometimes left unguarded. From there, town was a brisk walk away. Nurse was staying with her daughter. Lily had visited their home more than once. She knew she'd have no trouble finding it. Her heart began to race. The prospect of doing something forbidden, and perhaps a bit dangerous, pushed aside her disappointment and her shame.

The town was fortified, not as formidably as the castle, but it did have its own crenellated wall. She was obliged to slip in by the bachelor's gate, the door young men used to meet their sweethearts on the sly.

At this hour, only torches and the occasional candle in a window lit the winding streets. The shops had closed and she had wit enough to avoid the taverns. She'd grabbed a cloak from the empty guardroom. Though her velvet gown showed beneath its hem, the few people she passed paid her no mind. A wonderful sense of freedom filled her. Her strides lengthened on the cobbles. Tonight she was not a princess, not an heir, just a woman on a journey to meet a friend.

She passed a shuttered bakery and smiled as a skinny cat darted from an alley.

Without warning, hands yanked her off her feet and dragged her backwards into the shadows. They covered her mouth, preventing her from crying out. For a second she thought Grae had followed her, but the hands were too rough and the body smelled too foul.

"Well, well, well," said a grating voice. "What have we here come slumming in its fancy slippers?"

The hands spun her around and thrust back the hood of her borrowed cloak. Three men faced her, two young and one old, all wearing the brown and gold of the Tanner's Guild. One of the young ones held her by the shoulders. He was tall and wiry and had a skinny hooked nose.

The old man whistled. "Don't that beat all. It's her Ladyship's brat."

"I've come to visit friends," she said with as much dignity as she could muster.

"I'll bet you have," cackled the one who held her. "Come for a taste of town rough, eh? Three slavey boys ain't enough for you castle ladies. But you can forget about getting your slap and tickle here, Princess. We've higher matters on our minds."

"Like a charter," piped the other young one.

"Aye." Hooknose's grin bared crooked yellow teeth. "And now we've got the leverage we need to ransom ourselves a bit of self-rule."

Her body tensed against a shiver of fear. "My mother won't give in to blackmail. This is not the way to get what you want."

"Oh, ain't it?" said Hooknose. He continued to cackle as he dragged her into the dark.

They stashed her in a root cellar with her hands tied behind her back, her ankles hobbled, and a cracked piece of leather gagging her mouth. She could hear them moving about on the floor above, arguing over the proper composition of the ransom note. From the sounds of their contention, she might molder here for weeks.

I should have screamed when I had the chance, she thought. But she had no experience with screaming. For that matter, she had no experience with being in danger.

Her captors, such as they were, left her in the cellar all night. Sometime before dawn she wrestled her gown above her waist so she could relieve herself in the corner. The last time the town had petitioned for the right to govern themselves, Lady Fortis had fobbed them off with a sewer system. And here her daughter was, making the place smell like a midden again.

She dreaded her mother's reaction to this fiasco more than she dreaded anything those would-be councilmen might do.

Overcome with frustration, she banged her head against the wall. Though she'd managed to free her ankles, her wrist bindings held fast, despite rubbing them against a stone until her arms felt ready to fall off. The tiny paper-covered windows were too high to reach. Nor could she raise much of an alarm with a soggy swatch of leather in her mouth. Not even her captors could hear her muffled shouts, or so she assumed, since they did nothing to silence them.

Damn, she thought, damn, damn, damn.

The clatter of hooves on the cobbles outside brought her head up. More conspirators, she thought, but then she heard shouting and the clash of metal. Was she being rescued? Was it her mother's men? Oh, God. If it was, she almost wished she could stay a little longer.

It wasn't her mother's men, though. It was Col and Ian. They burst into the shadowy cellar with an impressive splintering of wood.

"Mistress!" said Col.

"Princess!" said Ian.

Lily struggled to stand. Her pride might hang in shreds, but she'd meet them on her feet.

Ian clucked over her scratches like a mother hen. He worked the gag off, then sliced through the ties that bound her wrists. She immediately flung her arms around his neck. To hell with pride. She was so happy to see him she could have cried. She did, in fact, just a little.

"There, there." He patted her back. "It's all right now. There were only five of the rascals and the fifth was so scared of me and Col, he ran off with his tail between his legs."

Pushing back from Ian, she peered around him at Col. He looked as if he'd been through the mill. His clothes were bloody and tattered. The state of his face suggested his nose had been broken again. Ian, however, barely bore a scratch. He wore a hooded hauberk even finer in make than Ka'arkish war mail. Black as pitch and shiny, the rings were so closely linked she could not see between them. They flowed over his form more like cloth than metal.

Curious, she stroked the slippery sleeve. "Where on earth did you get this?"

"Er," Ian shuffled his feet. "It's Grae's. Corking good stuff. Fellow broke his knife on it. Grae gave it to me when he saw he wouldn't make it."

Lily put her hand to her throat, suddenly icy cold. "'Wouldn't make it?'"

"Oh, no, Princess." Ian squeezed her trembling shoulders. "No, Princess, he's fine. He's just, well, I don't believe he's ever sat a horse before and he couldn't get the beast to cross the last stream. Col was hot on your track. He's keen on hunting, you know. And Grae insisted we go ahead without him. When he found you missing, he said he had a feeling something was wrong. He didn't want us to wait."

"And he was right," Col said, sliding his precious dagger back into its scabbard. He shook his head morosely. "He's going to be angry that he missed this."

They all stiffened at the sound of hoofbeats, quite a lot of them, coming their way.

"Damnation," said Ian. "That last fellow must have gone for reinforcements."

Footsteps thundered into the house, shouts rising as fallen companions were discovered.

"Quick." Lily thrust a shovel into Ian's hand. "Bar the cellar door."

"We'll be trapped," Col protested, even as Ian jammed it through the handle.

"No, I'm small. You can shove me out the window and I'll run for help. The town is loyal—most of it." Lily hated the thought of leaving Col and Ian to their fates even for the few minutes it took to summon help. They might have taken down four men, but it sounded as if they faced a good deal more than that now. Already the reinforcements were pounding at the cellar door, slamming it with their shoulders. Tears coursed down her face as she ran to the tiny window. "Hurry, Col, give me a leg up."

Col hefted her towards the sill. The door creaked and began to splinter. Ian faced it, sword at the ready, preparing to defend her escape. Lily punched the oil-covered paper off the window.

"God keep you," she gasped.

But her shoulders wouldn't fit through the narrow opening. She moaned in despair, then sucked a deep breath. At least she could call for help.

"Wait!" said Ian, his voice sharp. Lily realized their enemies had stopped ramming the door, even though the uproar had increased. Ian trotted up the stairs and pressed his ear to the wood. "I hear fighting. My God, Grae's out there. He must have run here on foot."

Lily dropped to the floor and flew to him, closely followed by Col. Ian yanked the shovel from the door handle. "I can't leave him alone out there. You stay here and guard her, Col."

"Like hell," Lily and Col said as one. The odds were bad enough.

Ian conceded with a brusque nod. He thrust the shovel at Lily. "You take this, Princess. If anyone comes through this door, you clobber him first and ask questions later."

She waited in terror, jumping at every crash, straining for the voices of her friends. Grae's rose loud and sure, directing Col and Ian, heartening them, warning them of danger. Once, she heard him grunt in pain and clutched the shovel so hard one of her nails broke. He's out there with no armor, she thought, against God knows how many men. She tugged the doorhandle, meaning to help, but he must have been close because she heard him curse.

"Stay there, damn you," he ordered, almost slamming it on her fingers. "We're coming."

Finally, after what seemed like an eternity, silence fell in the smoky little house. Weak-kneed and trembling, she poked her head around the cellar door. Bodies lay everywhere, bleeding, unconscious, more than a dozen by her count. Horrified, her gaze roved the scene of carnage until, like a homing pigeon, they found Grae. He leaned over his knees, panting, liberally splashed with blood but apparently hale. His expression was weary and drained.

"They're not all dead," he said, reading her unspoken dread. "Most just knocked out."

Ignoring her churning stomach, she examined the bodies, turning each onto his back so she could memorize the features. She might sympathize with their cause, but her mother would want to know who had been involved in the conspiracy. It was especially important not to accuse anyone unjustly, for the queen's response was sure to be fierce.

With the end of the fighting, townspeople began to arrive. Lily assigned a hostler and his staff to secure the house, and then she and her rescuers began the slow walk home. Ian led her along on his horse until they reached the spot where Grae had tied his own recalcitrant steed.

"Let her down," he said. "I'll see she gets home."

Ian looked at Grae's horse, stolidly munching grass beneath a shady oak. Clearly he doubted the wisdom of handing her over to an inexperienced rider.

"You take my horse and ride ahead," Grae said, the tightness in his jaw all that betrayed his embarrassment. "Tell the queen what happened and that her daughter is well."

"What about you?" Ian asked.

"The princess and I are going to walk. We have important matters to discuss."

Lily looked at Grae. He was pale and angry. She didn't want to face him alone but she knew she must. Men were dead today who would have been alive if she had not run from her troubles. She swore it would not happen again.

"It's all right," she said to Ian. "I'm sure the danger is past now."

Col gave Grae a hard look, but he didn't protest, either. "Don't be long," was all he said.

As soon as they'd turned the horses towards home, Grae took her arm, his fingers like steel on her elbow. He led her into a copse of trees that marked the edge of the royal game preserve, walking faster and faster until she was panting to keep pace.

"Please, Grae," she said, stumbling over a root. "I can't keep up."

Abruptly, he yanked her towards a fallen log and sat. Without a word of warning, he turned her over his lap and began to spank her. Hard, stinging smacks rained over her bottom from the small of her back to the top of her thighs. Lily cried out but she could not wrench free. He seemed determined to leave no inch of flesh unpunished.

"What," he said, with a particularly hard whack, "did you think you were doing?"

"Ow." She clapped a hand to her injured fanny. He immediately pulled up her gown so he could spank her bare skin. That stung even more. "Ow! Grae, stop. I was visiting my nurse."

"In the middle of the night! By yourself?" He let fall another volley of blows. "You are the heir. How dare you endanger yourself that way?"

Oh, her bottom was on fire. She'd never been spanked, never. How did children bear this? Each blow seemed to sizzle on her skin. And how humiliating it was! No doubt that was his purpose, for he showed no mercy. She wriggled to escape, but he held her too tightly, and spanked her all the harder for trying.

"I was upset," she pleaded. "Grae, you took my maidenhead. I was saving myself."

"Lord Almighty." His hand stopped and came to rest on her burning buttock. The blood pulsed in her skin. Her bottom felt huge. Like the center of the world. He was breathing hard. His little finger curved down between her cheeks. Its tip nearly touched her sex. Her sudden surge of arousal confused her. How could she be feeling *that* now? "You ran away because I took your virginity? When you'd forced your will on me exactly the same way?"

"I didn't run away," she grumbled, squirming under his hand. He didn't let go. In fact, though his hand didn't move, it seemed to caress her. "I went to see Nurse. She's very sympathetic. Haven't you ever wanted sympathy even when you knew you were wrong?"

He chuckled and now his hand did caress her, no mistaking it. His big rough palm moved in a winding figure eight over her cheeks. It hurt terribly, and yet it felt wonderful, too. Her sex liquefied and trembled, desperate to be filled. Then she registered the state of his lap.

"You're hard," she gasped.

"Aye," he said. "As a rock. You've got the prettiest bottom I've ever seen and right now it's glowing like a rose. You can't imagine what I felt when I thought I'd never hold it again."

"That's what you were worried about? My silly bottom? By God, you could at least pretend you feared for my life. You're a beast, Grae, an utter beast."

"I'd like to take you like a beast." The gutteral declaration sent a fresh thrill to her sex. "I want to rut inside you until we both explode. My cock is aching for it, Princess. I need you."

The way her heart jumped, he might have said 'I love you.'

She let him turn her so that her head faced his feet and her legs formed a 'V' around his waist. Her head was lower than her hips. She felt dizzy, off-balance. She gripped his ankles to steady herself as he worked his hose over his hips. His shaft fell free, settling against the crack of her bottom, its heat burning hers. She thought he would take her but he stroked her first, dipping his fingers into her welling sex and then playing them over her curves. The moisture was warm, then cool. Slippery. He smoothed it into her crease, tickling the bud of her anus, then back over the marks of his spanking. He pinched them lightly.

"Does it hurt?" he whispered, his voice tense with arousal. They were sharing a secret, something forbidden.

She shook her head. "It's hot, though. Sensitive."

"Ah," he said. He rolled his hips as if her words had destroyed his patience. Good, she thought, for she had none herself. He took his sex in hand. He pressed the head inside her sheath, then dragged her body up his legs until she held him completely within her. "Touch yourself, Princess. You can reach better than I."

She hesitated, but he coaxed her, praised her. When she did as he asked, his breath caught in his throat and his cock jerked inside her like a spawning fish. All he could see was the motion of her arm, but that was enough to excite him.

"Yes," he breathed. "Yes, that's beautiful."

His hands moved over her bottom. He spread her cheeks like a man preparing to split an orange. His thumb probed the little bud. His thumb was slippery. And it was sliding inside her.

"Oh," she said, as a strange excitement shimmered up her spine.

He began to move in tiny surging rocks, first his thumb, then his cock. Pleasure rocketed through her, multiplied, fractured, like prisms splitting each feeling into its rainbow parts. She came in a burst of color and light. He laughed, thrusting faster, stroking deeper.

"Again," he whispered, bending forward to kiss her spine, to lick it like the animal he'd claimed he wanted to be. Her gown was caught beneath her arms. His calves tensed under her hands. "For me, Princess, come for me."

"Together," she gasped.

"Quick then. If I let go, I won't last a minute. I've been starving for you too long."

"How long?" she asked.

He groaned, took a firmer grip on her hips. "Forever. Since I met you. Since you touched me that first day. Oh, I can't—"

And then she couldn't speak, either. They pounded at each other as well as they could. The position was awkward but they needed hard blows, deep blows. His thumb tensed inside her. He pushed further, stroking her with its pad. It was so unexpectedly delicious, that double penetration, that sense of being overfilled. She clutched at him, pulling for her second crest. He shuddered under the grip of her sheath. She was so wet. She could hear how wet she was. And he, he swelled. He strained. He grunted and bumped the neck of her womb, a subtle, delirious pressure. So deep. The heat rose in her belly, the blissful ache of need. He cursed and said, *please, please, please.* And he broke. Oh, it was lovely. Forceful. Noisy. He spewed inside her with a long, low moan and, like one wave pushing another to shore, his climax crashed into hers, a foaming, sparkling convulsion that receded slowly, sweetly, on a weary chorus of sighs.

Afterwards, he spread her stolen cloak and eased her to the ground. He had spanked her. She could imagine her mother's horror but, thinking back, she did not feel diminished. He had meant to punish her, but had ended up giving her pleasure, a pleasure in which he had been as rapt as she. The weakness, if weakness it had been, was shared. In its way, it had changed them as much as the morning's brush with danger. He seemed open to her now, as if he'd let down his guard. She teased a tassel of grass down his straight, proud nose. His eyes lifted.

"I thought you would pull back from me," he said.

"What do you mean?"

"When I refused to let you pleasure me unless you gave yourself completely, I thought you would keep your distance." He shifted onto his side to face her. "Since I met you, I have felt…"

Her heart beat a little faster. "As if you recognized me?"

His brow furrowed. "I don't think so. But I'd vowed that if I were chosen I would do what I had to do, but would take no pleasure in it." He smiled wryly and touched her cheek. "I wished to be miserable. I did not wish to like you."

"But you do."

He stroked her breast through her gown, his fingers making long sweeps over the peak, his expression shielded by his lashes. "You have your moments, Princess."

She judged he would offer no more compliments, so she turned the conversation to safer ground. "Tell me about the mail you loaned to Ian."

His mouth pursed. "My father discovered the secret to making this armor a decade ago."

"A decade. Why have I never seen its like before?"

He moved his fingers to her collarbone. "At the time, the king's cousin was the royal armorer. He was jealous of my father's skill. When my father refused to pretend this man was responsible for the invention, he had my father drummed out of the Armorer's Guild."

"I suppose your father was too proud to bend."

"It was more than pride." He stroked the hollow at the base of her throat, lost in memories. "The selling of the license would have made rich men of him and his heirs for many generations. Almost certainly, it would have meant our establishment among The Hundred, the families who rule in Ka'arkasba'ad. My father wanted us to be secure."

Lily rolled closer and nudged his knee with hers. "What did your mother think?"

His hand stilled. He spoke very carefully, as if the words were tripwires. "When my father was forced from the guild, he became angry and bitter."

"And sometimes he took it out on you?"

He shook his head, almost too forcefully. He must have realized she was thinking of the scars on his back. "No. That...that injury was different. Before that he never hit her, or me, never even shouted. But she couldn't bear his coldness." He drew a deep, slow breath. "When I was five, my mother left Ka'arkastan with my infant brother and returned to her people."

"What?" Lily went up on her elbow. "And left a five-year-old boy behind? Oh, Grae!"

His jaw tightened. He did not look at her. "It was not because she didn't love me. She must have believed my father needed me more than she did. That is how the Yskutians are."

"But what about what you needed?"

"I'm certain she took that into account."

"But if your father beat you—"

Grae threw himself off the cloak and stood over her, trembling with emotion. "He did not beat me but once, and he had cause. She loved me! She took my brother because he was too small. She did what she thought best." He covered his eyes. He was crying. Silent tears ran down his twisted face. She couldn't hold herself back. She did not know if it was what he wanted, but she rose and took him in her arms.

For a moment, he froze within her embrace. Then, like a glacier groaning with the spring, he cracked. His arms came round her and he held her so tightly she could barely breathe.

"Don't let go," he whispered, pressing desperate kisses to her cheek. "Don't let go."

"I won't," she promised.

"Never."

"Never," she agreed and he held her tighter yet. He was shaking like an aspen in a storm.

"I need you to love me," he said. "Someone has to."

She closed her eyes and hot tears spilled from the corners.

"I do," she said. "I will."

Chapter Seven

Explaining the night's events to her mother was not pleasant, but Lily was too exhausted to experience her usual anxiety. Lady Fortis had cleared the Audience room, then leaned forward on her black marble throne. She listened to the tale with pursed lips and shaking head.

"I don't know what's gotten into you," she said. "I'm not at all sure those slaves are a good influence."

Lily rubbed her aching temple. "It wasn't their fault, Mother. They rescued me."

"But they're not having their intended effect."

"And what is their intended effect?" she asked, too weary to guard her tongue. "To carve me into a precise copy of you?"

Her mother narrowed her icy blue eyes. "You could do worse."

Lily sighed and smoothed her bodice ribbons down the front of her rose pink gown. "You're right, Mother. My behavior was unforgivable and it won't happen again."

"I should think not!" said her mother.

Lily made her curtsy and turned before her expression could give her away.

"You need settling," her mother said by way of a parting shot.

Lily didn't want to ask what that might mean.

She trudged through the passage to her tower. The one bright spot in this day was the accord she'd reached with Grae. The thought of crawling into bed, with him to watch over her, was very appealing. He'd been so tender in the woods. They hadn't made love again, but she knew he'd wanted to. She smiled, recalling the way he'd held her, the way he'd kissed her hair. He didn't hate her after all. Her cheeks warmed and she touched her lips. Perhaps he loved her.

What had he said? She paused with her slipper on the first tower stair.

I've been starving for you. A honeyed warmth swept her sex. Maybe she didn't need to rest right away...

But Grae wasn't waiting in her chamber, Col was. His nose was taped and two blood spots marred his pretty blue eyes. "Grae's off to sharpen his sword, Mistress. In a foul mood, too."

Lily's heart sank. She didn't know if she could bear more disappointment.

"Did he say what was wrong?" she asked, hoping against hope.

Col touched the tip of his nose as if to ensure it was still there. "No, Mistress. And with a mood as black as his, I'd lief as not ask."

She found him in the cutler's room off the East gatehouse. He sat alone on a stool, sharpening his sword against the lathe. The sureness of his movements betrayed his familiarity with the task. But that shouldn't have surprised her. He was an armorer's son.

"Col told me you were here," she said over the whine of the grinding wheel.

He didn't look up. "Have you need of my services, Princess?"

The words were coldly polite. They lodged in her heart like splinters of ice. What had happened to the man who had begged her to love him, who had held her like the world was ending? She swallowed and pulled her courage together.

"Is something wrong?" she asked, knowing that it was.

He flipped the blade and sent sparks skittering off the second edge. "Why would anything be wrong?"

"Because," she forced her hands to unclench from her gown, "you're acting as if you hate me. And this morning it was the opposite."

He stopped pumping the foot pedal and laid the sword across his knees. His eyes glittered like stones at the bottom of a stream, hard, inscrutable. He said nothing. Somehow this was crueler than any insult he might have uttered. She squared her shoulders.

"I see. I'm an idiot to have read anything into what you said or did this morning. You were overwrought. You don't need me. You don't need anyone."

Silence. His foot moved on the lathe pedal. Before he could set it spinning, she trapped his toe beneath her slipper. No more running away, she thought. For either of them. She put her hand on his shoulder and leaned towards his closed, angry face. His jaw tightened, but she did not quail.

"You know what I think, Grae? None of this was ever about honor. It was about fear. Fear of being vulnerable. Fear of needing. You know your father didn't love you and you don't really believe your mother did, or why would she leave you behind when she took your little brother? Now you're so hungry for love it scares you. And it scares you twice over that you want it from me."

His eyes held hers, hard as obsidian and twice as steady. "Believe what you like, Princess."

"Oh, I will," she said. "I will." But it wasn't easy to remember the man who'd hugged the breath from her this morning. She stepped back from him, burned by his chill, needing distance to restore her fragile faith.

"There's something else you should consider," he said, his thigh muscle working as he put the wheel in motion again. "Col and Ian deserve a reward for rescuing you." He lifted his sword but did not press it to the stone. "I think you know what they want most, Princess."

Her heart thumped once in shock. Of course, she did. They wanted to give her their virginity. She clenched her fists. Did he think this proved he didn't care? Because he was suggesting she explore that final intimacy with other men? She spun around before he could read the hurt in her face and strode so quickly from the room she was almost running. She knew he cared. She did. But that didn't make her heart feel any less battered.

When the worst of her turmoil had faded and she stood in the sanctuary of her chamber, trembling but rational, she realized he had asked no reward for himself. He, who had braved twelve armed men, alone, asked for nothing—which did not mean Col and Ian deserved nothing. Grae was suggesting she repay them for the wrong reasons, but he was right. Col and Ian had risked their lives for her, because of her stupidity. If they'd wanted riches, she'd have showered them with coin, but neither had shown any interest in wealth.

She put the matter to them after they'd all prepared for bed. As usual, Grae was taking the first watch. Once she'd explained what she proposed, the two men exchanged a speaking glance.

"That would be wonderful, Mistress," Col said. He started to unwrap his kalisari, but Ian leaned over and whispered in his ear. Col drew back in alarm. "No, Ian, don't ask her that."

"Don't ask me what?"

Ian folded his hands together beneath his smiling mouth. "Col and I would very much like to take you together."

"Together?"

"At the same time."

"At the same—" A picture formed of Grae's thumb filling her bottom while his manhood filled her sheath. "Oh, I see. But would that count? As a loss of virginity, I mean?"

Ian laughed. "We were hoping to switch places, assuming you enjoy the first go."

"We've heard it's very pleasurable," Col said.

"For the woman, too," Ian added.

"Oh, yes, Mistress. Otherwise, we wouldn't want to."

"And we'll be very careful." Ian cleared his throat. "I myself have, er, had a bit of experience."

Well, thought Lily, there were virgins and then there were virgins. She smiled at the two men, as eager as spaniels for a treat. How easy it was to please them.

"Very well," she said. "I put myself in your capable hands."

After so many nights together, they knew her well: her pleasures, her weaknesses. They stroked her slowly, waking each inch of skin, praising her beauty, her softness. They caressed each other as well. Now that she knew their secret, and had expressed no horror, they lost their shyness of touching each other openly. The sight of male hands on male bodies fascinated her. It seemed oddly natural to her. They were so beautiful, two strangers thrown together far from home, kept from the usual expression of their sexuality. How could they resist each other?

Except, Grae had resisted them. Grae had not even seemed tempted.

Men were different, she supposed. But she didn't want to think about Grae. She wanted to lose herself among the admiring hands, to writhe between these two hard males like snakes mating in a nest of silk.

"Enough," said Ian. His sex pressed her back like sun-baked stone. "I need to take her."

Col reached into the night table for a corked brown bottle.

"A gentle oil," Ian explained. "The court physician's personal recipe."

She pressed her lips together to contain her amusement. "I won't ask how you got that."

"It would be better not to know," he agreed, then jerked as Col reached over her body and began to apply the oil.

She turned onto her back so she could watch. With only the slightest hesitation, Col worked the oil over Ian's thick, upthrust sex, his grip so firm she thought it must be hurtful. Ian, however, clearly enjoyed his masculine strength. His grey eyes narrowed to gleaming slits. Every so often they flickered up her body to her face.

"More," he said, his voice roughened by lust. His erection shone with oil already, so he must have meant he wanted more caresses.

"You like doing this in front of me, don't you?" she said.

"Yes. Your eyes—" He shuddered and touched Col's wrist to halt him.

Without further explanation, he held out his palm. Col filled its cup with oil. Ian nudged her onto her side and began massaging the oil between her cheeks. His progress was slow. At first he merely teased the entrance to her secret passage, gradually working deeper until his longest finger was buried to the webbing. She could not suppress her moans of pleasure. Tingling ripples swept up her spine. She could hardly wait to feel that warmer, thicker intrusion.

"I think, Princess," said Ian, "that it would be easier if I went first. Then, when you are comfortable, Col can proceed."

She could only nod. The pressure built as he pressed slowly, lasciviously inside. It was frightening and wonderful. He coached her through the process, warning her what she might feel, urging her to relax. All these instructions were punctuated by ecstatic sighs and groans as he entered by increments.

"It's like silk," he said when he was fully home. "I wish you could feel it."

"You're like silk," she said, "like hot, pulsing silk."

They both shuddered. Ian gripped her hips and steadied himself.

"Now," he said, "I'm going to pull back a bit and Col will enter."

Lily trailed her fingers down Col's damp, heaving chest. He'd taken himself in hand already. She swept her thumb over the deep pink head, marveling at the tautness of his skin. Col whimpered softly in reaction. His fingers tightened on his shaft. Ian lifted her thigh over Col's hip.

Together, she and Col positioned him at her gate.

"Oh, God," he said as the soft outer mouth closed over his glans. "You're so wet." He was trembling as he pushed inside, his eyes closed, his mouth slack with pleasure. He hilted with an endearing grunt, then shimmied a fraction deeper. "Oh, it's so marvelous. It's heaven. I don't think I ever want to leave."

Lily smiled and kissed him, gently, so as not to jar his poor nose.

"You're the best princess in the world," he declared.

Then they began to move. First Col thrust, then Ian. They rocked her between them, long alternating waves that inspired sensations so intense her throat tightened with sheer, physical joy. It was a dance of pleasure, perfectly timed. Neither man faltered. Neither missed his stroke. A thin wall separated their sexes. At the midpoint of each thrust she sensed a subtle increase in pressure as the rims of the heads passed each other. She noticed the men would slow each time they reached this point.

"You can feel each other, can't you?" she said.

The men shivered on either side of her. "Yes," they said in unison, then laughed.

Lily laughed, too, and stroked Col's thick red hair. "You are so sweet." She kissed his cheek and reached behind her for Ian's head. "Both of you."

"I can't last much longer," Col confessed.

"Neither can I," she whispered back, her laughter bubbling over. He was so dear. She kissed his mouth this time, parting his lips with her tongue. He sighed happily and joined her.

Some signal must have passed between the men because the pace quickened. Flares of heat burst at the increase in friction, shooting up her spine, melting her thighs. Her cry was lost in Col's kiss. It was too sweet. She couldn't bear it. Her skin ached with pleasure, her bones, her muscles. She could barely move between the two strong bodies that buffeted hers, each straining separately and together to get deeper. Arms twined around her. Legs. Someone kissed the back of her neck. Someone fondled her breast.

She groaned. She didn't know whether to thrust forward or back.

Col heaved against her, up and oh-so-far in. He groaned even louder than she. She wrenched her mouth free.

"Stay right there, Col." She reached behind her for Ian's hips. "Don't pull out."

"Yes," Ian said, his breath hissing through his teeth. He pushed, thick on thick, filling her, joining his eager, throbbing pulse to Col's, and to hers.

She tilted her hips a fraction lower and rubbed her bud of pleasure against the root of Col's shaft. That was all it took. She came like a banshee wailing in the night, drums pounding with heavenly violence through the tissues of her womb.

"Oh…my…God," she heard Col moan through her teeth-chattering spasm.

As one, the men spilled inside her. Their groans singed her ears, and their shudders set off another shower of spine-tingling sparks.

She wasn't sure when she noticed the shadow at the foot of the bed, or how she knew it had been there for some time. He had opened the hangings just wide enough to see. Beyond the reach of the bedlamps, his eyes alone caught the light, glittering, unblinking.

How could she explain this to him? The pleasure Col and Ian had showed her was sublime, but if it never happened again, she wouldn't shed a tear. She had not felt what she'd felt when Grae entered her, when Grae looked at her, as if her heart were being torn apart and made new. She stared at the silent shadow. He didn't have to watch. He had done it to hurt himself. To make himself hate her. He did not deserve an explanation, but she ached to offer one just the same.

"Your turn," Col said to Ian, sounding as if he were catching his second wind.

Ian laughed and kissed her shoulder.

The shadow turned away.

Chapter Eight

The Yskutian delegation arrived at sunrise. As far as Lily knew they had not been expected nor invited. And yet, and yet, the three maids her mother sent to oversee her toilette were very bright of face for women who should have been yanked but recently from their beds in town.

"What do you need them for?" Col grumbled, annoyed by the women's recall to duty.

Lily hid her smile. The maids had tried to shoo her slaves from the room, but all proved resistant, even Grae. He stood now by the window, his bare muscular arms crossed over his bare muscular chest.

"Oh, la," said Lyn, the senior maid, her eyes avoiding the display of handsome male flesh. "Men can't do for a woman when it's really important. There's a prince in that delegation."

Lily's brows rose. *A prince.* She held up her shift and lifted her foot so that Lynn could slide a stocking up her leg. Unlike Srucia, which was divided into city-states such as Ammam, the country of Yskut had but one royal family, and only six royal princes.

Her eyes found Grae's. A wordless message passed between them. She realized that he, too, suspected her mother was up to something. But what? On the surface, matchmaking seemed the obvious conclusion. An alliance with an Yskutian prince would be a coup for proud little Ammam. But why would Lady Fortis assume her daughter could handle an Yskutian? She barely credited her with handling her slaves.

Indeed, her mother's waters ran too deep for her to fathom.

Lyn smoothed the second stocking up her leg, then reached for the gown the other maids had removed from the wardrobe.

"Not the green," said Ian, who had been watching them with interest, and considerably less resentment than Col or Grae. The maids were pretty, after all. "The blue is more flattering."

Lyn's chin went up. "The blue is too low cut for a morning reception."

"Nonsense," said another voice. For a second, Lily couldn't believe it was Grae's, but he strode to the wardrobe and removed a sapphire velvet gown.

Lyn spluttered as he eased it over her mistress's head.

"Lady Fortis wishes to impress a prince," he said. "I assure you, the princes of Yskut are as impressed by a fine, fair bosom as any other men."

So. He thought she had a fair bosom. Bemused, Lily thrust her arms into the sleeves. The gown was closely fitted. Grae stepped behind her to fasten its tiny hooks, his fingers as deft as Lyn's had ever been. But then he did what the maid would never dream of doing. He reached into the bodice and resettled her breasts so that their curves swelled over the pearl-studded neckline.

The presence of the round-eyed maids could not quell Lily's reaction. Her nipples budded beneath his touch, lengthening, tightening. Her knees uncertain, she sagged into his embrace.

"You are ours," he whispered close to her ear. "This year is ours. If you think I'll entrust you to any man but those in this room, you are insane."

It was not something she had expected him to say. It was not something that, as his mistress, she should allow to pass uncontradicted. But she did not contradict him. She had too much pride to deny what she knew in her heart. Instead, she turned and stared. He was grinding his teeth in anger, but that look in his eyes might have been longing, or fear.

Either possibility gave her courage. How could she make him believe she loved him, that anyone loved him, if she wavered now? She stroked his whisker-roughened cheek. His eyelids quivered and she saw a fleeting shadow of the man-child who'd held her in the woods.

"I am yours," she said, and she didn't mean his and Col's and Ian's. She meant his. The truth had struck her the night before as she lay, limp with satisfaction, watching his lonely retreat from her pleasure bower.

He was her One True Love.

Nurse would have been proud. She had given her virginity to the man to whom it belonged, for all the good that did her now. Too bad the Yskutians couldn't give her Grae as a gift. Then she slapped both hands to her forehead. The gift! The blasted broken gift.

"Damnation," she said. Grae started back from her, his face stiff. "Oh, no, not you. I forgot to get the globe fixed, the one the ambassador gave my mother."

Frantically she dug through the chest where she thought she'd stowed it. "Oh, Lord, I hope the delegation doesn't notice it's missing. Ah! Here it is." She emerged, flushed but triumphant, and handed the broken halves to Ian. "Take this to my father and ask him, if he is able, to please repair it as quickly as he can."

"Wouldn't you prefer to speak to your father yourself?" Ian asked.

Lily blushed. It was a reasonable expectation, but surely one hurdle at a time was enough?

"I'll be too busy," she said. "You deliver and collect it, and then I'll sneak it back into my mother's office."

"Very good," Ian said, but she could tell he was perplexed.

From what Lily could see, the Yskutian prince was not the least bit impressed with her bosom. His eyes never left hers, not even when he bent over her hand to kiss it.

She, on the other hand, thought him the most perfect creature she had ever seen, even more beautiful than Col or Ian, even more exotic than Grae. His skin was smooth and creamy, his features as delicate as if they'd been carved in ivory. He was tall, well-formed, and wore the most sumptuous clothes: layered robes of heavily embroidered silk in varied jewel-bright hues, all gathered at the waist with a wide brocade sash. Set amongst all that glowing color was his silent, inscrutable essence, stillness amidst a fountain of noise.

His accent charmed her. His voice was as smooth and light as apple wine. He had such grace that the simplest of gestures, an adjustment of his robes, a tilting of his head, had the power to hypnotize her. She couldn't stop staring. But then, neither could he. They might have been alone at the official welcoming breakfast. They were alone for his tour of the castle grounds, Lady Fortis having dismissed her slaves for the afternoon.

Lily was not used to seeing a foreigner of his stature without bodyguard or armor. Of course, the men of Yskut did not wear armor into battle. And they used strange weapons, blades which never dulled and wicked black stars, *zhurim* they were called, which sliced like razors and returned to their owners after they were thrown.

When Lily questioned him about his current defenseless state, he paired the first two fingers of his right hand. "I could kill you with these, Princess, without you feeling a moment's pain."

'Science,' her mother called it. Lily preferred 'uncanny.' She did not, however, sense any danger from the prince. He might not have ogled her bosom, but he clearly admired her. And there seemed to be no anger in him. He was a still pond on a windless day.

Now they stood atop the east watchtower, gazing out over farmland towards the harbor.

The prince waved his deadly hand over the view. "This is beautiful country."

"But not as beautiful as Yskut," she said, alerted by an undercurrent in his melodious voice.

Turning, he caught the amusement quivering on her lips. To her relief, he burst into a warm, infectious laugh. "You think I'm arrogant, don't you? No, don't lie. I can tell. In any case, I am arrogant." He caught the edge of the battlement in his hands and rocked back on his heels, a gesture many young men might make, but few Yskutians. As if aware of her thoughts, he looked at her sidelong and smiled. "I forget, you see. Until I travel abroad and see those puffed-up foreigners strutting about. How many years of history do they have to our thousands? A hundred? Perhaps two? 'How foolish they are to be proud of *that*,' I think. And then I am caught. 'How foolish you are,' I tell myself, 'to assume that anyone who sees the world differently is a fool.' Perhaps that is why my father sent me on this journey. Perhaps he thought I needed the reminder."

"You mean you don't know why he sent you?"

He shook his head. His queued hair shone blue-black in the noonday sun, the same color as Grae's, but not as thick. His eyes resembled Grae's as well, though they had not his shadows.

"My father is a deep soul. He merely said I was needed. But I have not met anyone I felt drawn to help yet, except for you and I cannot imagine why." He grinned. "Perhaps I was blinded by how pretty you are and merely wished you were the one I was sent to help."

Flattered, Lily smiled and scraped her slipper along the wall. "My mother would tell you I need a great deal of help. She fears I am not sufficiently masterful to rule as Ammam's queen."

"Ah." The prince nodded at the waving fields of wheat. "My father would say that the most important person to rule is yourself. And the most impossible person to rule is anyone besides yourself."

"I'm sure that's very wise," she said. "Although I don't know what good it does me."

"Your mother is formidable," the prince agreed with equal sobriety.

They turned to each other, eyes sparkling like naughty children. Lily was the first to giggle, but soon both were lost.

"Oh, dear," she said when she could speak again.

The prince caught her hand and carried it to his chest. "I don't know about you, Princess, but I think I have found something I needed."

"And what would that be?"

"A friend," he said. "A friend who is not my own kind."

Eyes stinging with emotion, Lily bowed to him in the stiff, formal fashion of his people. "I would be honored to have you call me friend."

He smiled a serene Yskutian smile, then gave a little jump as if he'd just remembered something. "Oh!" he said. "So would I."

For once her mother did not make her stand on the carpet before her desk. They sat in the window in her jewel box of an office, each in her own chair. Lily stroked the carved arms and stared at the stained-glass roses while she waited for her mother to come to the point.

The prince had been in Ammam a week now, and his attentions to Lily had brought a smile to her mother's stern face. "He's so polite," she'd been saying since he arrived. "And so handsome. My goodness, I don't know how any woman could resist him." All of which was a thinly disguised attempt to find out whether Lily had.

She knew her mother was jumping to unwarranted conclusions. Or so she thought until her mother patted her arm and said, "Now. To the heart of the matter."

Lily turned from the window and prepared to listen.

"The prince has asked for your hand in marriage."

She squeezed her eyes shut, then opened them wide, as if her mother's words were a fever dream she could blink away.

Her mother laughed at her expression. "Yes, it's true. Rather precipitous, I admit, but for whatever reason you seem to have charmed him."

"But," Lily stammered and thought, how dare he? She did not feel flattered. She felt betrayed. The prince knew there was nothing but affection between them. After a week of intimate conversations, including a few on the topic of Grae, how could he not know? But perhaps Yskutians didn't believe in love matches. Perhaps he wished to live in a country that would perpetually remind him of his 'arrogance.'

"I cannot marry him," she said. "You must convey my regrets."

Her mother drew up in her chair. "I will not. He's just the sort of biddable fellow you need. Never forward. Never pushy."

"Unless he thinks someone *needs* him to push," Lily muttered.

Lady Fortis ignored the interruption. "And he's an Yskutian. Just imagine the potential for scholarly exchange."

Lily shook her head, startled to see how deeply her mother had misjudged the prince. She'd always considered her opinion on political matters to be infallible. But the Yskutians were anything but a 'biddable' people. Nothing, not marriage, not money, not threat of war, could induce them to part with their secrets. If her mother could be so wrong about this, what else might she have misjudged? Perhaps Lily wasn't as hopeless as Lady Fortis thought.

Buoyed by that possibility, she gripped the arms of her chair. "I cannot marry him, Mother. And it isn't fair to lead him on. If you won't tell him, I will."

Her mother leaned back, her smile gone. "I could order you to marry him."

"Mother." Lily pressed her hands to her head. "You can't order me to marry. That would undermine everything this year is meant to achieve."

Her mother digested this reminder. She smoothed her cloth of gold gown over her knees. "Very well. I'll make you a deal. Marry within the month and I'll give the town their charter."

"Their charter!" Lily lost her breath at the scope of the offer. "You've been resisting that since you took the throne."

"So I have. I suppose my priorities are shifting."

Lily pushed from her chair, paced three steps towards her mother's desk and turned. "I can marry anyone I want?"

Her mother smiled, a small cat-in-the-creamery smile. "Let it not be said that I forced the heir to marry against her will. You may wed a serf for all I care." A dimple appeared in her smooth white cheek. "I'm betting you won't, though. I'm betting you care too much for the well-being of our people to marry anyone who will not enhance Ammam's position in the world. And in the meantime, you will not refuse the prince's offer."

Lily stared at her smug expression. Her heart was pounding against her ribs. "You assume I won't find a better candidate within a month."

Her mother spread her hands as if to say, *of course.*

Damn her. How had she known Lily wanted to see the town get their council? She'd never said a word. She'd been careful to relate the tale of her kidnaping with the utmost objectivity. But perhaps that was the problem. She should have been angrier. She should have hated them all for what a few had tried to do.

She shook her head. That was water under the bridge. What mattered was that she had an opportunity to change the shape of her world long before she expected to. She could not throw the chance away without at least considering it.

"I will take your month," she said. "But I make no promises."

Still smiling, her mother inclined her head. She knew when silence was golden.

Chapter Nine

"I have news," she said from her perch on the steps at the foot of her bed. Col's head rested on her knee, Ian leaned against the carved bedpost and Grae stood by the window, polishing the hilt of his sword. It was the same sword she'd given him on her birthday. She wondered at that. If his father's mail were any indication, he must own finer. Like the others, he'd been quiet this evening. Perhaps her mood was catching.

Col leaned into her knee like a pampered hunting dog. "Bad news?"

"I don't know that it's bad." She glanced at Grae, then Ian. She didn't want to tell them. She knew her mother would disapprove. But they had a right to know.

"Pull the thorn," Grae advised. "We're all big boys here."

She closed her eyes. "The prince has offered for my hand."

Silence greeted her announcement. She opened her eyes. Ian put one hand to his head. Grae merely froze.

"Od's bod," said Col. "He's only been here a week."

"I know." She stroked his russet hair as much for her comfort as his. "Apparently, the men of Yskut don't take long to make up their minds. The point is my year with the love guard is meant to prepare me for marriage. If I marry earlier—"

"We'll have to leave," Ian finished, his expression grim.

Grae looked out the window. The men still wore their public clothes. It had seemed better to tell them while they possessed that small barrier.

Col scratched the knee of his hose. "I guess even an Ammami husband can't be expected to tolerate three slaves in his wife's bed."

"No," Lily agreed.

His words repeated in her mind. *Even an Ammami husband.* She thought of Vizier, her mother's former slave, her long-time lover. Had her father minded? Would she want to marry a man who didn't? Most of all, could she treat her own husband that way, whether she loved him or not? She did not believe she could. It would be hard to live without love, but it would be harder to live without self-respect.

"What's the rush?" Grae asked, his voice scrupulously level. He stared at the hilt of his sword, his lips white, his fingers tense. Lily's heart went out to him. He was so proud. So full of love which he dared not offer anyone. He did not deserve this from her. But how could she deny what her people deserved? How could she put her and Grae's happiness first?

She swallowed against the tightness in her throat. "My mother has expressed some doubts about my ability to rule my future husband. She seems to think this prince is someone I could handle."

Grae snorted.

"I agree," she said. "And I told her as much. But she said if I marry within the month, she'll license the town's charter. She didn't say I had to marry the prince, but she's betting I won't find another suitable prospect in so short a time."

Col craned around to examine her face. "You can marry anyone?"

"Anyone my people could live with." She twisted her hands together. "I'm not saying I will marry the prince. Just that, in good conscience, I have to consider my mother's offer."

"We understand, Princess," Col said. "In fact—"

Ian cut him short. "No, Col."

"But—"

"No. A man's word is his bond."

"I know, but—"

"No," Ian repeated, and this time he won Col's silence, not to mention a blush.

Before Lily could decide whether to probe further, Grae crossed the space between them and held out his hand. "Come with me, Princess. I need to speak to you privately."

The other men fell back. No doubt about it, Grae was king wolf here. Even she felt the pull to obey him. She put her hand in his and let him help her to her feet.

He led her down the stairs to the weaving room. The looms still sat against the walls and the prayer rug still covered the floor. She remembered how he'd lain there curled in sleep, a boy in sleep, a man whose heart could break as surely as her own. Her eyes stung. She prayed he wouldn't see the telltale glitter. When she turned to face him, he captured her hands in his. To her astonishment, his eyes shone as well.

"Princess." His voice throaty, he shook his head. "Just when I think I understand you, you surprise me."

She did not answer. She could not. His expression was for once unguarded. What it said made her throat close with emotion. His hands slid up her sleeves to her shoulders. His thumbs caressed the skin her neckline bared. He clasped her neck, then her jaw. His fingers fanned out behind her ears, the lightest, tenderest hold. Tendrils of heat unfurled in her breasts. He stepped closer.

"Princess," he whispered, the word ghosting over her lips.

"Lily," she said. "Call me Lily."

His smile brushed her mouth. "Lily then." He kissed her, soft as a breeze, skimming her mouth, her cheeks, her eyelids. "Beautiful Lily."

The kisses grew firmer, a gentle pressure, warm. Her arms rose, surrounding his back with the same light hold. He found a nerve on the side of her neck that made her shiver.

He laughed, low and soft. "Make love to me, Lily."

She stepped back and worked the sleeves of her gown over her shoulders. He unhooked the leather belt he wore wrapped thrice around his waist. The world fell away as they disrobed, each for the other, as if they had stepped into a dream. His eyes told her how lovely he found her, his eyes and the bold outward thrust of his sex. Her hands faltered when she saw it, shuddering and strong, in the last light of evening. He knelt before her. One by one, he undid the ribbons that rounded her thighs and peeled the hose down her legs.

He did not rise when she was naked. He kissed the gentle curve of her belly and turned his face from side to side. Arousal rolled through her in slow, liquid waves, a kind of drunkenness, one that heightened rather than dulled the nerves. She buried her fingers in his hair and stroked his scalp. Again she felt his smile against her skin, then her hair, then the secret purse of her sex. Here his kiss was deep and strong. He lifted the jewel of her pleasure and suckled it. She sighed, losing her strength, losing her breath.

He caught her before her knees could give way and lowered her to the rug.

"Simple," he said, as she opened to him. "You and me. Alone together."

"Yes," she said, and rubbed his hair-roughened legs with her smooth ones. He settled his elbows by her sides, the cap of his sex fitting neatly to her gate.

"You're wet," he said, his voice giving out a little.

"Yes," she said. "You made me that way."

He pushed inside. What a luxury this was, to feel this warm column of flesh sliding so smoothly into her body. She ran her hands down the wide sweep of his back and cupped his buttocks, lightly, the most polite of encouragements. He smiled and took her fully. She undulated beneath him, stretching into the wonderful sensations. He began to rock, long, slow strokes that lulled and aroused and dragged low, happy moans from her throat.

"That's it. Sing for me," he said and she knew her moans were music to him.

She sang until she could no longer hold him gently. Her hands fisted behind his shoulders, and her nails curled into her palms to avoid wounding him. Her legs she could not keep still. She stroked the soles of her feet over his calves, up his thighs. She locked her ankles behind his buttocks and dug her heels into the muscle there. Then she repeated the restless journey.

Through all this he was slow and steady. He caressed her with his sex, with his chest, with the hard clean line of his jaw. The end crept towards them, first with a quiver, then a tremor and finally a shudder that was weakness and strength and greed knotted together in a chain of gold.

"I can't wait," she gasped. "Bring me over. End it, Grae. End it."

His head dipped toward hers, his hair damp from their efforts, his breathing labored.

"I'll end it," he said, his strokes turning to angry hammer strikes. "I'll end it."

All his disappointments were in those thrusts, all his unrequited loves. Like a whirlwind, his passion caught her, disjointed her. She felt the thighs that pressed hers wider, the hand that tangled in her hair, the final swelling of his sex. His shoulders bunched beneath her hands. A drop of sweat fell to her breast. He licked it away and panted against her skin.

She gathered, arching, meeting his desperate blows with her own.

He broke a moment before she did. She felt his first hot burst, and his second and then she was lost with him, uttering cries that seemed to hold her heart. *I love you,* they said, wordless though they were. *I wish, I wish—*

She didn't know how long she lay with him sprawled atop her. She held him lightly, not wanting to cling but dreading the moment she'd have to let go.

"I need to tell you something," he said, and she remembered he'd had a reason for bringing her here, a reason beyond the pleasure they'd shared.

"Yes?"

He rose up on his elbow and his body slipped from hers. She winced.

"Col and Ian are princes," he said. "You could marry one of them."

She covered her forehead with her palm and stared at him, too shocked to speak.

"Yes," he said. "Ian is from Laravia and Col from Medellín. Col is a third son, but Medellín is a rich country. And he is very kind. I doubt even your mother would find him a bad match. Trust me, Princess. You don't want to marry the Yskutian. They have hearts, but they live by their heads. You wouldn't like that. You need to marry a man with a passion to match yours."

She could hardly take in what he was saying. She didn't know whether to be hurt that he could hand her so easily to another, or touched that he cared enough for her happiness to try. She squirmed out from under him and stood, needing distance to think.

"They're princes?" she said. "My slaves are princes?"

"All guard candidates swear an oath not to reveal their origins." He rolled onto his back and propped himself on his elbows. Lines scored the corners of his mouth. Perhaps this wasn't as easy for him as she'd thought. "Everyone knows that the best way to form alliances with Ammam is to send a slave. Ammam may be a small principality, but she is the Gateway to the South. The Choosing must be blind in order to be just."

"I don't understand. You told me your background."

"It doesn't matter if I break the rules. This was not my ambition. It was my father's, his way of redeeming the family after he was banished from the armorer's guild. Every coin he possessed went towards paying my entry tribute." His smile humorless, he touched the faint marks on his shoulder. "Do you know how I got these stripes? My father caught me behind a haystack with one of the village girls. I was thirteen. If he'd been a minute later, I would have been free today."

Her lips tightened at the bitterness in his voice. Did he honestly think of his time with her as imprisonment? Suddenly cold, she reached for her shift and pulled it over her head.

"Thirteen. That's young." She watched him from the side of her eye. "I suppose he locked you in a room after that, to make sure you didn't do it again."

He sat up, his glare more familiar than his kindness had ever been. "Are you saying I chose this? That I could have rebelled if I wanted to?"

"I'm saying it intrigues me that you care so much about your supposed oppressor's future happiness. That, having suffered so much, you risk disgrace by revealing the origins of your fellow slaves. A man who truly hated his position here would have asked for his freedom after he rescued me. You would have been sent home wreathed in glory. Perhaps you should ask yourself why you didn't."

She took no pleasure in his response, though it was no more than she'd expected. Immediately defensive, he got to his feet and grabbed his clothes. "Perhaps I didn't realize the woman who'd nearly raped me the night before would be so magnanimous. In any case, it doesn't matter now. Your efforts are better spent in deciding which of your slaves you'd like to marry."

"I've already decided," she said, for anger had made her reckless.

"Oh?"

She lifted her chin. "I've decided to marry you."

For a second his face went blank, eyes wide, jaw hanging, and then a look of pain crossed his features, a look such as she'd never seen on any man's face, and certainly not his. In that moment, she knew he loved her, truly loved her.

He soon recovered, or nearly. His laugh was harsh, but not as mocking as she was sure he wished to make it. "You can't marry me, Princess. I'm a poor man's poorer son."

It didn't matter what he said. That brief flash of longing had given her all the courage she needed. He was willing to sacrifice his happiness for hers. He had risked his life and his honor. A hundred times a day, he made serving her well a matter of pride, no matter how it galled him. And he had taught her some hard lessons about the true duties of a mistress. If those weren't princely actions, she didn't know what were. She closed the distance between them. She touched her heart. "You are a prince to me, the prince of my heart. When I rule you will stand beside me."

He stared at her as if she'd gone mad. She tried to smile but her lips quavered.

"Of course," she added, "we're not likely to rule for many years. By the time we wear the purple, you'll have lived here so long my people will have forgotten where you came from."

"You've lost your mind," he said, but his expression had softened. He wanted to believe it was possible. She could feel it.

"I can make it happen," she said, though in truth she didn't know how.

"You can't."

Again she heard the weakening, the longing. She rested her arms on his shoulders, clasped the back of his neck. "But if I could..."

"If you could." He shook his head. "I don't know, Princess. That's a lot to consider."

She tugged softly until his cheek brushed hers. "So long as you do consider it, my love."

He pushed back and looked into her face, his eyes once more naked. Tears sparkled in his lower lashes, more precious than diamonds.

"I do love you," he said. "God help me."

She laughed and hugged him close. Now she knew she could accomplish anything.

Lily sat up in bed as if a bolt of lightning had streaked through the window and pierced her chest. The armor was the answer. The bloody, blessed, Ka'arkish black armor. Her mother would move heaven and earth to outfit her garrison in the stuff. And Grae was the son of the man who'd invented it. All she had to do was tell her mother to offer his father a position as the royal armorer. Admittedly, this would make his father a traitor to his own people but after all this time, how much loyalty could he bear them? They'd betrayed him, spit on his genius. Surely he'd relish the chance to serve Lady Fortis. Especially if his son would one day reign as king.

She almost turned to wake him, to share her stroke of brilliance. Her hand stopped an inch from his shoulder. Would Grae approve? Grae wasn't sure he wanted to marry her. Grae was barely convinced she wanted to marry him. If she used his father as a bargaining chip, would he always wonder if she valued his father's skill more than she valued him?

Maybe she shouldn't tell him. Maybe only her mother needed to know. She could present marriage to Grae as an opportunity to make a useful alliance, not a promise, merely a chance. She sank back and pulled the covers to her chest. Yes, that would be easier all around. The cause was good. And she and Grae would be happy together.

One little secret couldn't change that.

Chapter Ten

Her mother rose from behind her desk, her face white with fury. "You want to marry your slave!"

The ornate crystal chandelier tinkled at the volume of her voice. Lily squeezed her hands together behind her back. Her fingers were icy, her palms damp.

"Yes," she said as steadily as she could. "I wish to marry Grae of Ka'arkasba'ad. He is a good man. He will rule well."

"Rule!" Her mother pressed both palms to her head. "No man will rule in Ammam while I have anything to say about it." She pointed at Lily, her finger trembling with passion. "No man will bring war to this country. No man will trod the women of Ammam beneath his heel."

"Grae isn't like that," she objected, even though saying he would rule had been a slip of the tongue. At least she thought it was. She shifted her weight. Last night, when she told him he was the prince of her heart, she had said he would rule beside her. Was that a slip as well?

"You cannot marry a slave," her mother said more reasonably. She smoothed her gown over the generous swell of her bosom. Today, she wore purple beneath her purple robes of state. The vivid hue made her eyes seem even paler. "I know we are not supposed to know such things but, whatever he may have told you, I assure you this slave's origins are humble."

"They are not as humble as you think," she said.

Her mother shot a skeptical look from beneath her brows. Lily's nails bit her palms. The queen could not know Grae's father had it within his means to grant one of her dearest wishes. The secret of the black mail would ransom a dozen princes. Once Lily told her about it, she'd be singing another tune. The words were in her throat, pressing on her tongue. Someone's hunting falcon flew past the window, screaming in triumph.

Lily's chest burned with a desire to wipe the disapproval from her mother's face, to claim her own victory.

But she had not consulted Grae. And she suspected Grae would not approve, even assuming his father would. She could not induce a man to betray his country, no matter how strained his relationship with it. They were not at war with Ka'arkastan. The only purpose this divulgence would serve was overcoming her mother's objection to the marriage.

It was the easy road.

If she stepped onto it, would Grae ever forgive her? Or would he believe she had once again set her will above his? She could not do it. With a quiet sigh, the words died unspoken. She raised her chin. "You said I might marry a serf. Do you mean to go back on your word?"

"Yes," said a voice from the door to the connecting chamber. "Do you?"

Lily expected to see Vizier, her trusty rescuer. Instead, she found her father dressed in his usual dusty black, his eyes lit with a fire she couldn't remember having seen there before. In his hand he cradled the Yskutian globe Ian had given to him to repair.

"William." Her mother sat, obviously shaken by his appearance.

"Yes, William it is." A faint smile played about his lips, more self-mocking than amused. "I bring you something you appear to need." He held out the hollow ivory sphere. Her mother looked at it, clearly confused. "I gather you broke it. Your daughter asked me to repair it so that its absence would not offend our visitors from Yskut."

"That's very considerate but I hardly think I need—"

Her father's laugh cut her short. What a strange sound it was, like the creaking of a door. "You don't know what it is, do you?"

"Of course, I do. It's a picture of the world. A trinket. Clever. But a trinket."

Her father leaned across the polished expanse of her desk, propping himself on one narrow hand. He held the globe before her face and turned it hypnotically from side to side. Lady Fortis watched him as a cat might eye an unexpectedly aggressive mouse.

"It is a meditation object," he said. "Years of work and thought go into making them. The creations of this particular artisan are highly prized. You see the tiny diamond chip set into the ivory? That is Ammam. Considering the recipient, I believe its message is that we inhabit a very small corner of a very small world. It is foolish to think that one man's perspective is the only perspective there is."

Her mother pushed her chair back from her desk. "One man's perspective, eh?"

Her father shrugged, his half-smile deepening. "Or one woman's."

Her mother's lips tightened. Vizier might have said *touché,* but Lady Fortis had too much pride for that.

"So," said her father, pressing his advantage home. "Did you or did you not tell our daughter she could marry any man she chose?"

"I did but—"

Her father touched his wife's lips. She started at the intimacy of the gesture, as did Lily. "And have you not taught our daughter that a woman is only as good as her word?"

"But she wants to marry a slave! Even *you* can see how impossible that is."

Her father dropped his hand and straightened. With a pang, Lily saw how gaunt he was, how her mother's scorn had tightened the skin above his beard. He stiffened his shoulders against the blow, but Lily saw his hurt. When he spoke, his voice was stiff as well.

"If my daughter admires this man, I suspect he is worthy. I have watched her over the years and she has demonstrated a great deal of sense. Fortis, please—" His voice broke but he did not pause. "If you love her, do not make her do as you did. Let her marry the choice of her heart. Then perhaps we can spare our citizens the spectacle of a queen who would rather sleep with her cabinet than speak to her king."

Lily knew then. She knew that he had minded all along. Theirs might have been a political marriage; her father might never have loved her mother, but insult by insult she had crushed his pride under her royal slipper, had made him the shadow man he was today. Lady Fortis did not know what she had lost, but now Lily did. Her father's mind was subtle and keen and under that silent black exterior a heart beat, a heart that was capable of courage and caring, even for a daughter who had shown him no more warmth or understanding than his wife.

But that was Lily's sin, one she would take care not to repeat. Who knew what he might have been, might still be, if someone he cared for treated him with respect, or love.

Never, she told herself. Never will I treat my husband that way. Never will I treat my people that way.

She curled her hands into fists and blinked back tears. All her life she had known she was different from her mother, that she did not, in her heart, even wish to be the same. She had bemoaned that difference, called it weakness, cowardice, when all along, in her own quiet way, she had been following her own path, because her conscience had not allowed her to do otherwise. Her father had called it good sense, Vizier, the ability to make her servants love her. She did not need to inspire fear in her people; she needed to inspire respect. And she could only do that if she ruled in a way that she herself could respect: a way that set love above fear. She would make mistakes, as her mother had, but her best would be sufficient. And she would have Grae's help, Grae's quiet strength, Grae's pride in a job well done.

With Grae at her side, her best might prove more than sufficient.

She barely heard her mother's surrender, barely felt her tearful kiss, barely heard her whispered plea to reconsider. None of that mattered. Victory had been hers the moment she began to trust herself.

She straddled his belly, not taking him yet, merely enjoying the anticipation.

His eyes slid shut as she ran her hands over his powerful torso. His own hands spanned her waist, kneading and releasing in a hot, restless rhythm.

The prince had sailed that afternoon. He had taken her refusal philosophically, even promised to begin contemplating a useful wedding gift. She wondered when he would realize he'd already given it to her, by acting as the catalyst for her marriage to Grae.

Now they were alone in her chamber. Col and Ian stood guard at the base of the tower. She had not asked them to remove to this position. If Grae had, she had not heard him do it. Perhaps they sensed their relationship had changed.

She was Grae's now. She would always be Grae's. The knowledge warmed her face, her body. She leaned back until the hard rise of his sex brushed her buttocks, bent back by the division of warm, rounded flesh. His body quivered, the part she brushed and the part she rode.

"Princess." His hands tightened on her waist. He rolled her beneath him.

"Bully," she teased, but she lifted her knees in wanton invitation. He did not laugh.

"I need to take you," he said, the 'take' a growl, his hands a pair of living manacles creeping up her arms, stretching them over her head. He notched her and pushed inside, one hard, quick thrust. He sighed with pleasure and pressed a fraction deeper. Their hands met palm to palm. Lily linked their fingers. Then they both were trapped.

"Mine," she said, with the most deliciously primitive satisfaction.

"Mine," he responded, and began the rhythm that would carry them both to completion.

But not without a satisfying struggle. She fought his rhythm. Pushed it faster with swiveling upward beats of her hips, with hidden tugs that massaged his pumping flesh and pulled him towards the very brink of pleasure.

"Too fast," he gasped, but he did not slow. Instead he pushed up on his arms, straighter, higher, until only his hips met hers.

Her hands freed, she caressed his taut, straining body. She teased the sweating cords of his neck and shoulders, the pinpoints at his breast, the small of his back, his buttocks.

"No," he rasped as she teased the hidden entrance. "Not this time. I'm too close."

She obeyed his request, though she smiled as if she might not. Her nails trailed lower, making him shiver. She cradled his swaying sac. Gently, she squeezed. Gently she pricked. It would hurt just a little, she thought, a sweet hurt, like a spanking.

His sex stiffened inside her. He groaned and closed his eyes. "Lily."

The world between the bed hangings spun. Sheets tangled and released her legs and then she was on top again, gazing into his beautiful face. His features were softened by the disarray of his long, thick hair, by the lust and love in his eyes. The sight made her clench inside, made her arch her back and press the thick, tensile strength of him against one wonderful, aching spot.

His lips curved in the subtlest, sweetest smile.

"Finish it," he said. "Finish us both."

She rode him, gracefully first, then with abandon. He squeezed her breasts, he stroked her hair, but those were dim sensations to the wild hard drive of his sex. She exulted in the greedy ramming in of him. She begrudged the reluctant pull. She clenched hard, struggling to keep him from going too far. Just to the rim of the swollen tip. No more. She enforced her will with a gripping tug, a gasp, and then down she flung again, taking him into her. Thick and smooth. His heat. His strength. Her liquid welcome.

She fed his shudders with her own and rode faster, losing control of her movements because the ache was so desperate, the fever so high. He held her hips. He slammed off the mattress to meet her. Sweating. Panting. A soft curse.

"Now," he said and pressed the point of gold with his thumbs.

Blindly they came, their hands locked together over the place their bodies met. She did not need her eyes. She felt their tremors, heard their tangled cries of relief. He pulsed inside her as she shook. The ease that followed, hers and his, warmed her like sunshine.

"Princess," he whispered. Had she fallen? She lay cradled in his arms. "Sweet Lily, I cannot marry you."

She laughed. She could not credit such foolishness when joy wrapped her so securely. In her heart, they were married already.

"Did you hear me?"

She kissed the hard, sweaty muscle of his shoulder. "I heard you."

"I love you, but I have thought carefully and I cannot live as your father lives. I would lose all respect for myself. And so would you. I could not bear that. I need your respect as much as I need your love."

The admission cost him. She could tell by the tension in his arms. So she did not laugh. She pushed up on his chest and smiled into his serious eyes.

"In some ways I am my mother's daughter," she said. "I can be stubborn. I do not like to admit I am wrong. And I hope I have a portion of her intelligence. But I am not my mother, Grae. I would never treat a man I loved as she treats my father. Nor would I deprive my people of the benefit of your wisdom, not to mention your sense of justice. I meant what I said to you before. When I rule, you will rule beside me."

To her surprise, he squirmed at that. "I don't know that I need to rule, precisely. I am only an armorer's son. I have no training for kingship. I cannot even sit a horse!"

Lily chuckled and snuggled back into his arms.

"Why are you laughing?" he said, endearingly aggrieved. "Kingship is a serious responsibility. I wasn't raised for this as you were. What if I—"

She silenced him with a soft kiss. "I laugh because I know you, Grae. You will not rest until you learn what is required. You are too proud not to do a job well, whether it is removing spots or making love or foiling an insurrectionist plot. If you have any doubts, Ian and Col can attest you are a natural leader, not to mention a cool head in a crisis. Trust me, you will learn to ride a horse and sit in judgment and remind your wife she has a responsibility not only to rule, but to serve."

A more flattering sort of man would have denied any necessity for the last. Grae merely scratched his jaw and looked doubtful. "You will help me?"

"Only if you will help me," she said.

That gave him pause. His arms tightened around her back.

"I will," he said with the seriousness of a solemn oath.

"Good," she said.

And they both smiled into the hush.

About the Author:

Emma Holly started out writing fantasy, wandered into romance and then jumped, headfirst, into the murky waters of erotica where she was rewarded with (gasp!) real publishing contracts.

Red Sage gave her her first chance to combine all her literary loves. For those interested in her even-steamier side, Emma Holly also writes for Black Lace. Her fan mail occasionally embarrasses her, but so far she's bearing up!

Men you've been dreaming about!

Secrets

Satisfy your desire for more.

*F*eel the wild adventure, fierce passion and the power of love in every **Secrets** Collection story. Red Sage Publishing's romance authors create richly crafted, sexy, sensual, novella-length stories. Each one is just the right length for reading after a long and hectic day.

Each volume in the **Secrets** Collection has four diverse, ultra-sexy, romantic novellas brimming with adventure, passion and love. More adventurous tales for the adventurous reader. The **Secrets** Collection are a glorious mix of romance genre; numerous historical settings, contemporary, paranormal, science fiction and suspense. We are always looking for new adventures.

Reader response to the **Secrets** volumes has been great! Here's just a small sample:

> *"I loved the variety of settings. Four completely wonderful time periods, give you four completely wonderful reads."*

> *"Each story was a page-turning tale I hated to put down."*

> *"I love **Secrets**! When is the next volume coming out? This one was Hot! Loved the heroes!"*

Secrets have won raves and awards. We could go on, but why don't you find out for yourself—order your set of **Secrets** today! See the back for details.

Secrets, Volume 1

Listen to what reviewers say:

"These stories take you beyond romance into the realm of erotica. I found *Secrets* absolutely delicious."

—Virginia Henley,
New York Times Best Selling Author

"*Secrets* is a collection of novellas for the daring, adventurous woman who's not afraid to give her fantasies free reign."

—Kathe Robin, *Romantic Times* Magazine

"…In fact, the men featured in all the stories are terrific, they all want to please and pleasure their women. If you like erotic romance you will love *Secrets*."

—*Romantic Readers* Review

In *Secrets, Volume 1* you'll find:

A Lady's Quest by Bonnie Hamre

Widowed Lady Antonia Blair-Sutworth searches for a lover to save her from the handsome Duke of Sutherland. The "auditions" may be shocking but utterly tantalizing.

The Spinner's Dream by Alice Gaines

A seductive fantasy that leaves every woman wishing for her own private love slave, desperate and running for his life.

The Proposal by Ivy Landon

This tale is a walk on the wild side of love. *The Proposal* will taunt you, tease you, and shock you. A contemporary erotica for the adventurous woman.

The Gift by Jeanie LeGendre

Immerse yourself in this historic tale of exotic seduction, bondage and a concubine's surrender to the Sultan's desire. Can Alessandra live the life and give the gift the Sultan demands of her?

Secrets, Volume 2

Listen to what reviewers say:

"*Secrets* offers four novellas of sensual delight; each beautifully written with intense feeling and dedication to character development. For those seeking stories with heightened intimacy, look no further."

—Kathee Card, *Romancing the Web*

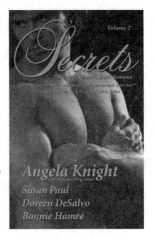

"Such a welcome diversity in styles and genres. Rich characterization in sensual tales. An exciting read that's sure to titillate the senses."

—Cheryl Ann Porter

"*Secrets 2* left me breathless. Sensual satisfaction guaranteed… times four!"

—Virginia Henley, *New York Times* Best Selling Author

In *Secrets, Volume 2* you'll find:

Surrogate Lover by Doreen DeSalvo

Adrian Ross is a surrogate sex therapist who has all the answers and control. He thought he'd seen and done it all, but he'd never met Sarah.

Snowbound by Bonnie Hamre

A delicious, sensuous regency tale. The marriage-shy Earl of Howden is teased and tortured by his own desires and finds there is a woman who can equal his overpowering sensuality.

Roarke's Prisoner by Angela Knight

Elise, a starship captain, remembers the eager animal submission she'd known before at her captor's hands and refuses to become his toy again. However, she has no idea of the delights he's planned for her this time.

Savage Garden by Susan Paul

Raine's been captured by a mysterious and dangerous revolutionary leader in Mexico. At first her only concern is survival, but she quickly finds lush erotic nights in her captor's arms.

Winner of the Fallot Literary Award for Fiction!

Secrets, Volume 3

Listen to what reviewers say:

"*Secrets, Volume 3*, leaves the reader breathless. A delicious confection of sensuous treats awaits the reader on each turn of the page!"
—Kathee Card, *Romancing the Web*

"From the FBI to Police Detective to Vampires to a Medieval Warlord home from the Crusade—*Secrets 3* is simply the best!"
—Susan Paul, award winning author

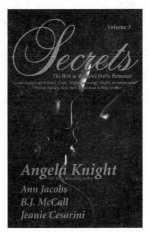

"An unabashed celebration of sex. Highly arousing! Highly recommended!"
—Virginia Henley, *New York Times* Best Selling Author

In *Secrets, Volume 3* you'll find:

The Spy Who Loved Me by Jeanie Cesarini
Undercover FBI agent Paige Ellison's sexual appetites rise to new levels when she works with leading man Christopher Sharp, the cunning agent who uses all his training to capture her body and heart.

The Barbarian by Ann Jacobs
Lady Brianna vows not to surrender to the barbaric Giles, Earl of Harrow. He must use sexual arts learned in the infidels' harem to conquer his bride. A word of caution—this is not for the faint of heart.

Blood and Kisses by Angela Knight
A vampire assassin is after Beryl St. Cloud. Her only hope lies with Decker, another vampire and ex-mercenary. Broke, she offers herself as payment for his services. Will his seductive powers take her very soul?

Love Undercover by B.J. McCall
Amanda Forbes is the bait in a strip joint sting operation. While she performs, fellow detective "Cowboy" Cooper gets to watch. Though he excites her, she must fight the temptation to surrender to the passion.

Winner of the 1997 Under the Covers Readers Favorite Award

Secrets, Volume 4

Listen to what reviewers say:

"Provocative... seductive... a must read!"

—*Romantic Times* Magazine

"These are the kind of stories that romance readers that 'want a little more' have been looking for all their lives...."

—*Affaire de Coeur* Magazine

"*Secrets, Volume 4*, has something to satisfy every erotic fantasy... simply sexational!"

—Virginia Henley, *New York Times* Best Selling Author

Volume 4

Secrets

The Best in Women's Sensual Fiction

Jeanie Cesarini
Emma Holly
Desirée Lindsey
Betsy Morgan & Susan Paul

Provocative...seductive...a must read!
— Romantic Times Magazine ✦✦✦✦

In *Secrets, Volume 4* you'll find:

An Act of Love by Jeanie Cesarini

Shelby Moran's past left her terrified of sex. International film star Jason Gage must gently coach the young starlet in the ways of love. He wants more than an act—he wants Shelby to feel true passion in his arms.

Enslaved by Desirée Lindsey

Lord Nicholas Summer's air of danger, dark passions, and irresistible charm have brought Lady Crystal's long-hidden desires to the surface. Will he be able to give her the one thing she desires before it's too late?

The Bodyguard by Betsy Morgan and Susan Paul

Kaki York is a bodyguard, but watching the wild, erotic romps of her client's sexual conquests on the security cameras is getting to her—and her partner, the ruggedly handsome James Kulick. Can she resist his insistent desire to have her?

The Love Slave by Emma Holly

A woman's ultimate fantasy. For one year, Princess Lily will be attended to by three delicious men of her choice. While she delights in playing with the first two, it's the reluctant Grae, with his powerful chest, black eyes and hair, that stirs her desires.

Secrets, Volume 5

Listen to what reviewers say:

"Hot, hot, hot! Not for the faint-hearted!"
—*Romantic Times* Magazine

"As you make your way through the stories, you will find yourself becoming hotter and hotter. *Secrets* just keeps getting better and better."
—*Affaire de Coeur* Magazine

"*Secrets 5* is a collage of luscious sensuality. Any woman who reads *Secrets* is in for an awakening!"
—Virginia Henley, *New York Times* Best Selling Author

In *Secrets, Volume 5* you'll find:

Beneath Two Moons by Sandy Fraser

Ready for a very wild romp? Step into the future and find Conor, rough and masculine like frontiermen of old, on the prowl for a new conquest. In his sights, Dr. Eva Kelsey. She got away once before, but this time Conor makes sure she begs for more.

Insatiable by Chevon Gael

Marcus Remington photographs beautiful models for a living, but it's Ashlyn Fraser, a young corporate exec having some glamour shots done, who has stolen his heart. It's up to Marcus to help her discover her inner sexual self.

Strictly Business by Shannon Hollis

Elizabeth Forrester knows it's tough enough for a woman to make it to the top in the corporate world. Garrett Hill, the most beautiful man in Silicon Valley, has to come along to stir up her wildest fantasies. Dare she give in to both their desires?

Alias Smith and Jones by B.J. McCall

Meredith Collins finds herself stranded overnight at the airport. A handsome stranger by the name of Smith offers her sanctuary for the evening and she finds those mesmerizing, green-flecked eyes hard to resist. Are they to be just two ships passing in the night?

Secrets, Volume 6

Listen to what reviewers say:

"Red Sage was the first and remains the leader of Women's Erotic Romance Fiction Collections!"
— *Romantic Times* Magazine

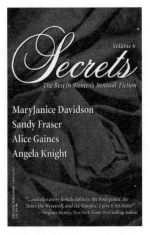

"*Secrets, Volume 6*, is the best of *Secrets* yet. ...four of the most erotic stories in one volume than this reader has yet to see anywhere else. ...These stories are full of erotica at its best and you'll definitely want to keep it handy for lots of re-reading!"

— *Affaire de Coeur* Magazine

"*Secrets 6* satisfies every female fantasy: the Bodyguard, the Tutor, the Werewolf, and the Vampire. I give it Six Stars!"
— Virginia Henley, *New York Times* Best Selling Author

In *Secrets, Volume 6* you'll find:

Flint's Fuse by Sandy Fraser
Dana Madison's father has her "kidnapped" for her own safety. Flint, the tall, dark and dangerous mercenary, is hired for the job. But just which one is the prisoner—Dana will try *anything* to get away.

Love's Prisoner by MaryJanice Davidson
Trapped in an elevator, Jeannie Lawrence experienced unwilling rapture at Michael Windham's hands. She never expected the devilishly handsome man to show back up in her life—or turn out to be a werewolf!

The Education of Miss Felicity Wells by Alice Gaines
Felicity Wells wants to be sure she'll satisfy her soon-to-be husband but she needs a teacher. Dr. Marcus Slade, an experienced lover, agrees to take her on as a student, but can he stop short of taking her completely?

A Candidate for the Kiss by Angela Knight
Working on a story, reporter Dana Ivory stumbles onto a more amazing one—a sexy, secret agent who happens to be a vampire. She wants her story but Gabriel Archer wants more from her than just sex and blood.

Secrets, Volume 7

Listen to what reviewers say:

"Get out your asbestos gloves — *Secrets Volume 7* is... extremely hot, true erotic romance... passionate and titillating. There's nothing quite like baring your secrets!"

—*Romantic Times* Magazine

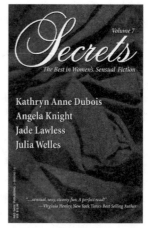

"...sensual, sexy, steamy fun. A perfect read!"

—Virginia Henley,
New York Times Best Selling Author

"Intensely provocative and disarmingly romantic, *Secrets*, *Volume 7*, is a romance reader's paradise that will take you beyond your wildest dreams!"

—Ballston Book House Review

In *Secrets, Volume 7* you'll find:

Amelia's Innocence by Julia Welles

Amelia didn't know her father bet her in a card game with Captain Quentin Hawke, so honor demands a compromise—three days of erotic foreplay, leaving her virginity and future intact.

The Woman of His Dreams by Jade Lawless

From the day artist Gray Avonaco moves in next door, Joanna Morgan is plagued by provocative dreams. But what she believes is unrequited lust, Gray sees as another chance to be with the woman he loves. He must persuade her that even death can't stop true love.

Surrender by Kathryn Anne Dubois

Free-spirited Lady Johanna wants no part of the binding strictures society imposes with her marriage to the powerful Duke. She doesn't know the dark Duke wants sensual adventure, and sexual satisfaction.

Kissing the Hunter by Angela Knight

Navy Seal Logan McLean hunts the vampires who murdered his wife. Virginia Hart is a sexy vampire searching for her lost soul-mate only to find him in a man determined to kill her. She must convince him all vampires aren't created equally.

Winner of the Venus Book Club
Best Book of the Year

Secrets, Volume 8

Listen to what reviewers say:

"*Secrets*, *Volume 8*, is an amazing compilation of sexy stories covering a wide range of subjects, all designed to titillate the senses. ...you'll find something for everybody in this latest version of *Secrets*."

—*Affaire de Coeur* Magazine

"*Secrets Volume 8*, is simply sensational!"

—Virginia Henley, *New York Times* Best Selling Author

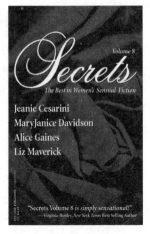

"These delectable stories will have you turning the pages long into the night. Passionate, provocative and perfect for setting the mood...."

—*Escape to Romance* Reviews

In *Secrets, Volume 8* you'll find:

Taming Kate by Jeanie Cesarini

Kathryn Roman inherits a legal brothel. Little does this city girl know the town of Love, Nevada wants her to be their new madam so they've charged Trey Holliday, one very dominant cowboy, with taming her.

Jared's Wolf by MaryJanice Davidson

Jared Rocke will do anything to avenge his sister's death, but ends up attracted to Moira Wolfbauer, the she-wolf sworn to protect her pack. Joining forces to stop a killer, they learn love defies all boundaries.

My Champion, My Lover by Alice Gaines

Celeste Broder is a woman committed for having a sexy appetite. Mayor Robert Albright may be her champion—if she can convince him her freedom will mean a chance to indulge their appetites together.

Kiss or Kill by Liz Maverick

In this post-apocalyptic world, Camille Kazinsky's military career rides on her ability to make a choice—whether the robo called Meat should live or die. Meat's future depends on proving he's human enough to live, man enough... to makes her feel like a woman.

Winner of the Venus Book Club Best Book of the Year

Secrets, Volume 9

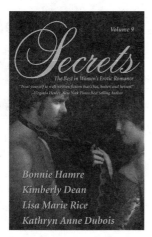

Listen to what reviewers say:

"Everyone should expect only the most erotic stories in a *Secrets* book. ...if you like your stories full of hot sexual scenes, then this is for you!"

—Donna Doyle Romance Reviews

"*SECRETS 9*... is sinfully delicious, highly arousing, and hotter than hot as the pages practically burn up as you turn them."

—Suzanne Coleburn, Reader To Reader Reviews/Belles & Beaux of Romance

"Treat yourself to well-written fiction that's hot, hotter, and hottest!"

—Virginia Henley, *New York Times* Best Selling Author

In *Secrets, Volume 9* you'll find:

Wild For You by Kathryn Anne Dubois

When college intern, Georgie, gets captured by a Congo wildman, she discovers this specimen of male virility has never seen a woman. The research possibilities are endless!

Wanted by Kimberly Dean

FBI Special Agent Jeff Reno wants Danielle Carver. There's her body, brains—and that charge of treason on her head. Dani goes on the run, but the sexy Fed is hot on her trail.

Secluded by Lisa Marie Rice

Nicholas Lee's wealth and power came with a price—his enemies will kill anyone he loves. When Isabelle steals his heart, Nicholas secludes her in his palace for a lifetime of desire in only a few days.

Flights of Fantasy by Bonnie Hamre

Chloe taught others to see the realities of life but she's never shared the intimate world of her sensual yearnings. Given the chance, will she be woman enough to fulfill her most secret erotic fantasy?

Secrets, Volume 10

Listen to what reviewers say:

"*Secrets Volume 10*, an erotic dance through medieval castles, sultan's palaces, the English countryside and expensive hotel suites, explodes with passion-filled pages."

—Romantic Times BOOKclub

"Having read the previous nine volumes, this one fulfills the expectations of what is expected in a *Secrets* book: romance and eroticism at its best!!"

—Fallen Angel Reviews

"All are hot steamy romances so if you enjoy erotica romance, you are sure to enjoy *Secrets, Volume 10*. All this reviewer can say is WOW!!"

—The Best Reviews

In *Secrets, Volume 10* you'll find:

Private Eyes by Dominique Sinclair

When a mystery man captivates P.I. Nicolla Black during a stakeout, she discovers her no-seduction rule bending under the pressure of long denied passion. She agrees to the seduction, but he demands her total surrender.

The Ruination of Lady Jane by Bonnie Hamre

To avoid her upcoming marriage, Lady Jane Ponsonby-Maitland flees into the arms of Havyn Attercliffe. She begs him to ruin her rather than turn her over to her odious fiancé.

Code Name: Kiss by Jeanie Cesarini

Agent Lily Justiss is on a mission to defend her country against terrorists that requires giving up her virginity as a sex slave. As her master takes her body, desire for her commanding officer Seth Blackthorn fuels her mind.

The Sacrifice by Kathryn Anne Dubois

Lady Anastasia Bedovier is days from taking her vows as a Nun. Before she denies her sensuality forever, she wants to experience pleasure. Count Maxwell is the perfect man to initiate her into erotic delight.

Secrets, Volume 11

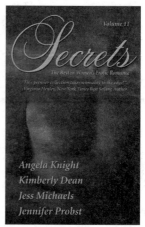

Listen to what reviewers say:

"*Secrets Volume 11* delivers once again with storylines that include erotic masquerades, ancient curses, modern-day betrayal and a prince charming looking for a kiss." **4 Stars**

—*Romantic Times BOOKclub*

"Indulge yourself with this erotic treat and join the thousands of readers who just can't get enough. Be forewarned that *Secrets 11* will whet your appetite for more, but will offer you the ultimate in pleasurable erotic literature."

—*Ballston Book House Review*

"*Secrets 11* quite honestly is my favorite anthology from Red Sage so far."

—*The Best Reviews*

In *Secrets, Volume 11* you'll find:

Masquerade by Jennifer Probst

Hailey Ashton is determined to free herself from her sexual restrictions. Four nights of erotic pleasures without revealing her identity. A chance to explore her secret desires without the fear of unmasking.

Ancient Pleasures by Jess Michaels

Isabella Winslow is obsessed with finding out what caused her late husband's death, but trapped in an Egyptian concubine's tomb with a sexy American raider, succumbing to the mummy's sensual curse takes over.

Manhunt by Kimberly Dean

Framed for murder, Michael Tucker takes Taryn Swanson hostage—the one woman who can clear him. Despite the evidence against him, the attraction between them is strong. Tucker resorts to unconventional, yet effective methods of persuasion to change the sexy ADA's mind.

Wake Me by Angela Knight

Chloe Hart received a sexy painting of a sleeping knight. Radolf of Varik has been trapped for centuries in the painting since, cursed by a witch. His only hope is to visit the dreams of women and make one of them fall in love with him so she can free him with a kiss.

Secrets, Volume 12

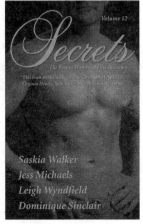

Listen to what reviewers say:

"*Secrets Volume 12*, turns on the heat with a seductive encounter inside a bookstore, a temple of naughty and sensual delight, a galactic inferno that thaws ice, and a lightening storm that lights up the English shoreline. Tales of looking for love in all the right places with a heat rating out the charts." **4½ Stars**

—*Romantic Times BOOKclub*

"I really liked these stories. You want great escapism? Read *Secrets, Volume 12*."

—*Romance Reviews*

In *Secrets, Volume 12* you'll find:

Good Girl Gone Bad by Dominique Sinclair

Reagan's dreams are finally within reach. Setting out to do research for an article, nothing could have prepared her for Luke, or his offer to teach her everything she needs to know about sex. Licentious pleasures, forbidden desires… inspiring the best writing she's ever done.

Aphrodite's Passion by Jess Michaels

When Selena flees Victorian London before her evil stepchildren can institutionalize her for hysteria, Gavin is asked to bring her back home. But when he finds her living on the island of Cyprus, his need to have her begins to block out every other impulse.

White Heat by Leigh Wyndfield

Raine is hiding in an icehouse in the middle of nowhere from one of the scariest men in the universes. Walker escaped from a burning prison. Imagine their surprise when they find out they have the same man to blame for their miseries. Passion, revenge and love are in their future.

Summer Lightning by Saskia Walker

Sculptress Sally is enjoying an idyllic getaway on a secluded cove when she spots a gorgeous man walking naked on the beach. When Julian finds an attractive woman shacked up in his cove, he has to check her out. But what will he do when he finds she's secretly been using him as a model?

Secrets, Volume 13

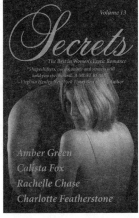

Listen to what reviewers say:

"In *Secrets Volume 13*, the temperature gets turned up a few notches with a mistaken personal ad, shape-shifters destined to love, a hot Regency lord and his lady, as well as a bodyguard protecting his woman. Emotions and flames blaze high in Red Sage's latest foray into the sensual and delightful art of love." **4½ Stars**

—Romantic Times BOOKclub

"The sex is still so hot the pages nearly ignite! Read *Secrets, Volume 13*!"

—Romance Reviews

In *Secrets, Volume 13* you'll find:

Out of Control by Rachelle Chase

Astrid's world revolves around her business and she's hoping to pick up wealthy Erik Santos as a client. Only he's hoping to pick up something entirely different. Will she give in to the seductive pull of his proposition?

Hawkmoor by Amber Green

Shape-shifters answer to Darien as he acts in the name of the long-missing Lady Hawkmoor, their hereditary ruler. When she unexpectedly surfaces, Darien must deal with a scrappy individual whose wary eyes hold the other half of his soul, but who has the power to destroy his world.

Lessons in Pleasure by Charlotte Featherstone

A wicked bargain has Lily vowing never to yield to the demands of the rake she once loved and lost. Unfortunately, Damian, the Earl of St. Croix, or Saint as he is infamously known, will not take 'no' for an answer.

In the Heat of the Night by Calista Fox

Haunted by a century-old curse, Molina fears she won't live to see her thirtieth birthday. Nick, her former bodyguard, is hired back into service to protect her from the fatal accidents that plague her family. But *In the Heat of the Night*, will his passion and love for her be enough to convince Molina they have a future together?

Secrets, Volume 14

Listen to what reviewers say:

"*Secrets Volume 14* will excite readers with its diverse selection of delectable sexy tales ranging from a fourteenth century love story to a sci-fi rebel who falls for a irresistible research scientist to a trio of determined vampires who battle for the same woman to a virgin sacrifice who falls in love with a beast. A cornucopia of pure delight!" **4½ Stars**
—*Romantic Times BOOKclub*

"This book contains four erotic tales sure to keep readers up long into the night."
—*Romance Junkies*

In *Secrets, Volume 14* you'll find:

Soul Kisses by Angela Knight

Beth's been kidnapped by Joaquin Ramirez, a sadistic vampire. Handsome vampire cousins, Morgan and Garret Axton, come to her rescue. Can she find happiness with two vampires?

Temptation in Time by Alexa Aames

Ariana escaped the Middle Ages after stealing a kiss of magic from sexy sorcerer, Marcus de Grey. When he brings her back, they begin a battle of wills and a sexual odyssey that could spell disaster for them both.

Ailis and the Beast by Jennifer Barlowe

When Ailis agreed to be her village's sacrifice to the mysterious Beast she was prepared to sacrifice her virtue, and possibly her life. But some things aren't what they seem. Ailis and the Beast are about to discover the greatest sacrifice may be the human heart.

Night Heat by Leigh Wynfield

When Rip Bowhite leads a revolt on the prison planet, he ends up struggling to survive against monsters that rule the night. Jemma, the prison's Healer, won't allow herself to be distracted by the instant attraction she feels for Rip. As the stakes are raised and death draws near, love seems doomed in the heat of the night.

Secrets, Volume 15

Listen to what reviewers say:

"*Secrets Volume 15* blends humor, tension and steamy romance in its newest collection that sizzles with passion between unlikely pairs—a male chauvinist columnist and a librarian turned erotica author; a handsome werewolf and his resisting mate; an unfulfilled woman and a sexy police officer and a Victorian wife who learns discipline can be fun. Readers will revel in this delicious assortment of thrilling tales." **4 Stars**
— *Romantic Times BOOKclub*

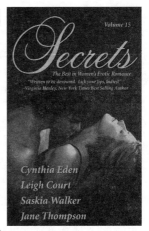

"This book contains four tales by some of today's hottest authors that will tease your senses and intrigue your mind."
— *Romance Junkies*

In *Secrets, Volume 15* you'll find:

Simon Says by Jane Thompson
Simon Campbell is a newspaper columnist who panders to male fantasies. Georgina Kennedy is a respectable librarian. On the surface, these two have nothing in common... but don't judge a book by its cover.

Bite of the Wolf by Cynthia Eden
Gareth Morlet, alpha werewolf, has finally found his mate. All he has to do is convince Trinity to join with him, to give in to the pleasure of a werewolf's mating, and then she will be his... forever.

Falling for Trouble by Saskia Walker
With 48 hours to clear her brother's name, Sonia Harmond finds help from irresistible bad boy, Oliver Eaglestone. When the erotic tension between them hits fever pitch, securing evidence to thwart an international arms dealer isn't the only danger they face.

The Disciplinarian by Leigh Court
Headstrong Clarissa Babcock is sent to the shadowy legend known as The Disciplinarian for instruction in proper wifely obedience. Jared Ashworth uses the tools of seduction to show her how to control a demanding husband, but her beauty, spirit, and uninhibited passion make Jared hunger to keep her—and their darkly erotic nights—all for himself!

Secrets, Volume 16

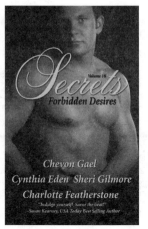

Listen to what reviewers say:

"Blackmail, games of chance, nude beaches and masquerades pave a path to heart-tugging emotions and fiery love scenes in Red Sage's latest collection." **4.5 Stars**
— *Romantic Times BOOKclub*

"Red Sage Publishing has brought to the readers an erotic profusion of highly skilled storytellers in their Secrets Vol. 16. ... This is the best Secrets novel to date and this reviewer's favorite."
— *LoveRomances.com*

In *Secrets, Volume 16* you'll find:

Never Enough by Cynthia Eden

For the last three weeks, Abby McGill has been playing with fire. Bad-boy Jake has taught her the true meaning of desire, but she knows she has to end her relationship with him. But Jake isn't about to let the woman he wants walk away from him.

Bunko by Sheri Gilmoore

Tu Tran is forced to decide between Jack, a man, who promises to share every aspect of his life with her, or Dev, the man, who hides behind a mask and only offers night after night of erotic sex. Will she take the gamble of the dice and choose the man, who can see behind her own mask and expose her true desires?

Hide and Seek by Chevon Gael

Kyle DeLaurier ditches his trophy-fiance in favor of a tropical paradise full of tall, tanned, topless females. Private eye, Darcy McLeod, is on the trail of this runaway groom. Together they sizzle while playing Hide and Seek with their true identities.

Seduction of the Muse by Charlotte Featherstone

He's the Dark Lord, the mysterious author who pens the erotic tales of an innocent woman's seduction. She is his muse, the woman he watches from the dark shadows, the woman whose dreams he invades at night.

Secrets, Volume 17

Listen to what reviewers say:

"Readers who have clamored for more *Secrets* will love the mix of alpha and beta males as well as kick-butt heroines who always get their men." **4 Stars**
—*Romantic Times BOOKclub*

"Stories so sizzling hot, they will burn your fingers as you turn the pages. Enjoy!"
—Virginia Henley, *New York Times* Best Selling Author

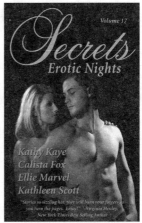

"Red Sage is bringing us another thrilling anthology of passion and desire that will keep you up long into the night."
—*Romance Junkies*

In *Secrets, Volume 17* you'll find:

Rock Hard Candy by Kathy Kaye

Jessica Hennessy, the great, great granddaughter of a Voodoo priestess, decides she's waited long enough for the man of her dreams. A dose of her ancestor's aphrodisiac slipped into the gooey center of her homemade bon bons ought to do the trick.

Fatal Error by Kathleen Scott

Jesse Storm must make amends to humanity by destroying the computer program he helped design that has taken the government hostage. But he must also protect the woman he's loved in secret for nearly a decade.

Birthday by Ellie Marvel

Jasmine Templeton decides she's been celibate long enough. Will a wild night at a hot new club with her two best friends ease the ache inside her or just make it worse? Well, considering one of those best friends is Charlie and she's been having strange notions about their relationship of late… It's definitely a birthday neither she nor Charlie will ever forget.

Intimate Rendezvous by Calista Fox

A thief causes trouble at Cassandra Kensington's nightclub, Rendezvous, and sexy P.I. Dean Hewitt arrives on the scene to help. One look at the siren who owns the club has his blood boiling, despite the fact that his keen instincts have him questioning the legitimacy of her business.

Secrets, Volume 18

Listen to what reviewers say:

"Fantastic love scenes make this a book to be enjoyed more than once." **4.5 Stars**
—*Romantic Times BOOKclub*

"*Secrets Volume 18* continues [its] tradition of high quality sensual stories that both excite the senses while stimulating the mind."
—CK²S Kwips and Kritiques

"Edgy, erotic, exciting, *Secrets* is always a fantastic read!"

—Susan Kearney, *USA Today* Best Selling Author

In *Secrets, Volume 18* you'll find:

Lone Wolf Three by Rae Monet

Planetary politics and squabbling over wolf occupied territory drain former rebel leader Taban Zias. But his anger quickly turns to desire when he meets, Lakota Blackson. Focused, calm and honorable, the female Wolf Warrior is Taban's perfect mate—now if he can just convince her.

Flesh to Fantasy by Larissa Ione

Kelsa Bradshaw is an intense loner whose job keeps her happily immersed in a fanciful world of virtual reality. Trent Jordan is a laid-back paramedic who experiences the harsh realities of life up close and personal. But when their worlds collide in an erotic eruption can Trent convince Kelsa to turn the fantasy into something real?

Heart Full of Stars by Linda Gayle

Singer Fanta Rae finds herself stranded on a lonely Mars outpost with the first human male she's seen in years. Ex-Marine Alex Decker lost his family and guilt drove him into isolation, but when alien assassins come to enslave Fanta, she and Decker come together to fight for their lives.

The Wolf's Mate by Cynthia Eden

When Michael Morlet finds Katherine "Kat" Hardy fighting for her life in a dark alley, he instantly recognizes her as the mate he's been seeking all of his life, but someone's trying to kill her. With danger stalking them at every turn, will Kat trust him enough to become The Wolf's Mate?

The Forever Kiss
by Angela Knight

Listen to what reviewers say:

"*The Forever Kiss* flows well with good characters and an interesting plot. … If you enjoy vampires and a lot of hot sex, you are sure to enjoy *The Forever Kiss*."

—*The Best Reviews*

"Battling vampires, a protective ghost and the ever present battle of good and evil keep excellent pace with the erotic delights in Angela Knight's *The Forever Kiss*—a book that absolutely bites with refreshing paranormal humor." **4½ Stars, Top Pick**

—*Romantic Times BOOKclub*

"I found *The Forever Kiss* to be an exceptionally written, refreshing book. … I really enjoyed this book by Angela Knight. … 5 angels!"

—*Fallen Angel Reviews*

"*The Forever Kiss* is the first single title released from Red Sage and if this is any indication of what we can expect, it won't be the last. … The love scenes are hot enough to give a vampire a sunburn and the fight scenes will have you cheering for the good guys."

—*Really Bad Barb Reviews*

In *The Forever Kiss*:

For years, Valerie Chase has been haunted by dreams of a Texas Ranger she knows only as "Cowboy." As a child, he rescued her from the nightmare vampires who murdered her parents. As an adult, she still dreams of him—but now he's her seductive lover in nights of erotic pleasure.

Yet "Cowboy" is more than a dream—he's the real Cade McKinnon—and a vampire! For years, he's protected Valerie from Edward Ridgemont, the sadistic vampire who turned him. Now, Ridgmont wants Valerie for his own and Cade is the only one who can protect her.

When Val finds herself abducted by her handsome dream man, she's appalled to discover he's one of the vampires she fears. Now, caught in a web of fear and passion, she and Cade must learn to trust each other, even as an immortal monster stalks their every move.

Their only hope of survival is… *The Forever Kiss*.

Romantic Times Best Erotic Novel of the Year

It's not just reviewers raving about *Secrets*. See what readers have to say:

"When are you coming out with a new Volume? I want a new one next month!" via email from a reader.

"I loved the hot, wet sex without vulgar words being used to make it exciting." after *Volume 1*

"I loved the blend of sensuality and sexual intensity—HOT!" after *Volume 2*

"The best thing about *Secrets* is they're hot and brief! The least thing is you do not have enough of them!" after *Volume 3*

"I have been extremely satisfied with *Secrets*, keep up the good writing." after *Volume 4*

"Stories have plot and characters to support the erotica. They would be good strong stories without the heat." after *Volume 5*

"*Secrets* really knows how to push the envelop better than anyone else." after *Volume 6*

"These are the best sensual stories I have ever read!" after *Volume 7*

"I love, love, love the *Secrets* stories. I now have all of them, please have more books come out each year." after *Volume 8*

"These are the perfect sensual romance stories!" after *Volume 9*

"What I love about *Secrets Volume 10* is how I couldn't put it down!" after *Volume 10*

"All of the *Secrets* volumes are terrific! I have read all of them up to *Secrets Volume 11*. Please keep them coming! I will read every one you make!" after *Volume 11*

Editor

Finally, the men you've been dreaming about!

Give the Gift of Spicy Romantic Fiction

Don't want to wait? You can place a retail price ($12.99) order for any of the *Secrets* volumes from the following:

① **Waldenbooks and Borders Stores**

② **Amazon.com** or **BarnesandNoble.com**

③ **Book Clearinghouse (800-431-1579)**

④ **Romantic Times Magazine** Books by Mail (718-237-1097)

⑤ Special order at other bookstores.
Bookstores: Please contact Baker & Taylor Distributors, Ingram Book Distributor, or Red Sage Publishing for bookstore sales.

Order by title or ISBN #:

Vol. 1: 0-9648942-0-3
ISBN #13 978-0-9648942-0-4

Vol. 7: 0-9648942-7-0
ISBN #13 978-0-9648942-7-3

Vol. 13: 0-9754516-3-4
ISBN #13 978-0-9754516-3-2

Vol. 2: 0-9648942-1-1
ISBN #13 978-0-9648942-1-1

Vol. 8: 0-9648942-8-9
ISBN #13 978-0-9648942-9-7

Vol. 14: 0-9754516-4-2
ISBN #13 978-0-9754516-4-9

Vol. 3: 0-9648942-2-X
ISBN #13 978-0-9648942-2-8

Vol. 9: 0-9648942-9-7
ISBN #13 978-0-9648942-9-7

Vol. 15: 0-9754516-5-0
ISBN #13 978-0-9754516-5-6

Vol. 4: 0-9648942-4-6
ISBN #13 978-0-9648942-4-2

Vol. 10: 0-9754516-0-X
ISBN #13 978-0-9754516-0-1

Vol. 16: 0-9754516-6-9
ISBN #13 978-0-9754516-6-3

Vol. 5: 0-9648942-5-4
ISBN #13 978-0-9648942-5-9

Vol. 11: 0-9754516-1-8
ISBN #13 978-0-9754516-1-8

Vol. 17: 0-9754516-7-7
ISBN #13 978-0-9754516-7-0

Vol. 6: 0-9648942-6-2
ISBN #13 978-0-9648942-6-6

Vol. 12: 0-9754516-2-6
ISBN #13 978-0-9754516-2-5

Vol. 18: 0-9754516-8-5
ISBN #13 978-0-9754516-8-7

The Forever Kiss: 0-9648942-3-8 • ISBN #13 978-0-9648942-3-5 ($14.00)

Red Sage Publishing Mail Order Form:

(Orders shipped in two to three days of receipt.)

Each volume of *Secrets* retails for $12.99, but you can get it direct via mail order for only $9.99 each. The novel *The Forever Kiss* retails for $14.00, but by direct mail order, you only pay $11.00. Use the order form below to place your direct mail order. Fill in the quantity you want for each book on the blanks beside the title.

_____ *Secrets* Volume 1	_____ *Secrets* Volume 8	_____ *Secrets* Volume 15
_____ *Secrets* Volume 2	_____ *Secrets* Volume 9	_____ *Secrets* Volume 16
_____ *Secrets* Volume 3	_____ *Secrets* Volume 10	_____ *Secrets* Volume 17
_____ *Secrets* Volume 4	_____ *Secrets* Volume 11	_____ *Secrets* Volume 18
_____ *Secrets* Volume 5	_____ *Secrets* Volume 12	_____ *The Forever Kiss*
_____ *Secrets* Volume 6	_____ *Secrets* Volume 13	
_____ *Secrets* Volume 7	_____ *Secrets* Volume 14	

Total _____ *Secrets* Volumes @ $9.99 each = $_____

Total _____ *The Forever Kiss* @ $11.00 each = $_____

Shipping & handling (in the U.S.) $_____

US Priority Mail: UPS insured:

1–2 books .... $ 5.50   1–4 books $16.00

3–5 books .... $11.50   5–9 books $25.00

6–9 books .... $14.50   10–19 books $29.00

10–19 books $19.00

SUBTOTAL $_____

Florida 6% sales tax (if delivered in FL) $_____

TOTAL AMOUNT ENCLOSED $_____

Your personal information is kept private and not shared with anyone.

Name: (please print) _____

Address: (no P.O. Boxes) _____

City/State/Zip: _____

Phone or email: (only regarding order if necessary) _____

Please make check payable to **Red Sage Publishing**. Check must be drawn on a U.S. bank in U.S. dollars. Mail your check and order form to:

Red Sage Publishing, Inc.   Department S18   P.O. Box 4844   Seminole, FL 33775

Or use the order form on our website: **www.redsagepub.com**

Red Sage Publishing Mail Order Form:

(Orders shipped in two to three days of receipt.)

Each volume of *Secrets* retails for $12.99, but you can get it direct via mail order for only $9.99 each. The novel *The Forever Kiss* retails for $14.00, but by direct mail order, you only pay $11.00. Use the order form below to place your direct mail order. Fill in the quantity you want for each book on the blanks beside the title.

_____ *Secrets* Volume 1	_____ *Secrets* Volume 8	_____ *Secrets* Volume 15
_____ *Secrets* Volume 2	_____ *Secrets* Volume 9	_____ *Secrets* Volume 16
_____ *Secrets* Volume 3	_____ *Secrets* Volume 10	_____ *Secrets* Volume 17
_____ *Secrets* Volume 4	_____ *Secrets* Volume 11	_____ *Secrets* Volume 18
_____ *Secrets* Volume 5	_____ *Secrets* Volume 12	_____ *The Forever Kiss*
_____ *Secrets* Volume 6	_____ *Secrets* Volume 13	
_____ *Secrets* Volume 7	_____ *Secrets* Volume 14	

Total _____ *Secrets* Volumes @ $9.99 each = $_____

Total _____ *The Forever Kiss* @ $11.00 each = $_____

Shipping & handling (in the U.S.) $_____

US Priority Mail:	UPS insured:
1–2 books .... $ 5.50	1–4 books $16.00
3–5 books $11.50	5–9 books $25.00
6–9 books $14.50	10–19 books $29.00
10–19 books $19.00	

SUBTOTAL $_____

Florida 6% sales tax (if delivered in FL) $_____

TOTAL AMOUNT ENCLOSED $_____

Your personal information is kept private and not shared with anyone.

Name: (please print) _____

Address: (no P.O. Boxes) _____

City/State/Zip: _____

Phone or email: (only regarding order if necessary) _____

Please make check payable to **Red Sage Publishing**. Check must be drawn on a U.S. bank in U.S. dollars. Mail your check and order form to:

Red Sage Publishing, Inc.   Department S18   P.O. Box 4844   Seminole, FL 33775

Or use the order form on our website: **www.redsagepub.com**